# STICK

# MAN

By

Richard Rossi

## Eternal Grace Publishing

## Hollywood, California

# ACKNOWLEDGEMENTS

I would like to thank my late father, Richard Rossi Sr. The loss I experienced over your passing became a catalyst for my writing this novel. I also want to acknowledge the rest of my family in Pittsburgh, my mother, brothers and sister. No matter what we've been through, we've always been a family and tried our best to support each other in trying times. Thank you as well to all my friends in Pennsylvania who shared my youth. I love you all.

I'm also grateful to my wife Sherrie, and my two children, Karie and Joshua. You provide a home and feeling of kinship and peace for me. I love you.

Thank you to Dr. Marlene Winell for encouraging my right to think for myself and recover from my past. I would also like to thank the following friends and/or fellow writers who read rough excerpts of Stick Man, and sometimes gave feedback: Sean Permutter, M. Spencer Wolf, Daniel Janik, Brandy Taylor, Jim Krusoe, Diane Arieff, Mary Trajan, Cathi Curen, Rick Setlowe, John Walker, Sherry Krueger, Abigail Parsons, and Louise Cabral.

I'm thankful to all of you for your encouragement in my life. The ups and downs I have been through have been a part of my journey and have made me who I am today. Writing is a deeply spiritual practice for me and an expression of grace that brings me reflection and healing. This novel has been a constructive outlet for me to take my thoughts, experiences, creativity, and imagination, and make something out of them.

And lastly, thank you to those I am not able to thank publicly. God bless all of you.

## ABOUT THE AUTHOR

**Richard Rossi** is a multi-medium artist. In addition to working as a writer, he is also a filmmaker, actor, singer-songwriter, guitarist, visual artist, and teacher. Richard lives with his wife and two children in Southern California. Stick Man is his first published novel.

## ALSO BY RICHARD ROSSI

### FILMS

Sister Aimee: The Aimee Semple McPherson Story
Live At Graffiti's
Saving Sister Aimee
Quest for Truth

### MUSIC ALBUMS

Stick Man Soundtrack
Full Circle
New Wine

### PLAY

Sister Aimee

If you enjoyed Stick Man you can contact Richard at: richardrossiactor@yahoo.com

# DEDICATION

For creative, wounded, and hurting children

the world round,

whose precious seeds

are too often choked by weeds,

snatched by birds,

and struggling to hatch in rocky ground.

Our lives may be determined less by our childhood

than by the way we have learned to imagine

our childhoods.

-James Hillman, *The Soul's Code*




Praising what is lost

Makes the remembrance dear.

-Shakespeare

# 1

My battle with Stick Man started one spring morning in 1970. I was seven. I have a superhuman memory for certain people who are burned into my recollection. I didn't think I'd make it to adulthood alive because Stick Man wanted to kill me.

Childhood in Pittsburgh was one of extremes. First loves hung like photographs on the walls of my subconscious. They lingered there, the one bright spot in my childhood, to battle their antithesis - Stick Man.

I had a foreboding feeling of doom, like death was floating in the room. There was a pungent smell, foul and bitter.

"Get ready, Jeremiah. No lollygagging, you hear me?"

I looked at Mom and smiled. She wore a dark blue men's button-down shirt and pink Capri pants. Her singsong voice followed a melody that ended every sentence with a low note. Her breath smelled like peppermint. God, I loved her.

I rubbed my eyes and rolled down my Batman bed cover. My dog Gabriel leapt on the bed and licked my face. I wrestled with him, rubbing his fur. I wondered if Mom was ready to snap again.

She tossed me a short-sleeved shirt and gave me a look that said *put it on quick or else.*

"The shirt's too stiff," I said. I buttoned it, but left the top unfastened. I grimaced when she rushed over and buttoned the top.

"There, there, dear. It's not that bad."

"It hurts."

"That's enough. We're running late."

She slipped a sweater vest over my shirt. "You're visiting God's house, you need to be on time."

Her voice was low again on the word "time." She was in a pretty good mood. When she was in a bad mood, all the words were high-pitched and screechy, like a B on the seventh fret of my first string.

*God's house.* That sounded interesting.

"Is that where He lives, Mom?"

"God is everywhere.   But this is His special house."

"How   come   Walker   can't   come?"   Walker   was   still sleeping, but the commotion stirred him.

"He isn't big enough yet."

"Hey…where  you  going?"  Walker  said.   He  yawned  and stretched his arms.

"I'm  taking  Jeremiah  to  church,"  Mom  said.   "You  be  a good boy while we're gone."

Mom  attended  mass  every  Sunday  at  Saint  Joseph's,  in  our little town of West View, Pennsylvania, a blue-collar suburb.

I  slipped  my  legs  into  the  wool  pants  and  suspenders  then watched her walk towards the hall.   I hated those pants.   They made my  legs  itch.   When  she  left  the  bedroom,  I  pulled  out  my  shirt, freeing it from the tyranny to hang out in front, so I could feel like a real boy again.   I tiptoed a few feet behind her.

I  saw  Dad  sprawled  out  like  a  bear  in  bed,  wearing  only  white boxers.   His penis hung out of his fly.   He was hung over from his gig  the  night  before,  so  she  snatched  his  keys.   He  didn't  notice. She  knocked  over  the  picture  of  Chuck  Corsello  on  the  nightstand. It  was  out  of  its  normal  spot.   Dad  had  probably  been  looking  at  it again.   Chuck  was  his  best  friend  in  high  school.   Dad  used  to  hold the  picture  and  tell  me  Chuck  looked  like  James  Dean.   At  the  time  I didn't  know  who  James  Dean  was,  but  I'd  learn  soon  enough.

"I  wish  he  was  over  him,"  Mom  said.   She  had  a  habit  of talking to herself.

Beside  the  photo  of  Corsello  were  pictures  of  Dad's  navy days  when  his  hair  was  dark,  before  it  started  receding.   His  sailor hat  tilted  to  the  left  like  a  lopsided  cupcake.   He  wore  his  naval uniform,  and  stood  on  a  ship  during  the  Korean  War,  flanked  by

Corsello and other seamen.    Dad seemed different in those pictures, happy and alive.

Next to the photos, was a copy of Hemingway's *The Old Man and the Sea*.    The book had a blue cloth cover with a dust wrapper. The spine was worn and lost some of its blue tone.    It was a first-issue, with only a few nicks at the corners and spine ends, and a tear at the lower rear panel.    The top of the cover had the name HEMINGWAY in capital letters against a grey-blue sea.    The bottom was four wooden shanties at the edge of the shore.    The title was in light letters set in the sand.

I heard Mom and Dad arguing over selling the book a few days prior, Mom red-faced and screaming in her screechy voice. When they fought, Dad would mutter "Dammit, anyway," under his breath.    Sometimes they'd keep me up half the night with Dad's "Dammit anyways" and her high-pitched yelling.

When they weren't fighting they played music together, Dad on guitar and Mom on piano.    Sometimes they co-existed in their solitude, Dad fixing guitars while she painted on a canvas.

I'm very much the genetic child of my parents.    I suppose I got the artistic gene from Mom and the musical gift from Dad.    I paint and play guitar.

I remember on Mom's side of the bed there was an autographed photo of Liberace.    She played his records when Dad was out.    When Dad was in, he played jazz like Wes Montgomery and Johnny Smith.    Those guys were real musicians.    They were musical encyclopedias who knew thousands of chords, chords with names an inch long, so difficult ninety percent of the guitarists alive couldn't play them.

Mom walked me down the stairs to the first floor of our brick house at 202 Oakwood Avenue, which she decorated in the Early

Colonial style. The ground floor was our store, Young's Music Studio. Dad taught a hundred students a week guitar, and Mom instructed thirty-six piano students. I knew the numbers exactly because when they fought, Dad reminded her.

Mom credited Saint Paul, Saint John, Saint George, and Saint Ringo for our cash-cow. The Beatles appearances on Ed Sullivan boosted interest when they opened their store in '63, the year I was born. Other teachers subcontracted space and offered drum, dancing, and martial arts lessons. I benefited from this, taking all the free classes I could.

I was uneasy about the cellar and the attic. The thought of walking the rickety stairs to either room made me shiver. I imagined being trapped down in the cellar and the power suddenly going out and something in the dark shadows waiting to eat me. Mom said I was silly and had a wild imagination. Walker said I was a scaredy-cat. Dad said if there were any monsters, he'd know about it.

Mom drove Dad's '66 white Eldorado Cadillac to church. It had a black roof, peeling in spots from the sun. The Caddy glided like a boat. We took Center Avenue south, around a winding turn called Horseshoe Bend, than up Chalfonte to a grey church with a purple roof. I didn't wear a seat-belt. Not too many kids did in those days. I never fell out of the car with Mom. She watched over me like a mother hen.

"Quit moving, you're distracting me," she said.

We walked up the cement steps hand-in-hand into God's house. She hoisted me an inch off the ground when I dragged my feet.

"Looks like rain," Mom said, gazing upward. I reached up to the sky but didn't feel any drops.

Once inside, she dipped her fingers in the holy water and made the sign of the cross.   I stuck my entire hand in the water and splashed.   I was having fun until Mom yanked my hand away.

"Don't," she said.   "Stay presentable."   She tucked my shirt in again, wrapping me like a mummy.   "What am I going to do with you?   I picked out your clothes and you messed them up, you goof."

When she was irritated, she called me a goof.   When she was frustrated, she called me worse things.   The next stage on the rage-meter was the high screechy yelling, a forewarning that I was in danger.

I heard a voice from inside.   "A reading from the Gospel of John," the monotone said.

A cacophony of parishioners answered back.   "Praise to you, Lord Jesus Christ."

Mom licked her fingertips and brushed my eyebrows again, slicking them down.   I wasn't fond of spit on my eyebrows, but there was no stopping her.   We walked the aisle in the center of the sanctuary.   The church looked gargantuan.   She found a seat, genuflected, and made the sign of the cross again.

I gazed at the man on the sticks with nails stuck into his flesh. My eyes were riveted to the blood.   We entered the pew, distracting the pious, wrinkled women around us who clutched their rosaries for dear life.   They shot me a glance that said, *"Be quiet little boy. Don't disturb our solitude."*

I stared at the man in the dress, and the rest of the stage - incense, the candles, the towering cross.   The bells and the smells were scary and sacred all at the same time.   The man in the dress was Father McCormick.   He was portly, balding with sideburns and wore a purple robe over a white vestment.   He glanced at me as he delivered his pronouncements of doom among the rattling of the beads.

"One day, God will purge our sins out of us in the stinking, scalding flames. You will burn in the light and heat of God's purging fire. Some sins are venial, and melted away easily. But other sins, such as adultery, are mortal. Mortal sins will damn your soul forever."

"What's adultery, Mom?"

"Sssh." Mom held her index finger to her lips.

"Those who commit adultery..." McCormick's voice echoed in the sanctuary through the speakers, "take heaps of burning coals into their own bosom. Some die in God's friendship and grace, but are still imperfectly purified. After death they must undergo purification in God's burning love, to achieve the holiness of heaven. Pray for the souls still in Purgatory."

"Have I ever committed adultery, Mom?"

"No. Be quiet."

I had a question and there was no relenting. "What's adultery? You're not answering."

Mom sighed. "Little boys can't. It's something bad adults do."

I stretched my neck to see over the hat of a heavy-set woman in front. "Satan has a stopwatch in his hand, and he sees his time coming to an end." McCormick pointed right to the section where Mom and I sat. "Therefore, he's chasing you harder and faster and more energetically than ever. He sees his time is running out and he wants you. His tactic is to tempt you with sin."

I squirmed. "I don't like this, Mom. I'm scared."

"Be quiet."

"The devil goes after the young," McCormick said. "Those who cannot fend for themselves."

I didn't understand it all. But what I did understand made me cry.

"Sit still," Mom said.

I wailed and wouldn't stop until we left. She had me by the hair while I kicked and screamed. When we exited the sanctuary, I looked up and saw the cross, high above the votive lights. The beams seemed to reach for me. For a moment, I was transfixed. I imagined my own body on the sticks. The volume from my crying increased and reverberated in the sanctuary. Father McCormick glared at me.

"Come on, you've embarrassed me enough." She yanked me away, and we rushed to the Cadillac in the rain.

That's when my nightmares started.

Later that night, Mom tucked me in with a ritual of eggnog and prayers. "I want to raise you to be a good and godly boy. Pleasant dreams." She kissed me goodnight and left.

I looked at the cross hanging above my bed then closed my eyes, whispering a prayer. "Now I lay me down to sleep, I pray the Lord my soul to keep, if I should die before I wake…"

I drifted off to dreams and a faint sound of scratching on the ceiling.

The house was still and black when I awoke, startled by rapping sounds. They were strange. Muted. Rhythmic.

At approximately one thirty a.m., my bed was shaking. I saw darkness, and then dancing sticks. They moved, crisscrossed, and formed into the beams of the crucifix. The sticks disappeared, and I saw a flash of a floating wooden face, manic yellow eyes with red pupils, and sharp teeth.   The face looked like a mask, but when I looked closer, I saw a detached wooden head.

A little whispering giggle came from the wooden head, in a breath of air wafting through the room.   He was mad and manic, and his little laugh, was the thinnest whisper of a rising laugh.   I felt it all up and down my spine.

I tried to scream, but lost my voice.   Sharp stabbing pains penetrated my stomach like knifes.   I rubbed my arms, trying unsuccessfully to make the goose pimples disappear.   I cowered under the covers but still heard Stick Man's voice mumbling the word "Soul, soul, soul."   His wooden mouth moved on hinges, snapping, coming to eat me.

I wet myself in the panic.   Stick Man clutched me through the covers.   I looked into the tortured eyes of the wooden face and felt a strange kinship for a split second, as if I'd known his eyes forever.

I felt the presence of absolute evil.   The room was cold, colder than the worse winter day.   The temperature must've dropped fifty degrees.   The cold was almost tangible, visible.   The degrading, sickening cold washed over me in waves.

The image vanished as quickly as it came, but I couldn't get back to sleep.   I worried that if I closed my eyes, he'd come back. He haunted me.   He hounded me, this hideous wooden face.   Even after he was gone, I still felt his cold breath freezing me.

I sensed he'd harm me in some unspeakable way, that there was no escaping this animal.   I couldn't outrun him.   He was omnipresent.

I thought of Beaver Creek where Walker and I swam.   By the Fourth of July it was warm as a bathtub, but then we'd hit a cold pocket and the thrill of an unexpected chill.   Minus the thrill, I felt the same quick onslaught of cold on my lower extremities and around my heart.

*Now*, I thought, *I will get my mouth to open right now and I will yell I will yell I will yell.* I found my voice and screamed. "STOP IT," I shouted. "MOM!"

The silence following my shout frightened me further, bringing panic up from the basement of my mind like an unwelcome guest.

Mom heard my yell. "What?" she said from up the hall, rushing to my room. "What, Jeremiah? What?"

"Close the door!" Dad said. "Dammit anyway."

"NO! Pray for me!" I said.

"Okay, okay," Mom said. "You're waking everybody up."

"Mommy, make him *stop*! He's trying to kill me. *Stop him, Mom!*"

"Calm down."

"I'm sorry. But he wanted to eat me, Mom. He wanted to eat my heart. Am I gonna live?"

"Yes." Mom moved stiffly. The sickening cold was gone, except for a little chill down my back when I looked at the crucifix on the wall. She sighed. "You're chosen, Jeremiah. Do you understand?"

"I think so, Mom."

We clutched our rosary beads. "The sorrowful mysteries. Jesus carries the cross." I was comforted by the soothing sound of her voice, and the rosary beads in my hands.

I believed.

I really believed.

Walker was awake by then and he prayed in unison with us. "Our Father, who art in heaven, hallowed be Thy Name…" When we ended the Lord's Prayer, we said a decade of Hail Marys.

"Hail Mary, full of grace, the Lord is with thee…" Even though Hail Marys were easier to say than Our Fathers, Walker lasted through only three more before conking out again.

"Pray for us sinners, now and at the hour of our death," I said.

After Mom and I finished, I saw a light dancing. I blinked and moved my hands in front of my eyes. I pinched myself to make sure I was awake.

"There's an angel in the room right now, Mom. Don't you see her?"

"Get outta town. Are you telling tales again? The truth is strong enough, you don't need to make stories bigger than they are. Don't overstate things, dear." She said "dear" when she knew better than me because I was just a stupid kid.

"But I see them." The light increased in brilliance, and floated to the window. "I want to go to the light."

"I believe that you believe you see them. Maybe they're real, maybe they're not. Wait and see. You experience the world like an Impressionist painter. The energy of emotions, the fantastic feelings. You're my little Monet. Hungry for transcendence."

"You sure use big words, Mom."

"Remember what I taught you to do, when you hear a big word?"

"Look it up."

"Good boy. Leaders are…"

"Readers."

She had taught me to read early after she noticed I was recognizing words in the Pittsburgh Press. She bought me a bunch of Disney books because I wanted to visit Disneyland one day, the happiest place on earth.

She reached by my bed and found the dictionary beneath the Disney books and baseball cards. "I know you're tired, so I'll read the definition." She cleared her throat like a bugle blast and began. *"Transcend. To rise above the ordinary limits. Beyond the material existence of reality."*

The dancing light was gone. When she'd said, 'ordinary limits,' my mind left the world of dictionaries, of all things clearly defined. I saw Stick Man's face again for a split second, and my hands were knotted in my bed sheet.

"I'm afraid to sleep. Stick Man will kill me."

"You're becoming a big boy. Almost ready for Holy Communion. When you receive Jesus, you'll end bad dreams. He'll take away your Stick Man. Now say the rest of your prayers."

"Okay. I promise. But don't leave."

"Gabriel and Walker are here."

"Walker's little and he's already asleep. I want you to stay." I batted my eyelashes and stuck my lower lip out. Sometimes I charmed her into feeling sorry for me. No such luck that night.

"Gabriel's a good watchdog. He'll bark if anything happens." Gabriel recognized his name, and his ears perked up like soldiers at command. "Get to sleep, tomorrow's the big day, you start preparation for Eucharist."

After she left, I started dreaming. Good dreams at first, of Disneyland, the circus and roller-coasters. Suddenly, I saw the decapitated wooden face again and smelled the monster's odor, a rancid smell of wet, rotten vegetables.

The room went immensely cold again, so cold I could see my breath in front of me. I grimaced and shivered. Panic rose in me like water in an overflowing tub. I lay perfectly still, a pale mannequin with a pulse beating in my throat. Stabbing pains returned, this time they clawed around my head like a crown of thorns.

I closed my eyes and prayed to fight against Stick Man.

"Jesus, help me!" I cried. My heart hurried in my chest.

The face vanished, and all was calm for a few seconds until a cross appeared. The beams detached and transubstantiated into dancing sticks. Then they blossomed into a man, with limbs made of wood. The face reappeared, baring his great big sharp teeth like a lion in the circus, and then the face floated to the top of the stick body. He wasn't headless after all. He was a wooden man with a stick body. He was the apotheosis of all monsters, and he was hungry for boy meat. He didn't have any hands, only sticks.

Stick Man.

# 2

I tried to slip off my pajama top, but it was glued to my belly. I noticed a brown stain. I peeled up my shirt, and it felt like removing a Band-Aid that was stuck on body hair. The stain was dried blood. The hair on the nape of my neck stood straight up.

I screamed.

Mom rushed back into the bedroom. "What the hell did you do?"

"I didn't do anything. I just woke up and I was cut."

"Do you remember falling out of bed?"

"Na-ah," I whimpered.

She ran her hand along the edge of the bed. "The bedpost is pretty sharp. Maybe you rubbed against the edge."

Mom wiped my cut, than bandaged it. She took my temperature and felt my forehead.

"Do you want to stay home today?"

"No, I'd better go to school." I figured I needed to be at Saint Joe's.

Mom was the handyman, so she sanded down the bedpost, and covered the sharp edges.

"Eat your cereal and get dressed. I don't want you to be late. And watch out when yins go outside, it's cold out there this morning."

I hardly touched my Cheerios.

I wondered if it was really the bedpost. Mom said so, and that settled it for the most part. The more I thought about the mysterious cut on my belly, the more my cold hands shook.

Soon I was at school. I hopped off the school bus, and went inside to join the other students. We tip-toed into the sanctuary, led by Sister Antonita. She was a large-breasted woman with a mannish face. Even though there were no masses going on, she told us to line up single file, and be quiet. I pretended to be tired and bumped into my friend Red Rawlings, who fussed back.

Red had unruly hair, crooked teeth, and an awkward gait. He wasn't allowed to have Communion because his family was Protestant. His father Mordecai was a Baptist preacher, but he sent Red to Saint Joe's because it was a private school and he hoped Red could witness and win us to their brand of salvation. Mordecai and Red believed the Catholic Church was the Great Whore of Babylon.

He still participated in the Communion practice, and walked with anticipation. Red was only a nickname, given because of his hair. His glasses were broken in the center, held together precariously by Scotch tape. The other children marched robotically with hands folded in front of their chests and mocked Red. I felt sorry for him.

My eyes were attuned to the high ceiling, vaulted upward to draw all eyes to heaven. There was a mural on the wall behind the altar of Jesus and His disciples. The artist rendered the shapes with simple lines, putting Jesus in the center.

We sat in the pews, engulfed by the stillness. The altar cradled a box in the center. Sister explained the Eucharistic hosts inside had been blessed by Father, transforming them into the body and blood of Jesus. The thought of the infinite God confined in a box in the suburbs of Pittsburgh was quite staggering. I longed to lift that lid and see Him. I wanted to free the Almighty from His limitations, but religion and the suburbs preferred formulas, pat answers, and above all, predictability - God in a box. There was another dark box, however that frightened me even more.   An old black chest in our attic, covered with cobwebs.   It was locked.   I preferred it that way.

"Please keep me from sin," I prayed.

If Stick Man turned out to be real, more than a bedpost or a bad dream, he might kill me, and I didn't want to be in Purgatory any longer than I had to be.   He terrorized me from the attic when it was dark, emerging late at night to ravage my dreams and he reigned from the top to the bottom of our house.   He peeked and popped from behind the heater in the basement, if I was alone.   He'd make a sound, like pigs being slaughtered, than retreat.   He lived in an alternate universe, a world subterranean and supernatural.

Often, when I walked down the first few steps towards the cellar, my heart would hammer in my throat and I would stop and run back to the first floor, sweat popping out of my arms and forehead.   I knew he was down there.

I told my brother Walker about Stick Man.   "He tried to get me and eat me."

Walker was roly-poly, but could run like a jackrabbit with Gabriel barking and nipping at his heels.   His belly protruded like a middle-aged man.   He was tough, with Popeye muscles.

"I'm not afraid of Stick Man," he said.   "I'm faster than he is."   Walker laughed when I talked about Stick Man.   I woke him on several occasions, moaning and thrashing, but he usually slept through my dark nights.

I tried to forget Stick Man by eating candy.   And I knew how to get plenty of it.

I had a collection of masks I interchanged, pretending to be a pirate, Santa Claus, Batman, Detective Dick Tracy, or Popeye the Sailorman.   Sometimes it was easier to be brave when I was someone else.  I returned home after trick-or-treating Oakwood Avenue.  I switched masks and went back five times, so I netted five times as much candy as Walker and Red.

I ate until my stomach ached.  I rested my thin fingers on my abdomen over my Stick Man scar, feeling the mixture of pleasure and pain.  My favorite candy was Mallo Cups, a Pennsylvania confection of chocolate and marshmallows.  Looking at the Mallo Cups, and the discarded wrappers I'd accumulated, I was struck with an idea to help the church.

The next day at school, I told Sister Antonita, "Saint Joseph's is like a candy bar that needs a new wrapper.  After all, ever since Elvis, people really like the guitar more than the piano, but the church is stuck in a time machine playing the organ. No offense, Sister." Sister smiled and quoted the words of Christ about new wineskins for the sacred wine.

The nuns tried their best to be hip in 1971.  Some wore street clothes rather than habits.  They played acoustic guitars for folk mass, singing songs like *Where Have All the Flowers Gone*, and *Blowing in the Wind*.  Sister Antonita's Joan Baez voice projected to the back pew.

They played guitars with the same strum pattern and used it for every song.  One-two-and-three-and-four.  One-two-and-three-and-four.  Sister Antonita once asked me if Dad and I would play for church.  She said she had too many other responsibilities at Saint Joe's, but I figured she knew the nuns couldn't really play rhythm guitar.

"I'll talk to him about it when I have my next lesson," I said.

Once a week, Dad sat me down for my lesson.  "You have soul, just like me, although not on my level," he said, tuning the guitar to pitch. "You feel the music pretty well and your sight-reading's coming along."

When we reviewed *Somewhere Over the Rainbow*, the song I selected for my first competitive performance, Dad couldn't curb his perfectionism. He exploded because I hit a wrong note.

"You lost the beat, goddammit," he said, punching me on the head with his beefy hands. "Straighten up and fly right, buddy boy."

*I won't cry.*

"You'll never have the audience if you lose the rhythm. When I play, I have them right there," he said, pointing to his open hand. "In the palm of my hands."

His fingers were too thick for a guitar player, but he was a master musician despite his huge hands. His rage proved pragmatic, for my performance of the song improved. I caught Dad listening outside my bedroom when I practiced on my half-sized Stella. I sensed he was there and got a glimpse of him through the crack in the door. I made absolutely certain to hit every note cleanly. My guitar playing elicited a good mood and a rare compliment from Dad, so I asked him if he'd play for Saint Joe's.

Dad and I took over the folk mass to help out, but the responsibility was too much and we handed the ball back after a few months. His band played in the bars every Saturday till the wee hours, which wasn't conducive to rising early Sunday to rehearse church musicians. The upshot was that he soon asked me to play with him at weddings. I learned how to play rhythm in the process. The downside was Dad yelled at me on stage until my hands shook.

Dad took me to Mass sometimes, but dashed out right after Communion, ten minutes before everyone else to beat the rush to escape the parking lot. This was no easy task, as the cars were stacked tandem in what was called "Catholic parking," maximizing the undersized lot's capacity.    Father McCormick's homily to "love your neighbor" was forgotten amidst the blaring horns.    Dad never received Communion.

Sundays were difficult for him.    One distinct morning stands out in my memory.    He lay snoring on the velvet bed, hung over from Saturday night's gig.    Walker and I could hear the grizzly bear noises no matter what floor of the house we were on.    We walked into his bedroom as quietly as we could.    When Dad had too much, Walker's job was to pile washrags on his forehead, and I was assigned to take off his shoes and socks.

After I removed the shoes, I assisted Walker, placing washrags on Dad as he came to.    When the washrags cooled, Mom replaced them with warm ones.

"Tell us a story," I said, shaking Dad from his stupor.    We lay beside him in bed.

Dad struggled to begin.    His voice was raw from singing for the barflies from ten p.m. till two in the morning.    He smelled of Pall Mall cigarettes and Old Spice.

He whispered, "Once upon a time, there were two little boys. Jeremiah and Walker."

"We're the stars," I said.

"They set off for a walk through the woods," Dad said. "They got lost."

"Uh-oh," Walker said.

"The day dragged on and it got very dark."    At this, we sat up.    Walker clenched his fist.    "They came to a haunted house. The windows were boarded up.    No one knew what was inside."

"I ain't afraid of ghosts," Walker said.

"Inside the house they saw a monster with a wooden mask."

"Stick Man," I said.

"Stick Man. Than Jeremiah climbed the stairs, up into the attic. There was a magic mirror next to the door. When Jeremiah and Walker gazed into the mirror, they couldn't see their faces. They saw the face of Stick Man in the mirror. Laughing." Dad cackled. "Jeremiah opened the door. He found the key to unlock Stick Man's mask, and learn the truth about who he was."

"What happened when he took Stick Man's mask off?" Walker asked.

"They saw that Stick Man was sad because everyone was afraid of him. 'I don't mean to do the things I do,' he said. 'Forgive me."

"Never. I hate you Stick Man," I said. "What happened next?" Gabriel was on the bed now, wagging his tail.

Mom was in the doorway eavesdropping. "I don't want you scaring them right now, Saul," she said, coming in with fresh washrags. "Jeremiah has bad dreams as it is."

"Finish the story, Daddy," Walker said.

"Why don't you finish the story, Jeremiah?" Dad asked. "You need to figure out the ending since you're the one who sees Stick Man."

"There are ghosts in the house, but we fight them and chase them away. And Stick Man is gone from our dreams forever," I said. "That'll be the end."

# 3

My favorite TV shows were broadcast live from downtown Pittsburgh on the weekends,    Chilly Billy and Kathryn Kuhlman. Saturday nights, Dad and I watched the wrestling matches on WPXI, Channel Eleven.   They were hosted by Chilly Billy Cardilly, who also was the emcee for the Chiller Theatre horror movie later at midnight.   My favorite wrestler was Bruno Sammartino, the world champion.   Bruno was a hairy, Italian man with big hands, like Dad. A working class hero from Abruzzi, Italy, he now lived in the North Hills of Pittsburgh, just minutes away from our house.   He'd once lifted a five hundred pound wrestler named Haystacks Calhoun clear over his head.   Bruno was part of my extended family.   Dad somehow called the TV station and got Bruno to call and wish me a happy eighth birthday.

I was a believer.

Bruno was a clean wrestler who defended the title against all challengers including Killer Kowalski, Olympic strongman Ken Patera, Nazi Baron Von Raske, George the Animal Steele, and Russian bear Nicolai Volkoff.   I pleaded every Saturday night begging Dad to drive me to the TV station for the wrestling show. Week after week, he said he couldn't because he was playing a gig.

The answer to my prayers came on a Saturday in June when his music job fell through.   Dad loaded Walker and me in his Cadillac.   We sat in the front row of the Pittsburgh Civic Arena beside Ringside Rosie, the most passionate believer of all.   A portly woman past sixty-five, she wore a gaudy hat with plastic bananas and apples.

"I design the hats myself," she said.

I wished I could climb into the ring and bounce off the mat and the ropes to hear the crashing sounds the grapplers made. The scent of popcorn and beer wafted past me as I fantasized that I was Bruno's tag-team partner for a title bout.

Bruno's enemies were monstrous, especially George "The Animal" Steele. He had fur all over his body, including his back, but his oversized head was completely bald. He didn't speak very much. He grunted mostly and ate the microphone and the turnbuckles.

Occasionally, the Animal yelled a hipster phrase like, "Hey, Daddy-O."

Bruno defeated him in a bloody steel cage match while I chanted "BRU-NO, BRU-NO, BRU-NO!"

Early Sunday morning, I crept down to our Sylvania TV set. Everyone was asleep so I had to be quiet. I had a tendency to blast the volume, so Mom marked a spot on the volume dial with her ruby red lipstick. I wasn't allowed to turn the volume past the red.

I turned on the TV and heard the announcer's voice. "And now, ladies and gentleman it's time for the Miracle Hour, with Pittsburgh's woman of power, Kathryn Kuhlman."

She glided out like an angel in her white chiffon dress. Everyone cheered in praise. The choir stood behind her in red robes.

"I believe in miracles," she said. "Do you believe in miracles?"

"Yes, Sister," I said. "I believe." My eyes were glued to the television.

She led the congregation in the repetition of phrases. The longer they chanted the more power came across the TV. "The power is in the blood," she whispered. "In ancient Egypt, the Israelites put the blood on the doorposts of their house, at the top of the doorframe and at both sides. The death angel had to pass right on by. Why? The blood," she said.

"The blood," I answered in sync with the TV congregation.

"The blood, the blood, the blood…" Kathryn said. "Say it with me."

"The blood, the blood, the blood…" we repeated until the masses were ready for deliverance. Sister's bemused smile changed to seriousness. She confronted any doubters, pointing into the audience.

"I am not the healer. I am only a witness to the power. With His stripes you were healed. Diabetics, cancer victims, high blood-pressure, those who are blind, deaf, and dumb, migraine sufferers…Receive the miracle!"

The theatre built to a crescendo as several hundred sick lined up like lambs for the touch. Kathryn's healing hands moved mountains and manifested miracles.

She was a mixture of sensuality and spirituality. Her religion felt erotic to me. Anything that wasn't Catholic was risqué. The nuns at Saint J's told me it was a sin to attend a Protestant church, and a mortal sin to watch Kathryn.

When she stretched out her hand to heal, the camera zoomed in for a close-up on her fingers. I placed my hand to the television, feeling the kinetic connection.

She stretched out her syllables in a whisper. "The Hoooo-lllyyyy Sssspirit is here…" Her uplifted arm displayed sleeves like angel wings on her white dress. "Many are talking about this new movie about demonic possession." I scooted closer to the TV. "There is only one power that conquers the Evil One. The power of looooovvvvvve," she said, elongating the word 'love' with the theatricality of an actress. "Perfect love casts out fear."

"Perfect love casts out fear," I said.

*****

I sat Indian style, cross-legged with Red Rawlings and my twelve classmates on the freshly-waxed floor at Saint Joe's. The aroma of disinfectant and paste drifted in from the halls.

"The word 'martyr,' is from a Greek word in the New Testament that means 'witness,'" Sister Antonita said. "I'm going to tell you about three witnesses willing to die for their faith. Would you be willing to die for Christ?"

I thought I would be, but in all honesty, I worried I might chicken out. I didn't want Stick Man to kill me.

Sister dramatized a tale of an altar boy who was tortured and killed by bullies, yet still protected the host he was carrying in his jacket. The body of Christ was held close to his chest. Then Sister's voice filled my head with images of Saint Sebastian's protection of the Christians, when the Roman troops tied him to a tree and shot him with arrows. Then I learned of the clairvoyant Joan of Arc, her visions from God, and her flesh burning at the stake in Rouen.

After religion class, came my favorite subject, Art. Sister rambled on, holding my drawings up before the class. "Look at the emotion. The faces. The eyes. They're not just stick figures. Jeremiah makes them three-dimensional."

I noticed these things for the first time as she raved about them. When I drew pictures, or played my guitar, it came out intuitively without much analysis.

"It's no accident you're part of Saint Joseph's, Jeremiah. Joseph was the carpenter, the patron saint of artists. You have special gifts," she said.    She pulled me aside and put her large hands on my shoulders.    "They're your weapons in the spiritual warfare. Keep painting and playing that guitar of yours.    Make something for Christ, Jeremiah," Sister Antonita said.    "Use your talents to win the warfare you are facing."

Mom taught me how to paint.    I was chosen out of all the students at school to train Saturday mornings with an artist who was a mentor to Andy Warhol when he was a boy in Pittsburgh.    I had an easel and paints set up in the attic, next to my Stella guitar.    That week, I overheard Mom and Dad discussing my paintings of the Savior.

"He's getting too obsessed with Jesus," Dad said.    "It's not normal."

"There's worse things," Mom said.

My model for painting Jesus hung in the center of our living room, above the TV and the shelves of green Bohemian glass.    Mom referred to it, in hushed tones, as the "Sacred Heart," because in the chest of Jesus was a burning heart, encircled by a crown of thorns, under a flame and light.    Jesus had hair parted in the center, like David Cassidy, the Partridge Family pop star who had a 1970's shag. The beard of the Savior was trimmed into a gap below His chin. Wherever I walked, the eyes of Jesus followed me.    I couldn't understand how this worked, but I concluded it was probably a form of heavenly magic.

I knew Stick Man's power was strong, but the blood of Jesus was stronger.    The painter who taught my Saturday art class at the Carnegie Museum in Oakland told me something strange.

"Artists always put their blood into each painting," he said. At eight years-old, I interpreted this literally.    When I painted Jesus, I pricked my finger with a pin and mixed my blood into the red paint.

Jesus began with a series of sketches. I tried various scenarios, drawing on a canvas with a charcoal stick. I drew Him with and without halos. Without halos was better, because Jesus was fully human.

The best sketches were the ones with blood. The moment the needle pricked I winced in pain, but I told myself I was a martyr, sharing in the fellowship of Christ's suffering like Saint Sebastian and Joan of Arc.

I cajoled Mom into buying me the linen canvases, but Dad yelled about the lion's share of the budget going to my painting. When Mom told me I had to do without, I panicked and protested, because I knew Stick Man wouldn't take a vacation from his assaults against me. Mom bought cheaper paper.

I lit the prayer candles one by one. They cast the glow that enfolded my easel with clouds of smoke.

"I hope I can be good enough," I said, "and do enough for You, so that Stick Man disappears forever. In the name of the Father, the Son, and the Holy Spirit, Amen." I blessed myself, making the sign of the cross.

For the hair of Jesus, I used burnt sienna. Yellow ochre worked best for the flesh tones. For the eyes of Jesus I mixed two blues, cobalt and ultramarine. For the robes, I wanted a strong white. I set up my palette, the burnt sienna on the right, the yellows at the top, and the blues and greens to the left.

The butcher up the street at Kelly's Drug Store on Center Avenue gave me reams of white paper. I spread the sheets over a piece of glass I found at the trash dump next to my house. This was my mixing surface. The remaining white sheets were spread on the floor, along with old *Boy's Life* magazines to catch the paint drips.

Mom bought me several straight palette knifes from the art supply store for mixing. "Use these," she said. "Wipe them clean before starting each new mixture. And don't tell your father I bought you these, or I'll beat your ass. Do you understand me?"

"Yes, Mom."

I dragged a portion of the yellow half-way down towards the blue, than pulled some blue up to the yellow, blending the two colors. I prayed as I mixed. "Jesus, help me." Mom told me to pray repetitively, like the biblical story of a woman that kept banging on a judge's door until she got what she wanted.

I mixed more of the blue into part of the medium green, to get a blue green on the other side. "Save me from Stick Man," I prayed.

I stirred more of the yellow until a clear yellow-green was achieved. I pulled another part of the blue towards the red and the red towards the blue. From these I combined a spot of purple.

I added blue to the purple to achieve violet, than red to deepen the purple for His robe. I continued mixing to achieve a range of chromatic possibilities on my palette. With white, I achieved half-tones. I pricked my finger a third time and let my blood drip into the reds and warm colors.

I adjusted the easel so it was at eye level. For the face of Christ, I started with three pencil guide lines. A vertical line the length of the face, drawn to divide it in half. A horizontal line the width of the face, drawn at the center of where His eyes would be. A third line was horizontal for the mouth. I had difficulties painting mouths, but this time I hoped I could master the sacred lips. I sketched Jesus, outlining the drawing in rose madder mixed with flake white and thinned with turpentine. I used a round sable brush and a broader bristle brush. I held the brush at the end of the handle and painted at arm's length.    After each brush stroke, I stepped back and looked at my work.

I made a mistake, smearing the face.

I panicked.

I turned around, feeling the breath of Stick Man, but he wasn't there behind me.    I knew how cunning he was, baffling as to when and why he manifested.    Like a Greek god, his attacks were unpredictable and irrational.

I erased the mistake with a soft rag moistened in turpentine and an eraser.    *"No, God, why?"*

I ripped a hole in the canvas and froze.    I stared at the blemish, slammed my fist on the palette, and knocked excess paint to the floor.    My shoe stuck to the newspapers and I couldn't dislodge my foot.    I shook my leg but the papers stuck, hardening around my foot.    I knew this was a counterattack.

"Cover me in your blood.    The blood, the blood, the blood."

I kept painting, ignoring as best I could the newspapers stuck to my shoe.    I wanted to give the face of Jesus a strong light from the right, throwing a strong shadow over the features.    I painted a little purple in the shadows of His face.    I finally got the mouth right, mixing from cadmium red and white, than I finished the features and unified the colors of the face.    In the bottom right corner, I signed my name.

I held up the mirror to see Jesus in reverse image.    To catch any flaws or wrong proportions.    The reflection was smoky.    The room filled with clouds.    I felt a chill, a cold presence.

There were yellow eyes looking back at me.

Stick Man was glaring in the mirror with his gleaming mad eyes, ready to bite like a rabid dog.    He was the image of all that was backward and reverse.    The manifestation of all that was flawed and insecure.   My heart beat in sixteenth note palpitations.   I gasped aloud in muted terror.   A voice, calm and reasonable spoke from the mirror.

*"Hello, Jeremiah."*

I blinked and looked again at his grinning, mad-staring face, at his cracked wooden lips grunting like a pig.   Stick Man's fox-like eyes glared from his round wooden face.   His head undulated like a cobra and his limbs were flailing.   He was worse than all my imaginations of the monster in the attic.

He seized my wrist with his stick-arm in one clawing stroke. *"These sticks are the cross that killed Jesus and they will kill you,"* his rotten voice whispered.   He hissed like a snake, salivating, coming closer to eat me.   He wanted to consume me, take me into himself, make me a part of his hellish horror.   I felt the dread of damnation.   For a moment, I was paralyzed.   I tried to scream, but nothing came out.   I tried to run, but my feet were frozen.   He pulled me into his terrible darkness.

Stick Man sang, mocking all that was sacred.   *"At the cross, at the cross, where I first saw the light, and the burden of my heart rolled away…"*

I dropped the mirror.   The glass shattered on the ground. The candles and lights flickered on and off.   I leapt down the attic stairs, screaming a shrill prayer into that horrific night in 1971.

"Pray for us sinners, now and at the hour of our death…"

Gabriel rushed to the rescue.   He barked towards the steps to scare Stick Man out of the attic.

"Good watchdog, Gabriel," I said.   "That's a good boy."

There was no doubt now.   Stick Man was real.   We would have to fight to the finish, like Bruno and George the Animal Steele.

And I was scared shitless.

# 4

The stretch of Oakwood where we lived was magical. Most of the families were Catholic and had four or more children. They filled the streets in those golden summers. I could round up a baseball game in five minutes and live out my fantasies, pretending to be the Great One, Pittsburgh's stellar right fielder Roberto Clemente. My street was only two blocks, but to our gang of kids that lived there, everything of import happened there. Our playmates and our play was our world.

Most of the fathers worked at one of the steel mills, J. & L., Bethlehem Steel, or the mills at the river towns of Ambridge and Coraopolis. An amusement park, West View Park, towered over the Center Avenue bend, holding an invitation to frolic. The magic of the merry-go-round cast a spell. My favorite ride was the carousel and the Racing Whippet rollercoaster.

That weekend, I ran a movie house out of Dad's basement with a Super 8 projector. I bought films like Abbott and Costello's *Ride Em Cowboy* and *Hold That Ghost* for the features. I showed Woody Woodpecker and Mickey Mouse cartoons for the preview. I charged a dollar per ticket to the neighborhood to raise money for the Muscular Dystrophy Association.

Gossip spread like wildfire about my movie night. All of the children crammed together in my basement. I avoided the cellar because of Stick Man, but the group kept him away. The kids generated electricity like they were at the Academy Awards. Mom made popcorn and divvied it up in brown sacks, sold for a nickel. The neighborhood kids clapped and screamed.

I sat with Walker, PK Red Rawlings, and his sister Savannah. "One day, I'm going to move to Hollywood and be in the movies,"

Savannah said, twirling her long red hair over her shoulder. "I won't forget you, Jeremiah when I'm a rich and famous actress in Hollywood."

"Actresses have to be pretty," Red said, dismissing her.

"One day I'll show you. You think I'm pretty, don't you, Jeremiah?"

I looked at her face, covered with freckles. I knew if I said yes, I'd get teased by Red and Walker, and feed into her crush on me. If I said no, I'd hurt her feelings. So I changed the subject and thanked everybody for helping the least of our brethren.

I sent the fifty dollars I raised to WTAE Channel 4. I scribbled on the envelope, "For Jerry's Kids, in care of Adventure Time."

Spring arrived on a Saturday, happy and green after the Pittsburgh winter. I climbed the hill next door to the top where all the daisies were. I picked armfuls to bring Mom as a love offering. She sat on a barstool in the kitchen where she made Kool Aid for me and Walker.

I handed her the flowers. "Oh, that's sweet." She probed my face. "What did you two do today?"

"Oh, stuff," I said.

"What kinda stuff?"

"Walker played with Lincoln Logs and I painted. Then we went outside to pick flowers."

"I built a fort," Walker said.

"Mom, can't we go see Spiritos at the Magic Shop?" I pleaded. "Can we?"

She smiled. "Go the bathroom and red up. Wash your face and hands and we'll go."

Mom supported my show business impulses, making me puppets and taking me to visit local magician "Spiritos the Magnificent." He had a magic shop on the first floor of his three-story theatre in Wilkinsburg. He wore a black turban with golden beads. His green eyes were wild, and his hair was jet-black.

When I'd first met him, he pulled half dollars out of my ears than made them disappear again. "Now you see it, now you don't," he'd said.

Spiritos tapped me with his magic wand. "Rabbit-child of Blackstone, son of Spiritos, and grandson of Houdini, I pass on the magic to you," he said, moving the glowing wand around the circumference of my head.

Spiritos Sabatino was a Renaissance man, a thespian who performed magic and music. He played guitars with my father, and acted in regional theatre. None of these things earned him a lot of money, but he didn't need to. That came to Spiritos through the mob.

He was the patriarch to Dad, and he was the godfather of the Cosa Nostra. The sanctuary at Saint Joseph's was paid in full with his dirty money. We gathered with the Sabatino family on Saturdays to play music, discuss business, eat, and play blackjack. After dinner, Spiritos smoked cigars and black Cavendish tobacco in a clay pipe. Before he lit up, he'd pass his finger through the flame of the lighter and I marveled how his finger never burned. I decided right then and there to smoke cigars when I was old enough.

Spiritos, Dad, and I played standards like *Satin Doll, I'm Confessing That I Love You, Tenderly,* and *Misty.* Dad played full harmony lead on his blonde Gibson.

Spiritos played rhythm using lots of ninth and seventh chords. I played chords in the first position. Dad smiled at the admiration in my eyes. Their melodies and skill swept me away.

"Who's your father?" Dad asked.

"The music man," I said.

"And what is your father?"

"A genius." We'd rehearsed this answer countless times so I'd answer by rote. Dad coached me, and then laughed each time, like it was something I came up with on my own.

"That's right. I'm M.G. Music genius. I discovered my talent, son, when I picked up your grandpa's mandolin. After that I explored the guitar, banjo, bass, drums. I discovered I could teach myself anything. When I was your age, you should've seen me, son. I was a wunderkind. You know what a wunderkind is?"

"No."

"Tell your mother to look it up in that damn dictionary of hers. Wunderkind. A kid that's so brilliant, they come around once every hundred years or so. I entertained the adults at the beer halls in the Southside, the Northside, all over."

"Your father's the best," Spiritos said. "I fool around on the guitar, but he's a real guitarist. I'd give a million dollars to play like him."

The bowl of spaghetti on the Godfather's table looked like a feeding trough. His black and white Manx cat perched on the table like a king and was treated like an equal. Spiritos named him "Loser," and Loser ate from the bowl of spaghetti when everyone was full.

"I hope Loser has babies soon," I said, rolling my spaghetti on my fork, the way Dad and Spiritos did. I wanted my own cat and was banking on Loser having kittens. The noodles never spooled very well, so I'd end up cutting them with a knife and eating them with my fork the normal way.

Spiritos laughed. His laugh was like warm thunder lighting up the whole room. "I promised you a kitten some day. Don't worry, I always keep my word."

"Another cat in the household will cause fights with Gabriel," Mom said, scooping the spaghetti.

"Don't worry. The lion shall lay down with the lamb," Spiritos said. I sucked on one end of a long noodle, feeling it slide up my chin and through my lips. I saw Spiritos grin at this. "When I give you a cat, what will you name him, Jeremiah?"

"Shadow."

"Who knows what evil lurks in the heart of man?" Spiritos said. "The Shadow knows."

Spiritos was feared, and no one wanted to cross him. Dad was a purist in his technique. Once when my thumb came up on the frets, Dad hit me. "Don't be a wisenheimer," he said. "Keep your thumb behind the neck."

"Don't be too hard on the boy," Spiritos said. Spiritos was the first person to really listen to me. He talked to me as an equal, just like he talked to his cat.

When Spiritos used his thumb to get the bass notes, no one told the godfather it was wrong. Despite his ability to knock someone off with an order, he was tender towards me, defending me and cherishing my drawings like they were Van Gogh originals. Spiritos taped a series of my work on his wall, sketches of Spiritos and Dad playing guitar. I wrote a caption beneath the sketches: *"i love Dad and uncle Spiritos."* Spiritos studied them as he smoked his stogie.

"Do you have to go away again, Uncle Spiritos?" I asked. He vanished periodically, but always came back.

"One day I'll be gone for good, so keep this note." He reached into a dresser drawer where he kept his ashtray, magic wand, and guitar picks. He pulled out a sealed envelope and handed it to me.

"Read this when I'm gone and remember what I tell you." There was a twinkle in his eyes. He puffed on his Cuban, than tapped me on the head with his electric wand. "Follow dreams!"

The tip of the wand touched my head. The moment it made contact with my head, the wand glowed orange and red.

We finished the evening with blackjack. Dad never looked as excited as when he yelled to Spiritos for another card. "Hit me, baby, hit me," he'd say. He peeked at his cards and said, "Freeze. I'm good."

The magic of Spiritos couldn't protect me forever. Like Moses escaping the wrath of Pharaoh by hiding in the bulrushes, I had an early brush with death. I fell in the yard, landing on a stick Dad pounded in the ground. We used it for playing horseshoes. The stick pierced through my neck, puncturing my throat. I struggled to breathe, and saw Stick Man's shadow, dark and nonhuman.

*"You've opened doors you can't close, little boy,"* Stick Man said.

My vision blurred, but I could make out Stick Man's arms forming into a cross. When they found my body and carried me to the ambulance, the neighborhood ladies gathered around our porch in a circle, crying and praying. I felt the warmth from their faces encircling me. All the ladies from my cookie rounds.

They were well-acquainted with me. I disappeared and was gone from dawn to dusk most days. "I don't know where you go or what you do," Mom said. "You're a bad boy. No matter how many times I spank you, you keep running away."

If I heard it once, I heard it a hundred times: *"Bad boy...,"* and *"You're gonna go to the bad boy home..."* I believed her story at the time, that I disappeared because I was 'bad.' Like a cat, I knew when to hit each house for treats.

"Where were you?" Mom asked upon my return each evening.

"I visit," I said.

She beat me for wandering off. It never curtailed me from making my rounds the next day. Women gathered around the porch and whispered after Stick Man stabbed my neck. I went in and out of consciousness, but heard some of their concern.

"He falls down a lot. Always bruised all over, poor thing," Mrs. Grace said. "Someone should keep a better eye on him."

"Such a beautiful boy," Mrs. Curen said. "He's too thin. I worry they're starving that child."

Mom stood there too, distant and remote. I saw their faces as I passed them on the porch and they transported me from the stretcher.

Exposed on the hospital bed, I realized the nurses could see me in my underwear. The doctor stood to my left, the nurses to my right. No one comforted me. They gave me a shot to calm me.

"What happened?" Doctor Bosley asked.

"Tripped."

"How did you trip?"

"A wooden leg. Stick Man tried to kill me."

"Hmmm. A stick bent on malevolence."

I recovered from the neck wound and Mom bought me more puppets and magic tricks, keeping her part of a deal she'd struck with me.  I was so worried about Stick Man, I couldn't eat. How could I even think of eating with Stick Man waiting to pounce?  When my stomach was full, I got sleepy.  When I got sleepy, I fell asleep.  When I fell asleep, I was more vulnerable to Stick Man.  Starving myself was part of my strategy to stay awake and stay safe.

Mom tried everything to no avail.  I sat at the table Saturday evening, my stomach upset at the thought Stick Man might appear.  I couldn't swallow a bite.  Dad and Walker were long since gone, having ate their plates clean.  I sat alone, my vigil and solitude scorching Mom with what she perceived as defiance.

"Why aren't you eating, young man?"

"Stick Man."

"That's enough out of you."

"I don't like it.   Round steak's like eating leather.   It hurts."

"I don't give a damn whether you like it or not.   You'll sit at that table until you finish what's on your plate," she said.

"I will NOT."

"You're free to leave the table as soon as you finish your dinner.   Until then, you sit there."

Four hours passed.

I stared at the dinner table.   Then I recalled that Spiritos anointed my head with the wand, imparting magic to me.   I blinked my eyes three times to make the food disappear, but the magic didn't work.

"This meat hurts my throat," I said.

I snuck a few pieces of meat to Gabriel under the table.   The carpet transformed into a clear ocean.   The blue water was crystal clear and sparkling like a diamond.   My eyes followed the fish swimming in figure-eight patterns below the table. Gabriel clawed at the fish with his paw. Gabriel belonged completely to me and was always on my side. He excelled any human in matters of loyalty.

A crocodile the size of the table drifted towards my feet. I lifted my toes just in time to avoid the snapping jaws at the base of my chair.

When Mom left the kitchen for a moment to check on Walker upstairs, I knew it was my chance. I swam the choppy waters of the dining room floor, clutching the meat in a napkin. I made it to the kitchen, hearing the *Mission Impossible* theme in my head as I threw the gristles into the garbage. Then I did an Olympic dive into the sea to swim back to my chair at the shore, eluding sharks and crocodiles.

"WHAT ARE YOU DOING SLITHERING ON THE FLOOR LIKE A SNAKE?" Mom's face was beet red. "YOU ARE SUPPOSED TO BE EATING YOUR DINNER, NOT DIRTYING UP YOUR SHIRT!"

The sea became carpet once again. I took my seat and held up my empty plate, feigning the pride of accomplishment.

"That's a good boy. I knew you could do it."

I scampered off to play, but my freedom was short-lived. Mom discovered the meat in the trash. She grabbed one of my toys, a paddle with a red bouncy-ball attached by a string. She disengaged the ball and string and beat me to a pulp with the wooden paddle.

Mom made a joke about "applying the board of education to the seat of learning." Her techniques didn't work. The spankings had no effect on my refusal to eat. I continued my hunger strike every evening for five-hour vigils.    I stared at my dinner, night after night.

The deal was cut one night during bedtime snacks.    For every week I ate my dinner, I received painting supplies, puppets, a magic trick, or guitar sheet music.    Dad went ballistic when my proclivities cost more money again.

"It's the only way I can get him to eat.    Do you want your son to starve?" Mom asked.

"Bullshit.    If he wants to be an artist, let him be a starving artist," Dad said.

"You don't mean that."

"I suppose he's not eating because of Stick Man."

I heard their arguments.    Their voices were loud and the walls were thin.

"Doctor Bosley said the night terrors are real to Jeremiah. We must go along with-"

"He blames Stick Man for everything.    That boy's got you wrapped around his finger."

"What kind of a father are you?"

"You encourage him," Dad said.

"Go ahead and blame me.    I'm tired of your guilt trips. You're good at that, you know."

"What's the doctor say?"

"Here.    Read it yourself."    She handed him the paperwork. I was on my belly, watching through the crack in the bottom of the door.

He read aloud.    "Won't eat.    Fantasies.    Eccentric behavior.    Possible nerve disorder."    He looked up to Mom for explanation.

"Go on," she said.

"Hysteria?      Consider    prescribing    methylphenidate. Insomnia.    Somnambulism.    Recurring night terrors continue..."

"Keep reading," Mom said.

"Repressed    ideas    in    subconscious.    This    repressed dissociated material splitting from mainstream of conscious mind could be schizophrenic psychosis.    Dissociation organized in subconscious, functioning as separate personality of Stick Man. Freud's conversion therapy, unconscious guilt feelings and need to be punished.    Child feels responsible for problems of parents."    He shook his head in disgust.    "What problems?"

"Just keep reading, Saul.    For God's sake."

"Dammit anyway."

"Read, read."

"Second Stick Man personality may be agent handling the punishing.    Or symptoms of parapsychic phenomena.    Patient's desires for affection thwarted by emotional deprivation, response is self-absorption, exacerbated by religious preoccupation.    Condition will likely remain until intense feelings are redirected to another, as defense against fears."    Dad handed the paper back to Mom. "Sounds like one fucked up kid to me."

Saturday night Walker and I watched *Chiller Theatre* on TV. Chilly Billy Cardilly was showing *Night of the Living Dead, The Creature from the Black Lagoon, and* the *Voodoo Curse.*    Chilly Billy had a cameo in the Living Dead film, playing a reporter. George Romero, the director, shot the low-budget classic in Evans City, twenty minutes north of West View.    The creature from the Black Lagoon reminded me of Stick Man.

Chiller Theatre was a school teaching me how to battle Stick Man.    I learned from *Night of the Living Dead* that zombies can be killed by hitting them in the head.    I made a note of this, in hopes I could somehow strike Stick Man.    I learned from *Voodoo Curse* a ritual that involved creating a chalk drawing of a circle, then making a voodoo doll of the enemy.

After *Chiller Theatre*, I drew a chalk circle on my bedroom floor.    I was considerably hampered because my hands were chilled by an extreme cold.    I couldn't hold the chalk for more than a couple seconds at a time.    Walker agreed to stay up all night with me.    He hung cloves of garlic from the ceiling, while I made a Stick Man voodoo doll and stuck pins in it.    We covered the chalk circle with colored sand, than danced around the circle, spinning like tops.

At approximately three a.m., I said a rosary.    I did this as quietly as possible, because Walker was already asleep by two-thirty. Kathryn Kuhlman gave a sermon that Sunday from the Apostle Paul's letter to the Ephesians.    "Put on the full armor of God," she said, "to battle the wiles of the devil."

I figured between the prayers, the voodoo, and the armor of God, I could sleep without worry.

"Good night, Gabriel," I said, as my dog scampered off the bed and out the door.    "Good night, Walker," I whispered.

I was sleeping.    A deep deep sleep.

Suddenly, I woke up.    The closet door started rattling. *What's in the closet?*    I looked into the closet and saw Stick Man. He glared at me from the dark closet, more demonic than all the monsters in Chilly Billy's horror movies.    My muscles froze and I gasped for breath.    A little winding shiver of sickness shot down my back.    Stick Man moved past the wall, floating through the curtains, then near the nightstand beside me.

*"You think that silly voodoo can stop me?"*    He growled deeply, ready to pounce on me and unzip my guts.

"Help me, Jesus," I said, the words stopping in my throat.

*"That wasn't the bedpost that cut you.    It was me.    And the next time, it will be worse."*

My nerves shattering, I collapsed.

I knew.

It was coming.

# 5

Stick Man's wooden hands lunged out of the hallway walls and grabbed me in a fit of frenzied fury.

*"Help me, Jesus.   The blood the blood the blood..."*

I fell backwards as if from a shove.

I heard Stick Man's breathing as he glided spiderlike behind me, slithering his rotted self and grabbing my ankle with his claw.

Nearing my parents bedroom, I heard them moan. Their groans blended with the sound of Stick Man yelping like a jackal. The door was open.   They weren't wearing clothes and were on their sides facing each other on their bed.   They seemed oblivious to me standing there.   They weren't nudists.   They just didn't lock doors.

I screamed, still seeing the wooden mask.

"Go to bed," Dad said.

"Stick Man's after me."

"Dammit anyway," Dad said.

"Poor baby," Mom said.

She wiped the tears from my cheeks and felt my breath.   In my distress, my nose ran.   She wiped it with a tissue.   She prayed Hail Marys and Our Fathers over me until my hand tremors lessened.

"Why are you and Dad naked?" I asked.

"It's only natural, Jeremiah.   This is how you got here. This is how everything gets here.   It's called intercourse."

"What's that?"

"After a man and woman fall in love and get married, a man puts his penis inside the woman's vagina."

I was stunned by this strange revelation. "Does every man do that with the woman he loves?"

"Yes, it's quite normal for grown-ups."

"Even Uncle Spiritos?"

"Yes, especially Uncle Spiritos."

"Did Nana and Grandpa do it?"

Mom covered her mouth with her hand and giggled, turning her head for a moment. "Yes. That's how your father came about."

"When I fall in love, she'll have dark hair and skin white as snow, like Snow White," I said. "And just like you, Mom. But do I really have to show her my penis and put it inside her? I don't think I want to."

"No, you don't have to. But when you get older you may want to, so just remember, honey, when you're with girls, keep your fly zipped up so you won't get into trouble."

"Yes, Mom."

"And forget about girls for now. You're too young."

Dad had an impatient look on his face, so she gave me a "How to Tell Your Kids About Sex" book by Doctor Spock, who I confused with Mister Spock from Star Trek.

*****

I called a meeting by the pine tree on the Center Avenue side of our house. Walker was the fastest runner of the trio, so he got there first. Reverend Rawlings conducted his nightly after-dinner Bible study and it ran long, so Red and Savannah were twenty minutes late. I told Red, Savannah, and Walker what I learned about the facts of life.

"The man's wiener gets hard and he sticks it in the woman's hole. Then he squirts juice. We all start out as juice in our Dad's wiener," I said. I wasn't as embarrassed as I thought I'd be.

Red laughed. "Jeez, oh man, that's ridiculous. I was never juice in my Dad's wiener," he said. "God made me. The Bible says so."

"Maybe God made you. But God's idea was to make you out of juice from your Dad's wiener," I said. I brushed pine needles out of my hair.

"You're gross, Jeremiah." Walker said. "Who would ever think of anything that stupid?"

"No, I'm serious. That's the way Mom and Dad did it. I saw it with my own eyes."

"Oooh, your parents are sick," Red said.

"Have any of you done this before?" Savannah asked.

"No," I said. "You?"

Savannah looked away to the distant woods behind Center Avenue. "The person that did it to me told me to never tell," she said. Her face changed and she looked older all of a sudden, like she possessed knowledge of the forbidden fruit while we were still innocents in Eden.

"Quit jagging around yens jag-offs. And stop making up stories Savannah," Red said.

Red told his parents, who confirmed the truth, and I was vindicated. Then Red told everyone at Saint Joe's. Somehow, it made me the coolest kid in the class all of a sudden. I was an overnight hero. What was once ridiculous, was now sublime.

Mom always bought me and Walker underwear and socks for Christmas. I didn't like it. I wanted battery-operated toys. She forced me to thank her. "Thank you for the socks and underwear, Mom," I said through gritted teeth.

"I went through hard years when I was your age during the Depression. Toys are a waste of money," she said. "When everything crashes again, you'll be glad I buy you underwear. You can't eat toys. Toys don't keep you warm."

I couldn't imagine being grateful for socks and underpants.

Mom was so worried about money she did whatever she had to. She placed bets for Spiritos and the mob out of the church basement. Sometimes I helped count the money. Father McCormick tolerated this since Spiritos was the benefactor of the church.

Mom also collected and sold figurines she encased in glass. They were for display only. She created them from kits and resold them for a profit.

"They aren't to be touched, or played with, is that clear?"

"Yes, Mom."

I was drawn to her collection of plaster-of-paris Disney figures. They came as a do-it-yourself set. The plaster powder, the rubber molds, and the paint and brush.

She had Mickey and Minnie Mouse, Donald Duck, and Snow White and the Seven Dwarfs. I coveted the figures. My fantasy was to one day visit Disneyland in California. I watched the *Wonderful World of Disney* every Sunday night on our black and white television. I longed to rescue Mom's Snow White and the seven dwarves from their glass incarceration and play with them in fantasyland. Suggesting this to Mom was blasphemy. To her, the figurines were sacrosanct, like the Eucharist on the altar at Saint Joseph's.

I remember the first time I sinned.

I was over at Red's on a December day. The Rawlings ranch-style house was rustic and plain, no cosmetics, like a fundamentalist girl's face. Plaques with bible verses hung on the peeling yellow wallpaper. I discovered Red had the same plaster-of-paris set. Red made the characters, but less skillfully than Mom. His paint-job made the figurines look grotesque, but at least they were free from the prison of display cases. Red's figurines were deformed from not filling the mold properly, and had missing legs and arms from living in the rough and tumble toy box world with GI Joes, Hotwheels, Etch-O-Sketch, and Lincoln Logs.

My eyes were riveted to Red's Mickey Mouse. When no one was looking, I snatched Mickey, hid him in my coat pocket, and raced home. I slid on the ice across Oakwood Avenue and through the door.

"Jeremiah! Close that door tight," Mom said. "You cost me money to heat this house. Were you born in a barn?"

"No, but Jesus was. You got something against Jesus?"

"Don't be smart with me. I'll smack your ass," she said in her screechy voice. "I know about Jesus and I don't need a sermon from you."

I shut the door with all my strength, and was overcome to think I could touch and play with Mickey. I had hours of adventure. Treasure hunts, conjuring potions, sailing and scaling castle walls, fighting dragons, and driving a steamboat across the dining room singing M-I-C-K-E-Y-M-O-U-S-E.

In an attempt to simulate the agony of the crucifixion, I made a makeshift cross from two Lincoln logs and taped Mickey to it. Mickey stared at me dispassionately from the cross.

Then the still, small voice of my conscience stopped me.

"Thou shalt not steal," the voice said.

I continued to play, ignoring it as best I could. With Mickey in my right hand, I climbed the dresser to the top, an imaginary Golgotha.

Mickey frowned.

I set Mickey down in the corner of the room and looked away. Out of my peripheral vision I saw something move. Mickey raised his arms and put them down. I broke out in a hot sweat and looked away.

When I looked back, I saw Stick Man in the corner of the room, licking his wooden lips with his furred tongue.

*"You're a bad boy, Jeremiah,"* Stick Man said.

"Leave me alone. Why are you bothering me?"

*"I need children,"* he said. Smoke poured through his wooden mask. *"Not just any children. The special ones. The outsiders."* He inched closer.

I remembered what Kathryn Kuhlman taught me. True love banished evil. I closed my eyes and thought about Gabriel. I felt Stick Man's energy lessen.

I fell to my knees, my head bowed. I looked in Mickey's eyes and saw them turn sadder.

Mickey does not belong to me, but to another, my conscience said.

I wouldn't trade the pleasure of those hours for anything, but I had to face the termination the moral law demanded.

Stick Man was playing possum, crouching like a lion. He leapt at me with furious speed, like a bullet. His wooden claws swiped at my head. I ducked. He barely missed, but I felt him grab my hair, pulling me into a hell-like horrible place.

*"You give me power because of your sin,"* Stick Man said. *"You're a thief. God's lifting his hedge of protection from you so I can ravage you."*

"I'm gonna take Mickey back," I said.

*"Shut up. Shut up, you stupid boy. Shut up. You stupid, stupid boy."*

"Help me, Jesus," I prayed. "Perfect love casts out fear."

*"You think your love for that stupid dog can save you? I'll murder your little dog."*

"NO! You leave him alone. God help me. God help me. God help me."

I broke free from Stick Man's claws and raced out with Mickey to return him to Red's right away. I smuggled him back into Red's toy box. I prayed God would forgive my sinful soul and that Santa would still come down the chimney at Christmas.

*****

Red told me something terrible about Saint Nick. "He's fake. Your parents put those presents under the tree," he said. "My Dad told me he's a plot from the devil to steal the glory away from Jesus. Satan and Santa are spelled with the same letters."

When I returned home from the Rawlings, Mom admitted there was no Santa, but only after I badgered her for the truth. "You're old enough to know. Santa's for babies," she said.

I walked mournfully into the dining room and saw Dad repairing pickups on a Les Paul. Disassembled guitars were spread across the table. Dad drank coffee from a cup that looked like a large soup bowl with a handle. I sipped my little cup, which was ninety percent milk and sugar, and ten percent coffee, because Mom was concerned about stunting my growth.

Dad's most cherished guitar was his Ramirez from Spain. It rested in the center of the table, freshly polished. This was the guitar father scrimped and saved for, the flamenco instrument for Dad's Segovia pieces. He played solos of *Romance De Amore, Lagrima,* and *Malaguena.*

"One day, this will be your guitar, son," he said. I felt privileged to be in a family where music was in the center. Constant guitarists came in and out, filling our home with full, harmonious notes. "So you're having nightmares?"

"Yeah. Bad ones."

"Let me explain, son, where dreams come from. The images we see during the day become the fodder for our fantasies. The details of our dreams."

"So, what you're saying, is because I went to Mass and saw the crucifix, my imagination created a monster?"

"Exactly, son. That doesn't make it any less scary."

"Hmmm."

"Something else on your mind?"

"Yeah. Daddy, is there really a Santa Claus?"

"Why do you ask? Of course there is." He tightened the screws on the humbuckers.

"That song, *Santa Claus Is Comin To Town* said he keeps a list of who is naughty and who is nice. So if I do something naughty, but then I do something nice, does it cancel out the bad?"

"Yeah, I suppose so. I need a break. Want to walk with me to the car, Jeremiah?"

"Okay, Dad."

*****

Dad brushed a coating of snow off the black vinyl roof of his Caddy with an ice scraper. We drove to the brewery at Horseshoe

Bend for Christmas spirits in his white Cadillac. I loved the big tires and cushy seats. I felt like I was floating on wind as we rode down Center Avenue, sliding around the icy bends. I forgot Stick Man for a few seconds.

"Is Santa real, Dad? Tell me the truth."

"What kind of a question is that? Why do you doubt?" Dad tapped out a five-four Brubeck rhythm on the steering wheel.

"Daddy, you can't fool me. Mom admitted there's no Santa."

"She's crazy. Who else?"

"My teacher."

"What do they know?"

"Mom said I was old enough to know the truth. So did Sister Antonita, and nuns can't lie. Can they?"

"They're women. Don't listen to women."

"Why not?"

"Ever since time began, a woman got the man to eat the apple. There are certain things I can tell you in secret, and you'll understand. What's your father?"

"A genius."

"That's right. Good boy."

"So Santa is real?

"It's an established fact. Santa Claus was a real person, Saint Nicolas. And what happens to saints when they die, son?"

"They go to heaven?"

"Good. So his spirit never really died, right?"

"Right."

Dad looked into my eyes with his dark stare. "Now, don't you think, on the one day every year when people remember him, the spirit of Saint Nicolas would return?"

"That makes sense, Dad."

"Don't even try to explain this to your mother, or Sister Amnesia, or whatever the hell her name is. Unbelievers don't understand the metaphysical. Especially women. A woman will steer you away from having faith in yourself."

"Thanks, Dad."

"Your welcome, son." He looked at me with his big brown eyes and smiled a roguish grin.

God, I loved him.

I supposed God rewarded me because come Christmas morning, Santa brought me the Disney plaster-of-paris set. I created the characters and watched them come to life. If that wasn't fantastic enough, I saw a purple Schwinn under the tree. Dad and Mom grinned at me. For once, the new socks and underwear didn't bother me.

# 6

I was in the bathtub on Saturday night with my newly created Disney friends. Mom came to look at her face in the mirror, studying her eyes and skin, and plucking her first grey hair. She grabbed her thighs, and pinched the excess with disgust. She stood back and rubbed her fingers through her hair.

"Where's Daddy?" I asked.

"Out playing with his band, dear."

I looked over to the door. Gabriel was blocking the exit, sprawled out and snoring. The soap-suds crown I placed on his head moments earlier was still there, but thinning out. I did my best to make his crown match mine.

Mom shaved her legs. I giggled. "What are you laughing at? There's nothing wrong with it," she said. "God made the human body. It's natural. Baring the body is baring the soul. Always remember, Jeremiah, an artist must be naked and not ashamed."

I looked away at the crown of Mister Bubble suds on my head reflected in the mirror.

Mom left the room and I fell asleep in the tub.

*****

Rusty nails popped out of the water, gliding in the bubbles towards my penis. A raw wooden hand formed a crucifix and poised it at my rectum. His other hand clawed at my genitals.

"Oh no, please don't. Noooo, *please*!" I wailed as his talons brought the crucifix closer. I strained to push him away and escape the tub.

Stick Man leered at me.

*"You'll do what I want you to do little boy,"* he crowed with throaty eroticism. *"You'll do it!"*

"No, PLEASE. No, DON'T."

He flared up at me with fury. *"You will or I'll kill you. You tell anyone about this and I'll kill your family."*

A sudden stench shoved into my nostrils. The water in the tub turned icy cold. I was frozen with horror. Stick Man's rusty fingernails stabbed me once in my stomach and twice in my testicles.

Stick Man thrust the cross into my rectum and roared his loud laugh, cackling joyously with demonic delight. With his other hand, he squeezed my scrotum with his iron talon. I screamed in pain, struggling to free myself.

"Mom! Mom, help me!"

Agony. Stick Man cackled devilishly then howled like a wolf.

Claws yanked me under the water. I struggled to keep my head above water but crumpled to the bottom of the bathtub in a daze of terror. I couldn't breathe. I swallowed water and gagged. My ears rang with dissonant distortions as I fought to raise myself.

"Jesus," I prayed. "Help me."

I thought of my lucky number, twenty-one. The number of the Great Clemente, formed by multiplying the two holiest numbers: three for the Trinity, times seven for the Days of Creation.

Stick Man vanished like a vapor. He must've heard Mom in the hall.

She rushed in, nearly tripping over Gabriel's leash. "Are you okay, dear? I heard you yelling."

Mom's face squinted up with anxiety. I didn't want her to worry. "I think so. Sorry I frightened you, Mom."

I dried off with my Batman towel.  She patted my body with Johnson's baby powder and handed me my PJs.

"What's this?" she said, noticing a smudge of blood on my towel.

"Oh, nothing," I said, remembering Stick Man's threat.

"I'm taking you to see Doctor Bosley again.  It's late, let's get to bed."  I watched her worried and weary form walk away from the bathroom like a hopeless prayer.

I sped into my bedroom to avoid Stick Man in the hall.  I closed the door and looked up at my walls.  A poster of David Cassidy hung next to my dresser.  A bully named Butch and some other boys who were his cronies called me faggot because of this, but I liked the romance of the Partridge family songs.  Songs like *I Think I Love You, I Woke Up in Love This Morning,* and my favorite *I'll Meet You Halfway.*  I sang the words of Keith Partridge to myself over and over.  *"I'll meet you halfway/That's better than no way/There must be some way to get it together."*

I stretched in bed, and spun visions of meeting a girl.  When I slept, I had a good dream for once.  I dreamt of a half-heart floating like a lonely kite through a storm, in search of a sweetheart.  Then a warm wind blew a girl with a matching half-heart to my side.  Like two pieces of a jig-saw puzzle they fit together and formed a whole heart.  The dream was dashed by Stick Man's dark claw ripping my heart to shreds.

I woke up the following morning and went downstairs.  After my breakfast of Count Chocula cereal, I listened to my Partridge Family records.  Their warm bubble-gum pop tapped into an inclination I had deep inside.

When the Partridge Family came to Pittsburgh to perform at the Civic Arena, they needed a guitar player.  Dad was well-known through the local Musician's Union and was contacted by the band's manager to play back-up.   I ran across the street to brag to Red, Savannah and the Oakland Avenue kids.

At the last minute, Dad backed out.   He told me about it when I returned home.

"I have responsibilities, son.   I'd have to cancel my students for the night, and that just ain't right.   I know my priorities."

"But Dad, you'd get to play with David Cassidy."

"He's good, but he'll come and go like the rest of them.   He caught a big fish, but the sharks will get him sooner or later."   Dad talked every so often about fish and sharks.   "I won't turn my back on Pittsburgh.   I'm a guitar teacher.   I don't need fame or fortune."

Like David Cassidy's music, old movies fed my romantic dreams.   In *Rebel Without a Cause* I liked the way James Dean rested his head on Natalie Wood's lap.   The next day after the movie was broadcast on Rege Cordic's Movie Show, I went to a poster shop in the Oakland section of Pittsburgh and bought an enlarged photo of James Dean resting with his girl in an abandoned mansion, his head nestled on Natalie Wood's thighs.   I tacked the photo above my bed, between the crucifix and the Partridge Family poster.

I looked up at the poster and made my wish for a girl.   A girl like Natalie Wood who would make me feel what I felt listening to those David Cassidy songs.   A girl that could help me beat Stick Man.   I knew she was out there somewhere.

*****

Saturday night, Dad and I played music for fifty bucks a piece.   Dad played lead and I was on rhythm.   Neon signs lit up the Pittsburgh tavern, and the atmosphere filled with blue smoke.

Dad mentored me in the tricks of the trade.   "If you make a mistake, or hit a bad note, don't telegraph it," he said.   "That's a sure mark of an amateur. A pro, like me, hears the mistake, and slides his finger into the correct note, not missing a beat. The audience will never know you goofed, unless you show it in your face."

He downed a Rolling Rock. I drew sketches of Clemente on the placemat and ate pistachio nuts.

Sam Tamerelli was our bass player. He had long hair and a beard like Jesus. He smiled a lot and had shiny teeth. Mom referred to him as the "druggie." Tamerelli also taught bass and piano at Dad's music store. Mom caught him stealing from the till and Dad was boiling over about it, like dynamite about to blow. I filled in for Sam at the bar gigs.

"I'm going to get him, son," Dad said. "I told him to straighten out and fly right, but he wouldn't listen."

A lady sauntered over, and sat beside me. She sung in my ear with Iron City Beer on her breath, *"Jesus loves me this I know/for the Bible tells me so/little ones to Him belong/they are weak, but He is strong."* She reeked of menthol cigarettes.

Above the bar, Steelers and Pirates memorabilia were draped above shelves of collector's beer cans. Photos of wrestler Bruno Sammartino, right fielder Roberto Clemente, and quarterback Terry Bradshaw hung slightly askew. I imitated the regal stance of the Great Clemente in the photo, swinging an imaginary bat, while I watched myself in the mirror. Mac the bartender smiled and shouted, "Arriba, arriba." The tipsy woman clapped. The ringing of pinball machines and the clanging of billiards hummed at a lower volume than the jukebox.

As members of the Musician's Union, we were guaranteed a fifteen minute break every hour, so Dad and I played a forty-five minute set, than we'd hit the bar. He stretched the fifteen minute break to a half hour, downing drinks and talking up the girls. Since I was under age, I had a Squirt then returned to the bandstand first.   I played solo until our break was up.   Or, should I say, until Dad made it back.   The break was up way before he was ready to return.   Dad said he wanted to give me a chance in front of the crowd alone, but I think it was so he could have a few extra moments for drinks.

The song I played, *Malaguena*, was easier than it looked.   I slid an E chord up from the first fret to the second fret and back again. I showboated, strumming with extra flare that seduced the crowd. When the applause died down, I walked back to the bar to remind Dad it was time to start our next set of eight songs.   Ignoring me, Dad noticed a flyer on the wall about a DJ spinning records the following Saturday.

"Mac, you're selling out," he said to the bartender.

"What're you talking about?"

"Taking work away from real musicians.   How could you?"

"I have a business to run here.   This ain't no charity.   With a DJ, I only pay one guy."

"Look, I'll play solo for you if you want, but don't sell out. You can't beat live music."

*****

In the middle of our next set, I noticed Mom slip into the back of the bar.   Her face was obscured behind cigarette smoke from a muscleman in a fireman's jacket on her right.   I concentrated even harder, coordinating my fingers into the precision of the chords.

Dad stepped up to the mike.   "I'd like to dedicate a song to my wife who's in the back."   Mom's smile faded as he sang Engelbert Humperdink's latest hit.

*"Please release me, let me go/for I don't love you anymore/to live a lie would bring us pain/Release me, so I can love again…"*

Dad thought it was the funniest thing in the world, but Mom cussed him out in the parking lot.

"I was humiliated," she said.

"That's the problem with you," he said. "No sense of humor." She left in a huff and Dad took me back inside. He told Mac he needed one for the road. One drink became another and another and another.

Dad drank one too many and skipped his medicine. I became an expert at spotting the cycle and the symptoms. Driving home, Dad was still fixated on the DJs.

"They're gonna take everything away, Jeremiah. Like Santiago's sharks in *The Old Man and the Sea*. Mark my words, the day will come, they won't have real musicians in the bars and clubs anymore, just DJs playing records. Before long, even the records won't be made by musicians, but by DJ's on turntables. Can you imagine, son? These damn DJs will dominate the charts. Guys that can't play an instrument to save their life."

Dad taught me to look upon DJ's the way Jews look upon Germans. The whole thing sounded crazy to me.

We passed West View Amusement Park around Horseshoe Bend. Dad went into one of his altered personalities. He talked with a Texas accent and went by the name "Rocky from Texas." He put on a cowboy hat and we popped in another rough and tumble tavern on Center Avenue known as Buddy's Bar. When Dad was manic, he chanted, "Things are looking up, Jeremiah. Things are looking up."

His car radio was tuned to the country station. Hank Williams was singing about a tear in his beer.

Four hours and fourteen beers later, Dad spray-painted the words "Fuck the world!" on his car and drove around the neighborhood just about the time everyone else on Oakland Avenue was getting up to face the day. In the morning, Dad swallowed his pills with long names like lithium and thorazine. I didn't know why, I just knew Dad was acting crazier.

He went down to the courthouse when they opened and filed papers to run for president of the United States. He put water in his car, convinced he could run on H2O instead of gasoline. "Fuck the Middle East, I don't need their oil," he said.

Dad was out of control, so I sequestered myself in my room and painted, than I played *Somewhere Over the Rainbow* on my Stella, escaping into an afternoon fantasy. Just as I played the bridge about "lemon drops on chimney tops," Dad busted the bedroom door down in a rampage, and threw my clothes, schoolbooks, and guitar out the third-story window.

Before this incident, Dad might have acted crazier than a cuckoo bird, but his madness was never directed at me. When his rage turned towards me, I felt like everything I could trust in was gone. The solar system crashed.

I escaped into a magical world of a surrogate father: Dick Van Dyke. I watched his movies over and over again. *Chitty Chitty Bang Bang* and *Mary Poppins*. I dreamt of wearing the same red and white ice cream blazer he wore on his jolly holiday with Mary. I imagined myself leaping with Bert the chimney sweep into a chalk drawing. We jumped in the air, shrank to a miniature size, and POOF, into a cloud of colored chalk dust.

I took some refuge in frequent visits to Red and Savannah's home. Their father Mordecai had a certainty about things. He gave me a red Bible. I clutched it for protection as Father drifted into his sea of madness.

The straw that broke the camel's back and sent Dad away for a while was when he decided to kill Sam Tamerelli.   Before going to Buddy's Bar to shoot him, he visited Spiritos.   I was drawing on the floor with crayons, but I heard the whole thing.

"So you're going to knock him off?" Spiritos asked.   He fingered a ninth chord on the Gibson.

"Damn right.   Motherfucker's been stealing from me to buy drugs."   Dad talked at a rapid pace.

"How do you know for sure?"

"I saw him take money out of the register.   With my own eyes.   And there's numerous unauthorized charges on the studio account.   Cash withdrawals on the credit card.   He even ordered a bass and a P.A. for himself.   On my dealer accounts."

"We can take care of this little fly.   But you don't shoot a fly with a machine gun.   Don't lose your head.   If you'd-"

"I'm killing him tonight.   And don't you try and talk me out of it."

# 7

Spiritos distracted Dad with small talk so he could empty the bullets from the gun. "On Satin Doll, do you prefer a D minor or a D minor seventh?"

"D minor," Dad said. "That's how Ellington wrote it. The D minor seventh adds a little spice to the dish, but if you want to be accurate, stick with the minor chord."

"Thanks, Saul." Spiritos strummed the D minor at the fifth fret. He adjusted the reverb on his Fender tube amp.

"You're a big boy, you can handle Sam. Just let me check the gun, make sure everything's okay," Spiritos said, winking at me.

Dad nodded and handed Spiritos the revolver. "Things are looking up. Things are looking up. Can I leave the kid here for now?"

"Sure, Saul. He's a good boy."

"You should see him at home. He's not so good."

"Don't be too hard on him. And be careful." He gave the gun back to Dad.

When Dad left, Spiritos opened his hands, revealing the bullets he palmed. He grinned at me. "Now you see them, now you don't," he said. The bullets vanished from his hand.

"It's magic. You're a good boy, Jeremiah."

From what I can piece together, Dad drove away from the house in his Caddy and headed to Buddy's. When he returned to the tavern to kill Sam, the gun wasn't loaded, so Dad and Tamerelli were both spared a worse fate. The police took Dad to Saint John's mental hospital in handcuffs. Even though he didn't kill him, brandishing a handgun in a bar was enough to send him away with the guys in the white coats.   It taught me that anyone can go crazy at anytime.

Dad was released after a while to visit on weekends on the condition he kept out of trouble.   He walked hunched over, shuffling in shame, his dignity ripped out of him.

It wasn't all sad, however.   We had some comic relief when he brought some of the other discharged mental patients home. Many of them had no place to go once their stays were up.   Their families didn't want the burden.   The misfits rambled in cryptic conversation around our dinner table.   They understood each other, but Mom got a headache trying to follow them.

After a while, I decoded their buzzwords enough to understand their distorted reality and deep discussions about "the essence of the realm" and "the connotation of the denotation."

Dad's face was beet-red as he pleaded, "What is soul?   What is soul?" and "I lost my soul in soul."   At the time, this was very strange but as months passed it was hard for me to think about it without laughing.

Dad's vacations in the nuthouse were a great source of camaraderie.   "Van Gogh painted in the asylum," he said.   "And Allen Ginsberg wrote his best stuff in the Columbia Psychiatric Institute."

Mom rolled her eyes at this, brought a tray of pork-chops from the kitchen and set it on the table.

Cathy, a schizophrenic art student with stringy hair chimed in.   She wore a tie-dye dress with a silver peace sign around her neck.   Dad befriended her in group therapy.   She spoke like she had a time limit and needed to cram an hour's worth into a minute.

"Absolutely. Crazy is normal, and normal is crazy," Cathy said. "Emily Dickinson knew it when she wrote about the divinity of madness. Crazy is a term the suburban robots use to suppress the dissent of anyone who will not succumb to the bribes of the game." She sprayed food in all directions when she spoke. "Fuck this whole nine-to-five gerbil wheel. They want us to get out there and kick that football again like Charlie Brown. The Man, he's Lucy, see, then they pull the football away, and we break our necks like Charlie Brown. I, for one, refuse to kick that ball again. I'm off that merry-go-round for good and crazy is a badge of honor because normal means thinking like the masses and the majority are always wrong. Who wants to be a normie anyways? The majority chose Barabbas over Christ for Christ's sake, and the problem with democracy-"

Dad applauded at this. "Here, here. Who wants to be a normie anyways? The woman's a genius."

"I don't know what the hell she's even talking about," Mom said.

"Why are you so irritated and jealous all the time? Don't be a pessimist. Things are looking up, things are looking up..."

"Yeah, I'm jealous. They're looking up, alright," Mom said. "You're driving me up the wall."

"WHO WANTS TO BE A NORMIE ANYWAYS?" Dad yelled like a triumphant battle call to defeat the restraints of convention, waving his fist in the air and wearing a Jack Nicholson grin designed to irritate Mom.

"Here, here," his merry band of psychotics cheered around the table, clinking their glasses together in jubilation. "WHO WANTS TO BE A NORMIE ANYWAYS!"

Most of them were failed writers, poets, musicians, actors, and painters who felt their meetings at Saint John's were destined so they could collaborate on creative projects that would enlighten the world. Their work was too inaccessible for the normies, so they self-published their books on mimeograph machines.

There was one thing Cathy was right about for sure. Crazy became normal to me, and normal became crazy, or at the very least, normal was boring. I encapsulated this with a little joke I said to myself. *"What's wrong? Nothing's wrong. That's what's wrong."*


A year later, Dad was back in Saint John's again after a manic episode. Mom signed me up for the Pittsburgh Talent Competition. A lot was riding on my performance because the prize money was one thousand dollars. Dad was a well-known music teacher in Pittsburgh, so expectations were high for me.

Mom sewed a blue outfit for me to match my eyes. "Pray, Jeremiah. Pray to win. We really need the money for back-taxes." I wondered about this as she buttoned up my shirt and vest.

*What happens if everyone in the contest prayed to win? How does God decide?*

"I can't find your Dad's book. It's not on the nightstand. I've looked everywhere. Have you seen *The Old Man and the Sea?*"

"No."

"That old fool. He was offered two thousand for that book." She combed my hair, than wet her finger and straightened my eyebrows. "What song did you pick?"

"My personal favorite song from my personal favorite movie. *Somewhere Over the Rainbow.*"

"That's a good one," she said. "That's the one your father arranged for you, isn't it?"

"Yeah, before he went in the hospital."

"What key?"

"C."

"Good, no sharps or flats. It's a big crowd, and when you get nervous, your hand shakes, and you hit bad notes. Are you nervous, dear?"

"Kind of. I got butterflies in my tummy."

She reached into her purse and pulled out a bottle. I read Dad's name on the label.

"Take one of these. They're tranquilizers. They'll keep you calm when you perform. Get rid of your stage fright." She handed me the pill. The texture was hard.

"I don't want to, Mom. It's a horse pill. I can't swallow something that big."

She sighed, and fished through her purse, finding a pill cutter. Mom held the capsule and sliced it in half. She hurried to the sink and poured me a cup of water in my Batman mug.

"Here, take half. That's probably better, it won't be as strong." I hesitated. "Come on, you goof. Swallow the pill."

I gulped as much water as I could then I took the half-pill in my mouth and swallowed. The pill got stuck in my throat.

"What a baby you are," she said. "Come on, we're late. Out to the car."

"I don't want to go to the show now."

"You don't listen, do you? Get your ass to the car."

I looked across the street and saw old lady Curen on her porch swing, shaking her head.

\*\*\*\*\*

A chorus of dancing girls wearing hula skirts for a Hawaiian number gathered around me in the dressing room. I looked at them and felt the softness of their feminine energy. On the far left of the coterie, was a blonde with eyes that danced like marbles. She told me her name was Sylvia. Her legs were muscular and tan. Beside her was Maria, an Italian girl with black hair that curled in long strands.

"Isn't he the cutest thing?" Maria said. She hugged me snug to her chest.

The rest of the chorus line fawned over me and escorted me to the stage and back again for each dry-run rehearsal. Their dance troupe included a Euro-Asian, an African-American, a redhead from England, and an Iranian.

Sylvia sat me on her lap while she applied makeup. She flipped her head, and her golden hair brushed my face like a feather. "You're the sweetest little boy in the whole world."

"You're pretty," I said.

"What about me? Ain't I pretty, too?" Maria asked. I giggled. "I've seen you at Mass little boy blue, haven't I? Next time, I want you to sit beside me, okay?"

"If Mom lets me."

"So you're a Mama's boy? You daydream during Mass. I'll hold the misalette for you and make sure you're on the right page. I'll keep you from daydreaming, okay?"

I nodded to Maria.

They walked me to the stage for the big performance, a gaggle of beauties in grass skirts. A half-dozen mothers, adjusting my hair, shirt, and belt. "Stand up straight," Sylvia said.

"Be bold," Maria said, "and mighty powers will come to your aid."

Sylvia and Maria kissed me for good luck. I felt calm. Maybe Mom's pill helped after all. Sometimes, I had an ability to rise to the occasion in front of an audience and perform better under stress than when I rehearsed. The stage put me in a surreal dimension, especially when I heard the applause of the crowd. I played *Somewhere Over the Rainbow* on my little red Stella guitar with pathos. I heard the cheers and ate it up. In retrospect, I don't know if they clapped because of the complexity of the jazz arrangement that poured out of a pint-sized performer, or because they thought I was a cute kid, or if they were just being polite. Everyone expected me to win first prize, including myself. The hula girls rambled on and on about it.

"You're a shoe-in," Maria said, with a dismissive wave of her hand. "An absolute shoe-in." She kissed me on the cheek.

They called all the performers out on stage to announce the winner. We lined up shoulder to shoulder. Hula girls, majorettes, jugglers, dancers, comedians, a drummer who dazzled the audience with his solo, and me. The MC had a Howdy Doody face and a Cheshire cat grin. He bounced up to the mike. "All right, let's hear it for our performers," he said.

The crowd cheered and we took our collective bow. I tried to bow at the same time as everyone else, but my timing was off. I knew Mom was praying in the audience when I saw her make the sign of the cross.

The MC ripped open a tan envelope with the judge's results. "And the winner is....."

The drummer with a lot of flash doing a *Wipe-Out* solo snagged first. He juggled his sticks and beat out rolls on his snare, his hands in a blur. I won tickets to see *Herbie the Love Bug* at the

North Hills movie theater for second place, but the drummer received the cash.

All of the cash.

When I arrived home, Dad called from Saint John's mental hospital to learn the outcome. The show was during the week, and the doctors wouldn't let him out.

"I lost, Dad."

"What? What you did was ten times harder, and took a helluva lot more talent. IT'S FIXED, DAMMIT!" I sobbed on the other end of the phone while Father fumed. "I'm going to talk to Spiritos, first thing tomorrow, we'll put a hit out on those judges."

"Don't do that, Dad."

Even a strange display, like wanting to put a hit on talent show judges, touched me deeply because it was one of the few, odd ways that Dad showed he cared. He didn't hug me or say "I love you," or praise me all that much, but if anybody doubted my talents, he was ready to kill them.

"I'm reading my favorite book in here for the sixty-sixth time, son. Not much to do in here but read. It's by Hemingway. *The Old Man and the Sea.* Your mother wanted to sell it for the tax money, but I outsmarted the old bat and packed it before I left."

"What's the story about, Dad?"

"This old man, he struggles to land a marlin, and after all his work, sharks attack and devour the big fish. It made me think of you tonight, son. You worked so hard, you played so well. But you can't hold on to it. Some dime-store drummer stole the prize. He was the shark. Look at me. All those years, I built up hundreds of guitar students and I sit here in the nuthouse while my business goes to pot. The DJs will steal the wedding gigs within the next two years. That's life for you, son. Everything you search for, and finally land, you eventually lose it anyway. And then it's just you, son. Alone. Like the old man Santiago. Look at Bruno Sammartino. Pittsburgh's wrestling champion for thirteen years. Seemed he'd never lose that belt. Than what happened last week in Baltimore?"

"He lost the belt to Superstar Graham."

"Exactly. Now you see my point, son. These DJs eliminate soul. All the musicians, who play their instruments with craft and pride, they're gonna be replaced. If Sammartino can lose the belt, why even the great Clemente will be gone from right field one day. Mark my words. It's God's cruel joke. You search your whole life for that one thing, and when you finally find it, you realize you can't keep it."

He talked like this whenever he was depressed. Dad was closer to me because I didn't win. We shared loss in a strange bond. He would've been jealous of me if I won, because it would highlight his own failure. I would've been his competition, and he didn't like me being the center of attention instead of him.

"We all die alone, son, and we can't take anything with us. So why even try?"

*Things aren't looking up anymore,* I thought.

"Get off that phone and come to the table," Mom said, as she set out paper plates for the party. "Every second you talk is another penny on the phone bill. Your father's not working. There's no money."

"Mom said I have to go."

"Tell that bat to shut up. Cheer up, son. I know you're the best. Who's your father?"

"The Music Man."

"And what am I?"

"A genius."

He chuckled.   "That's right, son."

I hung up and walked to the table.   Mom's stares froze into icicles.   She served chocolate cake to Walker and me to celebrate my birthday and what was supposed to be my first prize victory.   The letters on the cake said, 'Happy Birthday, Congratulations Jeremiah.'   I sat in my blue suit with my shoulders slumped.

"What have you got to be depressed about?" Mom asked. "You're not upset because you didn't win, are you, dear?   Now where are we gonna get the money?"   I couldn't hold back the rivulets flowing down my cheeks.

"Your mood's clouding your birthday," she said. "You're one year closer to your grave.   What have you done that will last?   Nothing at all.   You lost.   And you're too skinny. Your arms and legs are sticks."

This came from out of nowhere.   She wasn't just scolding my behavior, she was scolding my appearance.

*It's my fault.   Because of me, they don't have the taxes.*

I remembered Sylvia and Maria telling me I was great, despite the second place finish.   I wished I was with them.

"Go ahead and cry," she said in her parting shots before ordering me to bed.   "Little baby."

I climbed the steps to my room.   My vision blurred from tears as I overheard Mom talking to Walker.   "You're brother's too sensitive."

In the corner of my bedroom was a present.   A card on the outside said, "Happy Birthday."   I opened it quickly, ripping off the wrapping paper and throwing it on the floor.   It was a Roberto Clemente baseball glove, ball, and bat from Spiritos.   I put on the glove and created a baseball game in my mind. I threw the ball across the bedroom and Gabriel fetched it. He dropped the ball on my bed and barked. His ears twitched and he exhaled.

My bedroom became Three Rivers Stadium, and I was Number 21, the Great Clemente.

"You're number twenty-one too boy," I said, rubbing Gabriel's fur. "You're three, but in dog years you're really twenty-one, just like Clemente."

I reenacted imaginary at-bats, taking golf swings at low balls in the dirt. I hit pitches so far outside I had to run forward out of the batter's box to reach them. I envisioned the fans in the bleachers, the pennants and green weenies waving in the air. I imagined the raspy drawl of sportscaster Bob Prince calling the play-by-play.

Pretty girls like Sylvia and Maria sat in right field to savor my grace, my basket-catch, my slides into third base. I was Clemente, able to throw a runner tagging from third out at the plate from four hundred feet away at the Three Rivers Stadium warning track.

Mom and Dad were in the stands and they were proud of me. Dad munched down a ballpark hot dog. Mom was the organist. She played a Puerto Rican ditty as I caught a fly ball.

"You're definitely the best all around player, son," Dad yelled from the stands. "Hank Aaron may hit more homers, and Lou Brock may steal more bases, but no one holds a candle to you as an all-around player. Just like Roberto."

Melodies and lyrics came to me, a song about sports. I grabbed my Stella guitar and sang the newly formed song I was composing extemporaneously:

*"I saw Clemente catch a fly/His cannon arm/ His eagle eye/ I saw Bruno win the belt/I felt what Ringside Rosie felt."*

I called Dad from the upstairs phone to tell him the exciting news that I wrote a new song.    It took a long time for the nurse to get him to the phone.

"What are you talking about, son?" Dad asked.

"I want to write my own songs, about my feelings, things I think about."

"Why would you want to do that?    Stick with the standards, the great songs I teach you.    When people come to a bar or a wedding, they want to hear music they know.    Always do something the crowd is familiar with.    What do you think would happen, if in the seventh inning stretch of a Pirates game, the organist played a new song instead of *Take Me Out to the Ballgame*?"

"No one would sing along."

"Very good, son.    Stick with your old man.    How long have I been playing?"

"Thirty years," I said.    I knew this well, having heard him remind me again and again of his superior experience.

"That's right.    Thirty years.    And don't you forget it, buddy boy.    And who am I, son?"

"The Music Man."

"And what am I?"

"A genius."

"That's right."

"When it comes to music, there's a right way and a wrong way, and my way's the right way.    You're lucky to have me to show you.    Now forget about that stupid talent contest and that stupid song of yours and get some sleep, okay?"

"Okay."

I longed to follow my own creativity, to make something that was my own, from deep inside, but Dad suppressed my desire.    The music that tried to flow through me floated away in the air with the hotdog wrappers and the fly balls.

I lay in bed in the dark, feeling worthless. I thought about death, fantasizing and fearing what it would be like to cease to exist. Ever since I saw *Night of the Living Dead*, I remembered how the townspeople of Evans City were able to kill zombies by hitting them in the head. I kept my Roberto Clemente baseball bat next to my bed, in the event I'd get a good swing at Stick Man. I fell asleep for a while, than I heard slow rushing movements coming towards me. I felt something beneath me.

What's under the bed?

I noticed the cold. The room was icy. Cold talons crept up the floor and over my bed then touched my neck lightly.

I opened my eyes, awakening cold-skinned and gasping for breath.

I saw Stick Man.

*"This time, someone's going to get hurt,"* he said, hissing in his whistling wicked voice.

# 8

My pillow burst open, the feathers exploding in all directions. A glass of water beside the bed broke and shattered. Ants crawled on my arms, stomach, and legs, spreading out across my body.

In my nightmare, Stick Man assaulted Walker and Gabriel. He hated them both because I loved them so much.

Stick Man mauled at Gabriel with his wooden claws, the fingernails hacking him.

He sliced off both of Walker's legs. The legs scurried away from Walker's body, like an earthworm split in two. Walker saw his detached legs, and cried for me to rescue him.

All the while, Stick Man sang. *"At the cross at the cross/where I first saw the light/and the burden of my heart rolled away/I will steal Walker's legs and kill your dog/and you can't stop me anyway..."* He gleamed at me mockingly.

"Pray for us now and at the hour of our death," I said in my sleep. "Twenty-one, twenty-one, twenty-"

When I woke up I was in a pool of sweat. I shuddered and saw Stick Man still hovering above me. I reached quickly for my baseball bat to swing, but Stick Man knocked the bat out of my hands and choked me.

"The blood, the blood..." I said.

Kathryn Kuhlman was right.

He hated the blood.

Stick Man retreated.

After my nightmare, I waited for the residue of my dream to pour out of my pores, like sick sweat. I watched over Walker and Gabriel like a mother hen. Whenever I walked down the steps to the basement where Stick Man lived, I was cautious. I never knew when the enemy would appear.  I was vigilant and prayerful, ready for my foe to materialize.

Walker's legs were his greatest asset.  He was the fastest kid in West View and he excelled at every sport.  Pittsburgh was a sports town and the 1970's was the decade of champions.

Dad's psychiatrist successfully lowered the lithium in his blood levels to manageable levels so he was released from Saint John's mental hospital to come home for a while in September, 1971.

When Clemente led the Bucs to a World Series victory over the Baltimore Orioles, the city of Pittsburgh erupted in celebration.  Pirate fans poured into the streets.  They honked their horns and danced and sung.  Dad drove Walker and me down Center Avenue Saturday night, where parties, brass bands, fireworks and noisemakers filled the sky.

Walker threw a baseball with grace, like Clemente.  I wondered what would happen if Stick Man took his legs away for good.  I wanted to have a back-up plan, so I determined to develop my own athletic prowess.

Dad was lying on the couch on Sunday afternoon, recovering from another late Saturday night.

*From Here to Eternity,* Dad's favorite movie was on TV, but he slept through most of it.  Since he was back on his medication, he was calm.  I decided it was safe to risk waking him.  I roused him so I could ask my question.

"Dad, I know about baseball, football, wrestling, and basketball.  Walker and I are pretty good at any game with a ball.  But I want to be good at all sports.  Are there any other ones I don't know about?"

"There's one game," he said, a smile crossing his lips, "but you're a little too young to know about it, son. It's one I'm quite good at."

"Please, Dad. Tell me."

"Are you kidding? Maybe when you're old enough."

"That's not fair. Pretty please…"

Dad looked at my eyes. "If I tell you, you can't let your mother know about it. I'll never hear the end of it."

"Just between us, Dad. Scout's honor, I swear on the holy Bible."

"That sounds like an ironclad guarantee to me. Okay, son." He grinned mischievously. "Chasing girls."

"Chasing girls? That's not a sport."

"Oh, yes it is. Greatest sport there is. And the most pleasurable."

"Does it even have a ball? And how do you score?"

"You're too young to know about scoring, son. For your age level, let's just say if you catch a girl and kiss her, you score."

Maybe one day, when I scored with a girl and kissed her, I'd know the love David Cassidy and the Partridge Family sang about.

"What are you telling him?" Mom said in her high, mad-as-hell voice. She overheard from the kitchen.

"Nothing. Mind your own business."

"You'd like me to mind my own business, wouldn't you?"

Dad was in the doghouse. Mom found letters and photos from girls Dad scored with, and she caught a virus from him related to his scoring.

*****

A few days later, she told me her side.

"I've only been with your father and no other before or since," she said. "I was a good Catholic girl. And you better be a good boy and not listen to your father. Or we're gonna send you away to the bad boy's home."

She didn't describe in detail what the bad boy's home was, which made it all the more ominous. My imagination created images of Oliver Twist.

"And when your father's around, make sure he takes his pills. Count them, especially the lithium. He's tricky as a fox. Sometimes he puts them in his mouth and doesn't swallow. You're gonna have to be like a father to your father. Do you understand?"

"Sure, Mom. I'll make sure Dad's okay."


Something was wrong with Walker that winter. He seemed socially isolated from the other kids in the neighborhood. He called himself the Nowhere Man after the song by the Beatles.

He coped with Dad's illness by checking out on LSD he got from older boys in the neighborhood. They thought it was funny to watch a little kid trip. I escaped by putting my hands to work on my painting and music. Walker put his hands through the walls.

When the drugs increased, Walker turned on me. He came at me with a knife from the kitchen when I flushed his drugs. My relationship with Walker was becoming similar to my relationship with my Dad. I had to take care of them both and watch out for their dark side.

I never struck back. I wrestled Dad to the ground once to protect Mom, but I never hit him or Walker.

Walker threw tantrums without warning. He'd throw himself on the floor and pound his fists into the rug, kicking and screaming at the top of his lungs. Walker was the brunt of even more beatings than me.   He was blamed for things he had nothing to do with.   One of his tactics to retaliate was to stop speaking English. Walker made up a syllable, "thith," and than answered everyone with his new word.

"Walker, do you want more spaghetti?" Mom said.

"Thith," Walker said, biting a piece of garlic toast.

"I'm asking you a question, young man, do you want more spaghetti?"   She stood up, her fists on her hips.

I laughed under my breath.

"THITH, THITH, THITH, THITH," Walker said, mocking Mom.   She turned red and slapped him across the face.

"I DON'T WANT TO HEAR THAT NONSENSE!   You talk English around here, young man…"

I turned my head away, not wanting to see Walker get punched. I remembered how the beatings hurt, and the bruises from the last time were still on my buttocks and the back of my legs.   I put a pillow on the chair so my rump wouldn't hurt during dinner.

Walker sang to himself.   "I'm a real nowhere man, sitting in my nowhere land…"

SLAP.


November, 1971.   Dad was still at war with the DJs that would rob the land of soul and pillage gigs away from guitarists.   I taught bass lessons to Red Rawlings, so he could play with us occasionally.   Most professional bassists didn't want to work with Dad anymore because of his mood-swings, which caused him to yell and demean the rest of the musicians on the bandstand, humiliating them in front of the audience.

The corner of Center Avenue and Oakwood was busy that winter.   Just outside our front door was the PAT, (Pennsylvania

Transit Authority) bus stop. Gabriel and I watched the buses, reading the signs in the front to see where they were headed. I watched the circus parade of passengers en-route to various points of Pittsburgh. South Hills. North Hills. McKnight Road. Bellevue. Downtown.

It was inevitable on such a trafficked street that disaster loomed.

Gabriel escaped out the front door. He dashed by me, and then by two old ladies at the PAT stop. He sprinted straight across Center Avenue. I watched in horror. It all happened in slow-motion.

He was struck dead by a sports car.

The car took off, hit and run. It sped away towards Horseshoe Bend. Gabriel's neck twisted and his head hung over his shoulder against the pavement. Blood erupted like a volcano out of his mouth, gargling through his teeth and staining the road.

I walked like a zombie, trancelike towards Gabriel's corpse. I picked him up, than ran back to the house with Gabriel in my arms.

I dashed into the kitchen. Mom looked at his head, bent over my elbow.

"Oh, dear. I'm sorry." She looked at him.

"I'm going to catch the people who did this," I said. "I swear to God. And then give Gabriel a proper burial."

I remembered the license plate said "Rose," and that the driver was a man. In the passenger side was a blonde woman. I decided to be a detective. I organized a private investigators club consisting of me, Walker, Red, and Savannah.

I looked up Rose in the phone book and found "S. Rose" in the Hill district. The four of us rode our bikes there, which took four hours.   We discovered the residence of S. Rose was a black family with a Dodge Dart.

We followed the wrong clue, but when we told them what happened to Gabriel, they were sympathetic.   We made friends and played baseball with the two Rose brothers, Alvin and Jerome.   Then it hit me that Rose was probably the blonde woman's first name.

A dead end.

Since our detective work yielded no closure, I decided to have the memorial for Gabriel.   Oakland Avenue children gathered in our backyard.   I wore my best blue jean overalls and a striped shirt.

Red borrowed his father's ministerial book, entitled *Starr's Guide for Ministers*, which contained liturgies for weddings and funerals.

"Dust to dust, ashes to ashes," Red said, reading from the sermon his father used to send Baptists to their eternal rest.   "Our dearly departed is absent from the body, but present with the Lord."

I remembered the miracle message that Kathryn preached.   I clutched a bible Reverend Rawlings gave me and decided to interject more faith into the proceedings.

"God still heals and raises the dead today," I said.   "We all believe in miracles.   Gabriel's gonna come back.   Remember Lazarus, everybody."

Savannah stood to my left, in a checkered dress, her red hair in pigtails.   She reached for my hand and squeezed it.   Red bowed his head in prayer.   Walker dug a hole with a shovel.

*Why's he digging that stupid hole?* I wondered.   If Kathryn Kuhlman was right, our faith raises the dead, so it stands to reason that any lack of faith would keep Gabriel dead.

I looked at my brother. "We all believe except you, Walker. If you really believed, you wouldn't be digging that hole."

I placed the bible on Gabriel's corpse and looked down.

"You dumb dreamer," Walker said. "That ain't gonna work. Gabriel's dead."

"You didn't believe, Walker," I said, trying not to cry.

I fashioned a cross from two twigs and put it in the ground near the hole.

Long into the night, I still sat there after the others had gone. The roar of the wind blew the trees in the backyard. I looked up at the stars.

I walked towards the house, not wanting to stay in the dark any longer, in case Stick Man manifested.

Mom was there when I returned. "I waited for you to come home, honey." She sat on the glider, rocking back and forth on the porch. "Come over here."

I sat beside her, snug against her hips. Her voice soothed me. The scratchiness was gone. She was calm and kind. I noticed a large white bag on her lap. "I brought you something. A present." I hoped the bag didn't contain socks and underwear.

I unwrapped the present and saw it was a stuffed animal, a German Shepherd with a thick coat of fake fur and a plastic head.

"Thank you, Mom."

"You're welcome. What're you gonna name him?"

"I don't know. German Shepherds are good watch dogs. I'll keep him beside me when I sleep to scare off Stick Man."

There was no scolding, no shadow of turning from her gift. The dog was so lifelike, I could almost hear him barking. I put my arms around her neck and kissed her. "Thanks, Mommy. You're the bestest Mom in the whole world."

I decided then and there, to visit the one person I knew could help Gabriel. The following morning, I hopped on the PAT bus at Center and Oakwood. I sat in the front row so I could see the roads and bus stops. The bus smelled like the woods after a rainstorm. I rode down McKnight Road into downtown.

I hopped off at the First Presbyterian Church at six-thirty a.m. The church was already full. I sat in a pew just behind the ushers and occupied myself with a Partridge Family coloring book while I waited.

As the miracle service drew closer, I tried to contain myself. Kathryn Kuhlman arrived to begin the healing service at ten-thirty. She looked even taller in person, and her hair was redder than it looked on TV. She floated like an angel in her chiffon dress. Her assistant, a green-eyed girl with a black beehive, came over to me.

"My name's Connie. What's your name, young man?"

"Jeremiah."

"Are you okay? Why are you crying?"

"I don't know."

"Do you need prayer for healing?" she asked. I thought her smile was like the women in toothpaste commercials.

"No, but my friend Gabriel does."

"Is Gabriel here with you?"

"No." I squirmed. "He died. I really need to talk with Miss Kuhlman in private. I've come all this way from West View on a bus by myself."

"Where's your mother?"

"I don't know."

"Can you ask Kathryn to pray for me?"

Connie walked to the platform and whispered in Kuhlman's ear. Kathryn looked at me and smiled. Connie came over to me a second time and sat beside me. "Miss Kuhlman will talk to you after the service, just you and her."

"Thank you, ma'am."

Kathryn skipped the sermon and decided to go right into the prayer time for the sick. Miracles happened on cue. A lot of people were slain in the Spirit, falling backwards into the arms of ushers who caught them. The dark-haired pianist played like Liberace, and he had sparkling rings on his fingers. When the service concluded, Connie came for me.

*****

Connie sat with me in the back of the limousine that transported us to Kathryn's elegant hotel suite. There was a shop in the lobby that sold roses.

"Can we stop here for a moment?" I asked.

She looked at her watch and acquiesced. "Make it quick. Okay?" The clerk took in her beauty for a second before she could catch his eyes.

I emptied all the change in my pocket and bought a long-stemmed rose. I didn't have enough coins, but the clerk sold me the rose anyway, with a wink to Connie. I arrived at Kathryn's room, rose in hand.

The miracle woman greeted me at the door, wearing a green dress just past her knees. I handed her the flower.

"Awww…is this for me?" Kathryn was ladylike when she gushed.

I nodded, still a bit hesitant to speak. I looked down at her feet and noticed she was wearing sandals. She took my face in her long, bony fingers and raised my eyes to meet hers.

"You're not only a very handsome young man, you're quite generous." She smiled and kissed me on the forehead. I noticed her hoop earrings and bushy hair.

Kathryn took my hand and walked me into her suite, filled with candies and flowers from well-wishers. She put my flower in a vase, then opened a box of candies and offered me one with a smile.

The famed faith healer plopped down on the floor like a little girl, and patted the rug, signaling for me to sit beside her. I tasted the chocolate. It was luscious, almost as creamy as a Mallo Cup.

Connie left us alone sitting on the floor, talking and giggling.

"So, tell me about your friend who died," Kathryn said.

"His name was Gabriel. He was hit by a car."

"Awwww. That's sad. Gentle Jesus. How old was he?"

"Just a puppy."

She looked surprised. "Gabriel's your dog?"

"Yeah. But he was more than a dog."

"He was a member of the family," she said knowingly.

"Yeah." I nodded and scratched the rug. "I need to ask you something."

"Sure, what is it, darling?"

"You said that if we believe in Jesus, the same miracles He did, we can do also. So, I need you to speak life into Gabriel's body."

"Mmmm. Let's pray for Gabriel right now." She took my hand in hers and looked into my eyes. "Jesus, you know we love you. You know how much Jeremiah loved Gabriel, his best friend in the whole world. We know, Gentle Jesus, You can do anything so we ask you to comfort Jeremiah and touch Gabriel with Your healing hand." She was quiet and meditative for several moments.

Her pianist's room was down the hall.   He knocked on the door, interrupting our stillness, a signal that it was time for her to perform the next healing service.   She nodded to her pianist, than returned her attention to me.

"God's showing me that it was Gabriel's time to go to heaven, where all good doggies go.   You'll see him again, and you'll play with him one day, over the hills of glory."

"But I need him.   You don't understand, Miss Kuhlman, there's a monster, and his name's Stick Man.   He comes in my nightmares and hurts me.   And you said only perfect love casts out fear.   With Gabriel gone, I can't win."

"I'll send you another angel of love to protect you.   She'll come to you soon.   Very soon.   I give you my word.   And I want you to love your angel with all your heart.   You promise?"

"Scout's honor.   I will love my angel with all my heart."

I rose and walked to the door.   I waved goodbye and her expression changed.   "Jeremiah, come back here."

I walked towards Kathryn.   "Stretch out your hands to me."

I reached to her.   She placed her hand on top of mine and closed her eyes.   She squeezed my hand.   My fingertips tingled.

"My hands are hot, like I'm holding them over the stove," I said.

"Good.   You got it, the healing hands.   You will heal your angel, and your angel will heal you."

She gave me a small, wooden cross as a souvenir.   I slid the cross into my pocket.   She kissed me goodbye on my cheek and I headed out the door.

A week later, Walker, Red, and I were digging. We'd been up since dawn to see who would reach China first with our toy shovels.

Savannah heard an announcement on the radio that devastated Pittsburgh. She ran to tell me. "Did you hear the news? Roberto died."

When the gang played baseball, I always insisted I was the right fielder. I wanted to be Roberto, like so many other boys in Pittsburgh. Savannah told us how Clemente perished in a mission of mercy to Nicaraguan earthquake victims. His plane crashed and his body was never found.

I sat in the attic the rest of the day in a state of shock, thinking about my memories of the Great One. I remembered the smell of peanuts, Dad beside me, and Roberto's movements across the diamond. I recalled the 1971 World Series, how the Great One led the Pirates to a come-from-behind victory against the Baltimore Orioles. Clemente played on, despite his many injuries and ailments.

I could still smell the ballfield. I liked the scent of the glove and the feel of the seams against my fingers when I gripped the baseball.

Three days after Clemente's death, Dad had his breakdown.

The "big one."

He was volatile that morning, off his medication, and I prayed God would quell his tantrums. He lost it with Mom, who kept interrupting the Pirates game, even when it reached extra-innings. The bases were loaded. Slugger Willie Stargell was at the plate.

All through the game, Mom was nagging him about money, how he was foolishly lending it out to all his barroom buddies. When Dad went off his medicine, he spent and lent like he was Howard Hughes.

"Don't push me," he said, "or you'll regret it. Dammit, anyway."

Cardinals ace Bob Gibson had reached a full count on Stargell when Mom came in nagging Dad in her high-pitched voice. Like a dog sensing an earthquake, my muscles tightened in anticipation of a mood that would surpass all its predecessors.

*Stop. He warned you.*

I heard plates crashing, Mom screaming, and the thud of his fists.

I ran to the phone to call the police but he yanked the phone out of the wall.

"Dammit, anyway."

I ran to my room and locked the door. I checked the doorknob four times. I hid under my bed but Dad kept banging banging banging on the door.

He crashed through like a locomotive. The door flew in the room, unhinged as if a tornado ripped it like paper. I looked up at him and smiled, hoping to change his mood, but something snapped. His eyes swirled like the lights in a Van Gogh painting.

He kicked me again and again.

"NO, DADDY! PLEASE, STOP!"

He didn't slap, he used fists. Blows fell, jackhammer jabs as he punched me all over my body. I raised my hands in front of my face, but my position on the floor made me vulnerable.

I tried to run, but Dad grabbed me and threw me in the corner like a rag doll, attacking me again.   His fists and feet were all over me.

"Straighten up and fly right, buddy boy," he said.

"I didn't do anything," I said.   "Stop, Daddy."

"DON'T SASS BACK," he said, striking me again.   My body fell limp.   "Why do you have to act like a wisenheimer and get me mad?"

*****

Hours later, I came to.   He was gone.

I heard the piano playing and walked into the music room.

"They have to put your father away again for a while, dear," Mom said.   "It's kind of like when a dog bites someone and they have to put the dog to sleep."

After wiping off my face with a rag, Mom fixed a bag of ice to hold to my face.   She resumed Chopin's Opus 64 on the piano. She loved Opus 64 because it was the theme song for Liberace's TV show.   She played extra-slow, like a dirge.

Dad sent me a book about Clemente, as a token of his amends.   I slept on the downstairs couch because he injured my leg in the attack.   I opened the Clemente book and read the inscription:

> *I'm sorry firstborn son.*
> *Forgive me.*
> *I hope your leg heals soon.*
> *Love,*
> *Dad   XO*

After the deaths of Gabriel and Roberto, reading Dad's inscription in the book made me feel like things were going to be peaceful for a while.    I went to sleep, praying for good dreams for a change.

I should have lowered my expectations.

# 9

I awoke to the sound of hissing. I sensed Stick Man standing in the corner of my room, staring at the crucifix on the wall. His deep, demonic breathing grew heavier and more labored, like he was dying for air.

I heard Stick Man's reedy whisper.

*"Jeremiah."* He repeated my name, elongating the syllables. *"Jeerrrrr—aaaaaa—miii---aaaahhhh."*

I clung to my blankie in the deadly cold. I opened my eyes and saw Stick Man standing near me, six-feet tall, unearthly. His dark, big form was concealed by clouds of smoke. His eyes had red pupils, peering through the holes of his mask. He looked straight at me.

*"Jeremiah…"*

"Who are you?" I asked.

*"You're _mine_, firstborn son. God told Abraham to kill his son Isaac,"* he said, cackling. *"The firstborn is _mine!_"*

Stick Man's eyes blazed from the holes. He lunged at me, pouncing on me with grace, despite his size. I kicked and screamed. A blood-curdling scream. At the end of Stick Man's fingers were nails dripping with blood. They pierced my skin as he clawed my belly. He grabbed me, stretching out my body on his stick arms. Stick Man raised his arms to pound nails through my hands. I saw the holy number. I shouted an incantation of the two digits.

"Twenty one…twenty one…"

Poof. He was gone.

I heard Mom race down the hall. She burst through my bedroom like a mother lion defending her cub. I woke up, crying and sweating.

Mom sat beside me and consoled me. "There, there, dear."

"Make it *stop*! I'm *scared*! Please, Mom, make it *stop*," I cried.

She wiped my brow with one hand, and patted my back with the other. Though Stick Man was gone, I was still shaking and sweating. "Say to yourself, 'It's only a dream, it's only a dream. Stick Man isn't real.'"

I closed my eyes and folded my hands. "It's only a dream, it's only a dream, Stick Man isn't real."

After several seconds, I opened my eyes. "But I saw him, Mom. He *is* real."

"You're giving him power by saying that. How did this crucifix get knocked to the floor?" She picked it up. It snapped in the middle like a brittle toothpick, severing the carcass of Christ. "Remain calm, dear. Don't be afraid."

"Mommy, I'm scared."

I held my stomach and shuddered. "Your PJ top is stained, dear." She lifted my shirt and looked down at my midriff.

There were two cuts across my abdomen, forming a cross. "You still think that's from a bedpost, Mom? We better call Father McCormick."

"For what? What can he do?"

I remembered the movie with a priest and a young girl played by Linda Blair. "Perform an exorcism."

No one believed it was a bedpost anymore. Maybe I was marked like Cain, a devil-child like Damien. I worried that when

McCormick gave the command for expulsion, my head would spin around like a top, the way Linda Blair did. Then again, it would be a small price to pay to be free. If the darkness came from deep within me, I welcomed the light. I reasoned that when I turned on the light-switch in my bedroom, the darkness in the room goes away automatically.

Sister Antonita taught us that we're born into original sin. "Our natures are fallen," she'd often said. Yet it seemed like many good things in my life, the paintings I created, the songs I wrote, all came from somewhere deep inside.

The exorcism turned out to be much tamer than I expected. Father McCormick came into my bedroom with Mom. He was dressed in his black robe and carrying a copy of *The Roman Ritual*. I felt like a celebrity entered my house because I was used to seeing him on stage at Saint Joe's, transubstantiating the bread into the body and the wine into the blood.

"So how are you, Jeremiah?" McCormick asked. His grip swallowed up my hand.

"Okay," I said. I was anything but okay. Stick Man's attacks scared me out of my wits.

He glanced at Mom. "So this is where Jeremiah sleeps when the manifestations occur?"

"Yes, Father," Mom said. "This is his room."

Father McCormick opened a cork-tipped vial and sprinkled holy water around the room. He anointed the door and window, and said prayers in Latin. I remembered the priest in *The Exorcist* doing the same thing.

The priest splashed me with holy water. I made the sign of the cross. He capped the holy water and returned the vial to his pocket. He kneeled beside my bed and murmured the Our Father, then prayed for assistance. "God our Father, graciously aid me against this unclean spirit tormenting Your child Jeremiah."

"Amen," Mom said.

"Save your servant who trusts in You from the enemy of our souls." I made the sign of the cross and glanced at the copy of the *Ritual* in his hands. "You sent Your only begotten Son into the world to crush that roaring lion."

Mom and I lowered our heads in prayer.

"I'm going to ask you the questions that were asked of you at your baptism Jeremiah," McCormick said. "At that time, your godfather, Spiritos, answered the questions on your behalf In light of your reaching the age of accountability, you must answer these questions of your own volition. Do you renounce Satan and all his works?"

I was quiet, missing my cue.

"Answer '*I do,*' Jeremiah," he said, touching my neck with the stole.

"I do." I watched the clouds of incense and smelled the oblation.

"Do you refuse to allow sin to master you?" He kept the stole firmly pressed against my neck.

"I do."

"Do you believe in God the Father, the Maker of heaven and earth?"

"I do."

"Do you believe in Jesus Christ, His only begotten Son, begotten not made, one in being with the Father, who was crucified, buried, and rose the third day?"

"I do."

"Do you believe in the Holy Spirit, the Lord, the giver of life, who proceeds from the Father and the Son, and with the Father and the Son is worshipped and glorified?"

"I do."

Father McCormick lifted my shirt and examined the cut. "How did this happen?"

"Stick Man has nails for fingers."

Father McCormick sprinkled my head again, than removed the end of his stole from my neck. He revealed a crucifix and traced the sign of the cross on my forehead. He stepped back and commanded with lightning ferocity. "I cast you out unclean spirit, and every wile of the devil and attack of the enemy. Every specter of hell and savage companion, BE GONE by the authority of Christ who stilled the sea and the storm!"

I sat silent and still, shivering in the sudden coldness of the room. He watched me intently.

"Depart from him and go to the dry places!" McCormick traced the sign of the cross on my chest and exhaled deeply. He opened the window of the bedroom and I wondered if a spirit was an amount of breath or air that could escape out the portal.

"God loves you, Jeremiah," he said. His portly pure face shone with serenity and understanding.

He assured me I was safe from Stick Man. I believed Father McCormick was trying to do what God wanted, but I had doubts about the effectiveness of his exorcism. Stick Man's power was intense and electrical. Father McCormick's was ceremonial and ritualistic. Animalistic, fiery passion trumped religious ritual any day of the week.

"Now go see the doctor and get that cut checked out," Father said. "Promise me you'll take him, Medea."

"I promise, Father," Mom said.

The social worker from Children's Youth Services (CYS), a woman with cropped hair who walked like a cowboy, arrived with a police officer. Neither of them believed Mom's explanations for some of my bruises. Dad's history was well-documented with the West View police and the caseworker had a copy of the file.

"This isn't all Saul's doing. He's a bit clumsy," Mom had said. "Falls down stairs."

"We're aware of the attack from Mister Young. We don't want Jeremiah hurt again," the social worker said. She scribbled in a notebook and turned towards me. "Your father is being removed from the house by the authorities, Jeremiah. The police call it a three-oh-two."

"With his history of violence, you can call anytime and get a three-oh-two," the officer said to me. I noticed his silver badge. "We can't hold him forever, and he'll be back, but if he ever goes off his medication again, call a three-oh-two. You got that?"

"Three-oh-two," I said. "Will Daddy be all right?"

They didn't answer. I was asked to leave the room, but listened on the other side of the door.

After the deaths of Gabriel and Roberto, the triple blow came when Child Services forced me and Walker to split up. I overheard bits and pieces of the conversation between Mom and the Children's Services worker. I cracked open the door to watch.

"Is he going to be all right?" Mom asked.

"We'll have to move your son somewhere else for a while," the social worker said. "I can't imagine Jeremiah wanting to sleep in this house again for some time. It will be months, maybe years, before he's comfortable in the room where it happened." The social workers eyes fell lightly to my painting of Christ, resting on an easel in the center of the room. "Nice painting. The eyes follow me. Who's the artist?"

"My son Jeremiah," Mom told her.

"Very nice. Haunting."

"Look, I don't want him to leave right away. He's my little boy and-"

"He'll stay here a bit longer until other arrangements are made." The C.Y.S. woman sashayed across the room in her John Wayne walk and stood close to my painting and touched it. She stared into the eyes of Jesus then looked vaguely embarrassed. "That's quite a painting. Haunting, almost like it's alive." The social worker backed away from the painting and gathered her papers.

"Good luck, Mrs. Young," the officer said.

"Thanks." Mom smiled wanly.

When I heard them finish and the social worker neared the door, I scurried away. They nodded goodbye to Mom and left.

I would've lived with the godfather, but Mom gave me a newspaper clipping containing stunning news of Spiritos Sabatino's obituary. The papers called it an unsolved crime. Three deaths in a row. Gabriel, Roberto, and now Spiritos.

I closed my bedroom door and buried my face in my pillow, soaking it with my leaky eyes. I pummeled the pillow with my fists until I was exhausted. I wiped my face with my blankie then opened the letter from Spiritos, the one he gave me when we ate spaghetti.

*Dear Jeremiah,*
*    You've been blessed with many talents and great*
*intelligence. Pay attention to everything you like doing. And as*

*you get older, keep doing what you like.     Guitar, Art, magic.*
*Follow dreams!*
   *Love, Spiritos*

I wrote a note in reply, scribbled in crayon.


  *dear Spiritos,*


   *I can't believe you're dead. I don't know if this will*
*reach you in the afterlife, but I hope you always do what you like too.*
*Create magic.*
  *Love, Jeremiah*


  I walked to the mailbox on Center Avenue, and stood on a
bucket to reach the latch. I dropped the letter inside, than opened the
lid a couple times to make sure it went down.
  I was assigned to Reverend Rawlings home as my foster
family.
*****

  The following Tuesday, I was sitting in English class. I
couldn't concentrate. Within a few days, I was moving into the
Rawlings household. My world had been my family. When that
was stolen, nothing else was in balance. School didn't matter.
Friends didn't matter.
  Sister Antonita's voice grew soft and muffled, sounding like
a distant echo in a tunnel. I rose up from my seat, as if in a trance.
I left the classroom, sleepwalking past the lockers where my
classmates kept their coats and gym clothes.
  Stick Man waited in the hall by the lockers.
  I looked up and froze.

I stifled a gasp.

Stick Man's tumid tongue lolled loosely from his malevolent mask. *"I hate you,"* he said. He belched a hideous wolfish sound as from a rotted, putrid wasteland. The air suddenly turned foul, thick like a current, as the volume of his emissions increased.

I grimaced and pressed my hands tight against my ears to drown out the deafening noise. He floated rapidly, coming close behind me. I ran away from him, and ran right into his arms. I fell flat on my face. Stick Man swiped at my side. He cut me with his nails, hissing sibilantly like a serpent, his tongue flicking in and out of his mouth.

*"I'm going to crucify you,"* Stick Man said. *"Your family doesn't love you anymore. They want you dead. You deserve to be punished. I will kill you!"* I screamed, and ran away again with Stick Man's tongue snaking out at my thigh. *"You're mine, firstborn son,"* he hissed.

Wherever I moved, Stick Man followed, howling with hideous laughter, until I found myself back in the classroom.

"I'm calling Father McCormick," Sister said.

Go ahead, I thought. He can't do any good.

*****

In the rectory office, McCormick questioned me further. "What's really bothering you?" he asked.

I told him that I overheard Mom on the phone with a lawyer. "I'm tired of being married to a ward of the insane asylum," she'd said. "I'm filing for divorce."

Father McCormick took it upon himself to visit our house a second time to confront her later that day.

"Jesus wants you to forgive and honor your vows," he said. He was sitting at the kitchen table, across from Mom. "Your son needs his parents together.  He's in a battle with Beelzebub."

"But we're *not* together.  Saul's in Saint John's, and Jeremiah's moving to the Rawlings."

"God doesn't want you to divorce, Mrs. Young," McCormick said.  I was listening again from the hallway.  "Divorce is a mortal sin that excludes you from Communion."

"Does he want me to be married to a madman?  Does he want me to be a punching bag?"

Father McCormick stood up, larger than life squaring off eyeball to eyeball with Mom in a dramatic showdown.  He quoted a passage from Malachi that said '*God hates divorce*' and told her a second time the divorced are barred from receiving the Holy Eucharist.  She looked at him and refused to answer or respond.

After a long pause, she grinned.  Her sardonic smile gave away no trace of intention or emotion.  She reached out and took the crucifix Father was wearing in her hand and caressed the corpse.

Suddenly, she came to a decision, ripping up the legal papers and handing them to him.  Father McCormick raised his head to heaven and made the sign of the cross.  Dad had pushed her to the limit, but she told me she didn't want to bust up the family permanently for the sake of us kids.

I hated the way Mom and Dad fought, but I still felt a sense of relief when she called off the divorce.  After all, I thought, they still are my parents and they're the only ones I got.

*****

The night I was to leave for Rawlings, I wanted to cling to Mom and Walker and never let go.  I knew I was only moving across the street, but that seemed like a great gulf at the time.  Our final night together, Mom, Walker and I sat in the basement. She did most of the talking. Walker was engrossed with his spinners on the floor, making sound effects noises as his battling tops collided with each other.

"I should've listened to my mother. She saw through your Dad right away," Mom said. "I played polkas on my accordion at Croatian Park. I had my own band. I earned extra money, but when I heard your Dad on guitar, boy oh boy, I almost wanted to quit music, that's how good he was. He was charming. At least at first."

"What was the name of your band?"

"The Polka Dots. There were four of us. We didn't make a lot of money but we had fun. Some of the parties we played for, they just passed the hat for the band and we split whatever we got. When I left them to join your Dad's band, it wasn't that much fun anymore. It was more like a job as he was more critical and exacting about how he wanted it. It was his way or no way. My cousin Henry played bass. He's the one that sent me to the music school where I met your Dad. It was the summer of 1961, he was the guitar teacher at Spratt's Music on the Norside. He told me he couldn't help but notice me, he liked my dark hair. He said I was pretty."

"You *are* pretty Mom," I said.

She smiled and folded laundry. "I came on Tuesdays for my accordion lesson in the teaching room adjacent to his. He formulated a plan to have my teacher leave early. My teacher pretended to be sick, so your Dad could teach the remaining portion of my lesson. He had curly, black hair and brown eyes that flashed when he smiled. He played all the romantic songs. *As Time Goes By. Stardust. Tenderly.* He played with so much feeling, the way you do, dear. Your Dad fooled me. It wasn't fair. He seduced me with his melodies. He lied and said he never drank alcohol like other musicians. I gave everything up for him and for you boys," she said with her tired martyr's voice.

Savannah Rawlings interrupted us. I heard her footsteps on the cellar stairs. I tried to be tough, but much to my chagrin, I melted like a collapsing iceberg and hugged Mom. She hugged back as best she could. Savannah stood there and watched.

"We'll have fun, Jeremiah," Savannah said. "Besides, God spoke to me and gave me a bible verse for you. I'll tell you about it while we walk across the street."

"Don't worry, Jeremiah. We'll all be back together one day soon," Mom said. "It's only temporary." I ran back to her but she wouldn't embrace me a second time. "Be strong, Jeremiah. Like Queen Elizabeth. She's regal no matter what happens."

I shook Walker's hand and followed Savannah outside. We crossed Oakwood Avenue to her house. "The scripture God gave me for you is from the twenty-seventh psalm," Savannah said. "It promises God will be your Heavenly Father and care for you since you lost your earthly father. The Lord has a call on your life, Jeremiah."

"Why did He put me in a family like mine?"

"He always has a plan. He'll reunite your family, just like your mother said. Until then, you're gonna live with us for a while."

"How long?"

"As long as you need to, until your father gets better, I guess. What's wrong with him?"

"My father has a mental illness." It felt good to tell someone, but I felt guilty talking about Dad behind his back. Sometimes I wondered if I did something wrong that caused Daddy to get sick. One time, I told the TV repairman Dad was manic-depressive and Mom told me I was hanging out the family's dirty laundry. She reminded me that when Noah's son Ham uncovered his father's nakedness, he was cursed by God.

I could tell by the look in her face, Savannah knew I was entrusting her with a secret. In the childhood world of even-steven, she knew she had to ante up and tell me something.

"Let me tell you a secret about my family," she said, whispering a revelation in my ear about her father that was so prurient I could scarcely take it in.

"No way," I said. Savannah's secret was something that didn't fit with their house that set modestly behind trimmed hedges on the outside, and displayed biblical plaques on the walls inside.

"You calling me a liar?" She stabbed me with her stare.

"No, it's just that-"

Her eyes looked away towards Center Avenue. "You don't believe me."

"I believe you."

"You can't tell anybody. Cross your heart and hope to die?"

"Cross my heart and hope to die," I said, crossing my chest with a sweeping motion.

And with that, I left my family for the Rawlings. I left the frying pan of Catholicism for the fire of Christian fundamentalism, trading one house of horrors for another.

# 10

Sister Ruth Rawlings prepared my favorite goodies. There were plates of Mallo Cups and Reeses Peanut Butter Cups on the tables. In contrast to Ruth's ghostly face which was devoid of make-up (make-up was a sin to Sister Ruth), the table was decorated with multi-colored crosses and bright Sunday School paraphernalia. Her husband Mordecai stood by the tables displaying the candies. He was a stout man and his eyes were two different colors, which both repelled me and made me look into his eyes out of curiosity. He gestured to the candy like the girls on *Price Is Right* pointing to a new car or dinette set. I loaded up as much as I could shove in my mouth. Mordecai coughed and cleared his throat before speaking. "Do you know the Lord knows you?"

"Yes," I mumbled, my mouth crammed with candy.

"But the real question is... do you know the Lord?"

"I think so."

"If you *think* so, you don't *know* so. Those who *know* Him, *know* that they *know* that they *know* they have the Father's blessing. Let me speak plainly, Jeremiah. There are only two types of people in the world: saved and unsaved. You'll need to be saved to be a member of this household. When you ask Christ into your heart, you have peace, power, and purpose."

*Peace, power, and purpose.* It was the first of many times I heard Mordecai's penchant for three words spoken in alliteration.

Sister Ruth brought in another tray, with lemonade and cookies. Mordecai always referred to his wife as Sister Ruth, even in her presence. She wore her hair in a bun, and she buttoned her blouse to the top, lest she tempt others. She smiled demurely at me and left the room for a moment.

I noticed the books on the shelves. Jerry Falwell's *Liberty Bible Commentary*. *Criswell's Guide for Pastors*. Dr. James Dobson's *Answers for Family Questions*.

The requirement for salvation turned out to be simple. I had to pray the "Sinner's Prayer." Mordecai seemed to be making some of it up as we went along. He bowed his head and I repeated the words after him.

"Dear Lord Jesus," he said.

"Dear Lord Jesus," I echoed. I said the rest of the prayer with him. "I repent of my sins. I deserve Hell. Come into my heart today. Come into my heart to stay. I receive you as my Lord and personal Savior. Amen."

"Where does Jesus live now, Jeremiah?" Rawlings asked, lifting his head.

"In heaven."

I knew from the look on Rawlings face I didn't give him the answer he wanted. He swallowed and belched, covering his mouth with his hand.

"That's true, Jeremiah. Jesus does live in heaven, but where else does He live?"

He handed me the candy plate again. I took another Mallo Cup. "In my heart."

Rawlings face lit up. "Right! Yes, praise God, you got it. The key to joy, Jeremiah, is found in the letters J, O, Y. *J*esus first, then *o*thers, then *y*ourself last."

He opened the door and called Ruth, Red, and Savannah. "Welcome your new brother. Jeremiah just got saved!"

Red and Savannah bounded into the room. "If it's God's will for you to be my husband, its okay now because we're both Christians, so we'd be equally yoked," Savannah said. "Woo-hoo!"

"Savannah," Mordecai said sternly. "That's enough of that."

"She's just teasing, Mordecai," Sister Ruth said.

"That's nothing to tease about."

Sister Ruth shook my chocolate-stained hand, her fey wet eyes looking at me through steel-rimmed spectacles. "I just want you to know Jeremiah, that if you ever need prayer or someone to talk to about the hassles of life, I will be a spiritual mother to you..."

*You'll never replace my mother.*

"...because you've just been born again into the family of God. You can call me Mom Number Two. How do you feel?"

"I don't feel any different," I said.

"Being saved isn't about *feelings*," Mordecai said. "It's about the Word of God."

The Rawlings prayed for me to be an effective evangelist to my brother. As soon as I could, I rushed home for a quick visit to tell Walker. He lay on his bed in his red and white uniform, tossing a football in the air. Saint Joe's junior high sports teams were called the Crusaders, and the jerseys had an image of a medieval knight in the center.

Walker's legs hung over the edge of the bed. He was first string on both the basketball and football teams. He decimated opponents like the Crusaders decimated the Turks when they fought for the Holy Land. I wanted my brother in heaven with me, so I told him what I understood about the new birth.

"When you receive Jesus, you have eternal life in heaven, and the promise that God works all things for good in the here and now."

"I'll think about it, bro. I'm late for the game."

The following morning, during home room, a voice announced the scores over the speaker. "The Crusaders won again, led by Walker Young."

The school was abuzz about my little brother. Walker shunned other football players because the jocks shunned everybody else. He preferred to hang out with the "freaks" or drug crowd. He strutted through the school halls shirtless in a vest, outlaw hat, and steel-toed boots. They cheered at Walker's Herculean swiftness.

The Rawlings thought Walker and I needed an outing together. Saturday morning, Walker and I backpacked, hiking through the forest. I decided to rest, but Walker wondered off by himself, promising to circle back. I played my guitar at our campsite near the waterfall at Beaver Creek dam.

I remembered Walker saw a swimming hole earlier in the morning that looked tempting. My instincts urged me to check on him. I found Walker diving off the bank, but the bank was slick. His foot slipped on the bank.

My hand was shaking and my palm was wet with sweat. I firmed my grip on a tree branch and called him.

"Walker? Walk-"

I looked at the water and forgot how to finish my brother's name. I stared at the lake, feeling as solemn as I was on my First Holy Communion at Saint Joe's. In a moment, I'd react to save him, but for several seconds I stood like a statue in sacred solemnity until my shock transformed into adrenaline.

Instead of doing a shallow dive, Walker did a deep dive into the shallow water. He struck bottom and broke his neck, paralyzing him immediately from the chest down. Walker's form was still in the water, unable to move. He couldn't get any air.

I felt dizzy.  I never liked heights and I was paralyzed with vertigo for several long seconds.

Walker's graceful body lay lifeless, floating face down in Beaver Creek.  I pressed through my shock and dove in.  The water was cold as ice.  I swam over to his still, sinking body.  I put my hands under him and flipped him on his back so he could breathe. The water made him lighter to lift.  I pulled him out, laying him on the creek bed.  I looked up to the dark sky.  I must've made the sign of the cross a dozen times.

"Are you alright?"

"I can't move, bro."

*It's all my fault.  This is Stick Man's doing, his revenge against me.  Why didn't I keep a closer eye on Walker?*

I started to cry but suppressed the emotion.  I couldn't afford the luxury with Walker's life hanging in the balance.

I wrapped him with a blanket that was left on the shore, probably by a prior picnic.  "I'll be right back, Walker.  Don't worry.  I'll get help right away."

I'll never forget the sad expression on Walker's face, his last look at me before I left him.

I ran up the hill to a farmhouse and called the ambulance. Minutes seemed like hours.  The ambulance took forever, going to the wrong place before locating us an hour later.

Walker was sent to a hospital in West View.  They took X-rays and when they saw his neck was broken, and they couldn't do anything for him, they sent him to Allegheny General in Pittsburgh.

The doctor told him the break crushed four vertebrae in his neck.  "It was a clean break, a complete severance of the spinal cord, which means, humanly speaking, you will never walk again or do any of the things you've done before."   I was numb, incredulous at the prognosis.

Walker spent four months in the hospital and six months in the rehab center.   He hung in a Stryker frame, withering away to 120 pounds.   He missed a whole school year, but kept current through tutors.

"Do you still believe all things work for good, Jeremiah?" he asked me.   I sat beside his hospital bed, stunned and silent, flooded with a feeling of simple love for my brother.   "Even getting paralyzed in a creek?"

Mordecai Rawlings had told me God was sovereign. Nothing happens without Him knowing it.   He referred to the story of Job, how Satan had to get God's permission before attacking Job and his family.

"I know this hit you hard Walker, but God knows," I said. "Only believe.   He'll take care of you."

"No, you and Mom will take care of me," Walker said. "Say your prayers all you want, but if you don't help me, I'm fucked."   He turned his head away from me.

"I'm here for you," I said.   "Whatever you need."

"Look at me, Jeremiah.   I'm a freak."

"Who wants to be a normie anyways?"  I said.   This got Walker to smile.

I visited every day.   I offered to pray for Walker's healing. I told him I would lay hands on him the way Kathryn did in her healing services, and that my faith was high that he'd walk.   Mom urged this on.

"If there is a God," Walker said, "which I have some doubts about, He has all power to heal me.   He knows my condition, and He can do it.   He doesn't want to, or He would've done it already.   At the very least, He would've prevented me from having the accident to begin with. And I don't want to get hope up, for you, or for Mom, or for me, only to have that hope crushed when I'm still lying in this bed, unable to move. No prayers, thank you."

Mom fell deeper into despair. She had the blinds drawn shut for days. She sat sedated and sobbing hoarsely on the couch watching soaps, blasting Chopin, and drinking cheap red wine.

"What can I do to make it better, Mom?" I asked.

"Take care of your brother."

"Jesus first, then others, then yourself," I said aloud.

I bathed and dressed Walker every day. In the adjustment period, I split my time between home and the Rawlings.

I was bone-tired from the nursing duties. I turned Walker several times during the night to prevent bedsores. I was on the night-shift three times a week. This broke up my slumber, and once I was up, I couldn't fall asleep again.

I was exhausted. One night, I forgot to put the ointment on Walker's penis that was supposed to be applied before putting on his catheter, a condom-like device with a tube on the end. The tube ran to the leg bag to receive his urine. My error hurt Walker when the catheter was removed.

I felt terrible for my mistake. *I let Walker down, let Mother down, and let God down*, I thought. I told myself that taking care of Walker was taking care of Christ, remembering a song we sang at Saint Joe's, "*Whatsoever you do to the least of My brethren, that you do unto Me.*"

Mom confronted me about my sloppiness. "You've got to be more careful, Jeremiah. You are your brother's keeper."

"I'm beat," I said. "I need rest too."

"Do it without murmuring," she said. "He needs BT. He'll get really sick if you let him get backed up."

For BT (bowel training), I gave him an enema to release his stool. After waiting thirty minutes for the enema to loosen his feces, I sat under his portable toilet seat. I donned plastic gloves and waited the appropriate intervals to reach into Walker's ass and pull the shit out. For urination, I changed his catheter and emptied his leg bag into a silver pitcher.

"Be careful with the catheter," Mom said in her high-pitched voice. "I don't want piss all over the carpet, honey."

This continued into the fall of 1977. One October afternoon, I collapsed. Rawlings interviewed nursing attendants for Walker so I could stay with Mordecai more often and help his ministry.

"We need your music and artistic talents to aid us in soulwinning. You're called as an evangelist, not a nurse," Mordecai said.

Children's Protective Services extended my temporary surrogate family situation. Mom and Walker were to live together, while I stayed with the Rawlings indefinitely. I never understood the rationale for this, but despite the odd living arrangements, we carved out time together as brothers. Triumph came out of tragedy. We formed a deeper bond around music. Walker had an idea one Friday night. We were sitting in the living room, I in a beat-up love seat and Walker in his motorized wheelchair.

"I don't have much left, bro," Walker said. "I can't run anymore. I can't use my body. I got to use my brain. Are you still interested in songwriting?"

"Let's do it, Troubadour."

Walker's arms, once muscular, were now threads devoid of sensation. He flung his arms upward in birdlike motions, enabling him to cup and mouth a Special 20 harmonica while I strummed guitar. Together, we composed over seventy songs. I did the majority of the writing but Walker's lyrical contributions were literate and improved the music. He developed his talents as a wordsmith and also for playing the harmonica like Bob Dylan and Neil Young. We released an album entitled *From the Heart,* using one of my abstract paintings for the album cover.

Walker invited everyone over for a record release party. In the junior high days of Walker's athletic triumphs, his parties attracted hundreds. He set out a can to collect money so he could enter a motorized wheelchair race in Nashville, an Olympics for quadriplegics. To his disappointment, it was just me, Savannah, Red and Walker. Between the four of us, we came up with thirty-seven dollars for his can.

I brought my guitar along and played a song I wrote called *The Light on the Road.* It was a gospel rock song about the conversion of Saul of Tarsus.

"You see lights on the road," Walker said, "but all I see is darkness, bro. But religion's alright for you and Red right now." He added a harmonica part, a bridge, and vocal harmonies to *Light On the Road.*

Doors opened for us to perform our music. Our first performance was the Pittsburgh Talent Competition, the one I finished second place in when I was seven. There wasn't pressure this time from Mom to win the tax money, so Walker and I entered just for the fun of it.

Before we took the stage, we listened in the wings to two prior acts. A folk artist with a nylon string guitar sang *Annie's Song* by John Denver, than a black quartet with matching purple tuxedoes harmonized to a background track, moving with choreographed dance steps.

Red ran the PA system that night. The mix on the three microphones was just right. Savannah brought us water. We performed a piece I wrote called *The Ballad of a Brother*. It left few eyes dry and feelings untouched as I sang: *"Ladies and gentlemen/I tell the story of a friend/Who almost met his fatal end/When he dove to take a swim/I assure you, my friend/You will someday walk again/Please ignore a few defeats/You will walk on golden streets."*

I glanced down to the front and saw Savannah and several other girls crying. Mom sat in the second row. The audience gave us a standing ovation. Applause washed over us like rain. The curtain closed and the cheers rose to louder levels. The throng demanded an encore. Though it wasn't in the schedule, the show's director agreed.

A line of people came backstage to talk to us afterward. One shrunken man waited an hour in a grey raincoat, muttering to himself. We were distracted by the crowd around us but I caught a brief glimpse of the old man's hunched and hopeless carcass. He smelled like frozen urine and trash. He had lines on his unrecognizable face like bars under the windows of his eyes. He approached us tentatively, shielding his face as he started talking.

"I heard about your performance. People were talking, you got to hear these two kids. They cut the funding over at Saint John's, so a lot of us have been out on the street. But I had to come here tonight."

A security guard eyed the old man. The sound of the audience talking and leaving the auditorium echoed in the hall.

"When they took me away the last time," the old man said, "and I left home, my wife couldn't say she loved me. But you grabbed me and told me you loved me, Jeremiah. Remember? You're the only one. And that's kept me going. I know through the years I've never complimented you, I always told you that you'd never be the guitar player I was. I told you there were only three performers I've ever seen hold the crowd in the palm of their hand. You remember, Jeremiah?"

"Sinatra..."

"Good. That's right. Ol' Blue Eyes at the Paramount, Elvis in fifty-six, and Michael Jackson at the Motown show. But let me tell you something, son. The way your vocals harmonized and the way that guitar and harmonica blended, it soared like a kite in the wind. And those words. Those words ripped my heart out about Walker walking again in on golden streets. Let me tell you both something, and never forget it."

He paused a moment. He cupped his hand and tapped it with his finger. "You two had them right there, son. Right there in the palm of your hand. You're the music man, son. You're the goddamned genius. Your Dad's proud of both you boys."

His back bent over, he shuffled away.

A couple groupie girls pressed in close. Savannah stood nearby. She cast a glance in their direction, wanting to protect me for herself. I was disinterested in the girls because I was overcome by a moment of connection with my father. His fleeting approval was what I longed for all my life.

I once read in the Old Testament how the patriarchs blessed their sons. The sons put their hand under the thigh of the father, and the father spoke a blessing over them. The blessing prophesied all the good things that would happen to them and to their children.

I wanted to do something so great that he'd approve of me. Not just once in a while, but forever and ever. Walker was less emotional than I was, but I looked over and saw that he was crying too. I guess he needed the blessing as much as I did.

First prize was ours, hands-down, and the award seemed like a vindication. I ran outside to Mom to celebrate the victory. I remembered how upset she was seven years prior when I'd lost. She kissed me on the cheek in the parking lot. I smelled her scent, Trident gum and waxy lipstick.

"That song was fantastic," she said. "You need to get your music out there. But don't get all high-falutin about winning, dear. I warn you, self-praise stinks and will drive people away. Don't win anything more for a while or you'll make other people too jealous."

I looked down to her feet. She was wearing her fancy patent-leather shoes. Mom licked her finger and straightened my eyebrows.

When we got home, Walker and I hid the thousand dollars we won in a hole in his bedroom wall. We agreed to split it fifty-fifty. The money sat there until the following June, when I decided to give Walker the entire thousand dollars for him to enter and travel to the quadriplegic summer Olympics. He won the Quadralympics Worldwide Wheelchair Competition in Nashville and kept right on winning. Graceful nurses took care of him as he competed in one city after another, winning over a half-dozen races in a row. He managed to become a star athlete again, although now he didn't have to catch a football, he just had to move a red lever on his electric wheelchair.

*****

June, 1978. I awoke in the middle of the night. I shared a bedroom with Red Rawlings, who was asleep. A shadow floated past the window, a dark spirit that glided towards me, hovering above my bed.   I felt a chill and my limbs went numb.   The smoke congealed and became Stick Man.   He stood at the foot of my bed. I couldn't move my head to the left or to the right.   I huddled under the blanket.

*"What happened to Walker was your fault,"* Stick Man said. His voice was raw, a whistle of breath.   *"You're supposed to be your brother's keeper…you're a selfish sick little sow.   Soul, soul, soul. The soul that sinneth, it shall die."*

Stick Man bit and choked me, his oversized hands suffocating me.   I couldn't breathe.   He smothered my face, strangling me and laughing hideously.   I looked into the hollow red of Stick Man's eyes.   I writhed on the bed in a tangle of my arms and legs with his wooden extremities, making awful choking sounds in a melee of gasps and grimaces.

I broke the paralysis and rolled out of bed, battling my adversary.   The commotion and sound of Stick Man biting me and oinking like a pig woke up Red, who ran forward.

Sister Ruth Rawlings rushed in.

The minute she arrived, Stick Man's sinister spirit was gone.

"My God," she said, "look at those marks on your neck." Scratches and long thin claw marks were visible around my throat. "Do you see them, Red?"

"Yes, I see them, Mother.   The red marks look like fingers around his neck."

"There's bites on your neck, your cheek.   Oh my God," she said.   She turned on the lamp and examined me.   "More bites on your arm.   Red, look."

"Jeez oh man, there's a little chunk of meat gone from your forearm," Red said.   "Whatever it was, it really likes to bite."

Sister Ruth checked my pulse. "What's going on?" she asked in a haggard whisper. "We better get Brother Mordecai. Go wake your father."

Reverend Rawlings walked in wearing a bathrobe and slippers.

"Perhaps the devil is attacking you for a reason," he said. "The one thing young people respect is music. You can reach a lot of kids for Christ."

I pulled up my blanket. "What does this have to with-"

"If you get busy winning souls to the Master, Stick Man will be forced to surrender."

"Wouldn't that infuriate him more?"

"Every soul you win is another nail in his coffin. And come next summer, I want you to work in my ministry as a missionary."

*A missionary. That sounds serious.*

Mordecai chauffeured me to school in the fall. The red and gold leaves blanketed the ground. Rawlings drove his Buick. The sun was brightening, so he pulled down the visor, then adjusted his necktie. "Sister Ruth and I believe your music can reach the world."

"Thanks for your confidence in me," I said, "but that sounds like an awful responsibility."

"It's a privilege."

Much of what Mordecai said seemed grandiose, but he'd been a Christian for years. He was a seminary graduate, and what did I know? I was just a kid, how could I trust my inner instincts when Mordecai had the bible on his side?

"God will get them if they don't do His will. Look at your brother Walker. There's no doubt, his accident was God's chastisement for his sin, as it were."

I wanted to choke the life out of his sanctimonious face.

"Walker's doing pretty good, he just won another race."

"Has he accepted Christ yet?"

"Not that I'm aware of, but-"

"God sent the accident to get his attention and bring Him to the Lord.   Those whom He loves, He disciplines."   Mordecai laughed, baring his crooked teeth.

"Doesn't that make God out to be cruel?"

"His ways are not our ways.   You should thank the Lord He let Walker live.   He *killed* people for far less rebellion, like Ananias and Sapphira.   The sold their land and lied about giving all the profits to the church, so He *smote* them dead right on the spot.   They lied, they died, they fried."   Mordecai chuckled.   "Or how about Uzza?   God *struck* him down for touching the Ark of the Covenant. He tried to steady it when the oxen stumbled.   Big mistake."

*Mordecai's god sounds mean,* I thought.

"Or how about when the Lord told the Israelites to wipe out the Amalekites down to every last man, woman, child, and infant, but to keep the virgin daughters for themselves."   His multi-colored eyes twinkled when he said "virgin daughters."

I noticed the trees as we passed, shedding and scattering their leaves on Wexford Bayne Road.   My mind couldn't reconcile the Maker of the brown and gold leaves with Mordecai's Mafia hit-man god, the Old Testament jealous Jehovah.

"If you make a chair, you have the right to sit on it or burn it for firewood.   We're His.   He made us, and not we ourselves. We're just change in His pocket to spend any way He wants, as it were."   He saw he was losing me again so he changed the subject. "I hear you saw your father?"

"Yeah."

"How was he?"

"He said we had the crowd in the palm of our hands. We might start playing together again when he's better."

"I'd sure like to see your Dad get saved before it's too late. You must choose between your heavenly Father's will and your earthly father's will. He may try to get you back, playing in his worldly band instead of using your music to glorify Christ." He spoke with the authority of absolutes, a certainty that he was right and everybody else was wrong.

"What should I say to him?"

"Listen to me. You need to tell him you can't play with him anymore. Sometimes saving souls hurts those who don't understand. We have to be willing to let any relationship go that gets in the way. If any man would follow Me, he must hate father, mother, sister, brother. Luke fourteen, verse twenty-six."

"I thought Jesus wanted us to love."

"Don't listen to that liberal sloppy agape. He did not come to bring peace, but a sword of division in the family. He came to turn a man against his father. Matthew ten, verses thirty-four and thirty-five. There's a battle inside you, Jeremiah. Will God have your music or will the devil keep you playing in a carnal atmosphere of lust and debauchery?"

Mordecai's force prevailed and I became a summer missionary. I announced to Dad, without any forewarning, I was starting my music ministry for Mordecai and my father wasn't in it. I saw the vacancy in Dad's face when I visited him in the mental hospital and told him.

"No big deal, Dad," I said. "Nothing personal."

Dad was too doped up on fifty milligrams of soluble Thorazine to respond.

I didn't want to play in bars with Dad anymore. It brought back memories of him yelling at me in public. Thanks to Mordecai's indoctrination, I felt saved, on track with Christ, unlike my fucked-up father.

My concerts were now under the umbrella of Mordecai's BBC ministry, an acronym with varied meanings such as Baptist Bible College and Backyard Bible Clubs.

When I wasn't giving gospel concerts, I worked with the BBC team teaching children bible verses, and giving them prizes for memorizing scripture. The five-day clubs were fun for me as a teacher, and the kids enjoyed my guitar-playing.

Sister Ruth made spaghetti most nights. The noodles stretched well on the donations we lived on. Mordecai was authoritarian but lacked the charisma of more successful evangelists. He didn't have the Spirit like Kathryn Kuhlman. He was quite jealous of her, and told me she was a farce and a fake because the age of miracles ceased when the canon of the bible was completed in the first century. "Healings happened for a brief dispensation to authenticate the ministry of Christ and the apostles," he said.

Mordecai droned on in prayer before each meal, speaking in Elizabethan English. "We thank thee, Oh Lord, for the gifts which Thou hast graciously provided. We would be remiss, Oh God, not to mention the BBC missionaries we support around the world, carrying forth the gospel. Be with them, Oh God." I stared at the spaghetti, eyeing the largest meatball.

"...and be with Rev. Rutoona in Kenya as he leads boys and girls to Christ in that dark land. And be with Rev. Hough in Japan as he shares the gospel in a nation that for centuries has been going to hell in a hand basket, as it were."

Red opened his eyes, caught mine, and smiled. Savannah kicked me under the table.

For dramatic effect, Mordecai removed his monogrammed handkerchief from his breast pocket, spread it out on the floor beside the table, and knelt on it before continuing his interminable blessing over the food. His prayer denigrated into low moans.

"OOOooooOOOHhHh GGGGGaaaaaaWWWWdddd … "

Mordecai sounded like he was having a bowel movement. "OOOoooooghhhh GGGaaaaWWWWwwddd…"

The food was getting cold. I imitated Mordecai's prayers and facial contortions behind his back. Savannah buried her face in her hands, laughing in jagged spurts. Red stuck a piece of garlic bread in her red hair.

Sometimes the Rawlings family received donations of gift certificates to local diners. When Mordecai said the blessing at a restaurant, I was mortified, imagining the other patrons staring at us like we were aliens, although quite often someone would compliment us for the "nice gesture." Sometimes the waitress arrived, standing there through Mordecai's prayer until the final Amen.

One thing Mordecai had in common with my father was the reaction he provoked in me. It was a feeling of vigilance, walking on eggshells and monitoring my every move. I finished my junior year of high school without raising his ire. Until June, that is.

On the last day of school, Walker, Red, and I celebrated by blasting the Alice Cooper song, *School's Out for Summer*. The song evoked celebration, but the summer day turned sour when Reverend Rawlings overheard.

"I can't allow that music, boys," he said. "Alice Cooper is a tool of the devil. He staged a mock crucifixion. He worships Satan."

"How do you know that?" Red asked.

"I knew his father. He was a preacher but his son turned away from the faith when a demon named Alice Cooper possessed his body. He took on the spirit's name, selling his soul for fame. I'm going to have to ask for that record so I can destroy it. It's my job, as your spiritual covering, to protect you boys. What I bind is bound over you, what I loose is loosed. I decide what is allowed into your lives. Is that understood?"

"Yes sir," we answered together.

"Jeremiah, you of all people should know not to open any more doors to the devil." Pittsburgh's humid heat enveloped me like a black cloud. "You've given Stick Man a red carpet invitation to come back into you seven times stronger," Mordecai continued. "When a demon finds the house from whence he came swept clean, he brings back seven more spirits, all worse than the first. Matthew, chapter twelve, verse forty-four."

# 11

In the darkness of this religious zealotry, the light of Eve Vickers came to illuminate me. I believed her to be an angel at first, so I renamed her Angel. Angel Vickers.

Angel arrived to stay with Red's family for three weeks, so her mother Shara could organize backyard Bible parties to win boys and girls to Jesus. Shara Vickers toiled for Mordecai Rawlings as his Eastern Pennsylvania BBC director.

It was a summer evening, with fireflies and moonlight. Walker, Red, and I were in the back room recording gospel music. Red bought recording and mixing equipment and made tapes of our music to sell at concerts. Walker was wailing on a harp riff as I strummed an A minor seventh chord when we heard a knock on the door.

"I'd like you boys to come meet a girl. She's our guest," Sister Ruth said. "I made popcorn." Her smirk told me the girl was eye candy.

Walker grinned at me and whispered a vague obscenity. He was in his manual wheelchair because his electric chair was in the shop. I pushed Walker down the hall to the kitchen. Angel sat at the table. I almost couldn't look at her at first. After pushing Walker to the table and getting him situated, I pulled out a chair and sat across from her. Red and Walker were at each side.

I couldn't help but stare.

She twirled a dark strand of her hair between her fingers, than picked at her fingernails, examining them. She giggled when the conversation was serious and met my eyes with her brown eyes. This may sound corny, but the music in her eyes sang to me. They were dark brown, locking in on mine like a vise.

There was a big blast of energy and chemical synapses fired in my brain, branding a part of my heart that would be forever hers. Angel burned into me like a red-hot poker.

Her black shirt was modest yet could not conceal the shape of her breasts. She wore blue shorts with stripes on the side, not too short to upset her mother's convictions, but tracing the outline of her thighs like a wet finger. She was barefoot and curled her toes, moving her feet in a slow, circular motion that hypnotized me. Walker, Red, and Sister Ruth were invisible. I wanted to strum her like my guitar. We ate popcorn out of salad bowls. I couldn't look away. She wet her lips. I swallowed hard.

Time passed.

Vibrations swam between us like spawning salmon. There was instant chemistry.

"Jeremiah, put your eyes back in your head," Mrs. Rawlings said.

Never before had I felt this sweating in my palms, these goose bumps on my skin. I hesitated to speak, to spoil the dynamite with the inadequacy of words. I was convinced I had no shot at this goddess.

Walker and Red tried to talk with her, but she kept her gaze on me.

Walker knew how to talk to a girl, but Red squeaked awkwardly into adolescence. He was five-foot three with myopic glasses. He tried to act tough like Clint Eastwood's Dirty Harry, but he never did well in the social whirlpool. When he saw Angel alone later, he snatched her for a date for ice cream. She agreed to go, but when they returned Red took me aside. He seemed angry. "All she did was ask me about you the whole time, Jeremiah."

Sister Ruth Rawlings told us she was the May Queen of her school, and her boyfriend Tiger Ogerman played on the basketball team. "That Tiger, he's such a nice boy. You know, he raises money for our ministry by doing his DJ music," she said. "He makes me bust a gut laughing. He calls me Baby Ruth, like the candy bar. And he called Shara Vickers 'Mrs. Vicious,' instead of Mrs. Vickers. Oh, he's too much. He calls Eve 'Vicious Vickers.'" She struggled to get the last few words out because her prim laugh grew out of control.

"I don't think that's very funny," I said. "I could make her laugh, and it wouldn't be with jokes at her expense."

"Watch yourself. You're God's Pied Piper, and the call could be curtailed. She's a worldly girl. Don't get attached to her. I caught her listening to secular music on that radio of hers," she said, turning a page of her bible.

I wasn't dissuaded. To me, our eye-connection seemed like lightning striking. Sparks flew the minute we saw each other. I knew this kind of thing happened once every billion years.

The next day, I was eating a peanut butter sandwich at the kitchen table at noon when Angel came through the front door with Savannah. I decided right then and there to step out on faith.

I don't know what came over me, but I wrote a note to her that afternoon in large capital letters blaring, "I LOVE YOU, ANGEL!"

Nothing subtle. Straight and to the point. After all, she was going home to Mount Olympus, Pennsylvania soon. My audacity triggered Savannah yelling at Red within earshot of me.

"I know you always defend Jeremiah," she said, "and I know a certain level of eccentricities is a part of his artistic personality, but

I feel responsible to look after her as our guest. You didn't see the note Red, I did it. For God's sake, he just met her."

"Are you sure you're not just jealous?"

"You're the jealous one. You like her."

"Give me a break, will you?"

"Writing a note like that when he hasn't said two words to her."

I sat outside and awaited Angel's response to my note like a defendant awaiting the jury's verdict. Angel wore a red dress that hugged her ripening body. She glided towards me in red high-heeled shoes. The wind lifted her dress, Marilyn Monroe style. She slipped me a reply note, suggesting we go for a walk in the woods later, away from our chaperones.

*****

We snuck towards the forest. She carried her pink Barbie radio. We sat on a fallen oak log in the Rawlings woods and I looked into her face on that perfect June day in 1980. Alone at last with Angel, I was as helpless as a baby.

"I see you," I said. I wasn't sure why I said it.

"I know. No one else does," she said. "This is going to sound really strange, but I feel like I've known you forever."

"Me too," I said.

She looked down for a moment, and played with a twig. She averted my eyes. "I hope this doesn't hurt you, and I hope you'll still want me after I tell you this."

I took her hand in mine. "What, Angel?"

"Never mind."

"What?"

She hesitated, than exhaled. "I'm not a virgin. When I was twelve, this older man next door stole my innocence. I want to tell you right from the beginning. Tiger, this boy I've been going out with, he would condemn me, but I need to tell you, because with you I think it's different."

"I don't judge you," I said.

She smiled. "I know you don't. You make me feel new." Angel trusted me with her shadows, and lifted the manhole cover on my house of horrors so I could confide in her. "So tell me about your father. I overheard the Rawlings talking about him."

I opened up to her and explained my Dad as best I could, and the story of how I ended up with the Rawlings. "He's unpredictable. I have to always be guarded."

"Maybe that's why you believe what Reverend Rawlings teaches," she said. "He makes God out to be a heavenly father who is like your earthly father."

"How so?"

"The old man in the sky is angry. You never know when He'll attack."

"I wish I could tell the children about Jesus without the fear tactics, but Rawlings expects me to scare the hell out of the kids," I said.

"Do you really think God would create children just to dump them into Hell? They make Him out to be worse than Hitler and Nebuchadnezzar combined. Let me give you a present more real than anything they'll ever give you here," she said.

She touched the end of my fingers. The first time we touched, it was like someone threw gasoline on the strong flame between the two of us. Her face neared mine. And then it happened. We kissed. My first real kiss. I tried to copy the kiss Montgomery Clift gave Elizabeth Taylor in *A Place in the Sun*. We giggled, than she kissed me again. Her lips were like pillows. I felt pin pricks course throughout my body from my mouth to my neck and spine, then down the back of my thighs. Our second kiss was longer. Her mouth opened wide, and Angel put her tongue right inside my mouth, which nobody had done to me before. Our tongues darted and danced. Her lips were wet. I was dizzy. She cradled my face in her hands.

Time slipped away until we were interrupted by Red's voice. "Jeremiah...Angel...Mom says you two both have to come back in the house and you can't be together in the woods alone."

"Oh, please," Angel said, "it's not like we're going to have sex right here in the woods." Angel, quick on her feet, sent Red back to the house to get something, and returned her gaze to me. "Where were we?" she asked.

I looked at her and knew she was worth living and dying for.

I remembered my dream, about a half-heart floating in the wind that one day finds his match.

We walked through the woods, on a path through the apple orchard that spilled out into Beaver Creek. The trees welcomed us as if their branches were applauding. The leaves on the trees appeared shiny, as if angels cleansed them by hand.

I held her hand and carried her pink radio. Nothing mattered beyond the present. The black and white of the Rawlings world gave way to color. The fragrant flowers were red and orange and yellow. The sky was bluer and golden and the grass was richly, thickly greener. We entered the lake, downstream from the swimming hole. We heard the sound of a waterfall and inched toward the melody of the water. We climbed over rocks holding hands. I felt light on my feet.

"I don't want to get you in trouble with the Rawlings," she said.

"I'll take the blame," I said.

"Will he be too hard on you?"

"Maybe if it was someone else.   He lost his temper once, but I don't think he will again."

"Are you sure?   He bothers me."

"In what way?"

"The way he looks at me sometimes, eyeing me up and down."

The rumbling noise of water drew closer.   Flies and mosquitoes swarmed overhead.   We pushed through and there it was: a waterfall, pouring over the ledge.

Her perfume smelled like vanilla, and her mouth was a rosebud.   The scent of her tingled on my neck, answering all questions of adolescent angst.   Her lips curled upwards into a smile. Every molecule of my body was on fire.

"Let's dance," she said, turning on her radio.

"Mrs. Rawlings says dancing arouses the flesh and may cause us to miss the Rapture," I said.

"Arousing the flesh.   That's what I'm counting on."   She laughed.   The song spilling out from the radio was *Baby I Love Your Way*, by Peter Frampton.   I took her in my arms and she melted into me.

I thought about the Rawlings opposition to dancing.

"I'm not afraid of missing the Rapture, for I am enraptured," I said.

"You're such a poet."

We sang to each other as we swayed in circles.   *Ooh, baby I love your way...Wanna be with you every day...*

After we danced, we relaxed in the grass by the waterfall. I rested my head in Angel's lap and listened to the streaming water. She stroked my hair, just like Natalie Wood did to James Dean.

I remembered Sister Ruth saying when a man and woman are together, prayer was the most important priority. "The intimacy with God leads to greater intimacy with each other," she had said, "but after the vows. You boys remember that."

Mordecai taught us that sex outside marriage was a manifestation of Satan's power in the modern scene. I remembered him saying these things over the dinner table ten thousand times, that if I was ever alone with a girl I wouldn't be safe, unless it's consecrated, sanctified, and holy.

"Do you want to pray together?" I asked Angel.

She gazed down at me and chuckled, as I rested in her lap.

"You're silly. Our love is a prayer," she said. She kissed my neck again. I looked up at her. The sun shone on her hair, giving her face a luster.

When we returned to the house, Walker saw us when we emerged from the woods. "Hey bro, what're you doing?"

Red and Walker chanted, "First comes love, then comes marriage. Jeremiah and Eve with a baby carriage."

*****

"You're one lovesick puppy, Jeremiah," Red said. "I can see it."

I watched the dancing flames in the living room fireplace and grinned at Angel. I stuck my tongue out, panting heavy like a puppy. Savannah and Angel went back to their room to retire. She mouthed "I love you" to me as she walked away.

Reverend and Mrs. Rawlings were silent. There was no recrimination for our romantic excursion in the woods, although I overheard discussion between them later in the evening. They were in a back bedroom. I tiptoed toward their door to knock and heard them talking. I waited and eavesdropped.

"I will deal with Jeremiah in my own time, as it were," Mordecai said.

"Don't be too harsh," Ruth said. "The boy's convinced he's found his one true love. I'm worried about them. Eve told Savannah they were dancing in the woods. If I hadn't sent Red to interrupt them, Lord knows what could've happened."

"I don't need another battle at that camp. Savannah caused me enough problems with her stories."

"Are you sure they're stories?"

"Don't start that again."

I went back to my room and relaxed into the deepest slumber of my life. I dreamt of Angel. We rode Ferris Wheels and roller coasters. We ate popcorn at a circus, than leapt through the air, soaring off the flying trapeze. My sleep had restorative power, and the nightmares stopped. I couldn't dream of Stick Man if I tried. Kathryn Kuhlman was right. An angel did come to me, and her love cast out fear. I stumbled into an oasis, a promise of relief.

The following morning, I remembered the dreams and invited Angel to go to West View Park. The Rawlings had business at the BBC camp and they were away for the day. We knew at any moment the shoe could drop, but until it did, we wanted to savor every second of summer. Angel sat snug against me in a Rambler station wagon I borrowed from Mom. We headed towards Route 19 until we approached the sharp bend in West View and saw the Big Dips.

STICK MAN
138

"I want to take you to Danceland tonight," I said. "And we have to ride both coasters."

"This is phenomenal, Jeremiah. We don't have anything like this in Mount Olympus," she said. "Once a year, a little traveling carnival comes through, but that's about it."

We entered the park arm in arm on one-price day, getting in for a song. I smelled the cherry aroma of cotton candy and frying doughboys. We ran to the Racing Whippet. The Whippet was named after a dog, a cross between a greyhound and a terrier known for swiftness in chasing rabbits. The midway connected the two roller coasters, the Big Dips in the front of the park on Route 19, and the Racing Whippet in the back. The Whippet was built deep into the bottom of a valley with hills on both sides. The dips were steep and the banks were curved.

The loading station of the Racing Whippet was built on a bridge that crossed the valley, next to Boot Hill, a walk-through mirror maze and haunted house. Angel and I stood in line behind a girl with a ribbon in her hair.

"I'm riding the Racing Whippet for the first time," the girl said.

"So am I," Angel said.

"Are you scared?" the small girl asked.

"A little. But I got a big strong man with me."

"Is he your boyfriend?"

"He sure is." Angel smiled at me, giving my hand a squeeze.

I smiled back. "I've never been this happy before," I said.

"Never?"

"Never."

"Ever come close?"

"About ten years ago, Christmas morning. I got a new bicycle and a set of Disney characters. But it didn't come close."

"You like Disney characters?"

"Yeah."

"What's your favorite Disney movie?"

"Snow White. I saw it eight times as a kid."

"Ever been to Disneyland?"

"No, but I've always dreamed of going."

"Since you treated me to West View Park, I'll take you to Disneyland one day."

"Promise?"

"Promise." She sealed the promise with a kiss.

Angel looked above the coaster's dual tracks and read the signs aloud. "Positively no changing seats. Don't stand up. Please buckle your straps. No Repeat Rides." She noticed two tracks side by side.

"Oh, I get it," she said. "The two trains race each other." When we reached the front of the line, Angel squeezed me again as we entered the train and buckled the seatbelt.

The trains raced up and down the hills. Angel screamed. We careened at times running side by side with the other train and at other moments on opposite ends of the valley. Then the coasters rejoined together for the final chase. Our train won the race, as the brakes screeched and returned us to the loading platform.

"A long wait for a short ride," I said. "But being with you was worth it."

We ran to the Haunted House hand-in-hand. There were tilted windows on the outside of the dilapidated structure, and a gigantic bat at the top of the roof. We sat in the two-seater car which jerked as it started the ride down the five hundred feet of track.

She cuddled me in reaction to falling barrels, a spider staircase, corpses popping out of cellar walls, a torture chamber, and a graveyard. The power went out and our car was at a standstill in the cemetery.

"What's wrong?" she asked.

"I don't know. I guess we're stuck."

A pause. "Do you believe in ghosts?"

I thought of Stick Man. "I have nightmares and they seem very real."

"Tell me about them, baby."

I swallowed and tentatively revealed my nightmare. "When I wake up, whatever I dream about, I still see the monsters. I've seen insects crawling on my skin, lots of frightening things. There's this one monster made out of sticks. This may sound crazy, but he's so real to me."

"It's not crazy, baby. I have night terrors, too. The doctor told my mother to never wake me up when I'm having bad dreams."

"Really? That's what the doctor told my mom. You have them too?"

"Boy, do I. I've always been embarrassed to tell anyone."

"Since I met you, I haven't had any nightmares."

"Neither have I."

The power came back on and the car continued through the Haunted House. The rest of our day we rode various attractions. The Round-Up was a large wheel that spun us around, while we were strapped standing on the spinning wheel. Next was the Whip, the seven car Tilt-O-Wheel, the Scrambler, and the Bat Chute, an orange, two-story, mega-slide that winded around a white tower. We drove the Scooters bumper cars and collided into each other. I didn't want to hit her too hard, but I bumped into her enough to get her to laugh.

We saved the best ride for last, the Big Dips. The coaster ran from the arcade games building out to Route 19 along the West View Lake and back. The games building was covered with neon tubing and lit up as night fell during our final ride. In the center of the lake was an eight foot electric fountain. The coaster dipped out of the loading station into a dark tunnel, which gave us an opportunity to steal caresses. Her touch electrified me. We snuggled before launching into a rapid trek under the midway. The rickety train jolted and ascended the hill.

We glanced up at the sky. The moon was high that night and the low hanging stars shone unobstructed by trees. Darkness approached and the Big Dips ride ended, signaling us to run up the hill from the main midway to Danceland.

A cover band was playing a blues number from the stage to signify the crowd it was time to dance. We passed the main gate and walked into Danceland with arms around each others waists. We were sweaty, so we enjoyed the breeze from the air-conditioning units in the ballroom. The band was taking requests. Angel asked the bass player if they knew *Baby I Love Your Way*. He nodded and the lead singer put his mouth close to the mike to announce the song.

"This one's for Jeremiah from Angel."

We glided along the hardwood floor. "This floor reminds me of a bowling alley," she said.

The band played on the elevated stage. A crystal ball spun over our heads, revolving and catching us in the spotlight. She rested her head on my shoulder.

*Moon appears to shine and light the sky. With the help of some firefly...*

"I'm closer to you than I've ever felt with anyone else," I said.

"Me too, baby.   All my life, I've wanted someone to love me for me.   Not how I look."

"I love you, Angel."

"I love you, too.   Forever."

Our bodies blended.   We didn't have to think through the steps.   We danced as one through the soft night, under the summer stars.   I was the luckiest boy in the world.

*I wonder how they have the power to shine, shine, shine.   I can see them under the pine.*

"You won't ever go away, will you?" she asked.   "Never leave me."

*Ooh baby, I love your way...*

"Never."

God, I loved her.

# 12

Sister Ruth, Red, Savannah, Angel and I sat together in the tabernacle. The makeshift church was an outdoor structure with steel beams supporting the roof. The pulpit was elevated, front and center. The pews were benches made from two-by-twos and two-by-sixes. The main aisles were cement but the seating area was covered with wood chips. The sawdust smell blended with the humid air and the scent of teenage bodies deprived of hygiene and showers, underscoring the seriousness of the mission to rescue the perishing children.

I shared a hymnal with Angel, which covered our interlocking fingers caressing underneath. Angel's fingers spread open, and I laced my hand into hers.

We felt the wind and listened to the leaves swish against the sanctuary. "You look wonderful," I whispered.

"Thanks baby," Angel said. She counted the number of people at the revival, her fingers tapping against mine. "Seventy-six. Seventy-seven, counting Rawlings."

Mordecai preached in his simple, sterile style. He slid into his condemnation of sin, but I knew Angel's wet kisses were more divine than Mordecai's diatribes. At the first point of his sermon, meaning to say 'Jesus in your heart forever,' Rawlings twisted the words.

"Jesus in your fart herever," he said. A laugh welled up in Angel, escaping her throat and nose.

Sister Ruth and several spinsters turned their heads to Angel, triggering deeper spasms of laughter in her. She unlocked her fingers from mine to hide her face. Sister Ruth crossed her arms and scorched us with her glare.   This increased the staccato of Angel's nasal eruptions.

I never laughed harder in my life.

Rawlings saw the sparks between Angel and me and continued.   "The evils of temptation are there to seduce us.   Watch out for the three G's.   The gold, the glory, and the girls.   Or for you young ladies, the gold, the glory, and the guys."   Rawlings was fond of alliteration and making sure his sermons had three points.   No more, no less.   We watched the nervous way Mordecai rubbed his hand in his hair, and I catalogued his three points while Angel counted on her fingers how many times Mordecai used the phrase "as it were."

"The enemy is cunning.   Satan goes about as a roaring lion, as it were, seeking whom he may devour.   He tempts God's young champions through attractions to the opposite sex."

Angel whispered in my ear.   "The devil made us do it."   She laughed again.   Everything suddenly had a double meaning to us.

"There are only two types of people, believers and unbelievers.   People headed to heaven and people condemned to hell.   And the wages of sin is *death*!   I warn you, being a churchgoer is no assurance of salvation," Mordecai said, continuing his tempestuous bellowing as his forehead and face changed from veiny pale to pink.   "Some of you think more about dating each other than dating the Lord.   Shame on you.   You're falling short of redeemed behavior.   If you're not living as a Christian, then you're not a Christian.   Those in willful sin will not be saved.   Detractors will be damned.   We must put Spirit over self.   Repeat that after me.   Spirit over self."

"Spirit over self," the summer missionaries chanted in mindless unison, looking like colorless cardboard cutouts.

"Spirit over self," Mordecai repeated.

"Spirit over self," the summer missionaries echoed. They reminded me of the zombies from *Night of the Living Dead.* The 'Spirit over self' chant was repeated back and forth between Mordecai and his flock for what seemed like an hour.

"It's not easy, young people. Sex is the weak spot where Satan seduces us. Many of you here find yourself fascinated by the body of a brother or a sister in Christ. Sex is Satan's tool, as it were." Mordecai licked his lips and changed his voice. "So what do we do? Do we cut sex out of our lives? No, that's not what the bible says. Sex must be kept in its scriptural place. Ay-men? Keep sex in its place, a secondary place, in the Christian home. A part of marriage, consecrated as holy to the Lord." A pause again and whispered ay-mens. "And while you're here as summer missionaries, brothers and sisters, watch and pray that you be delivered from the evils of the flesh. There are those of you here in this holy place set apart for sanctified missionary service, that have sinned against God by living in lustful thoughts. I see your sinful thoughts so plainly, the delights of touching a young boy's belly, or a girl's soft breasts. Sometimes a certain woman will tempt you as it were, and it will be very, very hard," he coughed and continued, "hard to resist."

Mordecai stretched out his arm from his stiff blue blazer. An image of an erect penis flashed in my mind. Angel must've had the same thought, for a second later she cooed in my ear.

"When I tempt you, is it very, very hard?" Her giggles turned into a coughing fit and were so disruptive to the service she had to leave.

The other teenage missionaries were certain the eroticism passing between us would lead us to the pleasures of the flesh. Everyone's nerves were wound up. Most of the young missionaries were in love like me, or at least had a crush on someone at camp. We fantasized stolen kisses in the woods behind the tabernacle. We were sexually excited, and guilt-ridden about being sexually excited. We were warned about "fornication with the eyes," and reprimands were given for those making eye-contact longer than three seconds with the opposite sex. Right and wrong were magnified by Mordecai a million times more than Moses himself. Despite the warnings of our compatriots, Angel and I didn't have sex. We kissed and held hands and had three weeks of innocent bliss in which we fell into each other's arms at every opportunity. During lunch, we drank the camp's instant coffee and ate their dreary mashed potatoes, but we didn't care. We were in love. We stretched our legs to rub our feet together and steal touches of our hands as the saccharine songs piped through the speakers, insistent and innocuous, *'He forgave my sin, and He saved my soul, Cleansed my heart, and made me whole...'* while Mordecai roamed the dusty halls looking for couples to separate.

In the afternoon, I played guitar for Angel and rambled on about my philosophies. "I love listening to you," she said. "I could listen to you forever." My every theory was met with her acceptance.

The next hazy June day, Mordecai drove a group of us to several acres of land where he wanted to expand BBC's campus, which would include the bible college and missionary training center.

A group of fundamentalist businessmen followed Mordecai as he led the walk toward the acreage. We marched with thirty missionaries like a ticker-tape parade towards the land. Several spinsters who were solely dedicated to Mordecai and his ministry waved their hands in the air and prayed.

The ground was damp. The smell of manure was in the air. When we arrive at the site, Mordecai had a worried look on his face. "I could swear it was right here," he said, adjusting the knot of his tie. "Yes, here it is," he said, striding away from the group into a swampy section of the field.

The businessmen exchanged nervous glances. They were impeccably dressed and wore Jerry Falwell *Jesus First* lapel pins on their thousand-dollar suit jackets. I looked at the pins and it hit me that Jesus First and Jerry Falwell had the same initials.

The first man was in his mid-forties. He was a "Direct" in Amway, near the top of the pyramid. He built his network by visiting bible studies and converting them into Amway presentations. He carried a whiteboard and multi-colored markers to conduct impromptu sales-pitches in which he drew a series of circles to explain how God could make anyone a millionaire within two years. His favorite bible verse was Deuteronomy 8:18, "The Lord God gives me power to obtain wealth."

The second businessman was in his early sixties and a well-known fixture for his infomercials pitching household cleaning products. He had graying hair and a country club tan. On TV, he was gregarious and irritating. In person, he was stand-offish and irritated. Somehow, the two men's businesses were interrelated, but I didn't understand the synergism between the two.

Mordecai tried to act confident, stopping to pray for the property. He stood about twenty feet away from the rest of the group but we could hear him squeak when he spoke. Savannah groaned as Mordecai started.

"Brothers and sisters, I don't want this land for selfish reasons. Let me tell you who I'm doing this for. I'm doing it for a little boy in a red-hot oven. He's screaming to come out. He turns and twists in the divine fire. You can see the anguish on the little boy's face, the face of all the boys and girls in hell. The unfortunate lost boys who didn't have a BBC missionary to tell them how to be saved from God Almighty's wrath."

"Ay-men," Amway said.

"Can you see the torment, the desperate despair on the little boy's face? Let's pray for that little boy and all the little boys and girls we can reach for Christ if we claim this property by faith." Mordecai closed his eyes tight and bowed his head. "We thank Thee, Lord, for this property that Thou hast given to us, for the wealth of the wicked is being laid up for the just, hallelujah."

At this, the businessmen nodded. Mister Amway said, "Ay-men" again, spurring Mordecai to pray with greater intensity.

"Just as Joshua possessed the land of the Canaanites, we claim that every place our foot shall tread belongs to the righteous. Our faith is based on nothing less, than Jesus blood and righteousness. All other ground is sinking sand."

Just then, it became apparent Mordecai was standing in the wrong place, smack-dab in the middle of quicksand. Within seconds, he sunk up to his armpits.

"Quick," Amway yelled. "We need to form a human chain."

Amway grabbed Mordecai's hand and was almost pulled into the quicksand, so I grabbed Amway's other hand. Angel rescued me from the gravitational pull, holding me around my waist. Shara Vickers held on to Angel, and Mister Infomercial recovered from the paralysis of panic and grabbed Shara Vickers. Red and Savannah were next in the chain, followed by the other missionaries.

We were pulled into the mud, but we saved Mordecai and yanked him out. The businessmen ruined their Armani suits and lost their Rolex watches and Gucci loafers. Mordecai lost his glasses, bible, and clothes. The only thing he kept clean was his boxers.

Mordecai must've seen dollar signs float away. He told the businessmen he wanted to hold a board meeting the next day, but they said they weren't interested.

Mordecai warned them they were risking God's wrath. "Tithing opens the windows of heaven, but not tithing to God's work is robbing the Almighty and brings a curse on your business," he told them. "Remember Ananias and Sapphira. They held back in their giving, so God killed them. They lied, they died, they fried."

*Three points. Lied, died, fried.*

I couldn't understand why they acquiesced to the threat, but Amway and Infomercial said they'd be at the board meeting. I always heard you catch more bees with honey than vinegar, so I determined to help poor old Mordecai out this time, and use some fun to fund his efforts.

The meeting was set up in the BBC social hall to salvage the goodwill of God's philanthropists. Mordecai asked me to prepare the briefs for the meeting. This involved typing up an agenda of items he wished to discuss, pulling all related files, and putting them into his briefcase.

Angel and I were still laughing at the memory of Mordecai drenched in mud and standing dumbfounded in only his boxers while Sister Ruth wiped him off as she prayed, "We just come against the enemy, in Jesus Name."

I thought it would be funny to get Mordecai to laugh at himself, so I went through the men's dormitory at BBC and collected the underpants of every male missionary, packing them into Mordecai's briefcase.

Missionaries milled around, drinking their coffee from Styrofoam cups when Mordecai called the meeting to order. There was an opening prayer led by Shara Vickers, followed by the singing of two hymns. Mordecai rambled on for fifteen minutes about the weight of lost souls.

At the precise moment of the board meeting, when Mordecai said, "Jeremiah, may I have the briefs?" I handed him his briefcase. He opened the briefcase and boys briefs came tumbling out in a dazzling display of underwear, some clean and some putrefied. The spinsters were highly offended, and Mordecai turned red as a tomato.

Mister Amway and Mister Infomercial laughed their asses off, complimented Mordecai on his sense of humor, and coughed up money to expand BBC.

Something of far greater import than Mordecai's ministry happened that week. My marriage.

There was no priest or pastor. We officiated ourselves, marrying each other with our own vows. Our church was the great outdoors. Angel and I sealed our love at Beaver Creek. She wore white, and had daisies in her hair.

"You have awakened a heart song inside me," I said. "A dance that calls us to the rhythm of His spirit. A celestial music – a holy, purposeful rhythm. I vow to fulfill the sacred path that has brought us together. I embrace you close as my wife, enjoying heaven's dance." She placed her right hand in mine. "I, Jeremiah, take you, Angel, to be my lawfully wedded wife. To have and to hold, for richer or poorer, in sickness and in health, to death do us part."

"And I, Eve Angel Vickers, take you, Jeremiah Young, to be my lawfully wedded husband.   I, too, hear the call of heaven's dance and I say yes, to dance with you heart to heart and cheek to cheek.  Our passion flares forever as angels smile, casting light from their golden orb on the path we walk together.   I place my hand in yours, my head to your chest, hearing your heart beating unashamed as your express our love in your music and your art.   I vow my love to you forever as your faithful wife, forsaking all others and turning only to you.   To have and to hold, for richer or poorer, in sickness and in health, to death do us part."   She paused, than shook her head.  "No, correct that.   We'll never part, even in heaven.   I take you, Jeremiah from here through all eternity, Amen."

"Amen," I said.

"I'll always wait for you," she said.   A frog bellowed.

"That's our best man," I said.

I drank a potent first-love cocktail.   The hooks in my psyche were deep.   Angel was forever immortalized in my mind.   God, I loved her.

Angel cooked for me.   She asked my mother my favorite foods.   She grilled orange roughy outside on the patio and fried beer-battered shrimp.   Mordecai and Sister Ruth disapproved of her cooking with beer.

She'd packed the food in a wicker basket to celebrate our wedding with a picnic party on the grass.   Even though it wasn't a legal marriage we were entwined in a higher plane.   We spread out a checkered tablecloth.   Angel leaned over to take out a plate of bright fruit.   Hours slipped away.   Our eyes were blinded by the sun's rich light at first, but when we returned, we walked back in the black darkness.

And then it ended.   The best three weeks of my life.

She had to go back home.

Angel handed me a photo of herself before she headed back to Mount Olympus.   "This is so you don't forget me," she said.

"I'll never forget you."   I looked at the picture.   "I'll bet you never take a bad photo."

"Oh stop."   I loved it when she said, "Oh, stop."   She wrapped her arms around my waist.   "I'm not perfect, you know."

"You are."

"Don't lie."

"Practically perfect."

"That's better," she said, playing with the belt loops on my blue jeans.

She looked at me fixedly in the eyes.   "Whatever it takes, we'll be together one day."

I stroked her silky hair.   She was as magical to me as the day Spiritos pulled half-dollars out of my ear.   I believed in her as I did Santa, Clemente, Kathryn Kuhlman, and Jesus.   She excelled all fantasies and faith experiences, the summit of my dreams and longings.   I slipped a golden angel into her hand I'd bought for her at the Hallmark store.

I watched her drive away with her mother Shara.   In the three weeks we were together, Stick Man left me alone.   For the first time, I was having good dreams.   When I awoke in the dark, I saw her face instead of Stick Man's.   Her image did what Mordecai's prayers and Doctor Bosley's prescriptions couldn't do.   Dreams of waltzing by the waterfall liberated me.   She glowed like a celestial muse, radiant in my mental movies.

Like my earliest childhood, minute details had heightened significance and luminosity.   She inspired me to create.   After she left, she filled every canvas I painted, and every song I played.   I celebrated her in the chords and words.   I sent her a tape of songs I wrote about her.

The lyrics to the last song were, *"A three week visit from a girl sent from above/Why must she go, and take my love?/Angel, why do you have to go?/Angel, I'm going to miss you so…"*

Within days, I received a letter back.   The envelope smelled of vanilla perfume, bubble gum, and roses.

*Dear Jeremiah,*

*Let's write to each other every day.   Our day at West View Park was the greatest day of my life, I really mean that.   I miss your touch.   I long for it.   When you held me, I felt unconditional love.   I never want any man but you.   I don't write like you. You're a real writer Jeremiah, but I wrote a poem to express how I feel for you:*

*Outlasting centuries*
*Our love transcends time*
*For God is love*
*And love divine*

*Sealed With A Kiss.*

*Love,*
*Angel    Xoxoxoxoxoxo*

# 13

When my seventeenth summer faded, Angel and her mother moved away in tandem with Tiger Ogerman's parents. The two families had joined their fortunes at the hip for years, long before I'd come on the scene. They migrated like a colony to a hamlet in eastern Pennsylvania near Mount Olympus.

I'd warned Angel. "If you follow their pressure and marry him, he'll abuse you. Mark my words."

"I don't want to marry him, Jeremiah," she reassured me. "I only have eyes for you."

Sister Ruth gave me a small space where I painted and practiced guitar. I enlarged Angel's photo, using her picture as a guide. I sketched her face on canvas, lightly at first with a 6H pencil to prepare to paint her. I worked with detail and devotion. I displayed my paintings of her, along with my earlier work of Jesus, in the back of the Rawlings garage. The garage was in order under Mordecai's militarism, and the car was always clean. "Cleanliness is next to godliness," Mordecai had said.

I looked at Jesus and Angel every day when I arrived home from school. On a Wednesday in August, I gripped the handle on the garage door and raised it as I always did at three-thirty.

The paintings were gone.

*Oh my God. Someone stole my paintings.*

I saw the tools, the lawn equipment, a broken kerosene lamp, the jars of nails and cans of Turtle wax and WD40, but where were the canvases? I moved boxes and bikes, emptied pop bottles in a recycle bin, and still, no trace of my paintings.

I ran through the garage to the trash outside and discovered my artwork was broken and thrown in the garbage. I reached into the waste bin and pulled out my brushes.   They were snapped in the middle.   I saw the painting of her face, ripped in two.   I heard footsteps behind me and turned to see Reverend Rawlings.

He laughed at me.   "Now you're free," he said.

"Who could've done such a wicked thing?"

"You mean a *righteous* thing.   Congratulations," he said. "You passed the test."

"What test?"

"I wanted to see how much of an idol you made of your own creativity.   Whether you would cry at your toys being taken away, or"

"My toys?"

"-whether you would accept my putting away your idolatry with quiet obedience."

"I can't believe you threw out my-"

"The first commandment is to not make a graven image of anything in heaven and earth.   That includes your cheap imitations of our Lord, which are pale substitutes for the real Jesus.   You must worship the Creator, not your own creativity.   Creativity is God's domain, not yours, Jeremiah."

"How could you do this?   That painting's all I had to hold on to her."

"God doesn't want you to hold on.   Can't you understand? She provokes thoughts, even in me, that are not holy."

I staggered away.

*At least I still have her phone calls and letters.*

But before long, even our correspondence was gone.   Her letters stopped coming that fall, shortly after my paintings were destroyed.   Her mother refused to put her on the phone.   I kept mailing my letters every day, but they were never answered.   Sister

Ruth told me Angel was back with Tiger, and their wedding was set. I sent a letter to Angel's mother:


*Dear Mrs. Vickers,*

*As her mother who must regard her best interests at all times, you have a parental duty to insist Angel break up with Tiger and reunite with me.*

*Sincerely, Your future son-in-law,*

*Jeremiah Young*


I was confused at the wall that went up between us. For months, I hung in limbo, in a state of stagnant standstill. Angel slipped away, vanishing like a ghost. I tried to relax and do other things, but I couldn't get her out of my head. Angel's disappearing act threw me for a loop. I felt myself plummeting, spiraling down. The communication froze like ice. My only hope was that the ice would melt at the BBC winter retreat.

I returned that December to BBC winter camp to see Angel. I counted on seeing her at the winter retreat like a kid counts on Christmas. I rode with Mordecai up the Pennsylvania turnpike. He was occupied listening to a sermon tape he planned to mimic for one of his messages to the summer missionaries. All I could think about was Angel as I watched the scenery outside the car window.

*Maybe something happened in her family, a death or something, so she was overcome with grief and couldn't return my calls. Or maybe her mother intercepted my messages and never relayed them because she wants Angel to marry Tiger. What's that Partridge Family song say? 'We've been travellin' in circles such a long, long time tryin' to say hello...'*

When I first spotted her at a distance at BBC camp, resting her cheek in her hand, I repeated to myself the words of Romeo.

"See how she leans her cheek upon her hand!/Oh, that I were a glove upon that hand, That I might touch that cheek!" She sat a few yards from the retreat hall.

I ran to her and found her studying the BBC gospel lessons. She was in a purple flowered dress, one of the dresses she wore when we were together in the summer. I touched her shoulder-length brown hair and looked into her brown eyes. She stood and crossed her legs awkwardly.

"I can't talk to you," she said.

I reached for her hand. Angel glanced back at the missionary directors. She touched my hand for a second than pulled away.

"I can't," she repeated. A grim gust of December wind rattled the trees.

"What do you mean?" I reached for her hand again. She recoiled and pushed me away.

"No, Jeremiah."

"What's wrong?"

"We can't."

"What?"

"We can't I said."

My will to live was ripped out of me, my catechism carcass tossed in the trash behind the aluminum-sided retreat hall. I couldn't move, frozen in shock.

Rev. Rawlings ran the camp with rigid rules about the mingling of the sexes. He came over when we were talking and Angel scurried away. Rawlings sang a hymn under his breath.

Every time I tried to talk to her, Rawlings or one of the directors materialized like a prison guard circling the cellblock. The ground was hard and the wind slapped my face. I wrapped a wool scarf around my neck.

*Why?* The singular word reverberated in my mind. *Why? Why? Why? Why? Why?*

Seventeen, and my life was over.

I staggered alone to the woods.

*Rejected.*

I felt a shortness of breath, an ache in the bottom of my stomach.

I screamed through my tears to the trees. "I was nothing more than a diversion for a few weeks. You cheap, god-forsaken... I trusted you. I gave you my heart. I hope you burn in hell you fucking whore. How dare you treat me like this..." My fist pounded the ground. "Remember what you told me? 'Whatever it takes Jeremiah, we'll be together one day. I'll always wait for you.' Oh yeah, sure. Did you say the same words to Tiger? You lying fucking cunt..." I tried to call her a dry fucking cunt again but sobs came out instead of words.

I looked at the pine trees, the tall branches reaching like bony fingers into the black and blue sky. I remembered her tenderness when we sat on the log in the Rawlings woods. I caressed a tree, peeling a strip of bark in my hand, like picking the scab from a wound.

I heard Red call for me. I stumbled through the woods, back towards the campground. I fell, than my body curled up. I held my stomach, cramping up in abdominal pain.

"Jeremiah…"

"I'm coming."

The evening snow fell heavy and mixed with mud, an ankle-deep slush. The wind stung my skin raw. I looked up to the heavens. "Is it too much to ask to have someone? I'm mad at you, God. You owe me."

I listened for an answer, but none came. I wondered if I committed the unpardonable sin. The trees looked like Stick Man to me.

*I'm deteriorating into a permanent hellish place. This is the trigger that'll put me down for good. Down below with Stick Man.*

\*\*\*\*\*

I rode home from BBC camp with Reverend Rawlings who sermonized most of the way. "The enemy attacks us through females. If I see a pretty woman and I feel lust, I know she has a seducing spirit, like Delilah or Jezebel. When Eve Vickers broke your heart, I knew she was influenced by demons. Satan tried to use her to destroy you, because you're a young man called of God."

I replayed the breakup in an effort to make sense of it.

"Sister Ruth and I prayed and fasted for the grip of Eve Vickers to be released from your mind. We believed it to be an obsession, as it were, from Lucifer himself."

*I don't give a damn about the devil.* "What do I do now?"

"What do you do?"

"With the feelings I have?"

"Feelings are unreliable, as I said. Trust the Word of God. The heart is deceitful and desperately wicked. Who can know it? Jeremiah chapter seventeen, verse nine."

"But God gave me my feelings. Why would He give me something He didn't want me to use?"

"Your flesh is sin-cursed. Lean not unto thine own understanding. Proverbs three, verse five. Remember Jeremiah, Spirit over self, spirit over self."

"But I've worked so hard for your ministry. I finally want something for myself. Why is it wrong now?"

"Because of the Father's commands."

Rawlings entered the toll booth on the Pennsylvania turnpike. He handed the attendant change and a 'Turn or Burn' gospel tract then drove ahead.

"Whoever lusts after a woman commits adultery. Matthew five, verse twenty-eight. Christ is coming back soon, Jeremiah. You don't want to be caught in the arms of Eve Vickers when He returns in the rapture. There's something not right about that girl anyway."

Rawlings stretched over me and opened his glove compartment. He fumbled through maps, flyers promoting backyard bible clubs, and car registration papers until he found what he was looking for. A small golden booklet that fit in the palm of his hand. He tossed the leaflet into my lap.

"What's this?" I asked.

"A new gospel tract for leading souls to salvation. The Four Spiritual Laws."

I noticed a drawing of a train with two boxcars and a caboose. On the first boxcar was the word "Fact," on the second boxcar was "Faith," on the third, the caboose, the word "Feeling."

"Fact, faith, feeling," I said, reading aloud. *That's all I need now. Another three point sermon.*

"Let me explain the illustration," Mordecai said. "We must be led by God's bible facts, which stand outside of ourselves, holy and absolute. Our feelings come from the inside and are therefore unreliable. Feelings are only the caboose."

"What does this have to do with Eve Vickers?"

"Repeat after me. Love is a decision, not a feeling."

"I don't want to repeat anything." Mordecai pulled the car to the side of the road and parked. "We're not going anywhere until you do."

"Love is a decision, not a feeling," I said.

*****

Later that night, before I drifted off to sleep, Rawlings came in the bedroom with another book in his hand. "This should help you," he said. I glanced down at the title, emblazoned in bold letters: "*80 REASONS WHY CHRIST WILL RETURN IN 1980,*" by Reverend Mordecai H. Rawlings, M.A. Within seconds of skimming his self-published essay I noticed the numerous typos.

"You can read the Bible in one hand and the newspaper in the other," Mordecai said. "The stories on the evening news are the signs of the Apocalypse. We're in the last of the last days. The trigger for the end-times clock to start ticking was 1948 when Israel became a nation again. That guarantees we're the final generation, and a biblical generation is less than forty years. Jesus taught us that the believers who see the budding of the fig tree, the birth of Israel in 1948, will be in the rapture when the Lord returns. Christ will return in 1980. We'll be caught up together in the air. The unbelievers will look for us, but we'll be gone during the seven year tribulation."

"That means we only have a few days left."

"Yes, it's right at the door. We finally have the computer technology to make the mark of the beast a reality, praise God."

After he left, I struggled to unwind, unable to shake off my questions. It was two-thirty in the morning.

I woke again around three, feeling a presence touching my extremities. I looked up and saw a black cloud, a disembodied spirit. The phantom hovered over me. Stick Man's shadowy fingers choked my neck. The smell of sulfur seeped into my nostrils. The redolence of Stick Man mixed with the stench of a rotting corpse.

*"Jerrr----a-----myyyy----ah ... ,"* Stick Man hissed. *"She doesn't want you, Jeremiah. You're ugly and you're creepy and she doesn't love you."*

Stick Man's knifelike talons stabbed my stomach. I screamed in pain and flung myself face down onto the bed and tucked my legs tight under my tummy. I moaned in agony.

I called out to the Holy Spirit to deliver me, and the black cloud left, but the cross on the wall rotated and stopped when it hung completely upside down.

In the morning, Sister Ruth tried to get me to eat, but I had no appetite. "Teaching the word to children will help get your focus outward to the harvest," she said.

Sister Ruth had a flannel-graph board covered with felt and bible characters I drew for her. She cut out my drawings and attached Velcro to the back. They stuck to the board when she placed them on the felt.

"Story time," she said with a smile. She opened a multi-colored book made from assembling construction paper. Each color represented different points of the gospel. "And our story today is the Wordless Book."

"Now, Jeremiah, do you know what heaven is?" she asked. I nodded. Her Sunday School patter made me feel like a little boy again, drinking mother's eggnog and praying the rosary.

Mrs. Rawlings opened the wordless book to the gold page. "What does gold represent?"

"The golden streets of heaven," I said, having heard it before.

"Do you believe in heaven?"

"I have to. So far, this life has been hell." She tried to ignore this.

"Good, tell me about heaven."

"When I was in the woods with Angel, that was heaven."

"That wasn't heaven. Heaven's the place where God lives, where there is a street of gold, and a special tree that bears twelve different kinds of fruit, one for every month of the year." She stuck a cut-out picture of a tree, and an angel on the board. "Angel wasn't really an angel, but a girl named Eve. Everything was rose-tinted to you. She was puppy love."

I contrasted in my mind the love Angel gave me, tangible and present, with the golden streets of the hereafter. She was a real flesh and blood salvation, not a cardboard cut-out. "She will live forever in my memory, Sister Ruth."

"Call me mom number two."

"Mom number two."

She trudged forward, flipping pages of her bible. "Let's move on. The next color is black." She turned the page of the wordless book to black. "What does black stand for?"

"The darkness of sin."

"That's right. Since heaven's a perfect place, God can't allow even one sin in heaven. If we die in our sins, we go to Hell. Do you know what Hell is?"

"When she broke up with me, that was Hell."

"You're really trying my patience. You have a one-track mind. Children are lost, and you care more about Angel."

"When she left me, I was lost."

"Maybe we need a break," she said. "Angel, Angel, Angel, on your mind twenty four hours a day. Fight those thoughts, Jeremiah. Take them captive to the knowledge of Christ."

"How can I resist a tidal wave?"

"Brother Mordecai and I have a solution for you. I'm angry at that girl for how she treated you. She used you for her own pleasure. What were you to her? A summer fling. But you can recover from this wound by total surrender to Christ. We signed you up for Baptist Bible College next term. Wait till you see the wonderful things God has in store for you. He really wants to use you."

"I'm tired of being used," I said.

Gone was the divine romance. Winter was hard to bear. The cold days grew short and longer. The winds ripped through my body, rendering my frame brittle. During December, I hadn't washed my hair or had a night's sleep all the way through. The presents, the carols, and the lights only accentuated my agony. I didn't bother to open Mom's socks and underpants.

On January 1st, 1981, I drove to the Roberto Clemente bridge on Sixth Street. I chose this particular overpass in honor of my baseball hero, although the two adjacent sister bridges, the Andy Warhol and Rachel Carson, ran parallel and would've been adequate.

Rain poured from the dark sky like tears and splashed my windshield.   The windshield wipers kept time to the David Cassidy song playing on my eight-track.   His breathy voice sang of a summer romance that didn't last, encapsulating my feelings of obsession.

*I'm just a Daydreamer/Walking in the rain/*
*Chasing after rainbows/I may never see again…*

The U.S. Steel building towered ahead of me.   I saw the green exit sign and turned right off 579.   I prayed at the traffic light at the intersection of Fort Duquesne Boulevard and proceeded ahead. The tires strummed over the steel strings of the bridge.   I parked near the edge and scribbled a note telling my parents and brother to stay close to the Lord so they would join me one day.   I left the note on the front seat of the car.

I strapped weights to my arms and legs and crept to the edge. The yellow railing reached to my chest, so I climbed over to have an unobstructed jump into the Allegheny River.   I watched the choppy waves of the river and wondered what mysteries they contained in the depths.

# 14

I looked downstream to the convergence of the three rivers, the Ohio, Monongahela, and Allegheny.  I clutched the wooden cross in my hand that Kathryn Kuhlman gave me, and lifted it towards the pale sky.   The wind knocked the cross from my hand, and I watched it fall down into the Allegheny River.

Splash.

*We all die anyway.  If heaven's happier than earth, why wait, when I can be walking golden streets by morning?*

I glanced down at my red tennis shoes and then out at the dark watery tomb beckoning me.

"I can do it," I said.

*Others have.  Van Gogh.  Virginia Woolf.  Hemingway. One, two, three… JUMP!  That's all there is to it.*

I stood on the edge of the bridge.  I wasn't certain I had the courage to jump through the dull mist into the gray waters of the river.  I felt like I was a little boy all over again, afraid to jump into the swimming pool at the YMCA on Perry Highway.

Walker was brave in those days, running and leaping, pulling his chunky legs tight to his chest to do a cannonball.  He'd made a high splash.  I remembered how I was afraid of the cold water.  I'd stick my big toe in a teeny bit at a time, testing the temperature while Walker hollered, "Come on, bro, don't be a scaredy cat.  Just JUMP!"

I pictured Walker on the bridge with me, egging me on.  I readied myself to jump in the river and counted out loud. "One…two…"

I stopped, distracted by the envoy of notes from a saxophone under the bridge.  A homeless black man was mutilating Coltrane.

Amorous couples walking the river after dining at Christopher's on Mount Washington tossed quarters in the sax player's can. I didn't want to die with people around.

The street musician played *Amazing Grace*. I followed along in my head, playing rhythm guitar, envisioning the chord changes. D, D7, G, D. I listened to the hymn until the traffic noise drowned him out and my feverish torment over Angel returned.

I thrust my hands into my pockets, looked over the railing to the water and thought of Hemingway's old man.

*I wonder if there are any sharks in the river.*

I returned my thoughts to the task at hand.

*I can do it.*

*One...*

*Two...*

Suddenly, from out of nowhere, I saw Stick Man's face in the river, ready to welcome me.

*"I've been waiting for you to join me, Jeremiah. Welcome to Hell."*

The water below me turned to flames. Stick Man jolted my attention to questions of my destiny after death.

Will I go to the lake of fire with Stick Man? Will I enter eternity with the stain of suicide, a sin I won't have time to confess? If the nuns are right, I'll die outside the state of grace.

I didn't want to join Stick Man in the abyss.

I prayed for a reprieve from suicidal thoughts. The apparition I saw from the bridge made no sense to me.

In a strange way, Stick Man saved me. Was Stick Man and the Savior one in the same?

Did I want to kill myself? No, not really. I wanted relief and I saw it deep in the river. I thought it could've been an effective way to arrest Angels' attention.   She would've probably heard about the tragedy through the gossip grapevine.

She would've come to my funeral and gazed on my corpse, knowing I did it for her.   Then she'd be sorry.   I imagined her kneeling by my casket and crying, kissing my clammy cheek and whispering, "I love you, baby."   I'd be there, hovering mid-air in spirit form, smiling a ghostly grin, knowing my plan succeeded in winning her heart away from Tiger Ogerman.

I was determined to defeat Stick Man and find Angel.


A week later, I was in Walker's bedroom, which we referred to as "the troubadour cave."   We'd worked out a counterpoint harmonica melody that went well with a simple sequence of chords I came up with in the key of G.   The television and the stereo were on at low volumes simultaneously.   Barney Fife was on TV saying something like, "It's the principle of the thing, Andy, it's the principle of the thing," and Crosby, Stills, Nash, and Young were on the stereo.

I helped Walker arrange his Quadralympic trophies on the shelf.   He looked at them with bemused boredom.   "It's not a real race," Walker said.   "I can't run like I used to.   These wheelchairs races are easy.   I have a souped-up chair.   My stupid body can't do what I want, so I'm doing what I can.   I think life's like that sometimes.   Take you, for instance."

"What do you mean?"

Walker turned his wheelchair to face me.   "Listen to CSNY, bro.   Love the one your with.   Savannah's been hot for you since kindergarten.   Forget your fantasy of Eve Vickers.   Face the facts. I don't want you to get hurt.   It was only two weeks."   He tossed his harmonica on the desk in front of him.

"Three.   It was three weeks."

I played a C major seventh arpeggio on my guitar and acted indifferent. I noticed the TV was flipping, so I adjusted the vertical hold to steady Don Knotts and focus my body language away from my inquisitor.

"Whatever, three weeks. She was fifteen years-old. You're blowing it way out of proportion. Come off it, for cryin' out loud."

"Romeo and Juliet only knew each other for one day."

"Yeah, and look how they ended up." Walker chuckled, followed by several seconds of silence. He looked smug with a Stan Laurel grin on his face, as if he enjoyed making me look stupid with his razor-sharp wit.

"You don't know what went on between us," I said.

"Are you so obsessed, you're not going to date anyone else?"

"Of course not," I said, looking down to the threadbare throw rug.

"Then why don't you ask Savannah out?"

I shrugged. "I don't know."

"You need to fuck other women."

"I could do that. It might satisfy me physically, but it wouldn't satisfy me emotionally."

"I can see right through you."

"So you think you're psychic?"

Walker yawned. "Psychotic, maybe, but not psychic." He smiled, and shot me a look that said he'd let up for now.

*Am I a fool to believe there's a way win her back? Maybe Mordecai's right, the age of miracles is past.*

In the weeks following, I dated Savannah to try and get over Angel and to take away Walker's accusation with a contrary action.

I carried Angel's letters in my pocket. Everything reminded me of her. My first love still hung like a photograph on the walls of my subconscious.

Every hamlet where we played our music brought a girl who liked me, and competed with Savannah for my time, but none gave me what I had that past June. The summer with Angel cursed me with a standard by which all others fell short.

A wedding invitation arrived at the Rawlings home for the union of Eve Vickers and Tiger Ogerman. A Polaroid of Angel and Tiger was enclosed. He was a six foot DJ, who rode his Harley in a red, white, and blue Evel Knievel jumpsuit.

I looked at her smiling face in the photo.

*I hope you're happy. You left me cold.*

Sister Ruth went on and on about how Tiger fixed up old pick-up trucks and called Angel his future trophy wife. I wanted to challenge him to a duel, some ancient ritual to win back my fair maiden.

I rummaged through the top drawer of a dresser in the dining room and found a pair of scissors. I cut Tiger out of the picture and saved the remaining half of Angel.

During this dismal season, every song I heard on the radio made it worse. Bubble gum, golden oldies, disco, rock, country and western, R &B, it didn't matter. I'd find the meaning in the lyrics that applied to Angel, and the floodgates opened. I saw a poster at the local Murphy Mart department store at the intersection of McKnight Road and Route 19 that said:

*If you love someone, set them free*
*If they come back to you, they're yours.*
*If they don't, they never were.*

The image above the prose was a woman releasing a dove into the sky.  I bought the poster that Friday and taped it on my wall when I visited Mom and Walker at home.  I framed the poster between Natalie Wood and David Cassidy.  I prayed for the strength to let go and set her free, but it was easier said than done. Something deep inside, a still, small voice, told me the divine destiny between us wasn't over yet.

# 15

Red and I camped out under the stars.   We spread our sleeping bags on a level parcel of ground.   I looked around the woods and remembered my walk with Angel.   Red was reading his bible.   Lightning bugs cast their light.

"God told Father Abraham his descendants would be more numerous than the stars," Red said.

I looked at the stars and imagined each star calling, "Father Abraham, Father Abraham…"

"Can I see that?" I asked.   I took Red's bible and read further in the Genesis narrative and discovered the story of Jacob. He fell in love with Rachel at first sight, and waited seven years to be with her.

I thought about how seven was the number of completion. God made the earth in six days and rested on the seventh.   Seven times three for the Trinity, equals twenty-one.   The number of Clemente.

Even the unholy knew the number twenty-one was a doorway to destiny.   When Dad and I played in the taverns, a boy turning twenty-one became a man and celebrated.   I thought this was odd, to make such a big deal about a guy going to a bar for the first time, when I gigged on guitar every weekend at a bar with Dad since I was a kid.

Nevertheless, I made an inner vow to reconnect with Angel again before I turned twenty-one, the milepost of adulthood.   Every second that ticked off, drew me closer to her.

"What's going on in that head of yours?" Red asked.

"Nothing."

"Nothing.  Yeah right, Jeremiah.  I can tell when you're thinking of Eve Vickers."

"That's not too impressive, Red.  I think about her constantly so it doesn't take a mind reader."

The woods smelled like wet dog.  Moonlight shone on Red's face.  "You're the poster child for denial, you know that?  She's marrying Tiger."

"I'm not in denial."

"So you're denying you're in denial?"

"Real funny."

"Don't even think about going up there for the wedding."

Birds rustled in the trees overhead.  My eyes watered.  I blinked.  The woods grew darker so Red couldn't see my face and read what I was planning.


I drove northeast to the chapel.  A million things went wrong.  My car broke down in a redneck town.  When they told me the vehicle had to stay over the weekend, I hitchhiked.  A trucker with a king-sized hunger picked me up.  He talked on and on at a greasy spoon diner, ordering more meat and potatoes and ignoring my pleas to get back on the road.

When I finally made it to Mount Olympus Alliance Church, the wedding had just ended.

I got a glimpse of her through the window of the limo just as it took off.  The happy couple had to leave, because Tiger was shipping off for military duty.

*It's over.*

I ran towards the car calling out her name, but she never saw me.  I heard the faint sound of the cans on their car bumper clanging against the road.

"Hey come back here!"

The shout came from one of several burly ushers in blue tuxedoes who played on the football squad with Tiger. They ran towards me. I managed to clock one in the jaw before they subdued and restrained me. I wiggled like a worm and shouted for them to let me go. My foot tripped the biggest bully, a bulky redneck with a blonde crew cut. He retaliated with a sharp stinging slap across my face. When the car was out of sight, they relaxed their full-nelsons.

"Let the fool go," the ringleader said.

I staggered back into the church, struggling to keep my balance.

"Hey, stay out of there," crew-cut called.

I sat in the sanctuary and looked at the wedding invitation. I noticed a cross on the wall behind the pulpit.

I couldn't bear seeing her in a wedding dress marrying someone else. If I'd made it on time, I could've stood up to object, at that moment when the pastor says, "Does anyone know why they should not be married?" Even if I did, that didn't mean they would've stopped it.

Two of the ushers in blue tuxedoes returned to bounce me. When they grabbed me, I kneed one of them in the groin and punched the other one in the mouth. They charged me in retaliation and I grabbed the cross off the altar and swung it at them, smashing the cross in two.

"Now look at what you did," crew-cut said. "You broke the holy cross. Blasphemy. God's gonna get you for that."

I nursed my wounds from the wedding fight over summer break. I had a black eye and some pain in my lower back. Most of all, I had a broken heart. I was vulnerable to Mordecai's manipulations when I returned in the fall for his preacher boy class.

*****

"We will memorize the Jonathan Edwards masterpiece *Sinners in the Hands of an Angry God,*" Mordecai said. "Edwards describes God dangling humans over the flames. He views sinners with disgust, more loathsome than any insect." He quoted sections of the sermon. "Unconverted men walk over the pit of Hell on a rotten covering. There are black clouds of God's wrath now hanging over your heads. Your guilt is every day constantly increasing."

I tapped my pencil on my desk. I glanced at the American flag in the corner of the classroom, to avert Mordecai's eyes.

"He abhors you, and is dreadfully provoked. His wrath towards you burns like fire. He looks upon you as worthy of nothing else, but to be cast into the fire; he is of purer eyes than to bear you in his sight, for you are ten thousand times more abominable in his eyes, than the most hateful venomous serpent is in ours."

Mordecai smiled and talked about the importance of ministerial tones, putting on a pastoral voice of authority so the lost souls would respect what we had to say. "Even though ninety percent of humanity will be tortured eternally in the fires of hell, we must do our best to save souls because only God knows the remnant that will be saved."

With that, we left the classroom to blanket the city with gospel tracts. We headed to Fifth Street, the notorious section of the city, to sell salvation door-to-door like vacuum cleaners. We were ready to charge the gates of hell with a water pistol. One of the BBC students, a curly-haired southern boy, prayed for protection from angelic hosts, shouting above the noise of the city.

"HEAVENLY FATHER, we just ask you to bless us, Jesus. We just ask that you would just surround us with Thy holy angels. In the name of Jesus, we just command every demonic spirit that would hinder hearts from hearing our message to just be GONE."

I wanted to be a smart-ass and ask him, 'Why do you use the word 'just' as punctuation throughout your prayers? Are you able to say a sentence without the word 'just?' Do you do that because God is a *just* God?

Our evangelistic strategy was to pretend we were taking a survey to conceal our agenda to proselytize, and lower the guard of the lost souls. This concealment wasn't effective, however, because the first question was "*If you were to die tonight, and stand before God, and God asked you 'Why should I let you into my heaven?' What would you say?*" Unless the person answered, 'because I'm washed in the blood of Jesus,' we knew they were damned, so we urged them to pray the Sinner's Prayer.

My first victim, an erudite professor from the local college, shut me down immediately after question one. I asked him what he would tell God, when God asked "Why should I let you in the pearly gates?"

"First of all," he answered, "God wouldn't ask me such a stupid question. He's the Almighty, not Monty Hall hosting a quiz show. Even if he was inclined to play a game like that, He'd know the answer anyway because God knows all things." I felt silly and stupid and decided the professor was probably too hardened in his cynicism to be saved.

After a traumatic stroll through the streets with few converts, my heart melted like wax looking at one of the last women we witnessed to on her porch. She asked for groceries instead of gospel literature. The BBC students handed her the tract entitled, *Turn or Burn*.

"This piece of paper doesn't feed my baby son," she said, looking up with desolate eyes.   I heard hungry children crying inside her kitchen.

After a hard day of confronting strangers for Christ, I walked back to the BBC bus.   I sat in the back and made sure no one was looking.   I opened up my backpack, and pulled out my notebook to write my daily note to Angel.

*Dear Angel,*

*I just got back from street ministry   The rules here are strict.  I got in trouble yesterday, because my hair grows fast and it passed a quarter inch off my collar.   Jesus would've been kicked out for his hair and beard.   My biggest demerits came from skipping class to write songs.   They overheard me strumming.   I played a new song I wrote about you called "Area Code 814." They heard me sing: "Area code 814/she don't love me anymore/she don't answer the door."*

*The RA kicked opened the door.   He says, "I'm answering the door and writing you up for rock and roll, when you're supposed to be attending chapel."*

*The people here divide the world into a dichotomy of sacred and secular.   They indoctrinate us into a cold, cruel binary. We look at everyone we meet and decide if they're saved and on their way to heaven, or lost and on their way to the everlasting flames of hell.   I'm forced to write songs that save souls for Jesus, so a lot of my songs must include a line like "Accept Jesus into your heart, so a new life can start."   If I write a song about you, they tell me to toss the composition away.   I tried to throw the songs out so I could*

*forget you, but I ended up going to the trash depot and rooting threw*
*stacks of garbage to find them again.*

*After the evangelistic outings, there are campus socials.   I*
*date Savannah, but I can't attach my heart to her.   I sit beside her,*
*and wish it was you.   How can a guy be in love with one girl, (even if*
*she's gone and married), and date another?   I know I shouldn't keep*
*writing, now that you're off-limits, but I can't forget.   I hope I stay in*
*your head once in a while too.*

*With a love that transcends time,*

*Jeremiah    xoxo*


Spring came, ending the cold at campus.   Walker was concerned about me being "brainwashed."   He'd seen a news report about the recent mass suicides in Guyana under cult leader Jim Jones and worried Mordecai would do the same to us.

As fate would have it, Walker was competing in a Quadralympics race not far from the BBC campus, so he visited to make sure I was okay.   "Maybe we'll escape through the guard shack with you riding tandem on the back of my electric wheelchair," Walker said.

The week of his visit, BBC was hosting the much anticipated revival of Dr. Vernon Smith, the king of the circuit preachers.   The visiting evangelists scared the hell out of me.   The best bible-bangers could get anyone to go forward for salvation. Vernon Smith was the best of the best.   He was set to preach his ultimate fire and brimstone sermon: *The Heavenly Polaroid.*   Even Mordecai had concern that he might break down and answer the altar call.

I had a sensitive nature and was usually the first one to run to the front under the guilt-inducing diatribes.   It became a joke on campus that I kept rehearing the call to be saved over and over and over again.    Some of the pastoral students nicknamed me 'DJ,' short for "Doubting Jeremiah," because I doubted my salvation several times a week, usually after I masturbated.

If Walker were a character on *Star Trek,* he'd be Mister Spock.    Pure logic.    Impervious to the mental manipulation of revivalists.    Walker made a deal with me.    His electric wheelchair had a heavy motor.    It was impossible to move it unless Walker disengaged the parking brake and hit his red lever to accelerate.

"I'll tell you what I'll do, bro," Walker said.    "Let's tie a rope around my wheelchair and the other end around your ankle.    You'll sit beside me in the service.    That way, when the guy really gets going about hell, and you're feeling like he's breaking you down, you'll be tied to my wheelchair, so if you try to get up and run to the front, you're not gonna be able to."

"Sounds like an idea that would work."    To me it was worth saving the public humiliation.    The plan was good, but we'd underestimated Vernon Smith.

The auditorium was packed to the gills and wreaked of body odor.    My shirt clung to me and sweat poured out of my forehead.  Savannah was too scared to subject herself to Vernon   Smith, so she cut chapel and hid in the woods behind campus.    Red was in the front row and Walker and I were twenty rows behind him.

Mordecai introduced him as "Doctor Smith," but he'd never earned a doctorate.    Mordecai gave him an honorary degree for 'soul-winning.'    He had the white hair of a patriarch and a booming baritone that broke us down with forty-five minutes of repetition of every verse in the bible about death, hell, and judgment.

"In conclusion, God is showing me tonight, that He's taking a snapshot, a heavenly Polaroid," Smith said.    "When I give the altar call in a moment, the Holy Spirit will begin to draw and convict you. The Lord's gonna take a snapshot in a few seconds of who stays in their seat, and who softens their heart and comes forward to be saved. He's revealing to me that on the day of judgment, when you come before Him and His host of heavenly angels, and the decision is made whether you will depart from Him into the fire prepared for the devil and his demons, or be welcomed into the portals of glory, the Lord's gonna pull up the snapshot and look upon the heavenly Polaroid, and it will be displayed for all eternity and for all people, whether in that picture you were sitting in your seat resisting the Spirit's call, or whether you ran forward to this altar, putting aside the fear of embarrassment or the fear of man, and got saved. God will hold up that snapshot and say, 'You...you on my right. I see you came forward at my servant Brother Smith's revival. Here in the heavenly Polaroid, you're kneeling in the front getting right with God. Enter into the joy of the Lord. But you to my left, I see in the picture taken that spring night, 1982, at Baptist Bible College, that you remained in your seat, hardening your heart against the call. Depart from me, ye cursed, into everlasting fire.'

I'm going to count to three, and when I reach three, God will snap His heavenly Polaroid, and I want everybody here who wants to be in heaven to get up out of their seats and run forward to this altar."

The room sat in an intensifying silence. Every eye avoided every other. Mordecai sat on the platform behind Doctor Smith, nodding his head furiously.

"One..."

A scraping and rustling of chairs. One by one they rushed to the front. A pimply-faced preacher boy went first, head downcast. He was always depressed about his acne and his grades.

The rest of the congregation, heads bowed in prayer, peeked through squinted eyes, straining to see who it was. The silence intensified, tightening like a guitar string higher and higher, about to snap. I clutched my rickety chair like I was hanging on a cliff, resisting a strong wind.

    *Even if I wanted to, I can't. I'm tied to Walker's wheelchair.*

    "Two..." Another scraping of chairs. More students streamed forward. I pulled a loose piece of skin from my thumb until I bled.

    "Ay-men," Mordecai said, burying his head in his hands. Someone somewhere prayed softly, their whisper sounding like rustling leaves. A hymn book fell to the ground with a thud, breaking the silence, but not the tension.

    We sang softly with suppressed urgency, 'It's harvest time, harvest time. The grain is falling, the Savior's calling. Do not wait, it's growing late...'

    *God forgive me. I would go forward if I could but...*

    Doctor Smith cut into our silence with a shout. "THREE!!"

    At three, Walker broke down, disengaged his parking brake, and hit the red lever forward. RRRRRRRRRR... the motor roared and the wheelchair moved. I tried to stop him, but Walker sped forward to be saved like he was in the final lap of a Quadralympics race.

    I dragged behind him, my arms flailing, my free leg kicking. Walker dragged me like a rolling ball of trash. I couldn't untie the rope that tethered me. I bounced down the center aisle, much to the amusement of the onlooking pastoral students who teased me, coughing into their hands while saying, "DJ, DJ."

We arrived at the front, and Walker parked beside a kneeling Red Rawlings.   Walker bowed his head, closed his eyes, and prayed to accept Christ.   I lay in a heap beside him, battered and bruised with my left ankle still tied to his wheelchair.

*****

The social events were every Friday.   Savannah insisted I was her standing escort.   She wanted to do the right thing.   This led her into a compliant state in regards to the BBC universe that demanded strict adherence to the "Freedom Way," the voluminous book of do's and don'ts.

"We forbid movies, young people.   After all," Mordecai said in our daily chapels, "going to the theatre supports Hollywood, a modern day Sodom and Gomorrah."   This was tough on her, for she still harbored dreams of being a movie star.

Over Friday night dinner, I told Savannah about my disobedience of the edicts, including a transgression of sneaking off to a theatre to watch *Footloose*, a movie I thought had great parallels to BBC.   I identified with Kevin Bacon, suppressed by a small town ruled by a fundamentalist pastor who made dancing illegal.   An RA caught me at the local Cineplex.   This benign activity was treated as if I burned down a convent of nuns and lit a self-congratulatory joint off the fire.

Savannah looked at me with disapproval, swallowed a bite of lasagna, and looked at me.

"Jeremiah?"

"Yeah?"

"Can I ask you something?"

"Sure.   What?"

"I think we should get married."

"Are you crazy?

"No, I'm not. Listen to me. We've known each other since we were kids, and a friendship is a great foundation for a marriage. And God knows, we've had a bit of a challenge keeping our hands off each other sometimes. If we're married, we're not sinning, and I think if you marry me, I could help get your mind off someone else if you know what I mean?"

I saw three options.

Number one, go home, where my father was in the throes of mental illness.

Number two, stay on campus in Mordecai's concentration camp. Rigid religion twenty-four seven.

Option three, a sexy redhead begging me to move off campus for marriage and the attendant sanctioned benefits.

Sex, Savannah, Salvation.

I was blind to any other options. I couldn't see at the time that there were plenty of other possibilities like being on my own, having the experience of solitude, growing apart from the tentacles of BBC. And I didn't want to be alone.

I returned to my dorm room and weighed the odds of waiting for Angel to divorce. I went to the bathroom to pee, and when I returned, I found Savannah standing naked, looking in the mirror. This would be a bold move of seduction on any campus, but particularly BBC, where single dating was forbidden, and a boy must keep a bible between himself and a girl to enforce an "eighteen-inches of separation" rule.

I took her in with my eyes, from head to foot. Her long red hair fell, half on her right cheek, half on her ear, over her shoulders and breasts. She had a full, lovely figure.

"Let's make a movie. Rated X." She couldn't hide the desperation in her face. She looked like the faces after the Pittsburgh steel strikes, everything on the line.

She walked over to my bed and lay down. When I kissed Savannah, she was stiff. Her lips were closed. I remembered kissing Angel, the heavenly bliss transporting me. I closed my eyes and remembered her smell, bubblegum mixed with vanilla and roses. My thoughts of Savannah mingled with my memories of Angel. Savannah was in the mood to be reckless, bringing each other pleasure.

Savannah wore me down by keeping me in a state of constant arousal through heavy petting, and quoting to me a scripture out of Corinthians that it was "better to marry than to burn." I broke down and agreed to option three.


On a Saturday night in September, around 9:30 p.m., we were nearly busted. I was naked with Savannah in a car parked off campus. College security almost caught us, but we drove off in our birthday suits when the lights shone on us and the campus cop barked through his bullhorn. I knew I would've been expelled had I not peeled out of there. We careened at eighty miles an hour down BBC's mountain road. I drove the opposite way into oncoming traffic in the wrong lane. Cars barreled towards me head-on and I drove like the Dukes of Hazzard, naked as a jaybird. Savannah laughed her head off.

I wondered what would've happened had the cops not pulled up at that moment, right after Savannah asked me, "Do you want me?" I wasn't sure if I wanted her or not. I looked at her breasts and was turned on until I remembered the secret she told me the first night I moved into the Rawlings house. That muddy memory was a cold shower on my desire.

*****

After a breakfast in the school cafeteria of coffee, Rice Krispies, and toast with blackberry jam, Savannah and I set out on a Thursday morning to elope, driving together to the courthouse in a 1967 Ford I borrowed from the pimply preacher boy. Gray masking tape covered holes near the exhaust. I drove with a mug of coffee in my left hand and my right hand on the steering wheel.

I had no money for a tux, so I wore my dark blue three-piece preacher suit. Savannah had a white satin dress from Goodwill with tiny pearls. "Do you think its okay that I still wear white?" Savannah asked.

"In God's eyes, we're all pure," I said.

As we stood before the judge, I had one thought in my mind. My first love.

The judge looked over his glasses, down to his black book. "Do you, Jeremiah Young, take this woman, Savannah Rawlings to be your lawful wedded wife?"

# 16

Savannah looked at me and nodded. A nod that said, *"Go ahead, say yes."*

The walls of the judge's chambers closed in around me like a net around a fish. I was suffocating. The fishhook pierced through my lips. I knew I had only a moment to slip out or to bite the hook and be caught, captured out of the sea to be gutted and filleted. The judge looked at me, sensing the line was breaking.

"I'm sorry," I said. "I can't go through with this." I left the courthouse before the vows could commence.

Savannah let out a screech, piercing in its shrillness. I feared she would snap and exact revenge on me for jilting her as Angel jilted me.

*****

Several hours later, a dejected Savannah found me playing my guitar in my room and drinking fermented apple cider. Under the eyes of Mordecai's teetotaler college, I discovered leaving hard cider on the heater in my dorm room mingled in the night air and converted the sugar to alcohol as fast as Vernon Smith converted sinners to salvation.

My bicep was wrapped in a bandage. After escaping the courthouse, I'd snuck into a small tavern on Fifth Street, drank seven rum and Cokes, and sauntered into a tattoo parlor where I got a tat on my left bicep of an angel with the words "In Covenant" to reflect the vows I made to Angel my seventeenth summer.

The pain of the needle punctured my skin a hundred times a second. I blacked out for a moment. "You shouldn't have got drunk," the biker tattoo artist said. "It's making you bleed worse.

So many guys drink, thinking it's easier." The needle bobbed up and down in a blur through the skin on my upper arm.

"Hurt your arm?" Savannah asked, jarring me back to the present. A parade of preacher boys streamed out of my room so Savannah and I could talk privately. The preacher boys came nightly for the cider.

"I got a tattoo."

"Don't tell me. What does your tattoo say?"

"Something spiritual."

"Yeah right. You could've said something before we-"

"You wouldn't listen."

"Oh, for God's sake. Am I still your girlfriend?"

"I don't know," I said.

"You're still not over her."

I stood my guitar against the wall and decided to play dumb. "Who?"

"You know who. What am I supposed to do?" she said, wiping her eyes with Kleenex. "A girl looks forward to her wedding day from the time she's a little girl. I thought I could make you happy. Red's right. You're still a lovesick puppy."

"You're a really good woman, and any guy would be lucky to marry you."

"I don't want any guy. I want you."

"You deserve somebody that won't put you through so much."

"It's okay," Savannah said, taking my hand. "I don't want to spend the rest of my life with someone who regrets it. I want you to choose me as your first choice. I don't want to be your consolation prize because things didn't work out with her." I breathed a sigh of relief.

"What will you do, Savannah?"

"It's too painful for me to stay here and see you.   Every time I look at you, it triggers more heartbreak.   It would be hell to stay here.   I could've been a good wife to you, but you choose your imaginary world instead.   Her name's not Angel, its Eve.   She's not heavenly, she's earthly, and she chose someone else."   This stung me.

"No hard feelings?" I said.

"Yeah, sure."   I saw in her eyes a sudden resolution.   "I'm going to Hollywood to be a movie star," she said.   "These people are Neanderthals."

"With your looks, you'll have all the guys in the theatre."

"All the guys but one."   An awkward silence.   "If you're ever in LA, look me up."

I put my guitar in the case.   "Okay.   You can show me the ropes in California if I ever make it out there."

"Say goodbye to the hypocrite for me," she said, referring to Mordecai.   She kissed me on the cheek.   "Bye.   I'm gonna miss you."


Savannah's abrupt departure for California was the subject of gossip at BBC.   Mordecai added it all up and knew I broke her heart.   He popped in my dormitory room late one night.   I told him she wanted to get married but I backed out.   He seemed relieved.

"Seeing her get married to you would be like turning over a Stradivarius violin to a gorilla," he said as he exited the room.   "You wouldn't know how to play her right.   That takes a master who knows how to play her just right.   Someone who knows what he's doing."

Mordecai's remarks about Savannah creeped me out so I exhausted myself that night with fifty push-ups and a couple hundred sit-ups. I collapsed in bed and listened to the sounds of the RA yelling "Lights Out," throughout the dormitory.

After a couple hours of tossing and turning, I walked to the bathroom and peed. I'd drunk too much caffeine. Discharging the coffee enabled me to get to sleep. Soon I was sawing logs.

I sprung up screaming, in the throes of a night terror. I head Stick Man laughing. He whispered in my ear. *"You're a loser, Jeremiah. A worthless loser and a user. You used Savannah…"*

The RA ran into my room. I opened my eyes and saw Red, the RA, and Stick Man.

*"Now you have no one, silly boy. You've lost both girls and you failed with them like you fail with everything else and you will die alone and go to hell…"*

Stick Man tilted his head back in a torrent of laughter. His demon eyes glittered.

"He has spikes," I said, sobbing wildly and kicking in a tantrum. I rolled convulsively on the bed.

"Oooooh, I command you to leave him!" Red said, standing over my bed and looking down. "I rebuke you, in Jesus Name. Come out in the name of Jesus!" His voice grew louder with each command.

I hiccupped and breathed. Time passed.

They shook me in an attempt to wake me, inadvertently tearing the bandage on my arm. Blood emanated from my arms and wrists, pouring over the white sheets. My white tee-shirt was matted and stained red.

"What is it?" Red asked.

"Blood," the RA said. He sat on the edge of his chair, hunched over and tense. He reached down and felt my pulse then wrote on a pad.

"I plead the blood of Jesus," the RA said, stretching his hand toward my chest. I couldn't tell them I got a tattoo, so I hid my bicep under the smeared reddened covers.

"Let me wash you off," the RA said. He went into the bathroom and soaked a washrag and came back to scrub briskly at my arms and face. "You're filthy," he said.

He's such a square, I thought, watching him grimace at my soiled shirt. He took the washrag into the bathroom and let it soak in the sink.

"Watch out for him, Red," the RA said.

"He always does," I whispered.

Mordecai sat in the swivel chair with his hands folded and open body language. I'd researched cases of night terrors, and discovered some victims were cured through therapy. I mentioned this to Mordecai earlier that week. He responded by claiming to be a Christian counseling expert. To begin our first session, he bowed his head for a moment, than prayed out loud for my benefit.

"Gracious and Almighty God, we petition Thee for wisdom. We humbly acknowledge our exceeding sinfulness and Thy exceeding holiness. We do not presume to have any answers, only to be graced with the awareness that Thou holdest all answers in Thy sovereign hand, for Thou art the Wonderful Counselor..."

The prayer droned on like this for another ten minutes. I noticed Mordecai's pot belly pushing over the top flap of his waistband.

"…in the battle against this nemesis, we know we wrestle not against flesh and blood, but against wickedness in high places.  We are ever confident that greater is He that is in us, than he that is in the world.  Amen," Mordecai said.

*Finally.*

"Amen," I said.

Mordecai lined up the tips of his fingers, forming a church steeple.  "Well?  I'm waiting.  You can trust me."

"Waiting for what?"

"What do you want to talk about?"

*You're supposed to be the expert therapist.  You tell me.*

"I don't know," I said.  "This is my first time trying counseling.  I don't know what it's about.  I read that Freud helped people with their nightmares."

"The epistle of Romans says we are competent to counsel in Christ.  I'm a counselor of the gospel, not a student of sex-obsessed psychiatrists like Freud and other humanists.  Don't ever see a secular psychotherapist.  That opens the door to the enemy.  They get you focused on self, instead of focusing on God.  Spirit over self, remember?"

"So what's the difference between your approach and the other guys?"

"I'm superior to therapists who aren't Christian.  I have the benefit of certainty, the scriptural solutions to the dilemmas of life.  So what's troubling you?  Let's start with Eve Vickers."

I thought through my possible responses.  If I told him the truth, I set myself up for a lecture that she wasn't God's plan, or feelings were from the devil, and I couldn't trust myself.  But if I made something up, it would prolong the torment.  I ran this around in my head like I was playing scales on my Washburn guitar. I decided to tell the truth and let the chips fall where they may.

"You can trust me, Jeremiah."

I poured out my heart about the break-up with Angel, and my desire to woo her back.

"Your search for Angel is really a spiritual search, as it were. Now that she's gone, you still have the Heavenly lover of your soul. Only He can satisfy you now."

"But I still have feelings for her."

"Is love a feeling?"

"No," I said, saying what Mordecai wanted to hear.

"What is love?"

"A decision."

"Good. Feelings come from the enemy. Remember this, Jeremiah. Fact, faith, feeling..."

The sessions continued on like this for six useless weeks, until I completed enough school work to maintain a passing grade. Therapy proved ineffectual, just like everything else I tried against Stick Man.

Three hundred preacher boys sat in caps and gowns on the metal folding chairs in the BBC gym. I daydreamed during Mordecai's commencement address. He pummeling the pulpit with his fist and told us to be champions for Christ.

After Mordecai's sermon, he handed us our diplomas one at a time. Parents snapped pictures. Most graduates passed him within seconds, but when I got to the front he gripped my hand like an iron vise and wouldn't let go.

"You want your family to go to heaven, don't you?" Mordecai asked, pulling me closer to his chest.

"More than anything," I said.

Mordecai whispered. "Acts sixteen, verse thirty-one says if you'll dedicate your life to Christ, your entire household will be saved. Your father will be delivered, every whit whole. I guarantee it. I want you to write a letter to your parents about the burning hell. You, Jeremiah," he said, breathing heavily, "must warn them, or the blood is on your hands. If you do, you'll defeat Stick Man once and for all. Don't let them go to Hell."

That night, dreams of hell and Stick Man returned. Dad was at the juncture of three rivers, on the edge of an abyss.

"Save me Jeremiah," he said. "Help the old man, lost at sea."

I swam to Dad to rescue him. The full weight of saving my father and family rested on my shoulders. When I reached him, he turned on me and held me under the water in a death-grip. I was drowning, fighting for air and swallowing water. My struggle to breathe exhausted me.

*"That's it,"* Stick Man hissed. *"Drown him, Daddy. Kill your beloved son just like God killed his."*

I was about to give up the ghost when I woke up, grateful it was only a dream.

I didn't want to disturb my sleeping roommates, so I wrote the letters in the hallway light, scribbling with supersonic speed. I mailed them at four in the morning at the campus post office, sliding them into the off-hours outgoing-mail slot.

*****

When I returned home after graduation, Mom was waiting and ready, letter in hand. I heard her high-pitched holler in the driveway.

"JEREMIAH…"

She charged at me when I got out of the car, before I even had a chance to take my suitcase out of the trunk.

"How dare you shove scripture verses down my throat…"

"But Mom I only wanted to-"

"Who the hell do you think you are, telling me I'm going to hell? I changed your shitty diapers and wiped your ass. Is this what they teach you? It makes me sick, all those thousands of dollars you spent on that so-called college. I wish you would've given me the money. So you finished and graduated, you got your certificate?"

"Yes, Mom."

"I'm proud of you honey," she said, using her sweet voice again. "What subject was the certificate in?"

"Pastoral studies."

"Who the hell is going to give you a job with that? If you would've studied business administration, you could have worked anywhere in America and made decent money. You don't appreciate a dollar. If you had any idea what I had to do to stay afloat."

"The end does not justify the means."

"What's that supposed to mean?"

"Think about it."

"If you're talking about my taking the numbers as a bookie for Spiritos, you're a judgmental little shit." Her voice rose in pitch. "If the Almighty Reverend Rawlings cared so much, he wouldn't be electing politicians that cut every social net to support a woman who is poor and married to a mental case. I hope to God one day you meet a woman who's been through what I have.   We judge issues until we meet the people involved.   One day you'll learn, dear."

She walked back into the house and the screen door slammed behind her.   I recalled the socks and underwear every Christmas.

She stuck her head out the door again and wagged her finger at me.

"And one more thing.   Quit writing letters telling us we're gonna burn in hell.   Is that too much to ask, dear?"

# 17

I rented at 412 Martsolf Avenue, a couple streets over from Oakland where I grew up. My furniture came from the flea market at Saint Joe's. I picked up Father McCormick's old couch, table and chairs. Mom had told me the parsonage acquired new furnishings and I should jump on the old pieces right away.

"You won't have to spend money on expensive stuff," she'd said. "Every penny counts, dear."

My apartment was on the second floor of a three story house. I had a living room with a large bay window that overlooked Martsolf, a kitchen, bath with tub but no shower, and a bedroom in the rear that had a window with a view point of the Rawlings place. I monitored their house. Whenever Mordecai and Ruth left home, I walked into their woods, looking for Angel. I sat alone on the same log in the grove where I first kissed her, listening to the birds. I waited for hours, half-expecting her to come back. She never did.

I grew tired of sitting in the woods hoping to hear her soft voice behind me.

"Hello, baby," I imagined her saying.

I decide if I wanted to hear her voice again, I needed to take matters into my own hands. When I opened my old safety deposit box at Northside Deposit, the golden angel was still there. I had locked it up two years prior. When Angel left the Rawlings house after her three weeks with me, I bought two matching gold angels, giving her one, and keeping the second.

All day long I anticipated making the call. I had two years left in my pact, before I turned twenty-one. Before picking up the phone, I held the gold angel in my hand. I thought about her, wondering where she was and what she was doing.

I looked down at the gold angel in my hand and my mind drifted back to when I was seventeen. I thought about how I carved our initials in that old tree with my Cub Scout pocket knife. I caressed the gold angel, the present mingling with the past. After pressing the first few numbers, I hung up. Then I remembered the poster, still hanging on my wall.

*If you love someone, set them free. If they're yours, they'll come back to you…*

I fixed myself a cup of tea and I remembered how she savored her tea, dipping the tea bag in and out of the water. I flicked on the radio and recalled how she shouted out certain phrases of songs on the radio. Whenever I heard any of the songs that I heard with her, the music brought back all the memories, the ache in the pit of my stomach, the chill of the cold winter when she broke it off for good.

I remembered my heartbreak, maybe to try and talk myself out of picking up the phone. It all came back. The December wind. The frozen ground. Mordecai hovering over us. I wondered if I could've done anything differently. I didn't know then how much that simple kiss would cost me.

My stomach churned like the Scrambler cars at West View Park. Hearing her voice on the phone wouldn't be as sweet as seeing her, but I hoped it could tranquilize my longing.

I dialed her area code. Eight-one-four. I was grateful to Alexander Graham Bell for making it possible to reach her when we were separated not only by her marriage, but by the miles.

The phone rang and rang. *God, just let me hear her voice, that's all I'm asking from You.*

No answer.

My heart was drumming in my chest cavity.   Thump, thump, thump.

*Shakespeare was right.   The course of love never ran smooth.*

Suddenly, the ringing stopped.   Then someone picked up.

"Hello?" she said, answering on the sixteenth ring.

Silence on my end.   I couldn't say anything.   Tiger could be lurking nearby like a menacing shadow.   I heard the background noise of a TV, newscasters were talking about something somewhere in the world that was of far less importance.

"Hello," she said again.   Her voice poured into me like warm milk.   I smiled so wide that the corners of my mouth reached my ears.

I didn't answer.   I just wanted to hear her.   The battle between my conscience and   courage kept me from saying anything back.

"Who is it, goddammit?" Tiger yelled in the background.

"Crank call," Angel said, hanging up.   I wondered if she knew.


On a snowy January 22$^{nd}$, I went with Red and ninety-three BBC alumni to Washington, D.C. for the Pro Life rally.

Red's new fiancée, Millie, was a sandy-haired girl who smiled a lot and said things like, "that's nice," and "that's special." Millie was a nurse at Passavant Hospital and had to work a double, so she couldn't march with the Christian soldiers, but she assured us she'd be with us in spirit.

Millie specialized in caring for the dying.   She prided herself on saving their souls when they were at death's door, coaxing them to pray the Sinner's Prayer before they croaked.

"My main concern," she'd said, "is not their physical vital signs, but their spiritual vital signs. If they're not born again, we may prolong their earthly days, but we're only postponing their torment in the fires of perdition."

We were accompanied by the BBC Marching Band playing "God Bless America." Red was wearing a light brown cowboy hat, a blue dress shirt, and a thick dark winter coat.

I read the posters and found some of them quite clever. A lanky boy with protruding ears carried a sign reading, "*DOCTORS ARE MAKING A KILLING ON ABORTION...TWICE.*"

A doughy-faced girl with short-hair and no makeup carried a yellow sign that read, "*ABORTION...A Multi-Million Dollar Industry.*"

A nun-like woman held a sandwich board with her gloved hands that said, "*The unborn have Rights too!!!*" She had owl eyeglasses and a white flag between her teeth that had a red rose in the center. The words 'March for Life' were written in green letters at the top of the flag.

Many of the placards had graphic pictures of aborted fetuses in the trash, severed limbs and heads twisted together in dumpsters.

The protesters looked colorless and unhealthy, either too thin or too fat. I read as many of the signs as I could. The rest of them said things like "*BABIES HAVE RIGHTS TOO*" and "*CHOOSE LIFE.*"

A stern-eyed girl with a red knit tassel cap lifted a banner that read, "*ABORTION IS MURDER!*" (the most popular sign of the protest.)

Red waved a picket sign that said, "*DOWN WITH TED KENNEDY.*" "There's something about that Ted Kennedy," Red said, lifting his sign to the sky as we marched up Capitol Hill. I noticed some of the marchers faces were smiling under their winter hoods and others were grim.

My lips felt chapped from the wind, so I pulled the top of my purple winter coat over my mouth. The wind raked my hair back, so I drew my hood over my head and tied the black string to tighten it. The coat was a gift from Angel before we broke up.

"Why are you against Kennedy? Because he's pro-choice?" I asked.

"It's much more than him being pro-death," Red said. He explained he didn't like the term 'pro-choice' because the baby didn't have a choice. Red reframed his opponents semantically, calling them 'pro-death.'

"What then?" I asked. "Why do you hate him?"

"He caused the death of a young girl."

"He did?"

"He used and abused Mary Jo Kopechne. And he has the gall to still be in government after that. You never heard about it?"

"I heard."

"How do you feel about it? Doesn't it bother you, Jeremiah?"

"I suppose. Yes, of course. But at least he had the courage to keep going. Most people would've hid away after that. He stayed a senator. It's hard to keep living after something really traumatic. He could've hid away after something so bad, but he kept going."

"Jeremiah, what's wrong with you? He kept going because he has no shame. He lied and paid off her parents."

"How do you know?"

"I read all about the case in Reader's Digest. His brothers were the same way. John and Robert committed adultery with Marilyn Monroe. Shameful."

The BBC marching band ended "God Bless America," and flowed into "America the Beautiful."

"Be honest with me, Red, if you had a chance at Marilyn Monroe, would you be tempted?"

Red turned his face away from the wind. "Ooooh, you got me there."

"Maybe you're confusing morality with lack of opportunity."

Out of the blue, marching closer towards the Capitol, Red turned to me. "By the way, my sister still resents you for leaving her at the altar."

"Is there anything I can do?"

"Did you apologize?"

"Three times. Do I need to again?"

"No. She'll have to forgive one day." We passed a portly man carrying a small coffin with an aborted fetus inside. The sight repulsed me, so I looked up to the sky.

Red saw the dead baby and looked like he was about to vomit. "Jeez. Oh man," he said.

"Can't stomach the blood?" the man asked. His hazel eyes were huge, ablaze like a flaming meteor. "I speak to you as a prophet. The blood of the babies ascends to the nostrils of Almighty God. The blood of the innocents. The blood, the blood, the blood."

"Preach it, brother," Red said, trying to appease him without looking at him directly. "We're standing behind you."

He continued to harangue us. "Don't stand *behind* me, walk *with* me, brother. The doctors send their corpses out to the landfills by the truckload seven days a week. I heard the voice of Rachel weeping for her baby, because her baby was no more."

We walked faster and faster until we were a safe distance away. The prophet confronted the people behind us. I looked over my shoulder one last time at him and he flashed me a used-car salesman grin. "I heard the voice of Rachel weeping for her young..." His yell trailed off in the bitter cold wind.

"How's Savannah doing in California?" I said, slipping on the sidewalk. The snow and ice hardened in the noon sun to the consistency of glass.

"She got into SAG."

"What's SAG?"

"The Screen Actor's Guild."

"Good for her. That's something, isn't it?"

"I guess. I think she's doing it for herself and not for God. She's changed, Jeremiah. Last time I saw her, I barely recognized her."

The crowd of picketers started a war cry, "The little baby's heart so still, echoes God's words, 'Thou shalt not kill...'" The volume grew louder and louder. Red chanted with the multitude.

*"The little baby's heart so still, echoes God's words, 'Thou shalt not kill...'"*

"We're going to win this battle," Red said. "Roe v. Wade will be overturned."

"That wouldn't be complete victory for you," I said. "That would just put the decisions back in the hands of the individual states to decide." I admired the Corinthian columns and the white marble dome of the Capitol.

"Are you sure about that?"

"Women would drive to the states where it was legal, Red."

"But it would be a triumph in the larger battle. It would cut down the number of abortions. I watch these war movies, and God told me these films are a symbol of the Christian life."

Red liked to say 'God told me' a lot. 'God told me' was Christianese for whatever idea popped into his head.

"I watched *Green Berets* and *Rambo*. We're warriors, Jeremiah. We're fighting godless groups like the People for the American Way, and the ACLU. And I'm infiltrating Satan's territory as a soldier in the army." He smiled at this. "I got hired as a guidance counselor at West View Senior High. I'm one of God's footmen in a secular school."

"You go, General. Take the high ground."

I wished I could leave the protesters and the culture war and look at the paintings, sculptures, and wall carvings in the interior of the Capitol. Art fed my soul in a way that Red's Religious Right religion never could.

# 18

I knew damn well why I drank. It started with the night I demanded God heal my brother Walker. I laid my hands on him throughout the black night.

"Please God, heal my brother," I cried over and over. I impulsively did something I hadn't done for years. I leaned over and kissed my baby brother on the cheek. Walker pretended to be asleep, but I could tell he felt my kiss and heard my prayers.

He let me intercede all night long. I saw a trickle escape the corner of his eye. It was the last time he was moved by prayer.

I prayed all night to no avail.

Walker shocked me the next day. "Don't feel bad, bro," he said. "You know me. I'm a skeptic. I was manipulated by Vernon Smith to get saved, but it didn't take. But hey, I loved your praying. I'm sorry bro, but I honestly don't know if I believe in any one religion."

I gave Walker a half-ass speech to console him, platitudes and cop-outs of why God didn't always heal. "If God were small enough for us to understand, He wouldn't be big enough for us to trust," I'd said.

I saw his pencil-thin stringy legs, legs that once ran with the swiftness of a god. My rehearsed speech about God's failure to heal evaporated and I wept, powerless to stop.

The tables turned and Walker attempted to comfort me. "I still got a peace and a joy from your prayer, you touched me internally," Walker said.

"My prayer touched you, but didn't heal you," I said.

I figured if God was all-powerful, Walker would be cured. His disability defied everything divine. After that it was clandestine weeping or drinking, and the escapism of spirits was more subtle.

At least when I drank, the world really did have golden streets of righteousness, peace, and joy. Children were healthy instead of hungry, and people loved each other as they loved themselves, courtesy of Brother Jack Daniels. I slipped into oblivion, where the meek really did inherit the earth.

I threw parties. The wine flowed freely. I hid my drinking by pouring it into a plastic cup. Vodka worked well because it didn't have an odor. It looked like water, clear as glass.

"People are sensing you're in trouble," Red said. "You quit eating much at all and you're becoming very thin."

"Don't worry, General."

I came out once, every party, asking, "General, did you see her? She will have a red or purple dress. Dark brown hair. Brown eyes," I slurred. I hid the bottle behind my back in a feeble effort to preserve my dignity.

"I'm not stupid," Red said. "You need to let her go, not replace her."

"Are you going to help me or not?"

Loyal friend that Red was, he let me know whenever someone matched the description. Red found two women. One was an aide for the Governor of Pennsylvania and wrote his speeches. The second was a print model for hair salons. On both occasions, I walked out and held hands with them and rested my head in their laps.

I dated the Governor's Aide for six months and the print model for nine. The G.A had similar eyes to Angel, but the more I dated her, the more I realized she wasn't Angel. For one thing, she was obsessed with political power, something Angel never cared about. When I first saw her, the similarities between the two drew me in. But the illusion was soon dashed. The more time I spent with her, the more I saw the disparity.

The print model was a tiger in bed. I think that's why I dated her three months longer than the Governor's aide. In addition to having a similar hairstyle and coloring to Angel, the model had a way of busting out into an inappropriate laugh, just like Angel did. But once again, the more I dated her, the more I realized she wasn't Angel.

I made the mistake of telling the model the reason I was attracted to her. "You remind me of my first love," I'd said.

She thanked me for the compliment, then told me that was the "worse thing a guy could say to a girl." She had no more interest in dating me after that. "I want a man who wants *me*," she said. "I don't want to be a surrogate for another girl."

"I'm sorry," I said.

"I'm sorry too," she said. "It's so sad. You're obsessed." She touched my cheek and I felt kindness flow through her fingertips. "You break my heart. It's so sad."

Later that night, the model's pity and my own pitiful condition left me vulnerable. Stick Man approached again in the dark corridors of my mind with a bloody fetus in each of his claws.

*"Jerrrr-eeee-myyyyy-----ah.... The next time I come, I'm going to kill you."*

"Go to hell!"

*"I will, and I'm taking you with me..."*

"No, I belong to God."

*"God doesn't want you. Your mother and father don't want you. They would've aborted you if it was legal back then."*

"Stop your lies, Stick Man!"

I surrendered to the thought that he would murder me soon and the fight would finally be finished.

Red was keyed up about his upcoming wedding to Millie and bounded into the bedroom late. When he flicked on the lights. Stick Man's shape-shifting form scurried out the door like a big, black snake.

Red married Millie in the springtime. "God's really blessed me," Red said. "The Book of Proverbs says, 'Whosoever findeth a godly wife, findeth a good thing, and obtaineth favor from the Lord.'" Mordecai officiated.

After Red tied the knot, two opportunities dovetailed to point me towards California. I answered an ad in a music magazine to play back-up rhythm guitar for singers on records. I sent them a tape of me playing a sampling of songs from the 1940's through present day. I got the gig playing tracks at a Hollywood studio.

The next signpost pointing west was a phone call. I picked up on the fifth ring.

"Hello?"

"Jeremiah Young?" The voice was a woman, probably early twenties. I liked how her voice sounded.

"Yes. Who's this?"

"Teri Edison. How are you?"

"I'm okay." *Do I know her?*

"May I call you Jeremiah?"

"Sure."

"Jeremiah, I'm a curator here at a gallery opening in Pomona, California. We have a wonderful little arts colony here." I didn't say anything. "We're impressed with your work and want to open our gallery with an exhibit of your paintings."

"My work?"

"Your paintings are avant-garde, mystical. You paint from the subconscious. We really like it."

"How did you see my paintings? Most of my work's been destroyed."

"We have enough of your pieces intact to exhibit. We could use a few more, though."

"What do you have? And how did you-"

"Your paintings of Christ, and a female figure. You did a montage of her, a young teenage girl."

"Look in the corner of the painting of the girl. What's written? Bottom right."

"Angel."

"How did you-"

"A gentleman familiar with your work showed us some of your paintings."

"Who?"

"I'm not at liberty to say. He worked through an intermediary and insisted his anonymity be protected."

The next day, I sent slides of my remaining paintings to Pomona and wondered how in the hell they had their hands on my work.

That night I was unnerved. I kept running the California call around and around in my head. I didn't want to fall asleep and see Stick Man, and I remembered how Angel chased the nightmares away when we were together. I hoped if I went to California for a while, the distance could deliver me from my demons. I forgot to write my daily letter to Angel, so I picked up a pencil and wrote my feelings away.

*Dear Angel,*

*I pray for the power to let you go.   I know it's wrong, because you're married.   I must crucify the desires of my flesh, so I pictured myself on the cross, the nails piercing my hands, but no nails are strong enough to keep me there.   I still love you.*

*I have some opportunities because of my art and music in California. I don't want to leave my family and friends, and be three-thousand miles from you, but I remember how you always told me to go with my gifts wherever they lead.   Remember how you told me you wanted me to do what I love?*

*I haven't forgotten you, and I never will,*

*Eternal Love,     Jeremiah     xoxoxo*

# 19

I walked across the street to say goodbye to the Rawlings. Mordecai was perched on a footstool, painting his kitchen.

"There's something I want to tell you," I said.   I picked up a brush to help and started on the wall beside the sink.

"What's on your mind?"

"I believe God's leading me to California, to move there."

"What?"   Mordecai set down his paintbrush and stepped down from the footstool.   "Is it because Savannah's there?"

"No, although I can look in on Savannah while I'm there."   I dripped paint on the floor, missing the drop-cloth.

"Hollywood is Sodom and Gomorrah.   It's near impossible to be a Christian in a place like that.   I'd hate to see you slip into sin. You're not of this world, Jeremiah."

"Maybe Hollywood needs a missionary."

"Savannah tried to sell me that line, too.   She didn't bring Hollywood *up*.   Hollywood brought her *down*.   You can't make it out there.   You won't be safe."

"God's power in me is stronger and I-"

"So I suppose you want to paint out there?"

"You should know."

"What's that supposed to mean?"

"I know about the paintings you threw in the trash.   How much did you get from that gallery in Pomona?"

"What are you talking about?"   I pressed him further for information, but he denied any knowledge of how my paintings ended up in Pomona.

"If you're not gonna come clean," I said, "there's nothing more to say between us."

"Yes, there is, Jeremiah. In light of the shortness of time as it were, don't get caught up in the ego. This takes away from the real work of God's kingdom. Two men will be sleeping in bed. One will be taken, the other left," Mordecai said. "Two women will be working in a field. One will be taken-"

"The other left behind. I know the verse."

"Than you should know Matthew twenty-four says the Apocalypse is approaching with earthquakes. You don't want to be in Los Angeles when God sends the Big One to shake the wicked land. The West Coast will break off like a scab into the Pacific. Then it's game over. Do not pass go, do not collect two hundred dollars. Go straight to Hell." Mordecai looked up to the ceiling. "Even so, come quickly, Lord Jesus."

I looked to the same spot on the ceiling. "No, Jesus," I said. "Hold off on Your return. I'd prefer You wait until I get the chance to travel to California."

Mordecai scowled. "Don't scoff at me and at the Lord's soon coming."

I stared at Rawlings for a moment and realized his old time religion was becoming a glove that didn't fit me anymore. "Remember your booklet that said Jesus would return two years ago? Eighty reasons Christ will come back on September 13, 1980?" Mordecai looked down at the floor. "Maybe you're wrong again, Mordecai."

I put down the brush and walked to the door. Mordecai looked up, speechless, experiencing a rare moment in which he didn't know what to say.

I closed the door behind me.

# 20

I lived in North Hollywood, in an apartment in Laurel Canyon on a street lined with eucalyptus trees and bougainvillea. My building was deco, two-storied, with an underground garage. The front was landscaped violet jacarandas, growing alongside pink blossoms. The scent of honeysuckle and jasmine rode the breeze, and a fountain flowed between statues of naked cherubs. In the hall of my apartment, I tacked up a news article about me and Walker when we were teenage folk singers. The reporter called us "poets of song", and the story featured a photo taken after Dad gave me my Washburn acoustic. The cameraman laid on the floor when he snapped it, and the Washburn loomed larger than life in the foreground.

When Mom had seen the picture, she'd said I looked like a god at that age. Angel had told me the same in poems she wrote. "Eyebrows like crescent moons over your blue eyes. Your Roman nose, brown hair with streaks of blonde, curled at the ends, falling over your neck. The thin fingers of your guitar hands playing..."

California was a new experience, professionally and personally. Professionally, I taught guitar, played tracks for the recording studio, and collected commissions when one of my paintings sold. Personally, women let it be known they wanted to date me. If they reminded me of Angel, I'd take them out. Some even lasted a few dates, but they sensed I couldn't let them in. Trying to forget Angel wasn't the exclusive reason I came to California, but it was the most consuming. The weather was a motivating factor to stay. I hated the long cold winters in Pittsburgh.

Shadow accompanied me on the drive from Pittsburgh to Hollywood. He was a descendant of the cat Spiritos had when I was a boy, a farewell gift delivered by an associate of Spiritos, in fulfillment of his old promise. Shadow bit me when I tried to pet her tail. Before departing, I sat alone in the cab and took one last look around.

Dad had been released from Saint John's and stood in the driveway beside Mom waving goodbye. He wore a tee-shirt with the logo, "MUSIC MAN." He walked to the truck and slipped a piece of paper to me.

"This address is important. A friend of mine from Pittsburgh who's in California now. He'll help you defeat Stick Man," Dad said. "Trust me. Give him a call, but it's strictly on the QT, if you know what I mean." He whispered this like it was a government secret.

I stuffed the paper in my pocket. "Thanks, Dad." Most of his ideas weren't lucid, and most of his friends were psychotic, so I figured I probably wouldn't look up his "friend" in Los Angeles.

"And while you're out there, try out for a game show, son. Instant cash."

"My turn," Mom said. She pulled Dad's elbow and he backed away to let her approach. She gave me a peck on the cheek. "Goodbye, dear," she said. "Be careful."

"Okay, Mom."

"I'm worried that you're finished, Jeremiah," Dad yelled to me. "But I'll pray for you, son."

"Saul, that's pretty discouraging," Mom said. "Your father's obtuse, dear."

"I'm not obtuse. Whatever happened to you, son, I can see that it damaged you."

"What was it, dear?" Mom asked.

"I don't want to talk about it," I said.

"Judging by the songs you wrote," Dad said, "I think it was that girl, but-"

"If he doesn't want to talk about it, he doesn't want to talk about it," Mom said. I looked at them and knew I still loved them both. I wondered for a moment if my heartbreak over Angel hurt so intensely because it reminded me of how my parents broke my heart first.

Walker rolled out with his motorized wheelchair. "Don't leave," he said. I unlocked the cab of my truck. I wrapped my hand around his numb thumb. He motioned his finger to his jacket. I removed a pint from his pocket, took a look at the amber liquid and smiled. There was warmth in my bones as I drank. "I got a gig at the Blue's Café Friday, wish you could stay," Walker said, taking a sip as I lifted the bottle to his lips.

After I waved my final goodbye to everyone, I climbed into the U-Haul, and backed down the driveway, past the pine grove. I drove southeast on Oakwood, than made a right on Center. Shadow, frightened by the traffic, leapt around the truck. I put her in the cat transport to keep her safe. I drove down Perry Highway, past the orange-brick building of the beer distributor where Dad convinced me Santa still existed. I waxed nostalgic, making a left to merge on to I-279 South. I thought of the palms and golden shores that awaited me on the Pacific coast. I felt an impulse to pray for Angel. Whatever I did in Los Angeles, I hoped it would impress her. I wanted to forget her and remember her all at the same time.

I drove down I-79 south, merging with 70 West through Wheeling. Like most people who headed west, I went to escape something old and look for something new. I hoped the land of promise would be the place I truly was born again....again. I stopped at Dairy Queen, loading up on ice cream, and let Shadow do her business. I left 70 for 470 to roll through Columbus. I saw a road sign for an amusement park in Ohio and remembered Angel looking at me in the Tunnel of Love at West View Park, the red glow from the reflected rides on her face.

BEEEPPPP!!!!! A semi scraped by me, jarring my attention back to the turnpike. I pulled off the exit for a breather and stopped at the 7-11. I bought myself some wine, then cruised through Ohio, looking in the rearview mirror. I hoped Stick Man wasn't following me. I crossed the Indiana state-line. I sped to transcend limits and see how far I could push the U-Haul. The wind rushed through my hair like the Spirit at Pentecost. I sipped the cheap Chardonnay from a plastic cup and wondered if I was like Jonah running from God.

I stayed the first night in Indianapolis at the home of Rosalee Adams, a large black woman with enough love to mother an entire city. I knew enough musicians from former gigs to procure free lodging along the way, albeit a floor or fold-out couch at times. Rosalee used to sing blues with Dad and me in Cleveland.

"I'll never forget what you did for me, sugar," she said, making up my makeshift bed for the night. "Solid rhythm, you made me look good."

"It wasn't hard, Mama Rose," I replied. "You sing with soul."

"You're gonna do good out west. No weapon formed against you shall prosper, baby." Rosalee prayed for me. "Give him traveling mercies, Father." Her prayers were life-giving, like Kathryn Kuhlman's, rather than leeching and longwinded like Mordecai.

Although I was behind schedule because of a stomach flu I picked up in Missouri, I stopped at Oral Roberts University in Tulsa.

I stood under the large, 100 feet-high praying hands and took a snapshot. The first ORU student I saw was a paraplegic who reminded me of Walker. He wheeled under the praying hands. I thought again about praying for Walker's healing. Here at the healer's school there's a student imprisoned by a wheelchair, I thought. I figured the ORU Pentecostals probably didn't point out that the paraplegic student negated their claims to heal all who were sick. They were like the silent courtiers in the play, afraid to admit the emperor had no clothes.

I stopped to eat off the 44. A waitress in Dallas told me she tried to make it to California five years earlier but her car broke down. She didn't have the money to fix it and settled in Texas.

I drove through Arizona, stopping for a break at a diner surrounded by cactuses. A waitress with a bowl haircut and a pudgy face bragged about her home state as she poured coffee. I smelled the brew and reached for the cream. "Where you headed?" she asked.

"Los Angeles," I said.

"That's where I saw Kathryn Kuhlman at the Shrine."

"Funny you should mention her. I grew up in Pittsburgh, where she had her base."

"My mom was healed by her. Since you're headed west, you should visit her grave."

An irate patron yelled. "Enough with the history lesson, some of us need more coffee."

"Alright, alright." She turned closer to me before she left my table. "Remember, the anointing was in Elijah's bones. Visit her grave. You won't regret it."

When I crossed the California line, the state patrol inspected my truck for foreign fruit and I sang *California Here We Come.* I rolled down the windows to feel the warm, palm tree air.   I arrived in Los Angeles with eleven dollars cash.

# 21

I taught a lanky guitar student who wanted a transcription of Beck's boogie, and noticed it was turning out to be a blue ocean day. I drove to the Santa Monica pier, a quirky mix of Bohemians, fishermen, and tourists. The Ferris wheel reminded me of West View Park. Inhaling the sea air, I scanned the horizon, and picked out arpeggios on my acoustic. The Washburn was the second love of my life, my high school graduation present. Dad had bought it at a discount because it had a crack down the middle. I watched the seagulls overhead. I played my harmonica from a mouth-rack, and composed a song as I watched the carneys.

I hit a C and sang what I was thinking and feeling:

*"Going to Santa Monica tomorrow/Looking for a girl I used to know/Taking my harmonica and sorrow/Play a song the day is long and slow/And we dance/By the pier/Let your brown hair spin and then you disappear…"*

I played the pier for cash contributions, although I was busted once for not having a permit. My competition that day was a Jamaican drummer and an Asian karaoke singer. I glanced at my watch and realized she was an hour late. I heard the roller coaster at the far end of the boardwalk.

The girl I was supposed to meet rolled down the pier on roller-blades, wearing a flannel shirt and shorts, and sounding like a train clickety-clack on the boardwalk. She looked younger and freer than she did a couple years earlier at BBC. A modern-day Morticia Adams, white oval face and long black hair.

*I prefer her natural red hair*, I thought. Her lips were painted bright red, framing her Mona Lisa smile. Like most fixtures, the tourists and lovers on the pier took her for granted. Her feet and toes were painted with henna in a kaleidoscope pattern of flowers. Her legs were firm, but unshaven. She wore black lace around her neck, trimmed from a negligee. Her top was vintage French underwear. Around her left arm were bangle bracelets, around her right arm was a lace black glove. In her hand was a notebook containing prayers to the "God of Creativity."

"Sorry I'm late," she said.

"It worked out, I wrote a new song." I started into the chords, C, G, Am, Em, F. A small group of tourists listened. She complimented my song, than interpreted the subtext of the lyrics.

"Eve Vickers," she said. "She's the girl you danced with who disappeared."

"Very insightful, Savannah."

She invited me to join her for rice and beans her mother had sent her. Sister Ruth maintained contact, even though Savannah was no longer on speaking terms with Mordecai because he wouldn't admit the truth. He demonized her as an "apostate who defected" to discredit her sexual accusations. We walked back to her Ocean Avenue apartment. She told me she was called to be an actress but had endured a month of homelessness living in an abandoned van.

Savannah lit incense and asked me to pick out one of her records. I chose *Harvest* by Neil Young and played along with *Heart of Gold* on my harmonica and guitar. I played harmonica more in California, because back home the blues-harp was Walker's domain. When Walker did something, he claimed it as his exclusive territory and didn't like me doing the same thing.

"I know this place is small, but I'm grateful to have it after living on the street," Savannah said, fixing the rice and beans on the stove. She told me she didn't own a microwave. "The waves harm Mother Earth," she said. Savannah was among the remnant that knew this, she told me in a paranoid whisper. Seven cats roamed the studio apartment around the ubiquitous cat statues.

"It's a lovely little place. I like all the cats you have around here," I said.

"Their names are Helga, Bowie, Torquemada, Hendrix, Fellini, Coltrane, and Durgas. Durgas is the most powerful goddess of all." The cats sat on chairs and ate from bowls on the table, the way Loser used to when I had spaghetti dinners at the Spiritos house.

"I have a cat too. Her name is Shadow."

"So we're both feline owners. I collected cats after my boyfriend Daniel left, this guy I dated for a while. The cat's sacred, protecting the goddess, just like in ancient Egypt."

"Does your acting pay some of the rent?" I asked.

She rubbed my hair like I was a naive boy. "Talking about the odds is poison for an artist, but here's the facts. Ninety percent of all SAG members aren't working on any given day, and have to hold a second job. In all honesty, it's more like a third, fourth, and fifth job."

I remembered what Sister Antonita had told me as a boy, that my artistic gifts were a curse and a cure. I wondered why God gave Savannah a desire to act since she was a girl, but the limitations of her talent doomed her to this misery. She couldn't support herself acting. I wondered if sometimes passion was more of a burden than a blessing.

She cut a mango and handed me a piece. "But the journey's worth it. So I sell my homemade jewelry, teach acting, and cut hair on the side." She looked at my hair. "Come here, you need a haircut. It doesn't do your face justice right now. You always had a kind face." I glanced at her corkboard by the refrigerator, cluttered with decals and clippings of self-affirmations to boost her positive thinking.   I read them one by one:

I AM A STAR,
RADIATING MY LIGHT NEAR & FAR

MONEY FLOWS TO ME,
EASILY AND EFFORTLESSLY

LIVE YOUR DREAM

A small Buddha rested on an orange crate she used to store books under her burgeoning bookshelves.   I scanned her shelves, taking note of the titles.   *Lives of the Artists* by Giorgo Vasari. *Nostradamas: The Complete Prophecies.   The Communist Manifesto* by Karl Marx and Friedrich Engels.   *The Story of O* by Pauline Reage.   *Tantric Lovemaking. Complete Brothers Grimm Fairy Tales. The Hobbit* and *The Lord of the Rings* by Tolkien.   *The Prophet* by Kahlil Gibran.   Quotes from Walt Whitman's *Leaves of Grass* were scrawled on the walls.

"I like Whitman too," I said.

"He's in touch with the Infinite Energy," she said.

"What's the infinite energy?"

"Well, it's what you call God.   I refer to God as 'The Universe' now, or the 'Infinite Energy.'   I'm not comfortable calling God by the term Father anymore."

She snipped at my bangs.   Her kind eyes were deep green, like the ocean when the light hits.   "What's your favorite Whitman poem?"

"A Woman Waits for Me," I said.

Savannah knew the poem well enough to quote it. "She waits for the moisture of the right man. For if sex is lacking-"

"Than all is lacking," I said, completing the reference. Several seconds of sexual tension passed.

*If I act on it, I'm not thinking about the harm to her when I break it off again.* Savannah licked her lips and I saw her tongue was pierced now. After the haircut, she took the album out of her turntable and gave it to me.

"Neil will help you feel again," she said. "Oh, and let me give you one more thing to help you think of me." She handed me a photo of herself nude in a bathtub. "Do you still like my body?"

"Savannah, I…"

"Kiss me for old times sake…" She placed her hands on my shoulders.

I pulled away. "It's just no use…"

Her sensual leer turned to wrath. "Why, because of her? Oh, for God's sake." She let out a sigh. "You really got it bad. I thought by now you'd be over-"

"I'm sorry."

"No you're not. You're not sorry. Someone's gonna be another year older soon," she said, changing the subject.

"You still remember my birthday."

"Of course I do. It's coming up soon. I can do your chart for you."

"That would make Mordecai mad. He told me somewhere in the Bible it supposedly condemns astrology."

"Fuck him. He doesn't know what he's talking about. Daniel was in charge of astrology in Babylon and the magi were led to Christ by a star. They studied the charts. You're the archetype of a star child. Sensitive. You can't let love go. You'll never be a hack." I smiled at her assessment. She touched my cheek. "Did you know you're chosen?"

"Mom used to tell me that."

"I knew it since we were children. Don't hide your light under a bushel."

I knew two things. That she was even crazier than I remembered. And that she was right. She started throwing a pot as we talked, showing me her talents as a ceramist. I remembered the crude sculptures she made as a girl.

"I believe differently now than I did at DDC," she said. "Jesus is the Alpha and the Omega. That means all roads lead to one. Follow your inner path. Whatever road you choose will get you there."

"I'm glad you didn't give me New Age directions when I asked you how to get to Santa Monica," I said. "Following any street I wanted would've got me lost in El Segundo."

She smiled. "Touché! Funny, Jeremiah."

"What made you change your thinking?"

"I realized the road of fundamentalism is a dead-end. I don't believe in the abusive father-god of Mordecai. He's more godfather than God the Father," she said. "I'm undergoing a transformation. I'm learning to explore for myself. The chasms were too broad between what Mordecai said, and what he did. Some people have things that happen they can't get past for a while. We keep coming back until we get it right. Reincarnation. You must complete every circle."

I thought for a second and responded in a knee-jerk reaction. "The idea we keep repeating a cycle like a gerbil in a cage is depressing. And how do you know you ever get it right? Christ hung on the cross for our hang-ups. He saw we messed up, but he relieves us from coming back. He absorbs every ounce of bad karma."

She bent over to reach for the clay. I glanced at her form. "But you don't really believe it," Savannah said. "You of all people should know about unfinished business. I see the guilt in your face." She seemed free of guilt, at home with her body in a way she never was back east. Watching her work, it was like her fingers were massaging more than the malleable clay. "I'm not afraid of death. You are, Jeremiah. The Apostle Paul said everything must reach its perfected state."

"Where did he say that?"

"I can let you know." I knew she wouldn't. "I stay with the clay until it reveals beauty." She tossed an unused piece back in her cull-box. "Clay can be used again and again and again."

I realized my desire for her was a craving for Angel. I made an excuse about needing to go.

I walked down Ocean and saw a newsstand with ads for the Learning Center, a conglomeration of art and spiritual classes. The gaudy pages were dressed in bright type and caught my eye. I read the offerings: *P.R. for Actors, Screenwriting, How to Find a Mate.* Turning the pages, I read an ad that made blood flow into my gut and injected rhythm into the limbic system of my brain:

### *HOW TO FIND & FIRE UP A LOST LOVE*
*Relationship expert Deborah Cohen teaches*
*How to Reunite Relationship with*
*the One who got away...*
*BRING BACK THE ONE YOU LOVE!*

I found a payphone in the parking lot of a nearby Norm's Restaurant. I noticed a homeless man with a shopping cart full of pop cans sitting beside the phone. He had a long gray beard and wore army fatigues. I nodded hello and fed the phone a quarter. A Valley girl answered. "Hello, Learning Center. What class can I help you with?"

"How to find and fire up a lost love." She took my credit card information. I whispered the card number, in case the homeless man was able to remember the digits. He seemed inebriated though, unlikely to charge anything anywhere. I registered and hung up the phone.

"Lost love?" the homeless man asked, staring at me with yellow eyes. I nodded my head. He sighed and pressed his vomit-flaked hand on my shoulder. "Tell me about it."

I looked at him, not wanting to say anything, but figuring I had nothing to lose by telling him. "We were just teenagers. I'm almost twenty now."

His breath reeked of wine and garlic and stale sexual sins of his own. "You can never really recreate the past. You can't step into the same river twice," he said.

"I don't understand."

The tramp staggered. "You've changed. And the river's changed. Time moves on."

"I don't want to move on."

"All happiness is inside you, not in someone or something else. Trust your inner wisdom."

"Thanks." I pulled a dollar out of my pocket and handed it to him.

I hurried to my Jeep. The shadows shifted. The clicking sound of my key sliding into the ignition was crisp in the evening silence. Traffic was light on the 405. I heard a deep voice babbling as I drove in the rain. The steady sound was too low for words, but too steady for disbelief. I neared the 101 and the sound went on and on, falling sometimes to a whisper, lifting sometimes to a breath. Without warning, a bubbling laugh broke the babbling, rising up to a high C, and then broke off in a tortured gasp. The voice spoke again, articulating words.

"*I am the potter. You are the clay.*" My blood turned to ice and my grasp on the steering wheel loosened, than tightened. "*Clay in the potter's hand,*" the voice babbled again.

I looked in the back seat, imagining a hidden intruder about to strike. No one was there. I took a deep breath, wondering if I could speak yet. Then there came, suddenly a secret, creeping silence. I held my breath. I turned around to read the exit sign for the Getty Center and suddenly felt a little liquid hand on my shoulder. I jerked around and no one was there. My heart was running like a rabbit in my throat. Panic crept to the front of my mind like a rapist ascending the stairs and having its way with me. *Now*, I thought, *he wants to scare me. Well, he has.*

I exhaled and struck the dashboard in frustration, bruising my right hand. I glanced up at my rearview mirror and saw Stick Man's eyes in the darkness.

"GOD!" I screamed.

He reached out from behind. I swerved the car, veering off the side of the road and nearly hitting an abandoned Chevy.

I felt his glacial hand on my shoulder again, more palpable and firm. Stick Man's face was in the rearview mirror for a fraction of a second, taunting me with his malevolent bulging eyes. I jerked around, scanning the car floor and seats for Stick Man.

"Jesus, help me Lord, please God help me…" I exhaled and made the sign of the cross.

Stick Man was gone.

I exhaled. "God, Father God," I said, pulling off the 101, exiting my car and shuddering in the wind, "God, whose hand was on my shoulder?"

I'd hoped driving three thousand miles from Pittsburgh would've left Stick Man behind me. But there was no geographic cure to outrun this sinister spirit. I knew to defeat him once and for all, I had to reconnect with Angel. My three weeks with her dispelled him from my dreams and somehow I needed her to find a permanent cure.

*****

The class was on Saturday afternoon at a Holiday Inn on Highland, just south of the Hollywood Bowl. I was instructed to bring a notebook, a pencil, pictures of Angel, and a poster board. I had a couple snapshots Angel sent me in the mail before our break up, and pictures I stole from the Rawlings photo albums.

Deborah Cohen, the 'teacher,' was a sun-kissed Jewess, with a streak of anarchy in her hair. She wore a suede vest with fringes over a polyester floral jumper, vintage with a twist of dramatic flair. The class consisted of forty students. Beside me was a thin man named Devon "Smitty" Smith. He wore a leather jacket and black turtleneck. Deborah broke us into groups of two she called dyads.

"Reconnecting with your lost love isn't easy," Cohen said. "If it was, everyone would do it. You and your partner are going to keep each other accountable to follow through."

She paired me with Devon and told us to tell each other our stories in three minutes. I learned that Devon was heartbroken over a break-up with a lawyer named Allen. Devon earned his living by a multiplicity of jobs: a waiter at an Italian joint, a moving van service, playing guitar at the early mass at Saint Anthony's in San Pedro, and he moonlighted as a massage therapist.

I told him about Angel before a timer went off and Deborah gathered us into a circle for exercises. She explained that grieving a breakup drained us of endorphins and we needed to replenish our bodies for the quixotic struggle to find our lost loves. We stretched and breathed, as she repeated soothing encouragement.

"We're going to shout out things we're grateful for. Just think how lucky you are to be in California. Think of all the people who never get to see their lost loves, and today, you will learn my four tools to live happily ever after." She led us through contortions. We stretched our skin making funny faces.

"We're lucky to be in your class," Devon shouted. "You're a genius, chief." He called everyone chief, boss, or whatever new nickname flew out of his circus brain.

When the stretching was finished we created our Vision Boards. "We cannot achieve what we cannot conceive. You must look at your vision board every day," Deborah said.

She turned on a tape player to the song *"Reunited,"* by Peaches and Herb, than passed out crayons, scotch tape, glue, magazines, and scissors. I glued pictures of me and Angel on the poster board, along with images of Disneyland and the beach. The song played, *'Reunited and it feels so good, there's one perfect fit and sugar, this one is it...'* Devon's Vision Board had pictures of Allen and images of Michelangelo's David. We took turns showing the class our boards and clapping for each other. Deborah passed out a hand-out with her acronym L-O-V-E:

*L. ocate lost love.   Use your network.   If this fails, try public records and investigators.*

*O. pportunities to see them again.   Seize the chance.   Keep hope alive.*

*V. erify the feelings are there and are mutual.   If not, rekindle them.*

*E. rase the competition.   If they are in another relationship, break it up.*

She told us to write a time-line with specific deadlines to meet our lovers.   This was easy for me because I'd made a vow to find Angel by my twenty-first birthday.   Deborah read the four steps aloud then dove into her lecture.

"The biggest mistake people make when they want to recapture a love is they act desperate.   There's a principle in relationships called the one-up and the one-down.   The one-up is the dumper.   They have the power.   This is the one that takes their good old time to return the phone calls.   They are commitment-phobic."

Devon took notes with such intensity he ripped a hole in his paper.   "You're right, chief."

"The dumpees, because they're the one-downs with less power in the relationship, tend to be clingy.   Reverse the dynamic.   Go against your instincts.   When you're the one-down, you behave in ways that repel them.   Nothing makes a lover bolt like a vibe that says, '*I'm needy, please take me back.*'   There's something inside you that thinks they're higher on the desirability scale than you.   You don't think highly enough of yourselves."

A heavyset woman in front of me nodded like a bobble-head doll, and then emitted animal sounds.   Devon handed her a Kleenex and said, "Don't cry, boss."

"The obstacle you face is lack of sexual assurance.   You don't determine your hotitude by polling the public.   You alone decide you have hotitude and once you do, you'll draw them back to you like a magnet.   You become the one-up.   You and your dumpers are a rubber band.   When one of you pulls away, it attracts the other.   They'll come back when you decide you're worthy. Repeat after me, 'I am worthy of love…'"

*"I am worthy of love,"* we repeated.

"I am worthy of caring," Deborah said.

*"I am worthy of caring,"* we repeated.

I figured Deborah may be on to something because I never felt worthy of a princess like Angel.   I considered myself damaged goods right out of the gate because of my crazy family.   I was part of the mix of madness in the Young household so I felt like a repulsive frog instead of a handsome prince.


Back at my apartment on Sunday afternoon, I framed my Vision Board of Angel, mounting it above an indoor grotto.   I lit candles underneath it and added sketches I drew of Angel.   My Vision Board expanded to include more pictures of Natalie Wood and Elizabeth Taylor.

Devon's board had snapshots of Allen's other male lovers. Their faces had red X's slashed through them.   Sometimes Devon looked like a movie star, his black turtlenecks accenting his chiseled features.   Other times, he wore pleated wool skirts like the girls at BBC.   When he was depressed, he wore a shower cap on his head, a touch of eye shadow, and wandered Ventura Boulevard in his bunny slippers.   It soon became clear to me why Devon scared Allen away.

I thought about Devon's behavior and realized my tolerance for eccentricity was higher than anyone else I knew.   That's when I remembered the phone number my father had slipped me.   I remembered Dad telling me his buddy would help me defeat Stick Man.   I hoped the man wasn't another psychiatric patient from Saint John's.   I'd had enough insane people to last a lifetime.   I rummaged through my dresser and found the number underneath my boxers, buried beneath expired credit cards, handkerchiefs, socks, and old letters from Angel.   I dialed the number.

The smoky voice that answered chastised me for not knowing who he was from the "sound of his intonation."   This convinced me he was indeed one of Dad's mentally ill friends.   I was about to hang up, informing him I wouldn't be coming to visit.

"You still don't know who this is, my boy?   I'm Spiritos the Magician."

"I thought you were dead."

# 22

Spiritos was indeed alive in Sunland, California. He'd escaped Pittsburgh and a mob hit when I was a boy. He explained his obituary was a disappearing act that conned the newspapers with a fake death certificate. Now you see him, now you don't. He lived in a small apartment above a theatre called "Stage 12." He rented it out for plays, Bar Mitzvahs, weddings, and a Twelve Step Group for Love Addicts. His wild eyes, under stringy silver hair, came alive at my arrival.

Spiritos was seventy now and had Hollywood war stories, cigars, and bottle of rum to share. He wore black glasses and walked with a cane, not because he was decrepit, but because it made him feel regal. He wore a turban with golden beads. His shirt was white, with fraying cuffs and collar. The small studio was overflowing with crystal balls, top hats, silver rings, scarves, and boxes with hidden compartments. On the walls, yellowed by smoke, were press clippings and posters of his past performances as "Spiritos the Magnificent." He caught me gazing at him.

"I love that look of wonderment on your face. It's the same expression you had as a little boy." I smiled.

Spiritos had movie memorabilia, including the robot from *Metropolis*, posters from Universal horror pictures, Lugosi's cape, and a bandage from the original Mummy movie. He hobbled to the stereo and turned on Stravinsky. I noticed large photos on the wall of nude Marilyns, Madonnas, and Marlene Dietrich. The largest photo was a woman who looked vaguely familiar from my childhood.

"Who's that?" I asked.

"That's my late wife," he said. "We were married forty-six years. We were in Italy eleven years ago when she passed."

"Oh yes, I remember her now."

He did a trick with a silver dollar for me, just like the old days. We smoked Cuban cigars that he smuggled into the States by hiding them in the walls of imported magic tricks. In addition to his magic, Spiritos debunked fraudulent faith healers. I read a newspaper clipping on his bulletin board about how he exposed sleight-of-hand tricks an evangelist pulled with a radio transmitter that gave him inside information on those in the prayer line.

"So religion sure has a lot of charlatans, huh?" I asked.

"The only faith healer in Pittsburgh that was legit," he said, "was Kathryn Kuhlman."

"I met her when I was a little boy."

"I remember well." He smiled. "She was the real article, humble and trying to help others. My follow-up investigation of many ministers who claimed to do what she did, proved their miracles were nothing but frauds."

"Not everyone prayed for gets healed, though. Some are disappointed. Like Walker."

"But prayers are effective sometimes. It's still worth praying, Jeremiah. Maybe it's not for God's sake, but for ours."

"What do you remember of Kathryn?"

"The miracles were genuine, most of the time, allowing for the psychosomatic, those who believed in their head they were sick, and then believed they were cured."

"A waitress in Phoenix told me Kathryn's buried out here."

"That's right. In Forest Lawn."

"I wish I could find a real magic wand to heal me now."

"Why do you need healing?"

I told Spiritos about Stick Man and asked him to help me overcome my night terrors and my longing for Angel. "I can't stand these nightmares anymore."

"Maybe your nightmares help you."

"Help me? How so?"

"Like squeezing the puss out of a wound so it can breathe and heal."

"Maybe. But I need them to stop."

He walked to his bookshelf and pulled down a couple volumes with esoteric titles. "I've studied hypnotism and I'm gonna write a list of affirmations, tailored to you so you'll remember them. I'll record the commands, so you can play them when you go to bed at night."

"How does it work?"

"The cassette of our session will cure your night terrors and help you find Angel by reprogramming your mind." He put me in his leather reclining chair. "Breathe deep and slow. I'm going to give you twenty-six post-hypnotic suggestions, one for each letter of the alphabet. A, and Attracting Angel Again... All Anxiety Is Abolished, B, and things are Better and Better for you, Jeremiah...." I closed my eyes.

I'm not sure how much time elapsed, but I came in and out of consciousness as we moved through the letters. We cruised through the alphabet to the letter S. "Sensational Success in Songwriting...Seeing Angel Soon, Stopping Stick Man." When we finished with "Z, and You have a Zest for life," Spiritos called me to open my eyes. "By the way, no charge for the session. Consider it a twentieth birthday present."

Spiritos and Savannah threw me a birthday party at Stage 12. Devon and I hammered out melodies on our guitars. After we played, the reunited Devon and Allen put on the Village People and we all danced. When the music stopped, Spiritos stood up and spoke.

"A toast," he said, raising a glass of champagne. "To a great guitarist and powerful painter. May all his dreams come true."

"Here, here," the others said, clinking glasses.

"How about a dance?" Savannah asked me.

We danced like Ginger and Fred to an old Big Band record. On the third verse, Devon waltzed with the robot from Fritz Lang's Metropolis. After the dance, Spiritos, Allen, and Devon harmonized in three parts on Happy Birthday as Savannah led me to the cake. She sang, "Happy Birthday" like Marilyn Monroe for JFK, than gave me a hug.

The gang joined in. "Happy birthday, dear Jeremiah...Happy birthday to you..."

"Blow out the candles," Spiritos said. I was embraced by yays, whistling, and clapping.

After cake, Savannah pulled me outside. "What do you think of your party?"

"You do a great Marilyn," I said. Savannah had a faraway look in her eyes. We walked in the summer sun to a coffee shop next door. Youth, sex, and caffeine were in the air. U2 blasted on the sound system.

"I have such a good imagination, Jeremiah. I can sit for hours and leave my body, and travel to Paris or Venice. I can even go back in time." I noticed small cuts on her arms.

"What do you want to get away from?"

"Mordecai."

"I understand."

"I'm not as free and evolved as I pretend to be."

"None of us are."

We ordered cappuccinos and sat down. "Did you ever tell your mother what happened?" I asked.

"The first time, when I was eight."

"What did she say?"

"Nothing. She said nothing." I shook my head, puzzled. "How can a mother stay with the man who violated his own daughter?"

Savannah elaborated. "He told her it was a lie and I had a vivid imagination. I don't know if she really believes that, deep down in her heart. But she wants to believe it, so she stays. Mordecai reminds her daily that the bible says a woman must submit and obey her husband."

I started talking to end an awkward pause. "One of these days, I'll be able to face him, and tell him what he's done. To you and to me."

"You really think so?" She looked like a little girl all of a sudden.

"Money back guarantee." Savannah smiled.

We all stayed the night at the Roosevelt Hotel on Hollywood Boulevard. I took in the palm fronds and stone archways, than peeked at the pool. We roamed the halls looking for ghosts. About three a.m. we were sure we'd seen Marilyn's ghost, but it may've been imagination or sleep deprivation. Monty Clift had stayed in Room 928 when he was filming *From Here to Eternity*. He was one of my favorite actors ever since I saw *A Place In the Sun*. When I watched him walk to his death, condemned for murdering Shelley

Winters, I rooted for him. I saw the movie for the first time a year after Angel and I broke up, and took it to be a sign. When Elizabeth told Monty "Tell Mama all," she mothered him the way Angel mothered me. Director George Stevens did dreamy dissolves when Monty and Elizabeth kissed. The kiss was his final thought when he was executed. I knew then if I was a dead man walking, my final thought would be kissing Angel.

Later that night in the hotel room, I thought about how Elizabeth Taylor was the first to reach Montgomery Clift after his near-fatal car accident. Two of Monty's teeth were lodged in his throat and he was choking. Elizabeth pulled his teeth out and saved his life. He told her that she was his other half, and he wished the children she had with Michael Todd were his. I imagined myself in a car accident. Somehow, Angel heard about it and rushed to the wreckage. She saw the blood trickling out of the side of my mouth and told me she'd love me for as long as she lived, just like Elizabeth told Monty.

The following morning, Savannah, Devon, and Spiritos took me to the Disney El Capitan Theatre in Hollywood. Mary Poppins was there in person, in the form of a spot-on impersonator. Savannah found a costume place and rented Bert's red and white striped ice cream jacket and white pants for me. Savannah dressed as the Bird Lady and walked through the theatre calling, "Feed the birds, tuppence a bag." Allen and Devon dressed as chimney sweeps. Spiritos was Uncle Albert, singing at the top of his lungs, "I love to laugh." Mary Poppins called me to the front and wished me a "practically perfect" birthday and told me to "make two wishes."

"Chim chim cheree...." I said. I wished I could be free of Stick Man, and see Angel again.

Since Spiritos rented the theatre to Love Addicts Anonymous, I tried the Wednesday night meeting. I brought Devon, thinking it could help his relationship with Allen. They'd had a big fight the night before. We helped ourselves to coffee then found a seat. We bowed our heads for the Serenity Prayer than listened to members read laminated sheets with instructions about issues of sobriety. Sobriety in the Love Addicts group was up to the individual member to decide, but for most, it meant no contact with their "qualifier." Qualifier was their buzzword for the lover you were obsessed with. The painful relationship qualified you to be a member.

When they read Step One, *"We admitted we were powerless over relationships..."* Devon became unglued, raving, "You're NOT powerless, admit you have the power, chief!"

"We're going to have to ask you to wait until open sharing to speak," a woman with a German accent said.

*"Big mistake,"* I thought, knowing Devon didn't like anybody telling him what to do.

He stood and paced, even though everyone else sat. He continued his summation to the stunned jury, "You're trading addictions from one thing to another. You're addicted to this fucking group! Can't you see that? You want a sponsor, so you can have another father figure."

Devon got eighty-sixed from the Twelve-step group. In the parking lot, he was still ranting, "ADDICTED TO THE CURE!" Needless to say, he didn't find help. I knew I could never go back to the group with him again. If I decided to try recovery a second time, I'd have to do it alone.

"I'm sorry if I embarrassed you, Chief," Devon said as we drove home on Ventura.

"I was embarrassed, but more than that I feel upset."

"Sorry, Chief."

"I'm not upset at you. I'm upset because I wonder why Stick Man's been so quiet. This waiting is nerve-racking, almost worse than having Stick Man manifest."

"It's not us doing the waiting, Chief," Devon said. "It's Stick Man. He's biding his time. He's waiting until we think he's on the back burner." I watched Devon's apprehensive face and wondered at the uneasiness which lay just below the surface in both of us.

We pulled into my driveway and walked into the apartment. I shivered, started up the stairs, and punched my code, 6-8-0. I chose the numbers for the month and year I'd met Angel.


The following afternoon, Spiritos and I visited Forest Lawn. We made a left off Glendale Boulevard into the cemetery. A security guard nodded to us when we drove through the gate. When we were out of the car, the little boys in us took over. Spiritos lifted his arms and spread his black coat like a cape, pretending for a moment he was a creature of the night. He chased me around the tombstones, howling like a werewolf under a full moon.

A car stopped with a family of mourners carrying roses and teddy bears, so we straightened up and walked to Kathryn's grave. The grave was behind a locked gate. I scaled the wall, avoiding a small barking dog on the other side and opened the gate for Spiritos.

"I expected something more ostentatious," Spiritos said, seeing the simple marker. He knelt and laid his hands on the memorial stone. He closed his eyes and his eyelids fluttered. His silver hair yanked straight up in the wind. He pulled his magic wand out of his coat pocket and tapped the grave, then looked to the sky. I glanced around to make sure no one was watching.

"Abracadabra, Spirit of the great healer, visit and anoint Jeremiah," he said.

The wind swept over the cemetery. I zipped my jacket up to my neck. Seconds passed in a silence empty and still, like death itself. "It's all passing away, Jeremiah. Whenever I feel elated or defeated, I come to a cemetery. Puts all the highs and lows into perspective."

"When you come to the end of your life, I wonder what most people think about," I said. "We'll find out soon enough. One thing that lasts is the art. Your paintings and songs are eternal seeds. Fruit that remains. That's why I couldn't let Mordecai destroy yours."

"You knew about that?"

"Of course I did. How do you think the paintings ended up in Pomona?"

"It was you?"

"Yeah. When Mordecai threw out your paintings, you'd confided in Walker about it, and Walker told someone who told me. My emissary paid Rawlings a pretty penny to fish the paintings out of the trash and to ship them to our P.O. box. That greedy S.O.B. held out for a king's ransom. I hired some restoration specialists and-"

"And you made the deal to sell my work through the Pomona galley?"

"Yes, so your art will provide some residual income for you."

"I don't know how to thank you."

"No need to. You've always been like a son to me." He put his hand on my shoulder. We strolled through the cemetery, back on the other side of the wall to the section of Forest Lawn that was open to the public. The afternoon faded into a pleasant evening.

I read the words on the tombstones.  Beloved Mother.  Husband. Father.

"You ever think of going back home, Jeremiah?"

"Sometimes, but I don't want to spend so much money to fly back and be around all the chaos."

"They won't be around forever, Jeremiah," Spiritos said.


Savannah's desperation to make it got her into trouble in a myriad of ways, from auditioning for soft porn masquerading as legit projects, to being duped by an agent who convinced her to give him all her money for new headshots.  "I'll make you a star," he'd said, the oldest line in the book.  This led to her second homeless period. Besides not having the rent money, other tenants complained about the odor from her seven cats, which contributed to her eviction.

After not hearing from her for months, I'd found her living in a faded Ford woody station wagon in Malibu in the shadows of the Streisand estate. It was a rainy day.  She named the station wagon "Penelope Progress" and hand-painted peace signs and flowers on the exterior.  It reminded me of the time Dad spray-painted "Fuck the World," on his car.

Savannah moved the car to avoid overstaying her welcome. She drove north to Big Sur, than came back to Venice.  When she was asked to move the car from a spot by the LA River, she parked in front of the home of Elizabeth Whalen, the actress from the old Westerns.  Savannah wrote a screenplay that would star her and Elizabeth as modern cowgirls.  She hoped to show it to Elizabeth, who now had long white hair and hadn't acted in twenty years.

"They don't make good Westerns anymore," Savannah complained, sitting cross-legged on the car hood.  She dressed in layers, a pink tee-shirt over white thermals, and a frilly skirt over baggy sweatpants.    Her callused soles were dark from walking in her pink ballet slippers.

"I'm worried about you," I said, noticing the rear passenger side tire was flat.

"Me?   I'm not the one you should be worried about.    I'm free from the status quo.   I'm liberated from the incarceration of things and stuff.   I'm not crazy.   All the people chasing money are the crazy ones.   I only pay rent once a year when I send my car registration to DMV."

"Don't bullshit me with that Pollyanna princess nonsense. You're homeless."

"I never said it was Pollyanna.   Things aren't completely perfect, I mean I still have to rely on gasoline to get around, but I'm not a mental case just because I live in my car."

Rain started to fall on the roof of the wood-paneled wagon. A memory flashed in my mind, recalling Dad's friend Cathy from the mental hospital.    I laughed to myself remembering her sitting at our dining room table in her tie-dye shirt ranting about the "normies."

"I'd rest easier if you were in an apartment.    Aren't you concerned for your safety?"

"Yes, I worry about the crazies and the cops.    I sleep with one eye open, like my cats."    She smiled.    "They keep me grounded.    Coltrane and Durgas are better than an alarm clock. They keep me warm at night and they lick me at the crack of dawn so I remember to feed them."

"Who's feeding you?    How do you cook?"

"I don't need to.    I'm one hundred percent raw vegan now." The sound of traffic on PCH competed with the distant rumble of breaking waves.    "Can you help me move to the other side of the street, Jeremiah?   It's street cleaning day on this side from twelve to two."

"I want to move you *off* the streets.   How can you act when you're barely surviving?"

"Artists suffer."

"I want you to be an artist with a roof over her head.   Than we can deal with getting you acting roles, okay?"

She looked down to the ground and smiled, relishing my concern for her.   "Okay."   I moved her into a motel where tenants paid by the week.   Sister Ruth sent her money.   Fifty dollars a week, one hundred if Savannah worked a 'real job.'

I went to bed with Shadow on one side and my stuffed dog on the other.   I prayed for Savannah, turned on the tape of alphabet meditations and relaxed into sleep.   "M is for Mind Mastery…N is for Never Negative…"

My insomnia returned.   Not sure if I was awake or sleeping, I looked up and saw a ghostly swirling mix of sensuality and spirituality in the blue mist.

The spectral female form became clearer.   I recognized it was Kathryn Kuhlman, the evangelist who mesmerized me with her soul-saving TV broadcasts in Pittsburgh.   Her flaming red hair fell about her white chiffon gown.   A large cross hung over her ample bosom.   She looked at me and spoke.

"Hello there!   So we meet again.   And have you been waiting for me?"

"Yes, I have."

"Awwww, Jeremiah, you're precious.   Preachers like me are put on a pedestal, and the fall down can be long and hard.   But sometimes the fall lands you in a safer place.   Most people don't know, there's a secret about my past.    I had a big ministry in Denver, long before I came to Pittsburgh.    I fell in love with a married evangelist and had an affair that broke my heart.    He was my first love.    I couldn't find a church to preach in for years after that.    I turned my fall into a lovely dive, thanks to Gentle Jesus.    Sure they say I fell from grace, but I fell *to* grace.

"Why are you visiting me?"

"I'm returning the favor.    You visited me at my grave." She smiled.    "I died when I lost my first love, just like you.    His name was Burroughs Waltrip.    He was the last thought I had before going to sleep, and the first thought I had every morning when I woke up.    Just like you and Angel."

"How did you know?"

"On earth, we see through a glass darkly.    In heaven we know, even as we are known."

Clouds and white floodlights filled the room.    She took my hand and danced with me.    Kathryn was riveted to me, limb for limb.    Her breath burned my ear with intense heat.

"Life is a dance, with different rhythms," she said.    "We don't know where the steps lead, but God holds our hand and leads us one step at a time.    Some steps are more painful."    I looked down at my feet.    "Keep in step with the Spirit.    Don't break the rhythm of heaven's dance."    We stopped dancing and she looked into my eyes. "I loved with all my heart and lost him.    When you come to the end of your life, you remember one thing.    The person you loved."    She squeezed my hand and walked away, calling from the night with two last words.    "Find her."

# 23

A few weeks later, Spiritos and I sat on the roof of Stage 12. The cigars relaxed us. Moments passed in silence. "I have to ask you a favor," I said. "I need to see Angel again."

Spiritos shook his head. "I'm not sure about the timing right now. That could be trouble."

"I'm still in love with her."

"I know. But are you in love with Angel or the idea of Angel? What if you projected this? What if it wasn't real?"

"Then I wasn't real. If Angel wasn't real, and what she said to me wasn't real, than I don't exist because that's the memory I go back to over and over again."

"The memories that are most real are the ones that never happened. They're told six times over by our nostalgia."

"Don't you have memories of falling in love?"

"When I first met my wife, I thought I was seeing an angel too." He took his gaze from me and looked up at the sky, searching the stars. He tapped his cigar ash into a coffee cup. "After we got married, I realized it wasn't what I expected it to be. She wasn't the girl I remembered."

"Did you regret it?"

"There were moments I did, when I saw her idiosyncrasies. But we had kids together and she was a good woman. But she couldn't fulfill me. That's something I had to do for myself." He hobbled towards the roof, balancing with his cane. He looked out at the lights of the Valley. I walked to him to make sure he was steady. "I believed the myth once, just like you."

"What myth?" I asked.

"The Cinderella and Prince Charming myth. The belief that there's a perfect love, the one and only. She'll be our soulmate, a mixture of Betty Crocker, the Virgin Mary, and Marilyn Monroe. The perfect partner who will nurture us and know us through and through."

"Your wife did know you through and through. You were married half a century."

"She knew me in reality, which is something that's not true for you. My wife even knew I cheated on her with one of my assistants. And she forgave me. She knew me on the days I didn't feel like shaving, when I walked around the house in my bathrobe farting and belching. But even after fifty years, there were parts of me that she still didn't know, hidden like secret compartments in my magic tricks. There were things up my sleeves I could never tell her. She wasn't my salvation. Angel can't save you from Stick Man if you can't save yourself."

"So you think I shouldn't see her?"

"I didn't say that. We experience love through other people, and we need it. It's not good that man should be alone. Your heart wants what it wants. And the heart's stronger than the head. The heart has reasons which reason does not know." He patted my hand. "In the chess match between thoughts and feelings, feelings win. Emotions beat cognition. But you have to keep marching forward. If you look back, you'll turn into a pillar of salt."

"I want to march forward. I really do. But until I see her again, I don't think I can."

"You sure this isn't opening Pandora's box? The situation's delicate," Spiritos said. "I know through my sources that asshole she married abuses her. And some of the abuse is triggered by his jealousy over you."

"Believe me, I'm not going to endanger her."

"I don't like this guy, Jeremiah.   I can have him taken care of."

"Let's not go there.   At least not yet."

"You see this girl, without us taking care of him, it's asking for her to get hit again."

An idea flashed across my mind.   "Not if she doesn't see me."

Spiritos looked puzzled.   "I'm not sure I follow."

"I can see her, but she can't see me."

"One quick look at her.   No contact   There'll be a time for that, but it's not safe yet.   Understood?"   I smiled at him and nodded.   "You owe me a favor, Jeremiah.   It has to do with your father.   I'll tell you when you get back."

The sky grew black and we went back into the theatre.   We talked about trivialities for an hour, and Spiritos went to bed.   He was snoring soon but I couldn't sleep.   Lyrics and melodies swirled through me.   I kept paper by my bedside for such moments of inspiration.

At four a.m., I wrote a new song.   *"I know he treats you bad/In my heart I'm sad/I would die to live with you/I stay up every night/Can't erase your face from sight/God, I love her/What can I do?"*   I was keyed up from writing.

That night, I had my worse dream to date.   I saw Stick Man.   He was meaner than ever.   Claws like meat cleavers, dripping with blood.   He crouched over my head and threatened me in a voice so deep my entire body froze.

*"If you see her, you'll raise my ire higher.   Things will only get more violent, silly boy."*

"Shut up, Stick Man!"

*"You don't care about her.    You only care about yourself.*
*If you cared about her, you'd leave her alone…"*

"Shut up I said!"

He howled.    Despite his maniacal screams, all the powers of
hell could not quench my determination to get on the plane to
Pennsylvania.    If Stick Man was determined to stop me, it was
because she held the key to set me free, to make him flee like a
vampire from the break of day.

Red picked me up at the airport.    He arrived six hours early.
Same ruffled carrot-top hair and crooked glasses, but he looked well.
We owed thirteen dollars when we pulled out of the parking gate.
Red had no cash so I paid.    "Thanks, Hon," the lady in the parking
booth said.

"Now I know I'm home.    All the women in Pittsburgh call
me Hon."

"Everyone's buzzing about whether or not you'll move back.
God told me you were."    Red still acted like he had a direct line to
the Almighty.    He never grew beyond the fundamentalist trick of
manipulating others by claiming, 'God told me this and God told me
that.'    I sighed.    "Maybe you could come to church with me
Sunday, Jeremiah?"

"Not interested," I said.    "I don't go to church anymore."

"But Jeremiah, the church is the bride of Christ."

"I still love Jesus, but I can't stand his wife."

We listened to the oldies station as we veered on to 79 North,
the freeway towards home.    The four-lane seemed miniscule to me
after a year of living in LA, navigating the 405 and 101.    Red
considered it heavy traffic.    Dead winter trees flanked both sides of

the road.    I missed the western Pennsylvania woods.    New corporate chains gobbled up some of the rural area.

As much as I'd mythologized Angel in my mind, I knew she'd no longer be that same fifteen year-old girl.    A memory returned to me, unbidden, of her biting her fingernails, than twirling a strand of her hair between her fingers.

Elvis was singing, *"Does your memory stray, to a bright summer day, when I kissed you and called you sweetheart?"*    His voice warmed me.    The King reached the climax, when he stopped singing and spoke through the radio.    *"The world's a stage, and each must play a part.    Fate had me playing in love, Act one was when we met…You seemed to change, you acted strange and why I've never known…"*

Red updated me on his family.    He and Millie took in Mary, a seven year-old orphan girl.    They home schooled their adopted daughter, sheltering her from the world of liberals and evolutionists outside the sanctuary of their home in Hampton, a suburb of Pittsburgh.

We pulled up the driveway of my homestead, a repository of memories.    Mom ambled out in her nightgown and we hugged. Dad was back in Saint John's getting his levels checked or he would've been there too.    I lied to explain why I'd catch a bus in the morning.    Mom gave me a peck on the cheek.    She looked tired. Her breath still smelled like peppermint.    I opened the front door of the house as if it were a wound and went inside.    An odor of her soup cooking.    I looked around the living room and was overcome by guilt.    Her hair was starting to grey.    A tattered robe over her stubby, gnarled legs instead of Capri pants.    She no longer sat perched on a barstool making Kool Aid.   She heated dark coffee and sat at the table with cushions and pads for support.

"Yens eat yet?" Mom asked.

"Na-ah," I answered.

Mom served her soup and chipped ham sandwiches, a Pittsburgh specialty.   Liberace was singing *"I'll Be Seeing You"* from the turntable.   I listened to her talk for a while.   Uncle this.   Aunt that.   Mrs. so and so.   I avoided the pools of sorrow in her eyes.   *I never should have left.*

I gazed at the pines in Mom's backyard and remembered how I kissed Angel in the sun, sheltered by the trees.   Red finished his sandwich and headed home.

"There's some mail on the table for you," Mom said, interrupting my daydreams.   "One from Savannah."   I opened my mail as Mom made me another chipped ham sandwich.   "Eat," she said, "you need your strength."   The thin ham melted in my mouth.

I read Savannah's letter: *I know why you're there.   I know who you want to see.   You won't be free until you let it go.*

Mom's picture of the Sacred Heart of Jesus stared down at me from the center of the room.   The picture overlooked her shelves of green glass.   She noticed me glancing at Christ.   "It's yours one day.   And the books.   You always were the reader."

I walked into the dining room and saw the family photos.   I looked at a picture of myself as a boy, dressed in blue for the talent competition.   She still had first edition classic books on the shelves. *Tom Sawyer.   Moby Dick.   The Great Gatsby.*   I picked up Gatsby and started reading.

"The prodigal son returns home."   Walker's voice startled me.   "Let's kill the fatted calf."   I set Gatsby down on the dining

room table for later.   A petite blonde pushed Walker towards me.
"This is Doreen.   I met her at a gig a few weeks ago," Walker said.

Walker played blues harmonica and was the lead singer for
his band, 'Walker Young and the Iron City Bluesmen.'   Walker
tended to jump into relationships without looking first, inviting
women he barely knew to be his girlfriend and nurse.   "Hi Doreen,"
I said.   She had shiny teeth.

"I've heard a lot about you," she said.

I wished I could say the same about her, but she was one of a
string of girls Walker burned out.   This was the first I'd heard of her.

"So, how's the band, Troubadour?" I asked

"I've struck gold, Jeremiah.   I've struck gold."

Walker's "*I've struck gold*," had a similar timbre to Dad's,
"*Thing's are looking up, Jeremiah.*"   The same hollow futility.
While he jabbered, Doreen emptied his leg bag.   The urine made a
high-pitched sound as it tinkled into the metal container.   Doreen
turned her head away, wincing at the smell.   "That sounds
promising," I said.

"Doreen, check my catheter," Walker said.   She felt his
penis and traced the tubing down his leg.   His leg twitched with a
spasm.   She steadied his leg and he continued.   "W-Y-E-P is
playing my single.   I'm doing a concert, the news will be there.   I
just met someone with connections who can start the bidding war.
Your brother's on his way to the top."   Walker had an all-or-nothing
mentality, ready for the big gig with the right music mogul who
would make him a star.   "Maybe you can come up and do a song on
stage with me.   Like the good old days."

"You still owe me fifty bucks from the last gig," I said.

"Hey, I had to make the payment on the van."

"Yeah, I know. You got free rent here with Mom and I have to come up with seven hundred a month for an apartment in Hollywood."

"I'll get it to you, don't worry, bro."

After small talk, we retired to Walker's room, where he showed me several of his trophies from Quadralympics races. "I won this one in Phoenix," he said, pointing to a gold trophy. "I beat a guy who had a monster engine on his chair. And this one in Philly, all the money we raised with the race went to charity. And this one here, I won in Virginia, number sixty-seven. That race meant I've won more trophies since I've been paralyzed than I did before."

Doreen and I put Walker to bed, transferring him from his manual wheelchair. She broke a nail and was so upset she forgot Walker needed straightened out and undressed. I decided she wasn't tough enough to last more than six months.

At night, I lay in bed thinking about the Neil Diamond song that said something like, *"Nowadays I'm lost between two shores. L.A's fine, but it ain't home; East Coast is home, but it ain't mine no more."* The song whistled through the chambers of my soul like a lost, weeping wind.

*****

The house was still until morning. Red picked me up at six thirty a.m. to drive me to the Greyhound station in downtown Pittsburgh. From there, it was a five hour ride to Bradford, the closest town to Mount Olympus. The bus station was on Liberty Avenue, the main street of the city lined with massage parlors and peep shows. Adjacent to the red-light district, tall buildings housed the lawyers who did to their clients what the johns do to the girls in the massage parlors. Greyhound buses arrived and departed. I hopped out of the car.

The bus ride from Pittsburgh to Bradford was a parade of people getting on and off. I brought Mom's copy of *The Great Gatsby* to pass time. I looked up to notice passengers. A Spanish woman met my glance, than returned her gaze to a present she wrapped with a bow.

A baby cried at high pitch, and most of the passengers covered their ears. The helpless mother in her Madonna shirt was a child herself. I wished I could take the baby in my arms. I once had a rhythmic way of swaying the babies in the nursery at Mordecai's Baptist church that never failed to put them to sleep. I could thank Dad for my rhythm. "Tap and count," he'd say. "Don't you know how to count? Straighten up and fly right. One, two, three, four..."

New passengers boarded the bus. Their eyes all had the same vulnerability, "Will you let me sit with you on this crowded bus?" The empty seats were scarce. I moved my briefcase from the seat beside me and a coffee-colored preacher sat down. Sidney Poitier in a collar.

"Creflo Watkins," he said, introducing himself and shaking my hand. His fingers were long and thin. *He would be easy to teach guitar. His hands are like a bluesman.* "And you are?"

"Jeremiah Young."

"How's the Lord treating you today, Jeremiah?" he asked in his low throaty voice.

"Good, good."

"And how are you treating the Lord?" Creflo's dark eyes were animated.

I knew this patter from Pastor Watkins was a clever introductory line he laid on everyone. I liked the bass tones of his voice. I put my bookmark in Gatsby to save my place and conversed with Creflo for the final stretch. I didn't want to self-destruct and be a fool like Jay Gatsby. In the end, Daisy stayed with Tom Buchanan. She didn't return the pure love Gatsby carried all those years. Daisy killed him, at least indirectly. No one came to his funeral. Not even Daisy.

"Bradford," the driver said. My heart raced like the greyhound as the brakes screeched.

The Spanish woman got out first. The stench from diapers filled the bus. The teen mother in the Madonna shirt attended to the problem. The preacher handed me a slip of paper. He clasped both hands over mine. "God bless," Watkins said in his rich low tone. "Go with God, and He will go with you."

My eyes focused on the paper and I read:

*"Always keep me in your heart and remember me. The passion of love bursting into flames is more powerful than death, stronger than the grave. Love cannot be drowned by oceans or floods; it cannot be bought, no matter what is offered."*
*(Song of Solomon, Chapter 8, verses 6 and 7)*

I exited the bus, waved goodbye to Creflo, and left the station to look for her.

# 24

The country road was long and labyrinthine, and led up, up, up the hill to her house. It was late afternoon. I parked my rental car in a dirt lot that was muddy from the rain and walked two blocks. I checked the number on her white house with blue shudders, 43 Reginal Creek Road. A black pick-up truck sat in the driveway. I squinted to read the advertisement on the truck door. "*OGERMAN TREE SERVICE. Residential and Commercial. Pruning. Topping. Removing Clean-Ups.*"

The three-story house stood high above the rest of the row of clapboard houses. Tiger made theirs the biggest by building an addition. He made the cottages on either side feel bullied. The brown clapboard third floor didn't match the rest of the house, but gave them a view over the pines and maples. The well-groomed lawn had country décor, ducks and daisies. There were concrete steps coming up to greet a side door. In the gravel driveway, there were several cars in various states of assembly and disrepair.

A shivering breeze sprang up. I pulled the hood from my purple winter jacket around my face, shielding myself from the wind and concealing my identity. I crouched down and remembered Angel buying me the jacket at Marshall's department store on McKnight Road, just before she left the Rawlings house to drive way with her mother. She made me try on several jackets before choosing the purple one. "The inside layer will protect your chest in the winter," she'd said.

My knees cramped after a while, so I stood up. I had a long, thick cigar from Spiritos in my pocket. It took me forty-five minutes to smoke it, which passed the time and kept me warm.

I prayed aloud. "Give me a glance, that's all I ask. Red says what I'm doing is wrong, but my heart tells me its right."

I heard a hawk overhead. The smell of manure from the field next door floated by. I fantasized what it would be like to walk right up to her front door and see her. A red pick-up truck approached. I turned my head so the driver wouldn't see my face. I looked at the license plate as it passed. PENNSYLVANIA. THE KEYSTONE STATE.

*I can't believe I'm here.*

I reviewed the last couple years. All the times I cried for her. I remembered how I felt that seventeenth winter when she left me. My obsession froze me in time.

Then I saw her.

She walked from the house to the garage. She blew like the wind across the ground, swinging her arms. I wished I could break the silence and scream to her from across the street.

My pulse sped up and I cracked a smile. I was a great distance away, but there was no mistaking it was her. That silky brown hair, still to the shoulders. It was too far a distance to see her face. She walked twenty feet or so.

A few seconds passed.

I watched her drive away in her red Camaro. I took a Snickers bar out of my pocket I'd bought at a Sheetz store and ate it. I wondered if I should stay and wait to see her come back.

A nosy neighbor lady with her hair in a babushka glared at me and I recalled my promise to Spiritos. One quick look. No contact. There was something in my relationship with Spiritos that was a sacred trust. I had to honor my word. I drove my rental car, a white Taurus, back across the country roads towards the bus station.

I stopped at the DQ and ate a blizzard, then drove to the Enterprise rental lot to return the car.

     I decided to visit Dad before heading back to California.  I sat in the hospital room with its chipped green paint and stared at the crucifix over his head.  For one traumatizing second, the vertical wood became the legs of Stick Man, and the horizontal beams became his arms.  I made the sign of the cross and focused on my father.

     Dad wore a hospital gown open at the chest, exposing his grey hair.  He extended his hand.

     "Hi, Jeremiah."  His voice had the flat sound he got every time he was hospitalized, the fallout from the antidepressants.  "How have you been, son?"

     "Okay, I guess."

     I didn't want to shake his hand, knowing his penchant for self-stimulation when he was alone.  When I turned fifteen, he gave me an unsolicited lecture, advising me on the health benefits of masturbation, or "musturbation," as he called it.  Sometimes, he'd jack off with the door of his bedroom open and I'd walk in on him and turn around and pretend I hadn't seen.

     "We better not shake in a hospital," I said.  "To protect you from germs."

     Dad nodded silently and looked down at his large and powerful hands.  He struggled to sit up, asking me to help prop pillows behind his back.  I adjusted the blue pillows behind the small of his back.  He lifted his arm and I got a whiff.  He gave off an odor, a mixture of urine and Kenyan coffee.

     "I know what you're thinking," Dad said.

     "You do?"

"You think I've brought you nothing but nightmares," Dad said. "Maybe I have. But you know what your problem is, son? You're sleep-walking through life. Living in dreams. Fantasies about that girl. One day, you'll wake up and find out what life's really like."

I didn't want to argue. Dad always talked *at* me, not *with* me. He was too broken to manage a bilateral conversation. I wanted to run away but felt obligated to stay long enough to qualify for a visit rather than a drive-by. Dad rambled about Hemingway's Santiago, the sharks and the sea.

He had a way of going for the jugular, saying something that would trigger the most serene person into a rage. Maybe that's why the nurses who were assigned to him in the mental ward were given short shifts.

Just when the thought of killing him jumped out of my head, a nurse with Dolly Parton breasts came in and gave him his medication. After he swallowed, she made him open his mouth and examined his oral cavity to make sure he swallowed the pills. Her breasts hung over Dad's face and he enjoyed every moment of it. His arm lifted off the bed and she slapped it down.

"Keep you hands to yourself, Mister Young."

"I wasn't doing anything. I just wanted to introduce you to my special guest. This is my son, Jeremiah."

"Pleased to meet you," I answered, looking her right in the eyes.

When she left the room, I looked at her stature, a freak of nature. "I see why you're staying here," I said.

Dad smiled. "She could be in a Russ Meyer film," he said. "I tease her quite a bit. Don't tell your mother, but she's got a thing for me."

"Our secret."

"How's your mother?"

"Okay."

"Tell her to visit me."

"Yeah."    A pause.    "When are you getting out?"

"I don't know.    I don't belong here."

I hoped this was the last time.    I worried I might be next, because I'd read in *Psychology Today* that manic-depression was genetic.

Dad noticed the clock and asked me to hand him the remote so he could watch his game shows.    He zoned out just as Bob Barker's announcer said, "Loraine Gonzales, come on down..."

I waved goodbye, and walked out of the hospital into the windy breeze blowing across the parking lot.

*****

When I returned to California, Spiritos asked me over Stage 12 to collect on his favor.    He covered himself with Lugosi's cape. I noticed two cigars in the skull ashtray were lit with a couple inches unsmoked.    Spiritos reached to my right ear and pulled out a silver lighter in the shape of a wand.    His hands shook when he lit the flares.    We breathed out ghostly rings that floated like pale blue demons past the horror movie posters of Dracula, Frankenstein, and the Mummy.

"I have a theory about Stick Man," he said.

"Really?" I asked.

"Wanna hear it?"

"Go ahead."    I watched our smoke ghosts gather in the corner.

"I think your father being hard on you has something to do with Stick Man.    You're on the verge of good dreams, Jeremiah, if you do me a favor.   I notice an emotional block in your painting and when you perform," he said.   "You're extremely talented, but you seem unable to access certain feelings.   I'm giving you an unusual assignment."   I sat back in my creaky chair and braced myself.

"What?"

"Don't worry.   Do you trust me?"

I nodded.   "Yeah."

"Your obstruction is from the wounds from your father. Write a letter to him."

"A letter?"

"Put it in writing.   Tell him what you needed from him and didn't get, and what you want from him now.   You're writing for your own catharsis.   You don't have to send it."   He handed me paper and a pen.   "Write.   Quickly, without thinking."

"No, I don't think so."

He looked at me sternly.   "Write!"

I exhaled, not wanting to comply.   "Okay, okay," I grumbled.   I wrote the note quickly.

"Now read it to me."

I shook my head in rebellion.   "Do I have to?"

"Yes."

I held my letter and read out loud:

*Dear Dad,*

*Growing up, I always wished you would tell me you loved me.   I wanted you to hold me.   I wanted you to approve of me.   My guitar playing was never as good as you.   My efforts were ridiculed. I needed your love then and I need it now.   In the time that's left, I want to forget how you hurt me in the past, and I want you to forgive me for any way I've hurt you and I want to love each other for the time that's left.*

I fought back a rising tide of unexpected feelings that overwhelmed me. Unable to speak without losing my composure, I read the rest of the letter silently, than looked up to Spiritos. "Now what?"

"Send it, Jeremiah."

"But you said I didn't have-"

"I changed my mind."

"You lied."

"No, I didn't lie. I changed my mind."

"Can't."

"You have to. When you do this, you've become a man."

"There's no way-"

Spiritos prevailed. I mailed the letter to my father on Monday morning. I figured he'd never read it, and if he did he'd pitch it in the garbage.

Later that fall, my building had a vacancy in the apartment above mine. Devon and I moved Savannah and her seven cats from the hotel. "Now, I can keep my eye on you," she said.

*That's what I'm afraid of.*

Savannah unpacked through the night, clippity-clomping so loud above me I wore earplugs to sleep.

I awoke to the scent of bacon and eggs and the sound of Spiritos voice on the tape he'd made for me. "Q is for Quality of life and Quantity of income increasing. You surely will do it, Jeremiah..."

Savannah fixed breakfast as her way of thanking me.  Her refrigerator was bare, so we ate like kings.

Spiritos came over with Cubans to celebrate Savannah's new apartment.  I lit the edges with a Bic lighter until they blackened before we inhaled.  Devon and I played guitars for a few moments until everyone was done eating.

Savannah kissed me for good luck.  "It's a tradition when one moves into a new home," she said.  "This is a perfect day, a day unlike any other."


On bad nights, when Stick Man came, I wandered in my sleep, leaving the apartment.  One morning, my sheets were wet with blood because I jumped off the steps in the front of the apartment.  Stick Man chased me shouting, *"Die, motherfucker, die..."*  I landed in the bougainvillea thinking I was escaping.

The next night, Savannah barricaded my doors before retiring upstairs.  The tape of Spiritos still played every night to ward off the parasomnia that haunted me.  "T is for Transcendence Over the Past... U is for United with the Universal Intelligence..."

On good nights, I still battled Stick Man, but I had twenty seconds of the fresh memory of Angel walking from her house to her garage.  This image graced my dreams and kept my hopes alive.

Savannah made me breakfast most mornings.  "I'm worried for you, Jeremiah," she said, serving up the toast.  "I noticed the trip back home made your obsession worse."

"Don't preach at me."

"I just want you to look at the root of your problems."

"Enough."

"Okay, I'll drop it. I cooked casseroles for later. I'll leave them in the fridge. Look at your hair. I need to give you a haircut."

Savannah snipped at my hair while she smoked a cigarette and talked on her cordless phone to her new boyfriend, a bass player in alternative band. She cut my ear when she cut my hair, but the bleeding was minimal.

We all shared Thanksgiving that year. It turned into a party, with too much wine. When Savannah said, "It's a potluck. Everyone bring something," everyone brought a bottle.

Devon and I jammed on guitars, and Savannah's boyfriend, a lanky guy who looked like Ichabod Crane, played bass. The climax of the night was when Devon had sheet music to the Patsy Cline song *Crazy*, Savannah's personal favorite. I started the song, but the chording was complex, and I was the only one with enough skill to play it.

I kept going, but Ichabod and Devon were lost and dropped out. Devon blamed Ichabod for throwing him off with "some ass-backwards bass beat," to which Ichabod erupted.

"You're a few fries short of a happy meal, Smitty."

Savannah tried to calm the ruffled feathers, provoking Devon to attack her next, and before long insults flowed in every direction like pastries in a Three Stooges pie fight. Savannah left the living room in tears, and Devon and Ichabod were inches from blows.

"Stop it, we can play the song another time," I said.

They calmed down, as if snapped out of a trance and agreed to choose peace over power. I knew we needed a simple, three-chord song to play together, so I started *"Blowin in the Wind,"* in the key of C, and before long everyone was singing.

# 25

A few weeks later, on a cold evening on December 14th, I watched President Reagan on television. I went in the bathroom and started a shower when I yelled out "DADDY!" My fingers froze like ice. I felt terrifying chills than a flush of fever. My spirit knew something happened to him. I called Walker, trembling as I dialed.

"Get home now," Walker said. "Dad's getting worse. Really sick."

"What happened?"

"We were watching *Price Is Right*. A woman from the Burg won a show case to Hawaii. She kissed Bob Barker and hopped like a pogo stick. Dad jumped up and down too, celebrating with her, and then he collapsed like a crumbling pillar to the floor."

"He always wanted me to go on a game show," I said.

"I'm worried," Walker said.

I dreaded the day Dad or Mom would die. I pushed it out of my mind and buried my head in the proverbial sand. "He's gonna be okay, Walker," I said.

"I don't think so. I've been here watching him decline while you're three thousand miles away in La-la land. Here in reality, there are only two things for sure. Death and taxes."

*****

Walker met me at the airport and told me about Dad's final days as I wheeled him through the parking lot. "Dad watches *Little House On the Prairie*. He longs to journey to another world, bro," Walker said.

For years, Dad seemed to be existing, not living.  I reasoned that the anti-depressants, the physical rejection of his wife, and an absence of hope made him an empty shell.

Rare moments of passion seeped through, when he'd shout out an answer during his favorite game shows.  After these outbursts, he became a zombie again.

I remembered his regular nagging on the phone ever since I moved to L.A.  "It's your ticket to wealth, Jeremiah.  Try out for one of Merv Griffin's game shows.  All the auditions are out there in California," he said.  "Easy money."

"It's easy at home, in the comfort of your living room," I'd say, "but under the stage lights and pressure, that's another matter."

After I arrive in Pittsburgh, I watched Dad grow sicker and sicker.  When his condition took a turn for the worse, I took him to stay at the Veteran's hospital.  He was capable of only one word sentences, muttering commands from his hospital bed.

"Bathroom," Dad said.  Mom or I assisted with the bedpan.

"Here, Dad.  Go in the pan."  He lifted his robe and Mom held his penis for aim.

"Water."

I lifted the glass to his lips, careful not to tilt it too high and spill it on his chin.

"Pray," Dad said.

There was a look of death in his eyes, facing the final aloneness.  I led the recitation of the Lord's Prayer.  Mom and Dad followed in lockstep.  Walker resisted at first, than cooperated for Dad's sake.

When I played blackjack with him, he came alive again.  I adjusted the hospital bed to the upright position, pulled the food tray in front of his chest and dealt the cards, one up, one down.   He made all the right calls.   "Hit me," and "Freeze," he said.

In his last moments of awareness I talked with him, although I did most of the talking.   After years of Dad's monologues at me, this was a role reversal.

"Dad, I kept having these dreams about West View and going home.   I think heaven might be like that.   Like going home."

Father smiled at me.

I heard a knock on the door of the hospital room.   Red and Millie came to visit with their adopted daughter Mary, now a freckled teenager, who crept in behind them.

"Hey, Mister Young," Red said.

Dad managed a nod.   They brought him a stuffed teddy bear that he barely noticed.

"It's real special your family is all here Mister Young," Millie said, managing a nervous smile.

Red and Millie showed us pictures of Grace and Luke, two children they were adopting who were abandoned on the streets of China.   Their compassion enabled me to overlook Millie's self-righteousness.

Millie looked at Dad with the bedside manner that came from years as a registered nurse.   She pulled me aside.

"Do you think your Dad knows the Lord?" she asked, looking for reassurance.

God knows *him,* I thought to myself.   *That's what matters.*

"I think so," I said.   I wore the mask of civility but felt like slapping her out of her Amish-like rigidity.   "It's been a struggle for him to walk things out sometimes because of his mental illness, but God understands all that."

"But is he SAVED, Jeremiah?"

"He's my father and God understands and knows that-"

Millie couldn't swallow mercy theologically. "My mother is probably damned," Millie said. "She died in our house four months back."

"I'm sorry, Millie. I don't think-"

"Narrow is the way that leads to life, few there be that find it," she said. "Mom never talked much about her faith, so I question whether she was saved."

"God's big enough to understand your mother's hesitance to discuss spiritual matters," I said.

"It's in the Word," Red interjected. "Whoever confesses Me before men, I will confess him before My Father on the day of judgment. Whoever denies Me before men, I will deny Him."

"Millie, you couldn't enjoy heaven if your mother was being tormented in hell," I said. "You're too selfless of a person. You're the essence of everything good a nurse should be. Kind. Selfless. Caring. Motivated to relieve suffering. You hurt when others hurt. Unless God performed a lobotomy on your brain to forget your mother, you'd be miserable."

"Maybe that's what God does," Red said. "Removes the memory of our unsaved relatives."

"Then heaven wouldn't be based on truth, General."

"Maybe I'm one of those branches that don't bear fruit and I'll be cut off and thrown into the fire," their daughter Mary said, with a worried look on her face. "A true Christian loves everyone and there are some people I don't love."

"God would never do that to you, Mary," I said.

"Hell is real, Mary. You can be sure," Millie said.

*I'll tell you what Hell is,* I thought. *Loving a woman your whole life and not being able to be with her. That's hell.*

"What about the bad people?" Walker asked. He'd been drinking, and I hoped he would be just drunk enough to tell Millie off. "What if God let everyone into heaven? What if He forgave His enemies, and had mercy on all the broken souls? God commands us to forgive our enemies, so He has to, right?"

Red tried to clue him not to provoke Millie.

Walker chuckled. "It would be easier than trying to keep track of everyone's stupidity," he said, playing with the switch on his motorized wheelchair. "If God exists, maybe He's so tired of sinners and sin, He'll say, 'the hell with hell.' Surely good is strong enough to eliminate evil one day."

At this, Millie shook her head. "I'll pray for all of you," she said. I marveled at her ability to deliver words of concern in a way that turned them into an indictment.

"Thank you," Walker said. "But your prayers and your question about Dad aren't called for. You may be well-meaning, but that's very insensitive. So I request that you jag-offs get the hell out of here."

"Look," I said, "You and Red are the nicest people on the planet, but-"

"That's okay," Red said. "This is a trying time. We'll let you be with your Dad."

Red, Millie, and Mary left the room.

Walker pressed the red accelerator lever on the arm rest of his motorized wheelchair and drove out of the room, chasing after them. His wheelchair lurched at Millie and Red in the hall. He raced around them in a series of circles, twirls, and figure-eights.

"God, save me from your followers," he said, transforming his motorized machinery into an extension of his rage at religion. A nurse rushed over and stopped the commotion, grabbing Walker's wheelchair as Red, Millie, and Mary scurried to the elevator.

Walker was worn out and slept during the ride home. Mom stared out the window, catatonic. I drove on McKnight Road, past the new Ross Park Mall.

I recalled my seventeenth year, as I passed Pizza Roma on Perry Highway. I remembered having pizza with Angel during our three weeks together. I felt the loss of her and the pending loss of my father swirling together. I remembered talking about heaven with Angel as we held hands and walked through the apple orchard in the summer.

"It won't be heaven unless I'm with you, baby," she said.

I tried to imagine what heaven was like. *Maybe the moments of life that are timeless are previews of heaven. The kiss with Angel is a foretaste of an endless ecstasy, the beauty of being with her multiplied beyond imagination, in a place without death or disease.*

I exited back to West View. Dad's death disturbed my theological assumptions. I struggled with Mordecai and Millie's interpretation of scripture that sends all non-evangelicals to hell forever. It was too cruel. It wasn't something a loving God would do. Something inside me, something decent and humane, shone through the cracks of Mordecai's indoctrination and let me know my father would be okay.

I thought of this as I turned on Oakwood. I arrived home and my legs ached.

"You can sleep downstairs, dear," Mom said. "I fixed it up real cute."

When the call came the following evening from Veteran's that Dad was on the way out, I was in the living room. I read a few scriptures from the bible Mordecai gave me, and set the Good Book on the dining room table. I stared at the Christmas tree, watching the red and green lights flash off and on. I remembered my eighth Christmas when Dad restored my faith in Santa, and my unbounded joy when I saw the Disney characters and purple Schwinn under the tree.

I walked to the tree to adjust a drooping strand of silver tinsel and noticed *Mary Poppins* was on TV. Christmas week the cable channels showed the family classics. Bert the chimney sweep escorted Jane and Michael Banks into chalk drawings. He wore the red-striped ice cream jacket with white pants. I was lost in the show, realizing I preferred pretend to reality. Everything turned out happily ever after. The father realized the error of his materialism and incarceration to his job at the bank. The family skipped off together to fly a kite in the wind.

I wished for a happy ending for my family I knew didn't come. But Mary Poppins redeemed the father. Mr. Banks found grace at the end.

Mom raised her voice. "Jeremiah, turn that TV off. Your father's dying, we need to go to the hospital."

I started singing with the movie. "Chim chiminy chim chiminy, chim chim cheroo…"

"Jeremiah, what are you waiting for?"

"Blow me a kiss, and that's lucky too…"

"Don't be a bad boy and ignore your mother. Jeremiah, do something!" I looked at her and wondered how the young girl I worshipped as a boy was now suddenly old.

I wore one of Dad's baseball caps perched crooked on my head. I drove to the hospital in the rain with Mom and Walker in his Econoline van that was equipped with a lift for his wheelchair. I put the hood up on my jacket so my hair wouldn't get wet. The van's wiper came off on Moreland Street, increasing my visibility issues and frustrating Walker, who gave me a lecture about servicing the van. I thought about how we put off vehicle maintenance and other necessities because we both followed in Dad's footsteps, living the feast or famine life of an artist and musician.

*Like Bert the chimney sweep, I does what I likes and I likes what I do*, I thought. *Chim chiminy, chim chim cheroo*

"I can barely see," I said. The rain pounded harder on the window. "I'm going back to Moreland Street to get the wiper and put it back on."

"It's no good now. I'm sure it's been ran over by all the other cars," Walker said.

"But I can't see out the window!"

"Just drive slow, bro."

"Thanks, Troubadour. Good advice. The blind leading the blind."

"Take it slow," Mom said. "Both hands on the wheel. And don't tailgate."

The hospital walls were liver-colored. There were no windows in the ICU. The air-conditioning was turned on high, blowing cold air that made me quiver. We gathered around Dad's bed and watched him take his final breaths. His eyes were glazed. On my left was Walker's wounded face, still reeling from his girlfriend Doreen's departure a few days before. Walker told me the story.

She'd dressed him every morning, changing his catheter, lifting him into his wheelchair. Doreen woke extra early weekday mornings to shampoo his hair and brush his teeth before she'd get herself ready and head to her job at a book bindery. She'd done this consistently for over a year, but the last six months she'd quit caring for Walker. "I'm tired," she'd said. "Who takes care of me?"

Just when I was feeling a sliver of mercy for Doreen, Walker interrupted my thoughts. "She ignored me, bro, and let me lay in bed all day."

When Walker spoke of his ex, the pain in his eyes was immense. She moved her new lover into their house in Millvale when Walker was in the Harmarville rehab recovering from bedsores. Walker had to move back in with Mom. He'd planned to murder them both, but his drummer called while he was lying in wait with a forty-five hidden under a towel. He probably would've been unable to fire the gun. The ringing phone stopped him from a crime of passion.

Walker looked lost. "This feels like a double whammy," he said. "Dad's dying, and I catch Doreen cheating."

"I always told you that Doreen was no good," Mom said. "You boys never listen to me."

"There's no time for that now," I said.

Mom whispered over and over, saying something about "the light." I couldn't quite make out what she was chanting.

Walker flipped his rock and roll hair. "I don't want to see him like this," he said. "This is bullshit. Sitting here, waiting for him to die."

"We can't let him die alone," I said.

"The numbers in the family are shrinking by death and Walker's breakup," Mom said, frowning.

"Doreen's fucked up," Walker said.

"She was," I said. "Fucked up people from fucked up families tend to gravitate like a magnet towards fucked up people from fucked up families…"

Mom looked at me with her bird eyes. "Watch your language, honey," she said. "And our family's not fucked up."

"…so no one has a clue how a healthy family functions," I said. "Everyone does the best they can, but we're in a dance contest where no one has any legs. Everyone's paralyzed like you, Walker. And she probably had a sick need to rescue and take care of a man."

"Thith, thith, thith, thith," Walker said.

"Don't start that nonsense at a time like this, dear," Mom said.

"Thith, thith, thith, thith, thith."

"Stop that meaningless gibberish, dear."

"It's not meaningless. You just don't know what it means."

"Oh? What does it mean?"

"You really want to know?"

"After all these years, I want to know. I really want to know."

"T-H-I-T-H. Trapped Here In the Headlights. I'm like a deer, trapped here in the headlights." Walker wheeled out of the room into the hall. "I can't watch this anymore."

Dad had a look of goodbye in his face. Like a laser, he found me with his gaze. "God refuses to forgive me. He's going to damn me to hell," he said. He got out two last words, "Pray, Jeremiah." He was about to burst through the cocoon of his mortal body.

*He's looking right up into the ass of death.*

I'd watched old movies that week on TV. I recalled the final scene of *A Place in the Sun*, where Montgomery Clift was the dead man walking. After the final kiss from Elizabeth Taylor, a priest quoted a medley of scriptures to give him courage. I recalled the verses and moved my face within inches of Dad's, standing over him by the bed. I grabbed hold of his fierce brown eyes that held sway over me all my years and now seemed so helpless. I quoted the scriptures, the ones that were in the movie because they comforted the dying for so many years.

"Though I walk through the valley of the shadow of death, I will fear no evil, for thou art with me…I am the resurrection and the life, he who believes in Me, though he were dead, yet shall he live… In My Father's house are many mansions, if it were not so, I would have told you, I go and prepare a place for you…" Dad's fear lifted and peace returned to his face. "You're going from here to eternity, Dad."

He gave me a long look, with kindness. "You were a good kid, all the way through." He smiled. "I'll always be with you," he said. My eyes clouded over.

I glanced at the vital signs monitor. We prayed the Lord's Prayer again in unison. "Our Father, who art in heaven, hallowed be Thy Name…"

Dad's lips moved, praying the words, than his mouth was wide open, struggling to breathe. His face, once animated all those years, was ghostly pale.

Then Mom repeated her mantra louder and I understood it now. "Go to the light, Saul. Go to the light…"

She'd read New Age books about people who claimed to have clinically died and came back. They all described going to a white light. Walker wheeled back in the room and heard the incantation of "Go to the light, go to the light..." and burst out laughing.

"What's so funny?" Mom said. "People that die have to go to the light or they get stranded. I don't want his ghost floating around and bothering us at the house."

"He's either going to the light or he isn't," Walker said. "If there even is any light, which I doubt. Your saying it doesn't effect where he goes."

"Leave her be, Walker," I said. "It's okay, Mom. God takes him to the light. He doesn't need your help anymore. You can rest."

Mom wasn't deterred, in fact, she chanted louder. "GO TOWARDS THE LIGHT, SAUL...GO TOWARDS THE LIGHT..."

I recalled how Mordecai once told me that near death experiences were a deception. "The Bible warns Satan appears as an angel of light," he'd said. "I have to question it. Why do so many people who aren't saved claim they were welcomed by white light? The light at the end of the tunnel is the blistering flames of Hell, not the divine glow of Heaven."

I always had the right words when a crying friend lost a loved one. I held them in my arms, becoming a father to people twice my age. But none of this prepared me for losing my own Dad.

I imagined his ghost floating off to the sky like the kite we flew together at the Cub Scouts picnic when I was eight years-old. Dad was put on lithium and thorazine that year in 1971, and he seemed momentarily stabilized by the medication. He was full of pain-killers now.

Suddenly, a vacuum filled the room. He drew one last breath. I stared at my father's shell.

He was gone like a puff of smoke.

Dad died.

I whispered, "I love you, Dad."

I pictured a shaft of light filling the room and taking his spirit. I saw myself as a small boy again, holding his hand, traveling in the light with him, up, up, up through the ceiling.

Everyone else was strong. Stone-faced. I glanced again through my wet eyes at Dad's dead fish eyes staring up at the ceiling.

I left the death room and walked down the corridor. Sobs flew out of my throat.

A black cloud dropped over my head. Walker followed and wheeled closer. "I have something I want to tell you. I know I've always been uncomfortable with feelings. But I just want you to know, Jeremiah, I really love you, bro."

I bent down and hugged Walker.

"I love you, too." The day Dad died ended with the most vocal and visible expression of love between my baby brother and me I'd ever experienced.

Mom rushed down the corridor and caught up with us.

"I helped him get to the light," she said.

"Sure Mom," I said, putting my arm around her.

# 26

I arranged the viewing at Thomas funeral parlor on Route 19. I hung balloons from the ceiling of the mortuary and a blown-up picture of Dad playing his Ramirez. I looked at his corpse and placed a pick in his hand.

Musicians who played with Dad through the years showed up. Harry "the Highhat" Parisi hobbled with a walker. My last boyhood memory of him was when Dad's band, *The Starlites*, played West View Park Danceland the night before a fire burned it to the ground. It was the year after I danced there with Angel. All the girls were in love with Harry the Hat in those days.

Before Dad's casket was transported to the church, custom dictated the immediate family said goodbye first. Mom wanted to walk to the casket with me. When I saw Dad for the last time, my legs turned to rubber.

"Jeremiah's having another breakdown," I overheard one of my Mafioso uncles say as he watched us walk.

"Be strong, like Queen Elizabeth," Mom said, clinging to my arm. "Look at all she's been through. She never cries. Be like steel."

"Queen Elizabeth may be your hero, but she's not mine. I'd rather be like Lady Diana," I said. "And besides, steel is hard and cold."

The procession led from Thomas Funeral Home to Saint Joseph's, escorted by the West View police. I thought it ironic that they were the same cops who knew Dad's long rap sheet from all the times they 302ed him. They blocked traffic so our family could drive down Route 19, following the hearse from Wexford to West View. The familiar route jarred my memory of riding to church for the first time, how I didn't wear a seat belt and distracted Mom with my movement.

The bells of Saint Joseph's tolled seven times as we entered the sanctuary. Most of the convent next door was torn down and rebuilt as a boarding house because of the declining number of nuns. The grey church building looked the same, but worn from wear since Spiritos built it for Father McCormick in the early sixties. The purple roof was in need of repair and the paint was chipped around the light fixtures inside.

I looked up the high ceiling of Saint Joseph's. The sanctuary seemed smaller than I remembered, but still awe inspiring. I was glad to see the mural behind the altar of Jesus and His disciples was still there, all these years later. Jesus was in the center, conducting the Last Supper. I still admired how the artist rendered the shapes with simple lines. This pleased me aesthetically as it did when I was a boy. I sat in the pew, dark-suited and engulfed by the stillness. The ornate purple altar cradled the Eucharistic box in the center. God in a box.

I thought of the other dark box that frightened me. The old black chest in Mother's attic, covered with cobwebs. It was locked. I'd always preferred it that way. Something was inside. I knew it intuitively. The smell of rotted flesh had seeped through the black chest and floated through the attic, and down the stairs to my room. I'd heard the clanging of the rusted brass handles of the old black chest and wondered if Stick Man was moving them with his nasty little claws.

Father McCormick said the funeral Mass in his thin voice. "Remember Thy servant, Saul Young...Lamb of God, who takes away the sins of the world...through Him, with Him, in Him, in the unity of the Holy Spirit, all glory, honor and power is Yours forever... " His hair, what was left of it, was white. He was hunched over, almost a corpse like Dad.

I avoided looking at the crucifix but a very steady very strong wind blew the length of my pew. A hymnal crashed to the floor and startled, I looked up at the cross. The beams reached for me, forming Stick Man's arms. He clawed at me with his meat cleaver fingers.

*Now we are going to have a new noise*, I thought, listening to the inside of my mind. I heard a pounding, and then a swift movement up and down the aisle, a hungry jackal pacing back and forth with impatience. Then I heard Stick Man's babbling murmur which I remembered. Am I imagining that? I wondered, is that me? And then I heard his lunatic laughter mocking me.

I hid under the pew, hearing his cackling. *"Dead... dead... Daddy's dead..."* Stick Man laughed out the words.

Mom reached over and shook me. I huddled down near the kneeler and then realized no one else saw Stick Man and I was disrupting the funeral.

I sat back up on the bench and shook off the shadowy presence of Stick Man. When I looked back up at the crucifix Stick Man was thankfully gone.

After Father McCormick's feeble homily, I walked to the altar to say a few words.

"Are you all right, Jeremiah?" Father McCormick asked. "Are you sure you can do this?"

I nodded, made the sign of the cross, and quoted scripture from the lectern. "When we are absent from the body, we are present with the Lord. Being back here at Saint Joseph's, brings back memories of attending school here."

I told the story about Dad convincing me I could still believe in Santa based on the belief in immortality of the soul, then I sang a song I wrote to honor him.  The chords were simple, D, G, and A. I played finger-style on my Washburn and sang:

*"One last thing to say/Papa listen yet/Your hands our my hands/Playing on the fret/Your song is in my soul/Your music in my heart/As long as I have my guitar/We're never far apart."*

I stood my guitar back in the stand and took my seat.  I thought about how Dad died long before he was laid to rest.  He chose the safety of the shore rather than the life of the sea.  His fear of the sharks forced him into dullness, imperceptibility, and boredom, The polar opposite of life.

Father McCormick resumed the Mass, blessing the Host and transubstantiating the wine to blood, submerged in ritual.  "For this is My body," he said.

*Is that really Christ's body?   What if it's just bread?*

"Lord, I'm not worthy to receive you," I said.  "Only say the word and I shall be healed."

I joined the Eucharistic procession and when I made it to the front I closed my eyes and let Father place the Host on my tongue.  I made the sign of the cross and walked back to my pew, swallowing the bread like lost idealism.  The Eucharist stuck in my throat, dry and parched from repressed sobs.

When the funeral ended, I walked down the cement steps hand in hand with Mom as I did years before as a boy.

Dad was sent off with a second funeral, a military memorial by the Navy.  He'd served his country at great personal cost, his own sanity.  He was never right since the war.

The sky fell as the naval officers carried the flag-draped coffin and lowered it into the ground.  They gave Mom the flag "on behalf of the President of the United States" and played taps. I looked at the flowers one last time before walking away with the wind hitting my face.

Dad's gravestone blended in the crowded cemetery with rows and rows of identical government-issued markers, flanked by daffodils and crying for breath. I looked at the marble tombstone, reading the words to myself:

Saul M. Young
AT3 US Navy Korea
Dec. 15, 1932
Dec. 27, 1983
Music Man

*Music Man. I'm glad Mom added that as I suggested.*

I watched them lower him into the dark hole, his entrance into the world with no windows. Mom touched my shoulder. "He's at peace now, honey," she said.

*Please let it be so, God.*

Relatives spoke briefly to me, assuring prayers and offering sympathies. My Aunt Rita braced her hefty frame against me. "He's in a better place," she said.

*I hope he's in a better place. I hope it's not all mythology to comfort our fears and sadness.*

I wiped the wetness from my eyes and choked on my sobs and bittersweet memories. I looked at the Sacred Heart of Jesus on the Mass card and tucked it in my wallet.

Walker and I performed a tribute concert that night for Dad at The Verity Room, a new space showcasing artists in Pittsburgh's Strip district. We spoke of him in glowing terms, calling him

"Music Man" and the "Leader of the Band" and pretended our grief over Dad was new, rather than lifelong.

After the gig, Mom set out food but I had no appetite. Walker and I opened a bottle of Chivas Regal and drank from coffee mugs. He tried his best to make me laugh. I packed my suitcase to return to North Hollywood and went to bed.

I slept.

I dreamt about Dad and death in the chilling particular, thinking again and again of his body beneath the sod…Darkness…Nothing moving except the worms…I wept.,, *I will die just like my Dad, I won t be, I WON'T BE, God, how sad, forever and ever, oh please no Dad, don't let me die, don't let me be nothing forever and ever, decomposing disintegrating and melting and Death will eat me like Stick Man* banging and clanging, the banging-

The attic! The dark chest in the attic!

*****

I awakened in tears and sprang up in bed with my heart pounding and no air in my stomach.

"Come upstairs, dear," the voice called.

The attic! The dark chest in the attic!

*Must we open that up?*

"Come upstairs dear," Mom called. Hours before I left, she was busy organizing Dad's belongings when I entered her bedroom. "Close the door behind you. I don't want your brother to overhear."

I shut the door.

"I want to give you some of your father's stuff." She walked to the closet and pulled out his Ramirez guitar. It glistened in the light. "It's worth a lot of money. Made in Spain. I think he'd want you to have it. You're the only who can play the music he loved, all those old songs. The good songs."

I held the guitar and played *Romance De Amore* in E minor. "Wow. Thanks," I said.

"Music was his escape. It brought him joy, until he was traumatized in the Korean War and nothing could ever bring him joy again. Come follow me," she said, leading me up the stairs to the attic. The air was bracing. She struggled, holding on to the sides of the wall. I pushed the cobwebs out of my eyes and peered into the darkness, readying myself for Stick Man's gleaming red eyes.

There it was at the top of the stairs. The dark box that frightened me as a child. The old black chest was in the same spot in the attic, still covered with cobwebs and dust. I hesitated in the doorway of the attic, glancing around quickly before following her. I told myself that I wasn't a frightened boy anymore, I was a man.

When I came inside, Mom grabbed a blue rag from the floor and examined the dark box like a fruit inspector. The rag was soiled with dark stains. She spit on the rag and polished the rusted brass handles of the dark box, than unlocked it with a skeleton key she kept in the pocket of her flannel robe.

"I can't look in there," I said, surprising myself. I backed away, overcome by the cold air of dead earth and mold that rushed at me. "Father-" I said, not knowing what I wanted to say. I pressed myself against a chair and shut my eyes.

"The smell is awful," I said.

"What's it smell like?" Mom said.

"Blood. It smells like blood."

"Don't be silly, dear."

She unpacked the box slowly. A deceptive scent of cedar rushed out like a waterfall, covering the scent of blood and calming my nerves. The aroma filled the air with memories of Christmas trees and driving through the snow with Dad. I remembered his story about Santa being a symbol for something real and transcendent, and I wondered if the same was true of Stick Man.

"His personal treasures. I'm giving its contents to you. Reach in, take them out, dear."

I removed items one at a time as she described them. The first thing I saw was a picture of Chuck Corsello, yellowed and frayed around the edges. "Your father loved him. He never got over him. He looks like James Dean, don't you think?"

"Yeah."

I pulled out a second photo of Dad with his trio, the Starlites. Dad was in the middle, playing full harmony lead on the twelfth fret of his blonde Gibson L5. Spiritos was on his left, playing a bar chord on the sixth fret of his white Gibson SG, and Harry the Highhat Parisi was playing the drums, a silver Ludwig set. They wore matching blue blazers, black pants, and white sweater vests, over white dress shirts and dark blue ties.

"I like this photo. They sure were good in those days," I said.

"Oh yes, he played so well. I gave up my career to support him. I could've been a concert pianist, but I sacrificed my dream for your father and you boys."

Next, I pulled out the letter I wrote my Dad. "He read that constantly, probably thirty times a day," Mom said. "Only time I saw him cry, except for when his own father died. Go ahead, read it."

"I'd rather not. It's personal."

"Read your dear mother a few lines. You always were a good writer, honey."

I exhaled unevenly, then read:

*Dear Dad,*

*Growing up, I always wished you would tell me you loved me. I wanted you to hold me. I wanted you to approve of me. My guitar playing was never as good as you. My efforts were ridiculed. I needed your love then and I need it now. In the time that's left, I want to forget how you hurt me in the past, and I want you to forgive me for any way I've hurt you and I want to love each other for the time that's left. We have some really good childhood memories together, before things got bad. Now that I'm a man, and living in California, I need you to support me and believe in me and not criticize me. We don't know how much time we have left on this earth and in the time that is left, I want to be able to say we love each other and we support each other. All the past with your manic depression, I forgive it and I ask your forgiveness for the times I tore you apart. Whatever love we have, let's give it now, before it's too late.*

"That was nice, dear."

I reached into the box, and pulled out a piece of sheet music. I smiled. "*Somewhere Over the Rainbow.* This was the arrangement Dad wrote up for me when I was seven years-old for that talent competition."

"Your father was furious you lost. He woke everybody all night, making collect calls from the mental hospital. 'It was rigged, it was rigged, I'm going to have Spiritos put a hit on the judges,' he kept saying over and over. I guess that's how he showed he believed in your talent. He loved being a big-shot, playing the role of the Mafia musician.   It wasn't rigged.   You lost.   You came in second."

I decided in that moment to go against the grain.   The long established protocol in my family, to not confront Mom for fear of hurting her.   "I wish you could've said, 'I'm proud of you.   That's the best you've ever done.'"

"You're too sensitive, dear.   There's more."

I opened a small box encased in light blue wrapping paper.   Inside the box was a note: *For my first born son, Jeremiah.   The secret of what life is all about.   Read and remember.   Love, Dad*

I peeled off the remaining wrapping and saw it was his first issue copy of Hemingway's *The Old Man and the Sea.*   I caressed the blue cloth and dust wrapper.

"He saved it for you, dear.   He wanted you to have it.   He always refused to sell that book.   'Chuck Corsello gave it to me, and I'm giving it to Jeremiah,' he'd say."

Half-dazed, I reached my hand again into the old black chest.   I didn't know what to expect.   My heart pounded, sensing a monster, a dark and dangerous creature.

"Stop," Mom said.   "Don't look."

I looked into the black chest and couldn't believe what I saw.

# 27

Mother clutched the handle tight, but I forced the dark box out of her fingers. With trembling hands I opened the lid and felt inside, my fingers closing around something solid with three holes. Two of the holes were parallel. The third hole was beneath the other two and attached by hinges.

"LET GO," Mom said. "GIVE IT BACK."

"NO!"

My fingers found the openings, and slid into the sweaty holes. I lifted the object out of the box.

I pulled out the wooden mask of Stick Man.

I dropped the face at first. I remembered his canine teeth jutting out from the mask. I picked it up slowly and gazed face-to-face into the visage of my nightmares. I looked in Mom's eyes, but only for a second. I turned and looked out the window. My head was spinning. I tried to make sense of it all.

"Wha, what wa..." I struggled to speak but could only stammer at first. I shook my head side to side in disbelief.

"Please, don't be mad, Jeremiah."

"Mother," I said, shaking my head. "Stick Man." I fixed my gaze on her. She stared at the ground, trying to hide her shame, tightening her mouth in stubborn defiance.

"Please, Jeremiah."

"Mother," I said, still shaking my head *No, No, No.* She slumped back in her seat and cocked her head back. "Oh, Mom." I chided her again with another headshake. I picked a piece of dirt off the mask and flicked it to the floor. "Wow," I said, rubbing my lips as the truth sank in.

"Jeremiah, I..." It was her time to stammer. "You see, dear, I..." My collar felt tight. I loosened it to make sure I could breathe. We sat in stunned silence for a long time, speaking now and then in half-phrases trying to tell one another something primal and ineffable, between pauses, held back emotions, partial answers and breakdowns.

She looked at me with maternal love, with the softness she once had. "You were such a beautiful boy." I looked away, first to the right, than hurriedly to the left. I exhaled. "Oh, you wouldn't want to keep that old thing, dear."

"SHUT UP."

"DON'T YOU TELL YOUR MOTHER TO SHUT UP."

"Don't you try and hide-"

"I won't have you speak to me like that, you don't..." her voice trailed off and she started sobbing.

I laughed. There wasn't anything funny. But I laughed. I didn't know what else to do. The mask seemed so small. It was inanimate and much less frightening now. I needed answers and I hoped she'd stop whimpering and come clean. After blowing her nose and wiping her eyes, she stared at me.

"Listen to me. I don't know why your father kept it," she said. "It was a souvenir from overseas. He kept it, and-"

I sighed. "There's more to this,"

"...to remember his navy days."

"...a lot more." I stared her down, looking her right in the eyes until she came out with it.

"There's something I never told you about, dear. When your father was in the Korean War, he fought alongside Chuck

Corsello.   They were best of friends since they were little boys.   In the heat of combat, your father went out to sea with Chuck and the rest of his crew on a minesweeper ship.   Their mission was to fire shells at enemy targets on shore, to help our troops land.   A storm hit, and they prayed together for protection.   After they said 'Amen,' shots rang out.   That's when Chuck's face was blown off by enemy fire.   His remains were all over your father, dear.   The bombs thrust your father back on his right side and destroyed the hearing in his right ear.   The boat was split in two.   He went kind of crazy, dear."

*So that's it.   That's why he lost it.   Why didn't anyone ever tell me?*

I remembered ten years earlier seeing the hint of a feeling in Father's face when he looked at the photograph of Chuck Corsello on his nightstand.

"The Navy put him in a psychiatric hospital in a strait jacket and that wooden mask.   They experimented with several electroshock treatments.   Your father was the guinea pig.   The doctors didn't like to see his face when they gave him the shock treatments, his eyes bugged out and he grimaced in pain, so they made him wear that hideous Korean mask."

"Where did it come from?"

"It came from the Communist torture chambers in North Korea.   It was believed to have special powers to call forth the spirits of the dead.   It was used in shamanistic ceremonies.   This mask was the most horrifying and grotesque of all the masks of the dead.   It was used for its ability to evoke terror in ceremonial rites."

I knew this was a trick of hers.   She used it whenever the horrors of our house were exposed in any way.   She became detached, matter-of-fact, and clinical, describing something in a pedantic lecture instead of facing the emotions in the room.   I looked away from her and tuned her out.   My collar felt tighter.   It was choking me, just like when I was little and she always had to fasten that damn top button.   I loosened my shirt and wiggled my neck.   I distracted myself by playing with the hinges that made the mouth on the mask move, but I caught the tail end of her history lesson.

"...the mask was called the 'Hahoetal,' it was the mask considered the most fierce."

I held it up to my face and looked through the eyes.   I felt numb with the combination of my boyhood fear from the first time I saw the mask, coupled with the reality of the lifeless mask before me. "I can't believe it.   This is what scared me all those-"

"He scared me too.   The first time I saw it was after we were married a few months.   Your father had a nightmare.   I woke up to him wearing that hideous thing and swinging at me like I was the enemy.   He was screaming about the movements of the Communist artillery and something about Seoul, Korea.   He kept saying 'Seoul, Seoul, Seoul.'"

*So that was it.   He mumbled 'Seoul, not soul.'*

I wanted to erase all the volcanic videos in my mind, the electrically charged childhood I'd repressed, but I felt trapped in a pattern of not challenging her version of reality.   She looked at me for a moment, anticipating my response but it was all too much for me to put into words.   I wondered if she could read my shocked expression.   My face felt frozen like ice.   Mom cleared her throat and continued.

"Saul was dangerous to himself and everyone else for a while.   Everything good was shattered with Chuck Corsello's death. His hearing.   His back.   His heart.   They finally discharged him from the service and ever since, they pay for everything.   He got a monthly pension. They even paid for his funeral. They sure take care of the veterans, dear."

I had deified Mom as the innocent victim. I thought she was unaware of the full extent of Stick Man's campaign to destroy me. For years, I saw her as a mother lion, protecting me as her little lion cub. My first reaction upon awakening to the realization she allowed Saul to torment me was a profound disappointment settling in on me like a chilly Pennsylvania snow. She knew more than she'd ever let on. I felt an explosion shoot up my chest like a rocket.

"You knew."

"I knew what, dear?"

"You knew Stick Man was real all along and you never told me."

She nodded, looking relieved to unburden her secret complicity. "Yes, I knew. Sometimes I wore the mask, but mostly your father did. I went along with everything, like the Tammy Wynette song, '*Stand By Your Man.*' That's the way it was for women in the sixties. We didn't talk openly about violence in the home. I didn't like putting you and Walker through it. Your father had two personalities, the charming storyteller, the master musician. Then there was the other side. What could I do, dear?"

"You could've at least-"

"When he'd remember the horrors of war, the torture they put him through, he'd put on the mask and go crazy. Hissing, yelling about Seoul, scaring the hell out of everybody. And that damn thing stunk like the smell of a thousand corpses. Well, that's past. He can't get you anymore, dear. He's dead."

"All those years," I said, staring down at the carpet.

"I realize now, we beat you too much.   That's the way it was back then.   It was wrong and I'm sorry.   You were a hard kid to raise.   You were a bad boy."

"Don't say that."

"Always running away."

"Yeah, I ran away.   I wonder why?   Maybe because I was scared."

"We had to use fear to keep you in line, dear, the way my mother did with me.   She beat me with a belt."

"You knew the whole time what he was doing to me."

"He did it to me too, dear."

"And enough with the dears.   Your dears sounds like daggers.   You're dearing me to death.   It wasn't just him.   It was you, Mother."   She looked down to the stained rug and turned her head from me to hide her anguished face.   I looked at her steadily. "You kept me as a punching bag all those years.   You were my mother," I said, my finger grazing her shoulder.   "You should've protected me a little bit.   You should've taken care of me so I didn't have to be hit like that."

"I kept you from a lot.   There's a lot you don't know-"

"YOU DON'T UNDERSTAND."   I waved my arms in frustration.   "I could've grown up and been someone without all this stuff in my head, without this circus of thoughts tormenting-"   I stopped, starting to sob and not wanting her to see me cry.   She avoided my eyes.   I sensed she was remembering it all, in painful detail, just like I was.   "It wasn't just Dad.   It was you, Mom."

She looked at me now in disbelief.   I averted her eyes.   We both knew I'd broken the unwritten rule of silence.   The truth was finally spoken out loud after twenty years.

"Okay, okay," she said calmly. Suddenly, she had a final burst of defiant defensiveness. She raised her voice. "What was I supposed to do? Be out on the street?" Her pitch grew higher, straining towards a high B. "A single mother with two little boys? Where could I go? I couldn't make it without him. It was different back then for women."

"I know that, but-"

"But that's all gone. I'm sorry, honey. What about Jesus forgiving your father and me?"

*Dammit anyway.*

An awkward silence stretched out and suspended the passing seconds. I wasn't ready to forgive. I knew I eventually would, I had to, but I didn't want to cheapen the pardon by glibly dismissing something so horrific. I wanted to break down and cry completely but I couldn't. Then I wanted to scream at the top of my lungs, but it was like one of my Stick Man nightmares where I'd lost my voice. An invisible umbilical cord broke between Mother and me with the realization she was part and parcel with the crazy swamp I grew up in.

She snatched the wooden mask from my hand. For a half-second, I saw rusty nails growing out of her fingers. "It's high time we throw this out with the trash, dear."

"I want to keep it," I said, grabbing the mask.

"Why, what on earth for, dear?"

"I want to keep it."

"That's your whole problem. You can't let things go, dear."

"I can't let go until I face the truth and know what I'm letting go of. When I was a little boy, I was never allowed to be angry or tell anyone. We all were walking on thin ice, afraid of setting Dad off. I looked up to both of you to protect me." I gripped the Stick Man mask in my hands.

"When you and Walker were little boys, every mother and father on our street gave their children spankings," she said, her voice quivering. "That was our generation."

"He not only beat me to the ground physically, he beat me down mentally. He made me believe I was a failure, because he perceived himself to be a failure." I paused a moment, trying to repress my sobs. "And all his talk about *The Old Man and the Sea* made me feel that if I ever by some miracle did succeed, it would never last. The prizes I attained, I could never maintain. But as many times as he read this book, he got Hemingway all wrong."

"Over one hundred times, dear. He read it over one hundred times."

"But he missed the point. Can't you see? The point of *The Old Man and the Sea* isn't that Santiago lost the great fish, it's his courage under pressure to venture out and land the fish. I refuse to be a zombie like him. I'm not gonna sit on the shore and watch the water pass by the way he did. I'm not gonna waste my life. I'm not going through my days asleep. I'm gonna grow and learn and I may stumble and bumble, but hopefully, I'll take some of the knowledge I gain with me wherever I go beyond this world. But even if the shark devours me and takes everything away, I choose to live."

She stared at me. Her guilt was palpable, like a weighty black cloud hovering between us. "I'm sorry," Mom said. "But I wish you could see, I did my best. I never meant any harm. I was dealt a bad hand, and I played it as best I could."

"That's not the point."

I stood away from the black chest. My hands were cold and I wanted to cry. I turned my back to the door of the attic. "I don't want to come back to this attic again," I said, trying to speak softly. "Not with that smell, the smell of death up here."

"I hadn't noticed a smell," Mom said. I was afraid she would break, shattering into tiny crystal pieces.

She dragged herself downstairs, pulled the covers of her bed around her and curled into the fetal position. I followed her and tucked her in. "I'll be right back, Mom."

She removed her rosary from her nightstand and prayed. "Hail Mary, full of grace, the Lord is with thee…"

I went to my bedroom and added the mask to my collection of items I packed for California. I determined to follow my heart like Santiago. My thoughts drifted to Angel.

*I'm gonna wake up and see Angel again. I'll look for that woman, by God, and even if I lose her again, I'm going anyway.*

After I finished packing, I walked to the kitchen, mouthing the prayer. "Blessed art thou amongst women," as I sliced apples and prepared eggnog for Mom. I looked out the kitchen window to the giant pine tree where my fort had been as a kid, my secret cave where I hid from Dad's manic explosions. Away from Mom's sight, I finally released my pain for a moment, saturating my cheeks with a flood of salty tears. I wiped my eyes and walked down the hall with the snack on a tray. "And blessed is the fruit of thy womb, Jesus," I said, reaching her bedroom.

I heard the sounds of Liberace playing *Chopin's Opus 64*. She'd put her music on the turntable beside her bed and it made me think of her when she was younger, and still had life in her. I knew she was warped by fear and by years of a loveless marriage. Even in my anger, I couldn't help but look at her with pity, no matter what she did to me, or what she allowed Dad to do to me. There was a still a little boy inside that remembered. I finished praying the rosary with her.

"Everything's all right," I said. I saw the toll the years had taken on her face.

I walked down the rickety steps to the basement, not knowing where Stick Man was. I approached the green heater and heard the clock ticking. I heard noises in the heater and in the walls. "Twenty-one," I said to myself. "Twenty-one…"

Seconds passed.

*I have his mask in my hand,* I thought. *I'm safe.*

I conquered the basement than walked to the attic with the wooden mask in hand, waiting for him to manifest.

In my vigilance I realized something so obvious that I missed it all those years. My instincts as a child were correct. Stick Man was in the old black chest. In a flash of blinding insight, I added up and connected the dots of my life.

*Every time I listened to myself, I was successful, whether writing my own music, or trusting my own instincts.*

"By the way," Mom yelled, startling me. "There's a message for you by the phone, some woman in Mount Olympus who said she knew you."

Angel tracked me down. I dialed her number and realized I just might reach my goal before I turned twenty-one.

# 28

Ring.

Ring.

"Hello?"

"Angel?" I clutched the phone tighter.

"Is this who I think it is?" Her voice had the same melody, slightly huskier. I kicked the door closed.

"Is this the girl I fell in love with three and a half years ago?"

"That's a long time."

"Seems like yesterday. Thanks for remembering me."

"Are you kidding? How could I ever forget you?" she said. "I heard about your Dad. I just had to reach you."

"How did you find out?"

"Mrs. Rawlings told my mother and she told me. How are you?"

"Pretty well, considering. I can't believe I'm actually talking to you."

Mom was up again. She came in the room, bringing me a plate with chipped ham, applesauce, and Pittsburgh pretzels. I took the plate, nodded thank you, and escorted her out. "This phone call's private," I said.

"Excuse me," Mom said. "Who's the lucky woman?"

"Queen Elizabeth," I said, closing the door.

There was static on the line from the winter winds. "Is my voice different?" Angel asked, her voice wrapping around me like a warm coat.

"Even better than I remembered."

"Oh, stop." Angel caught me up, telling me the details of her life.

She talked about her husband. *I don't want to hear this*, I thought. "I left him once," she said. "I got an apartment by myself for a few months, and he found me, busted through the front door. I was listening to the tapes you made me back in 1980, singing the songs you wrote for me. Tiger destroyed the tapes and put me in the hospital. I'm heartsick that I don't have those tapes to listen to anymore but I can still close my eyes and hear you playing your guitar and singing. Those days are etched in my mind, more real than the present."

"Me too. I think about you every day," I said. I heard Mom stir upstairs in the kitchen.

"I was so upset when the tapes were gone. I knew then what you still meant to me. I couldn't deny it anymore and pretend to be happy. My marriage was a farce and a fake. But for some unknown reason, I believed Tiger's apologies and got back with him. Mother taught me marriage is forever and God hates divorce. Soon, I was pregnant with my daughter. Tiger made me have a procedure. And then-"

"Procedure?"

"An abortion."

After the word abortion, my mind disengaged in the space between her words. I was grateful in that moment we were talking on the phone and not in person because my face revealed the squeamishness I felt in my stomach. Images of dead fetuses from the placards of the March for Life flashed before my eyes.

"...she'd be a year-old now."

"I'm so sorry."

"I gave her a name. Sarah."

"That means 'princess' in Hebrew."

"I know."

"You've been through so much in the last few years, haven't you?"

"I sure have, Jeremiah. I've been to hell and back."

I played a tape in the background of Dad performing classical guitar. Mom returned with a glass of Iron City Beer in a chilled mug.

"That was your father's favorite glass," she said. "Be careful with it." She walked across the room and turned the music off.

"I was listening to that." I turned the tape back on.

"You shouldn't do that to yourself," Mother said, glaring at me as she left.

"Was that your mother?" Angel asked.

"How did you guess?"

"She seemed upset."

"I'm listening to Dad playing guitar. She thinks I'm torturing myself."

"It must be hard for her to see you in pain, but you have to deal with this in your own way. After the procedure, I made a memorial for her. My husband got very angry with me. He didn't want to deal with it and he thought I was making it harder on myself. We didn't grieve together, so our marriage suffered further. We almost parted for it." Somehow the years of not speaking were a mere interruption to me. We picked up right where we'd left off several years before. "I have to ask you something, Jeremiah."

"Sure. Anything." I pressed the phone tighter to my ear with expectation, to hear her better and shut out the noise from the TV upstairs. Mom was blasting Lucy reruns.

She paused for a second like she was getting up her courage. "Why didn't you stand up to Reverend Rawlings?   Why didn't you try for me in 1980?"

"You left me cold.   I wanted to go for a walk in the woods with you and you said, 'No.'"

"How could I after the meetings?"

"What meetings?"

"Rawlings called a conference with me and my mom, and told me you were too important with your music and preaching and I was a distraction.   He said you wanted me to stay away from you."

"What?"

"Mother was a director in his ministry, as you know, for McKean and Potter County and she felt Mordecai was God's man, and he knew best."

I cradled the phone between my shoulder and ear and absorbed the shock.

Reverend Rawlings, I learned, met with other leaders of BBC.   Angel remembered his words verbatim.   "He's writing anointed music on that guitar of his.   The ministry is growing." Then he told Angel and her mother, "He must focus on winning boys and girls to Jesus.   Eve, you'll be in big trouble if you ever talk to him again."   His threats were vague, and her imagination filled in the rest, she explained.   "Right before the winter retreat, he met with me and Mother again to make sure I didn't talk with you, or we'd all be in trouble."

"All these years, you thought I pushed you away and vice-versa," I said.

"Yes.   I cried to my friends.   Why isn't Jeremiah standing up?   Why isn't he coming back for me?"

"You mean to tell me I had a chance?"

"More than a chance.   I was waiting for you to come for me."

"If I knew I had a snowball's chance in hell, I would have begged you to marry me legally for good, right then and there.   I've tried to make sense of that moment ever since."

I remembered driving home from BBC camp with Rawlings, when I told him my heart was butchered into tiny pieces.

"I'm sorry," Rawlings had said, still humming that tune, "leaning, leaning, leaning on the everlasting arms."   I remembered how the wind beat me down that dark December day, how the white crystals clung to the car windows.

"I had complications, Jeremiah.   Reverend Rawlings came to the hospital once to visit me.   He didn't know about the abortion. To this day, no one does, not even my mother.   I asked him if you ever married.   He told me you didn't.   I asked him to say hello to you from me."

"He never did."

"I figured that."

I looked out the window to the traffic on Center Avenue, then across the street to Mordecai's house.

Mom made creaking sounds as she came down the steps again.   "Walker needs your help to get to bed," she said.

I walked into the hallway to yell back.   "In a minute."

We talked on the phone for another twenty minutes, reconstructing how Mordecai sabotaged our relationship.   Maybe if we were older and more sophisticated we could have done more to be together, but Mordecai used fear and fabrications to pull our strings like a master puppeteer.

After we hung up, I lifted Walker out of the wheelchair, undressed him, and put him to bed.

"I got a chill in my legs," Walker said.    I wondered how he could feel the chill.    I told him about the phone call.

"Why would Mordecai do that?" Walker said.    He asked me for a Vicodin.

"You don't need that, Walker."

"Give me a Vicodin, bro."    I acquiesced and decided I needed to numb my own pain too, so I sat in Mom's yard and drank Chardonnay.

I looked out at the mist of the lawn.    There were no cars on the street.    The air was humid and heavy.    I sipped my wine and concluded those who preach righteousness are often the most wicked.

After knocking off a bottle, I saw the bible with a red leather cover Mordecai gave me on the dining room table.    I carried it to the backyard.        Lightning bugs danced in the bushes.

I remembered Angel's face, staring at me that June night.    I thought of this as I tossed my bible among the twigs and sticks.

I recalled how she stroked my face and gave me a knowing laugh.    I doused the bible and sticks with lighter fluid.    I watched the moths swirling around Mom's porch light in figure-eights.    I piled Pittsburgh Press newspapers on the sticks.

I lit the news articles on the corners.    The wind blew them out, so I poured lighter fluid, and lit them a second time.    The flame hit the fluid and presto, the flame jumped and danced.    The cover of the bible curled when the flames turned it brown, than black.    The Old Testament was the first to go.    Leviticus evaporated in the heat and light.    Pages of the gospels turned when they burned.    The epistles of Paul were devoured in the blue hot fire.    The Apocalypse, John's revelation, burned the easiest.

I walked back into the house and checked on Mom. She was snoring with her mouth wide open, emitting piggish noises from deep in her throat.

I went to bed, but wasn't able to sleep. I remembered Devon's warning that Stick Man was waiting for me to feel secure so he could pounce with more power than ever before.

Thoughts of Angel and Mordecai leapt through my mind like scatterbrained rabbits. All night long, I rehearsed what I'd say to Mordecai, knowing what I planned to say never was what I actually said.

*****

The smell of morning coffee floated through the hallway and under my door. I heard the ringing clicks of Mom's spoon stirring milk into her first cup of coffee.

I slipped out of bed and dialed a few friends. I compared notes with three people from BBC, which confirmed Angel's story was accurate. After three cups of coffee, a bowl of Life cereal, and two strips of bacon, I walked over to the Rawlings house for an unannounced visit.

I crossed Oakwood Avenue, and thought of my boyhood, remembering when Dad went to Buddy's Bar to kill Sam the bass player. For years, I thought Dad was psychotic to want to murder another man. But I knew now I was his son and the same passion for blood boiled in my veins. I knew murdering Mordecai would be the most honest act of my life.

*A vampire can only be killed by a wooden stake.*

A stick.

I grabbed my Clemente baseball bat, and stepped into the gathering gloom of the street. I moved closer to the Rawlings house, knowing it held darkness within. The smug certainty of the house watched me quietly.   I felt a vague prickling at the base of my neck as I ascended the crooked driveway of Reverend Rawlings, and steeled myself.

There were long shadows on the lawn as I came up the sidewalk of the Rawlings house, blessedly hiding its sanctimonious face in the growing darkness.   Mordecai heard my unsteady knock and opened the door.

"What a surprise.   Come on in, Jeremiah," Mordecai said. "Sorry about your father."

"Thanks," I said.   He looked into my eyes, reducing me momentarily to an insecure adolescent.   I struggled to regain my equilibrium.

"Playing baseball?" he said, noticing the bat in my right hand. "Yeah."

"You and Walker were good hitters back in the day."

He stared at the bat.   The house felt chilly.

"How are you and Mrs. Rawlings doing?" I said, clutching the bat with my left hand and shaking his hand with my right, even though I didn't want to touch him.

"Good, good.   Sister Ruth's come down with a bit of a cold. She's resting in back.   We're taking one day at a time, trusting Him."   I followed him to the kitchen, and saw the same table where I first saw Angel.   "Say, would you like a glass of Cranberry juice?"

"No."

"It's good for you."

"No thank you," I said in a firmer voice.

"Suit yourself."   He poured himself a drink.   I sensed with this small refusal I had more power.

I saw a folksy plaque on the wall that hung in the same spot it always did.   I read the inscription:

*Only one life, twill soon be past*
*Only what's done, for Christ will last.*

I sat for a moment in the same brown chair I sat in when I looked across the table and stared into Angel's eyes, when I first took in how breathtaking she was. I remembered the shape of her and the touch of her silky skin, smooth like jazz. I could almost hear her voice aloud, rich like a minor seventh chord.

I stood, and walked over to the chair where she sat. I caressed the wood, closing my eyes. I looked up and saw Mordecai watching me. An awkward pause, then I started into it. "I have to bring something up that happened."

"What is it?"

"Eve Vickers called to express her sympathies and she told me something I was unaware of, and it upset me to just learn of this now."

"What?"

"Her and I, as you may recall, met and fell in love, the summer of my seventeenth year."

"Oh, yeah. I remember that all right."

"The next winter, at BBC camp, she was cold to me. You told her she was to stay away from me. Your exact words were 'you're here to be summer missionaries and not a summer romance.' And she asked me last night why I didn't defy your prohibition back then. And I thought, 'What're you talking about?' I was unaware of your meetings. She told me there were two of them."

"You know, Jeremiah, I can hardly remember that. Why are you bringing this up now?"

"No one had a right to do that. It was my life."

"There is a concept known as spiritual authority. The Bible clearly states, 'Obey those who have the rule over you, for they watch for your souls. Submit unto them as unto God.' Hebrews thirteen, verse seventeen. Like an umbrella that protects us from the rain as it were, the covering of pastoral leaders is the place of safety. You were a new believer, a babe in Christ. And a baby cannot determine what is good for him, he relies on his parents, as it were. I was your spiritual father. I took you in."

"I'm grateful for what you did for me when my Dad was sick, but you're not my father and had no right. I was desperate when I came to you. I went along with it all. I was young. I absorbed your judgments, that we were the remnant, the righteous, and the rest of the world was going straight to hell in a hand-basket. I was invisible unless I echoed you. But I exist. Apart from your doctrine, I am. I am that I am."

"You're going through a hard time," he said, putting his hand on my shoulder. "Normally, these blasphemous comments would upset me, but I know it's the grief talking. I love you and I'm here for you."

"Your love's conditional." I removed Mordecai's hand from my shoulder. "You care about me as long as I believe the way you do. You slandered me because I went to California." I sat to balance myself from a sudden dizziness.

"I told you why I opposed that. I've told you many times, creativity is God's domain. You want praise for yourself when all praise is due Him. Music and painting are expressions of your ego wanting to be the center of attention."

"What about your ego, Mordecai?" I asked, pointing my finger at his chest. "Your pride to perform in the pulpit, the high and mighty apostle. Your ego's draped in a cross, but it's the same as everyone else. You taught me to look at people, even little children, as objects to be used. Conversion statistics to report to the BBC board. Notches on our belts of salvation. Decision numbers to be transferred from the ledger of the lost to the column of the converted. You don't really care about some child's soul. You just want to feel important for saving them."

"Maybe I was a little driven in those days, for the sake of souls. I'm sorry you have the stress of Eve Vickers contacting you at a time like this. And I'm sorry if I don't sound understanding enough, Jeremiah," Mordecai said, his tone more indignant. "I'm trying here. But the Bible says 'forget those things which lie behind and press towards the mark of the high calling.'"

I stood and glanced out the window to the Rawlings woods where I first kissed her.

"You sabotaged us. How dare you play God? I needed to make that choice on my own. The bible you preach from says, 'Love never fails and many waters cannot quench love, neither can the floods drown it.' So you couldn't stop the love I feel for her."

"With the hormones of adolescence as it were, you and that girl were headed for nothing but trouble. I spared you that wretched path. I sent her away for your own good."

"You never did anything for my own good."

"That's a lie. Dating is not even scriptural, Jeremiah, it's an ungodly part of our American culture as it were. I challenge you to find the word *dating* in the scripture." Mordecai pointed to his black bible, openly displayed on his desk. "All the answers are right there."

"That book doesn't bring her back to me. You use it to justify whatever you want to do. I'm starting to do something that's really dangerous in your world."

"And what would that be?"

"I'm thinking for myself."

"Sounds like Satan to me. Remember how he questioned Eve in the Garden of Eden? Hath God said?"

"Can't you listen to me for once as a human being, instead of measuring every word I say for orthodoxy?"

"Your focus needed to be on Christ and on the call of God. God was sparing you from being unequally yoked with a woman that didn't have the same calling you have. That decision came out of Sister Ruth and me praying about what to do."

"No amount of prayer meetings will save you. Take that flannel graph board of yours and shove it up your ass sideways."

"It's obvious from the way that you are talking that you don't have the love of the Lord in you heart."

I was suffocating from his smugness, enveloped in the cloud of Savannah's secret.

"Where do you get off judging me? I know what you did to Savannah. You raped your own daughter."

Rawlings revealed the truth for a half-second in his face, and then the falseness returned. "Don't believe her slanderous stories, Jeremiah."

"She wouldn't make something up like that."

"Satan is the accuser of the brethren and I am going to insist you leave now. I won't listen to lies."

I no longer could restrain myself. I breathed out deeply and let Mordecai have it both barrels.

"Do you have any idea what you did? Or are you completely blind? Do you have any idea how you destroyed your own daughter because of your monstrous perversion? You represented not only her earthly father but her heavenly father in some strange mixture. You're not the great man of God, you're a pedophile." I tightened my grip on the bat, waiting for the right moment to swing and crush his head like a melon.

"Calm down, Jeremiah, I-"

"You're a child molester. Savannah may never, ever, regain her trust in life, in men, in goodness, or in God ever again. How ironic. You were the state director for a ministry that supposedly exists to save children, and you were a sexual predator on your own child. For once, I'm going to quote Jesus words to you. 'Woe unto you who harm one of these little children, for it would be better for you to have a millstone hung about your neck, and that you would be drowned in the depths of the sea.'"

Mordecai's lower lip quivered and his body trembled. He looked like he was about to faint. He steadied himself against the wall. I heard a pounding, throbbing sound in the walls, like a kettle drum beating. THUMP, THUMP, THUMP! The walls behind Mordecai bubbled and bulged in and out like they were breathing.

I raised my bat and raised it to my shoulders like Roberto Clemente, picturing red stitched seams across Mordecai's mouth. I was God's millstone of righteous judgment, about to hit his head over the right field wall.

Sister Ruth heard the commotion and emerged from the hallway. "Jeremiah, STOP!"

I knew if I didn't leave then and there, I'd split his skull like Clemente spraying a line drive.

Slam.

I heard the echo of the door behind me. I couldn't get out fast enough.

I walked around the back of the house to the yard. I looked out at the woods again and ventured forward.

There was a slight drizzle. I heard the cars on Center gliding on the wet road. Twigs cracked beneath my feet as I set out, searching for the log. I circled around the vicinity where I first sat with Angel. I heard a noise behind me and saw Sister Ruth and Mordecai approaching.

"I don't think you'll find it," Sister Ruth said.

"The deer cleared a lot of this out," Mordecai said. His tone was gentle and conciliatory again. They kept a bit of distance since I still had my baseball bat. I sensed they were nervous about me exploring their property.

"The grandkids built a tree-house back here," Sister Ruth said, crossing her arms around her chest for warmth. She coughed nervously. I realized finding a log three and a half years later was futile and I walked back with them.

"You're acting mighty strange tonight, Jeremiah," Sister Ruth said.

"Who wants to be a normie anyway?" I said.

I waved goodbye and headed home. I looked back for a final glance. The Rawlings house stared at me, and the dark sky shrouded its shame. *The house is vile.* I trembled and thought, the words coming freely into my mind. *The Rawlings house is vile, it is infested; get away from here at once.*

"Mordecai," I called across the street.

"What?"

"You owe me money."

"For what?"

"My paintings. The ones you destroyed, just like you destroyed Savannah. When I was a child, I thought as a child. I really wanted to believe. But I know the truth now. Red may act

like it's no big deal what you did to Savannah.    But it is, Mordecai.
It is.    I know who you are."

    I turned my back to him and walked away for good, knowing
I'd probably never see Mordecai again.

# 29

Mom drove me to the Pittsburgh airport in a used silver Buick she purchased from Dad's life insurance money. We snaked through West View's windy byways, visual reminders of my childhood. We made our way towards the terminal, driving down Ohio River Boulevard as she narrated Dad's war experiences in greater detail.

"It's such a relief to get this whole Stick Man thing out in the open," she said. "I can still hear him sometimes, the way he'd wake up kicking and flailing in the dark of night. 'Medea,' he'd say, 'Do you know what it's like to be in a war for three years and you're not allowed to unleash your power politically or militarily? It builds up and it builds up and I can only shove it down for so long before that monster comes up out of the manhole cover.'"

This made sense to me. A memory of Mom and me on the amusement park boardwalk resurfaced. "I remember an arcade game I played as a boy at West View Park," I said. "There were a bunch of holes, and a frog would pop out of one of the holes and I'd strike it down with a mallet. But the frog would pop out of another hole and before long no matter how good I was at smacking the frog down, it would always pop up somewhere else."

"You spent all the change in my purse smacking those slimy toads," she said, smiling fondly. "Your father never could keep the frogs inside him from jumping out like a biblical plague. He used to say, 'The war's over everywhere but in my head.'"

"I feel sorry for Dad."

"So do I sometimes. The way his shrink, Doctor Corrado, described it was that your father suffered Post Traumatic Stress Disorder. Certain things and places triggered his memories and it was like he was right back in the war."

"Did he get much counseling?" I asked.

"No, not really. He met with Corrado once a month, but that was only to get his drugs. Your father acted like everything was fine and put on a show for the doctor. Saul was a chamber of secrets."

Rain drizzled down our windshield. "Can you see, Mom? Do you need me to drive?"

"I'll be all right." She turned on the wipers and squinted. For a moment, the sun shone through and she remembered more of the war stories.

"What else did Dad tell you about Korea?"

"I remember him saying, 'The Asian summer of 1950 was a nightmare, Medea. We had the atom bomb,' he told me. 'But it didn't matter, Medea. It didn't matter,' he said. 'This peasant army, from an unknown nation, was slaughtering us left and right. The army ambushed us. The Communists from North Korea in their masks."

"Stick Man."

"Yeah, Stick Man. They thought their military might would snuff them out, but in a few weeks, Korea pushed them off the peninsula into the bloody sea. Their all-enveloping army was better equipped. Your father had no idea what was going on or where he was. They couldn't stop the North Korean steamroller. The Communists went around them, behind them, and through them.'"

I saw the Dairy Queen. "Pull in. The airport food is expensive. I'll eat at DQ."

She looked at me with surprise that I could eat as she described the fiery battle, but she knew me well enough to know DQ was a safe form of self-medication

"Be quick about it, Jeremiah." We went through the drive-through and I ordered a chili dog, onion rings, and a blizzard and sat in the car eating quickly in the parking lot.

"Want an onion ring, Mom?"

"Maybe one." She ate an onion ring and continued. "The Forgotten War. That's what they called it. But your father never forgot those three terrible years of bloodbath. And neither did Stick Man." She looked away from me to conceal her eyes. "Your father's personality split in two over there, right down the middle, like the 38th Parallel divided North and South Korea."

I finished the food and noticed the clock in the car. "We'd better move out." We veered into the traffic on Route 65 and headed toward the Pittsburgh Airport. "How did Dad and the rest of the Navy get involved in that big battle?

"The North Korean Communists marched into the South and captured Seoul. Thirty-four thousand men were killed, captured, or missing. So the U.N. met and voted unanimously to combine the navies of a bunch of countries. They went there with their battleships to capture control of the Yellow Sea and the Sea of Japan. He was dispatched with the seventh fleet. The Communists left Seoul to move south."

My heart raced when she talked, like I was there on the ship with Dad. "This was about the time Senator McCarthy was working everyone up about the Communists?"

"Yes, the way McCarthy described it, the Reds infiltrated us at every level of government and society. Your father and everyone with him in the war were our heroes at the time."

We crossed over the Sewickley Bridge and I remembered how Dad had panic attacks driving in Pittsburgh, the City of Bridges. He avoided the bridges at all costs, working out alternative routes whenever possible. I was connecting the dots, figuring out Dad's pathology. "What happened when the Communists left Seoul?"

"In the searing heat of July, they bombed the bridges, killing seven hundred troops." She shook her head. We drove by a strip of chain restaurants and airport parking lots. "Our government embroiled them in a hopeless cause. They battled in the perimeter for weeks, defending and fighting until the end in the U.N. apocalypse. 'They butchered us,' he said over and over." Mom made the left into the airport and eased into the lane for departing flights.

"There's something I never understood about him, Mom. Why was he so afraid to try and be more successful? Like when the name acts came to town and he could've played with Tom Jones, and Engelbert, and David Cassidy. He always had some lame-ass excuse to turn them down. Why did he stay in Pittsburgh? He was such a good guitarist."

"He gave up his dreams in Korea. Opportunities came up, and he'd always say, 'It ain't the same without Chuck Corsello.'"

"Why did he think he needed Corsello?"

"Chuck Corsello was a part of his dream. They wrote songs together in the navy. Scores of songs. They had dreams of being the next great songwriting team, and they could've been like Lennon and McCartney. I heard an old reel to reel tape of the two of them playing guitars together and they were fabulous. Corsello stimulated your father's creativity. He brought out the best in your father. They were great collaborators, like you and Walker. After Corsello died in the war, I encouraged your father to keep composing."

"Did he write any music after the war?"

"He wrote one or two songs on his own, but they weren't as good. And your father ingested the military mindset of discipline and perfectionism. If he couldn't create a perfect song, why do it?" She read the signs for departing flights aloud. "Southwest. TWA. United. Delta. Here we go, American."

We pulled parallel to the curb behind an airport shuttle van. I watched the teary goodbyes of the other passengers and their families as they grabbed their suitcases. I noticed a wrinkled man hugging a short kid about my age. "Bye, Dad," the kid said.

"It's not fair, Mom," I said. "I can't believe he's really dead."

"Things could've been worse," she said. "We're still lucky. He could've died in Korea before we had you and Walker." She smiled and patted my hand. "We've had a hard life, but it's still good to be alive, Jeremiah. Isn't it?"

I smiled. "Yes, it is, Mom."

I needed to ask her one more question, since she was in a rare mood of disclosure. "You explained why he quit writing music, but I still don't understand why was he afraid to go to the next level as a guitarist?"

"He was in charge of firing the cannon off his schooner. The sound of the cannon blasts partially destroyed his hearing. He can't hear the high notes. He figured, 'I lost my songwriting partner, I lost my hearing. Why try?' So he settled. And when he saw so much death in the war, something died inside him. He didn't want to be like Hemingway's old fisherman and try for something he wouldn't be able to keep."

"Poor Dad."

Mom clutched the steering wheel with both hands and looked up to the planes arriving overhead. "The Korean War was the first jet war. What a waste. So many young men died. And the ones who didn't, walk around like zombies from the wounds of war. Truman sentenced your father to a lifetime of PTSD. When the killing is over, who can really say what it was about? To this day, I don't know why we were there."

"Do you think we should've gone to war?"

She watched a jet land and swallowed hard before continuing. "On the Fourth of July, we'd take you and Walker to see the fireworks at West View Park, and we'd all dress up in red, white, and blue, and I'd get a bit choked up when someone sang the National Anthem. But once in a while, when I think what defending the country did to your father, and what he did to us, I guess we're all casualties. Some politician in Washington plays chess with real men as pawns and sends us off to die prematurely."

I heard the rumble of a jet overhead. "Need any gas money, Mom?"

She looked at her gauge. "No, I'm all right. Still got a quarter-tank to get back." She looked out at the landing strip and cleared her throat. "Don't get me wrong Jeremiah, I'm still gonna wave my flag and say 'God bless the U.S.A.,' but I can't help but wonder if someone somewhere gets rich off these wars. They pile up debts for the rest of us and we pay the price when Stick Man shows up."

I reached over to her and pulled her in for a hug, a real one this time. No patting each others backs and quickly disengaging, just holding my mother still and steady until she broke the embrace. "I love you, Mom."

"Love you too, dear. You better get moving. I don't want you to miss your plane, honey."

"Yeah, I guess so," I said wistfully. "You're a good mother. You did the best you could."

"Thanks, dear. Get going now. No more dilly-dallying for chit-chat."

I walked to the back of the Buick and lifted my suitcases from the car trunk. "Bye, Mom."

"Bye, dear." I stood at curbside check-in with a new understanding of my father.

The second day after I returned to California, I had dinner with Savannah. She told me she was concerned for me and she wanted to keep me company that evening while Ichabod was on tour.

"I don't think you should be alone," she said. "I want to make sure you eat."

I chose Mel's 50's Diner on Ventura Boulevard. Mel's had mini-jukeboxes on each table. I put quarters in and chose *Strangers In the Night* by Sinatra. I remembered the night of June 17th, 1980, when Angel and I blasted that song from the car radio of Mom's station wagon and pulled into West View Elementary. We jumped out and danced in the school parking lot. Angel was giddy as I spun her in circles. *Dooby, dooby, doo…*

"So tell me about your confrontation with my father."

I ate my hamburger and told her all of it, how Mordecai denied molesting her, as we both expected. "He didn't want me using his head for a baseball, so he filed a restraining order against me. But I was flying home to California before the paperwork went through. Mom told me about it."

She smiled. "Thanks for standing up for me."

After dinner at Mel's, we parked on Mulholland overlooking the lights of the L.A. basin. Savannah booked a shuttle to pick her up there and take her to LAX for an out-of-town film role. Her star was rising. She booked three independent movies that month and was leaving town to shoot.

"I'm not sure about spiritual things anymore, Jeremiah," she said. "I see a child on the evening news, gunned down by a gang-banger, and I wonder, was that really his appointed time to go? Some killings seem so arbitrary. People squashed like ants on a sidewalk. What if it's survival of the fittest with no benevolent God planning it all?"

"But all your life you were taught to believe."

"Mordecai's been wrong about so many other things he taught me. What if he's wrong about heaven?"

"What about the Infinite Energy and praying to the Universe?

"The New Age was a safe place for me for a while when I still had a modicum of faith left. I needed something different from the religion that hurt me growing up. I wasn't ready to let go completely."

"What does it feel like, to stop believing completely?"

"It's scary to think of letting go of faith. Breaking up is hard to do. It's like taking a leap off a cliff and not knowing where I will land. But I'm getting tired of making excuses for all the bad things a supposedly good God allows. The excuses are getting flimsier and flimsier, like broken Band-Aids."

"So after this life, there's nothing? It's all meaningless?"

"Not necessarily."

"How can there be meaning without God?"

The roar of the shuttle approached and Savannah flagged them to stop. "Because it's not about a pie-in-the-sky somewhere else, some time in the future, Jeremiah. Life's gone so quick. If it's all we got, we really have to seize this short sliver of existence."

Savannah looked up at the night sky. "If this is all there is, maybe we should appreciate it more, not less."

She extinguished her cigarette on the ground, kissed me goodbye on the cheek, and boarded the airport shuttle.

I gazed at the evening sky, savoring the moon and the stars.

*****

I struggled to sleep that night. I thought about Mordecai and Millie, how arrogantly they sat on the judgment seat and divided everybody into their two-category binary of saved and unsaved.

I felt for a moment a love inside me for the whole world, a realization that for every Mordecai marching lockstep to legalism, there were people like me and Savannah who struggled to believe.

I sensed something rising up in me, an understanding for the skepticism of Savannah, and the messiness of my father. I never had the father I needed, and now it was too late to ever fix it. I hoped the oppression of religion was buried for me with the burial of my father.

*Go to the light, Saul.*
*Maybe when Dad went to the light, so did I.*

I pulled into the Sunset-Bronson studios where I was set to audition for a pilot for a new game show. Dad's presence was with me when I passed the audition and became an instant contestant because someone scheduled to compete that day was a no-show. I was shocked I made it through the initial tests.

I waited in a green room with a middle-aged Southern woman who talked about her barbecue recipes to anyone willing to listen, and a blonde-haired twentysomething surfer boy. I closed my eyes and took deep breaths to relax, remembering Dad sitting in his chair watching *The Price Is Right*. Dad almost always came up with a winning bid on the luxury showcases and ridiculed the contestants who came up with losing numbers. I knew it was an escape, a safe way for him to land the big fish he didn't have the courage to catch in real life, where real sharks could devour his prizes. Dad never stood under the stage lights or had to bid under the prodding of Bob Barker and the pressure of a real game.

After initially freezing from stage-fright, I answered a string of questions correctly and built up a cache of several thousand dollars. The game show was structured so that the winner is the one who answers the very last question. The twenty-something surfer kid who missed questions the whole game answered the last question correctly, something about the Mighty Morphin Power Rangers. He took all my money, but he seemed to need it more than I did. I got a concession prize, a watch with Merv Griffin's signature on it.

Driving back to the Valley, I passed a street with low palms at sunset. The trees were silhouetted black. I realized California was almost feeling like home. I loved cruising Hollywood or Sunset Boulevard, seeing the tourists at Grauman's Chinese Theatre. I smiled when I saw the Hollywood sign, the magical white-lettered meme up Beachwood Drive.

Traffic was heavy when I headed home, a hypnotic movement of people dancing like bees on the 101 and 405. I exited the 405, and drove by the Veteran's Cemetery. The grave markers were identical and symmetrical, like the cemetery where Dad was buried. I thought about his decomposing body in the grave and hoped the resurrection was true.

I remembered Sister Ruth telling me heaven's a place with a golden street, a tree that bears twelve different kinds of fruit, one for each month of the year.

*Dad's got to be somewhere. His corpse can't be all that's left of him.*

I drove to DQ on Lankershim for dessert before heading up Cahuenga. When I reached my neighborhood, I avoided the main streets. I liked exploring alleys in the evening, smelling the seediness. The quiet corridors of fences, the smell of garbage mingling with night air, the domain of crows and giant green dumpsters. The same reasons I lived on the edge as an artist. To find reality, a glimpse at real people on tossed-out couches.

I arrived home and looked around my studio apartment. I looked at the picture of Dad hanging on my wall, the photo of him in front of the bandstand, playing his blonde Gibson with Spiritos beside him strumming rhythm.

That night, I went to bed after watching Johnny Carson and played the tape of alphabet affirmations, spoken by Spiritos. "Y is for Your Youthfulness..."

I was tired, but my mind was active, thinking about my phone conversations with Angel. She kept in touch with greater frequency. When I knew she was calling, I felt like a kid on his birthday.

We'd been writing each other since Dad's death. As days turned into weeks, and weeks turned into months, I got to know her through daily calls and letters. I fell in love a second time for the woman she'd become. Though not religious anymore, Angel embodied to me the essence of religion. She'd often give the last dollar in her purse to a poor person.

I remembered how her ability to nurture me was beyond her years when we were teens. She couldn't wait for me to taste her peanut butter pie or bread pudding. The satisfaction of knowing I'd relished her cooking brought her joy. She prepared and delivered meals to shut-ins, visited the sick and the elderly in nursing homes, and collected toys for needy children.

Our letters were sometimes a tease, sharing turn-ons. Mostly it was the day-to-day. I talked about teaching guitar and painting. She talked about her work as a home caregiver for a disabled man.

When we talked on the phone long distance, I liked the way she listened. Everything I bottled up burst forth. She never interrupted, never was offended.

"I'm sorry to make you hear all this," I'd say.

"Oh, please. I like listening to you, baby," Angel replied. "Talk about anything. All night if you need to."

Everything I did was for her, to impress her, to present my accomplishments at her feet. I wondered if there were other men somewhere who remained frozen at seventeen years-old to the memory of a girl whose name possessed some seraphic sound to them.

Separated by three thousand miles and the logistics of life, our eroticism became verbal. I knew in my gut her husband was nuts, and I didn't want him to find out.

I couldn't sleep. I was still up at four a.m. thinking about Angel's husband. The thought of him beside her in bed drove me into a fit. What was it about her that provoked my jealousy? I couldn't quite put my finger on it. It had to be more than her unmatched beauty. I couldn't bear the thought of Tiger's hands on her soft skin.

At five a.m., I had a dream about Angel and Sarah, the baby girl Tiger made her abort. Sarah was wearing a white dress. She came out of a cloud and spoke a poem to Angel. *"Mommy if I was with you today/you would let me live/so hear me say/Mommy, I forgive...”* I wrote down the words and drifted off.

At dawn on Thursday, the Santa Ana winds blew through the canyons. I woke to the rhythm of the cars whizzing by on Laurel Canyon and the sound of my doorbell. I looked at my Vision Board, the ever-expanding collage I created from a mishmash of photos and magazine clippings. In the center was a picture of Jesus. To the right of Jesus was Angel. Clippings of Natalie Wood and Elizabeth Taylor blended with pictures of guitars and ocean scenes. At the top was the number 21.

I walked down the hall of my apartment past photos of the Great One, Roberto Clemente, and the newspaper clippings of Walker and me, heralding us as best new artists of 1981.

After starting coffee and looking in the mirror, I missed my father for a moment and felt tears sloshing inside me, like waves against a ship that would burst out any moment. I looked out the window and saw Ichabod ringing my bell and remembered we had a music appointment. We had a few well-paying gigs lined up together. The sky was overcast and foggy when I opened the door and greeted him.

Ichabod unpacked his bass and tuned to an electronic tuner. I petted Shadow’s black and white tail, and he nipped at my finger. I wrapped a Band Aid around my finger just in time to answer my ringing phone.

It was Angel.

“What are you doing, baby?” she cooed on my answering machine. I was screening calls and her melodious voice caught me off guard.

Ichabod heard Angel on the message machine. I excused myself and left the room with the cordless phone.

"Conducting a meeting with a bass player. Savannah's boyfriend. He's co-writer for my next album project and we're playing at the Whiskey next week."

"I'm driving to grandma's house," Angel said. "I'm sorry, I'll let you go. You're busy."

"No, wait. I wish you were here. What's it like there?"

"Sunny. I'm passing by houses in Mount Olympus, toward a willow tree, and now I'm turning into Grandma's."

"Wish I was there."

"Want me to hang up?"

"No. Hold on."

I decided to end the meeting. "Sorry, that was an emergency," I said to Ichabod. "I have to ask you to go."

"But the gig's next Friday and we haven't rehearsed one time."

"I know, but we're both pros and we'll be fine."

He left, perplexed at my firmness. I watched him slide his lanky frame into his car and drive off.

"I'm back Angel," I said into the phone.

"We need to see each other again," she said. She picked up on my hesitation. "What's wrong? You want to see me, don't you?"

"I want to see you, but I don't want to risk triggering Tiger."

"He doesn't hit me anymore. Not for a while. He won't find out. I need to see you again."

I remembered Father McCormick teaching me adultery was a mortal sin, but if anyone was worth dying for and committing a mortal sin, it was Angel.

After I hung up, I drove to the Studio City library. I read up on domestic violence and how to know if a situation was dangerous. Tiger fit all the signs of an abuser that would go off the deep end if he found out about us. I had to find a way to stop it for her sake, but I was powerless over my obsession.

The next day, I attended the Wednesday night meeting of Love Addicts Anonymous at Stage 12. This time, I didn't take Devon with me to the meeting. Until I was further along in my grief process, I cut off contact with him. I didn't have the energy.

Spiritos greeted me at the door and we had a cup of coffee in his upstairs apartment for a few minutes before I went back downstairs for the meeting. "Maybe you'll get some practical tips in the meeting that can help you," he said.

"I hope so."

The metal chairs were set up in a circle around the table. In the middle of the table was coffee, a collection basket for the Seventh Tradition, and pamphlets about the program.

I had no problem with the first step, admitting I was powerless over the relationship. I told my story in the open sharing portion of the meeting.

An older guy in the group talked to me afterwards and explained the only hope for me was to cut it off cold turkey. He was a bodybuilder with a black tee-shirt and bulging biceps who spoke in a string of Recovery phrases.

"One day at a time, Jeremiah. Progress not perfection, I always say."

I poured myself another coffee. "That sounds good," I responded, not understanding why he communicated almost exclusively with twelve step buzzwords.

"Willingness to go to any lengths, Jeremiah, willingness to go to any lengths.   Throw away all the songs you wrote about her," he said, "then you go through a withdrawal process.   It works if you work it, and you're worth it.   I know.   I've been there."   He handed me a Hefty trash bag.

"What's the bag for?"

"Put everything in here.   Any gifts from her.   Letters, reminders, pictures, that type of thing.   Ask God to remove any defects of character.   Progress, not perfection."   He flexed his bicep and smiled.   "Keep coming back, it works if you work it."

"I don't want to do that.   The letters, and pictures, and my songs I wrote are all I have left of her that's tangible."

"To thine own self be true," he said.   "Your true, best self knows what is ethical."   His advice had the opposite of the intended effect however, because I reasoned if I was true to myself, I'd follow Angel rather than the maxims of the Recovery Movement.

"My true self is in love with her."

"That's self-will run riot.   Remove the bondage of self that we may better do the Higher Power's will.   Principles, not personalities.   It's a passing fancy, Jeremiah."

"If it were a passing fancy, it would've passed already," I said.

He sighed and shook his head.   "The requirement for this meeting is a willingness to be sober," he said.   I tried not to look at him.   "You lack willingness."

"I'm sorry to disappoint you," I said, walking away.

"It works if you work it," he yelled after me.   "Fear of people and economic uncertainty will leave us..." he said, his voice trailing off in the distance. "A power greater than ourselves, one day at a time…"

Angel decided to fly to California, despite my repeated need for assurance that it was safe. She knew I held a precise vision of her from the past, photographic and exact. She wondered if I'd find her attractive as our meeting approached.

"I'm not that same fifteen year-old girl," she'd told me on the phone, just before booking her flight to come see me. "I have stretch marks."

"And I'll kiss every one of those stretch marks."

"Can I get that in writing, Mister?" she said flirtatiously.

"Signed, sealed, delivered."

On the eighteenth of May, I played the Spiritos meditation tape, and felt like I was finally defeating Rawlings. Mordecai couldn't keep us from seeing each other this time. I fell asleep to the alphabetical meditations and prayed I'd have a night free of Stick Man.

"Z is for Zest to accomplish your goals…You will accomplish your goals, Jeremiah, nothing can keep you from success," Spiritos spoke into my subconscious.

*****

When I woke up, the room was brutally cold and thickly dark. I felt the unreal cold and heard the noise of wind, knocking on my door. The knocking echoed in the hall. I rocked to the pounding, which seemed inside my head as much as in the hall. I hid under the blanket, and the sickening, still cold surrounded me. I had the odd sense my life was about to end.

It's inside my head, I thought, putting my hands over my face, it's inside my head and it's trying to get out, get out, GET OUT!

"*Jeremiah,*" a voice said distinctly. I smelled the odor of decay.

"Father?" I said softly, and then again, "Daddy?"

"*Help me.*"

"Coming, Dad, coming," I said, feeling a tingle of goose bumps and fumbling for the light. "I'm coming, it's all right."

*Jeremiah,* I heard, *Water, Jeremiah.*

"Coming, Dad, coming," I shouted, annoyed. "Just a second, I'm coming.

"*Jeremiah, help me.*"

Then I thought, with a violent shock which brought me awake: *Oh yeah, Dad's dead.*

I was shivering and cold, out of bed and alert. My father was knocking on the wall. It was terribly cold, terribly, terribly cold. It's only a noise, I thought, not my father knocking on the wall. It's not at all like Dad drumming on the wall. I'm dreaming again.

Dad's voice was replaced with a low, strident growling and a thickening tension in the air. The animal sounds stopped and I heard the labored breathing of Stick Man, invading my dreams again.

I tried to stay calm but I was so very cold. Icy chills started in my stomach and crawled up and down my spine in waves, like someone alive. Or some thing alive.

It's just a noise.

"Go away," I shouted wildly. "LEAVE ME ALONE, GO AWAY!"

I thought, Now I am really afraid. There was complete silence, except for the sound of my teeth chattering. The old cold crept and snapped at me. I felt feverish and I shivered.

The reptilian clicking on the door started up again. I thought you were dead.

It knew I was afraid.

I leapt back against my bed and lifted my eyes in terror. The hammering in my heart was echoed from both the hall and the corner of my bedroom, the sound of wood against wood.

My apartment shook and shivered, the curtains danced against the window, the furniture swayed back and forth, and the noise of nightmarish pounding in the hall became so furious that it pushed against the walls. I heard breaking glass as my pictures of Dad crashed down from the wall.

The floor moved beneath me. Holding to my bed, buffeted and shaken, I put my head down, bit my lips against the cold and closed my eyes to pray. "Lord, help me," I said. I felt the room fall beneath me, a stomach sickening drop. In the churning darkness I fell, nothing was real except my own hands clutching the bedpost. I could see the fingers on my guitar-chording hand white and tight on the bed when the bed rocked and the walls leaned toward me, then the room righted itself and filled with mist.

Suddenly, a strong stench assailed me, the stench of decaying flesh and decaying memories. The tomb cracked open and Stick Man flew out again.

He hid in the shadows, waving and crossing his stick arms, his mouth stretched taut in a feral grin. I opened my eyes, responding to the presence of the cunning predator. I straightened and stared. That horror. That thing. Watching me. His long claws and sharp teeth. Full of hate. Full of power.

It's just my fear. It's just my fear.

Stick Man hovered in the doorway, singing. *"At the cross, at the cross where I first saw the light, and the burden of my heart rolled away..."*

I jerked my head around at the sound of Stick Man smashing his wooden limbs together, then forming them a cross. He erupted in diabolic laughter.

*"I can't take my eyes off you,"* Stick Man said, licking his black, wolfish tongue and mocking me with his stare. *"You're one of my favorites. I need the sensitive children to survive."* I felt a blast of icy stench. A smothering black stillness hovered over me. *"Well, first-born son,"* croaked the demon. *"At last you know the truth about me. But it won't help you. This time you're going to lose."*

Still staggered by the cold, I traced the sign of the cross in the air above me. "Pray for us sinners now and at the hour of our death," I said, averting my eyes from his hideous Hahoetal wood-mask.

Stick Man lifted me off the bed. I stared down at the bed incredulously. Three inches. Six inches. A foot. It's not happening! It's only a mask! I floated, transfixed. He lifted me up, a foot at a time and then he threw me down and I fell with my breath jerking out of me. The up and down movements ceased suddenly.

He roared frenziedly at me in a cackle of evil glee. *"You've lost and you know it!"* The mask was turned sideways now, as Stick Man continued to rage. *"Look at you, frightened with your cock in your hands!"* A glob of Dad's decomposed flesh hit my eye and I fell to the bed.

I stared numbly at Stick Man, his yellow eyes bulging behind the mask. He was in a murderous mood.

I didn't move.

I prayed fervently. "Twenty-one, twenty-one...Pray for us now and at the hour of our death. Our Father..."

Stick Man spat and hit me in the face with an orange glob of vomit. It oozed slowly down my face. The hair on my arms prickled up. The lights in the room flickered, than faded to an eerie grey. I shivered, my body felt like ice.

"Thy kingdom come, Thy will be done..." I continued my prayer without a pause while my hand found a box of Kleenex on the nightstand and I wiped the bile from my cheeks. I heard Stick Man hissing. His tongue flicked in and out swiftly, his mask weaving back and forth like a python about to strike. The room jolted with a muffled pounding. The walls shuddered steadily, throbbing like the beating of a diseased heart.

"*Seoul, seoul, seoul...*" he hissed, undulating.

I looked at his manic red eyes. "Be silent! Depart from me!"

Stick Man cowered, but still cackled his maniacal malevolent laugh. The poundings grew louder and faster, accelerating to a terrifying tempo. I made the sign of the cross again over my body for protection from his tricks and torments. "O God of the angels and archangels help me..."

"*You will lose! You will die!*"

"God of the Angels..."

"*Put your holy cock in Angel's mouth and cleanse her-*"

"Deliver us from evil..."

"*Hypocrite! You're not holy. You want that whore who married someone else. You want to make her scream with perverse pleasure. She fantasizes nightly about you, first-born son. She masturbates, dreaming of sinning with you. You're an adulterer and you'll burn in hell for your lust! Go fuck that whore! Have your cunt!"*

I heard his yelping laughter, coming thin and lunatic, rising chromatically in his crazy little tune, followed by a torrent of frenzied obscenities.

Dread seeped into my mind. Stick Man's footsteps approached, coming at me like a bird of prey with his talons extended for the final kill. *"You're mine, buddy boy, prepare to die,"* he said, his hideous voice bristling with venom.

I had an epiphany. Stick Man is like every bully, I thought. His taunts and teasing formed his mask, a mask that covered fear. Stick Man's energies come from other entities. He is the fear from every father, the betrayal of every beau, the punitive guilt of every golden god, the universal dispenser of worldwide feelings of unworthiness and worthlessness.

And then resolutely, quivering, I faced him squarely. "You son of a bitch!" I seethed in a whisper that sizzled in the air like Pittsburgh steel, forged in fire. "I KNOW WHERE YOU GET YOUR STRENGTH," I said. "FROM MY FEAR AND GUILT. I TAKE BACK ALL THE POWER I GAVE YOU. YOU HAVE NO AUTHORITY OVER ME!"

Stick Man eyed me with malevolence. He stopped laughing.

"Yes, you're very good at scaring little boys!" I said trembling. "Innocent little boys."

*"You were never innocent, you were sexual-"*

"HUSH! Let's see you try someone bigger. Come on, Stick Man!" I extended my arms like big, fleshy planks, beckoning slowly. "Come on! Come on, Stick Man. Try *me*! You want a piece of me? I'm a man now. I'm not that scared little boy anymore. Leave the boy and take me! Take me!"

Stick Man cackled, winked fiendishly at me and vanished.

Mercifully, it was over.

I exhaled deeply and cracked open a window.

I opened the drawer of my nightstand and found a rubber band. I slid the rubber band around my wrist and made a covenant with myself to snap the rubber band if any Stick Man thoughts returned, a ritual to condition myself to replace his negative accusations with positive truths. I determined to nip his distortions in the bud, at the root of the thoughts, before they blossomed into fiery, full-blown imaginations. I realized I had the power to keep and defend the ground I gained within my own mind.

I drifted off to sleep, knowing I'd finally won the round with Stick Man.


I awoke again at six a.m., exhausted from spiritual warfare. The room was quiet, and between the still curtains at the window I could see the California sunlight.

Savannah leaned over me and said, "You're okay." I sat up in bed and shook my head.

Back from her shoot, Savannah brought down breakfast and complained that I never bought new furniture. The flea market couch and table had been stained brown countless times by my coffee and tobacco.

"Close your eyes, Jeremiah," Savannah said, washing my face and towels with a wet towel. "I want you cleaned up for breakfast."

I ate the scrambled eggs and fried potatoes she set on my lap on a TV tray and listened to Savannah haranguing me about my "rudeness and lack of professionalism" for kicking Ichabod out when Angel called during rehearsal. I knew she was more upset about Angel calling than she was about how I treated Ichabod.

I promised I'd make it up to him and stay focused on our work on the album.

I anticipated Angel's arrival. She'd booked the flight thirty days out to get an economic rate.

When Savannah left, I opened my journal and scribbled my letter for the day.

*Dear Angel,*

*It's eight-thirty in the morning on Saturday. My first guitar pupil, an Asian stock broker from New Zealand, is set to arrive at nine. After my morning students, I'm gonna grab lunch at In-N-Out Burgers. I can't wait to take you to the beach and the Santa Monica Pier while you're here.*

*Our meeting, forthcoming in just a few days, will be the one event of my life I will cherish more than any other, an adventure that will surpass all that has gone before. Finally, I'll feel your breath on me once again.*

*Outlasting centuries*
*Our love transcends time*
*For God is love*
*And love divine*

*Till then,*

*Jeremiah        xoxxoxox*

# 30

In the dreamland of Hollywood, I never knew what a day would bring. Ever since I'd moved there, I had a feeling I was one step closer to a dream coming true.

I read the slip of paper with her arrival information. American Airlines. Flight 379. 4:00 p.m. Angel was flying out to the land of dreams to make my dream come true.

I walked to Gate B at 2:12, carrying a sign I'd made. I wrote the letters S-O-F on the homemade sign. I held it up waiting for Angel to arrive. S-O-F was a joke between us. It stood for 'Sick Obsessed Fuck.' On the phone late one night, I was reflecting on how I could never let her go. "God, I am one sick, obsessed fuck," I'd said. The way I said it struck her as funny and she laughed so loud the outburst startled me. S-O-F became her pet nickname for me.

I stood by her gate and waited near baggage claim. I waited.

And waited.

And waited.

Finally, it was 4:00 p.m. I caught a glimpse of my reflection in the glass of the window. I wore a white tee shirt and jeans. She'd always liked me in jeans. "I'm a simple girl," I remembered her saying. "I like it when you dress simple."

Angel, once a lost memory, was nearing closer as I focused on each passenger arriving through the tunnel. Sweat formed on my neck. I watched the people push and stream past.

The first cluster of passengers emerged from the tunnel, but didn't contain Angel. I scanned each one to be sure. An old woman crept with a cane. A businessman in a brown suit hurried around her, doing an end-run. In the bustling baggage area, he dodged in and out of the crowded clumps of travelers like a running back.

And then it happened.

I finally saw her.

The sight of Angel carried me back to my young, hot hopes, the simple love I had when I was God's sweet innocent fool.   I had faith again, hope that my brief hours with her would usher me into the angel's palace.

She remained fit, swinging her hands and shoulders when she walked.   Angel moved gracefully, flowing towards me, like a dreamy river.

Our eyes met.

She smiled.

We embraced, standing in a timeless moment, together in tight enfoldment for the longest hug of my life.   When we released our arms and looked into each other's eyes, I studied her face.   The same thin lips and high cheekbones.   Her tan face had thickened. She looked like a young woman, rather than a girl.   She had a tiny touch of crow's feet, a slight wrinkle around the outer corner of her eyes when she smiled.   I reached out and touched her neck.   My fingers coursed through her dark hair.

We hugged again, squeezing tighter and longer.   Her caress calmed me like warm milk at night.

"It's been centuries," I said.

"Hey, mister," she said.   Like my Washburn, the tone of her voice aged just right.   She laughed at my SOF sign.

I cupped her chin in my hand and turned her head towards mine.

I kissed her.

"Hey.   You look even better than you did in 1980," I said.

"Oh, stop."

"My eyes don't lie."

I kissed her again. We locked in a stare like four summers before.

"You still send shivers down my spine," she said.

I took her hand and led her away. "I love you," I said, whispering in her ear.

"I know, baby," she said. "You're my heart. I love you too, Jeremiah."

We walked to the baggage area, joining others clustering around the conveyor belt. She rubbed against me while we waited, grinning. I touched her behind the neck again.

"There's that smile," I said.

"This is the most important day of my life, Jeremiah."

"Mine too. I'm proud to be standing beside you."

The baggage belt started moving. I stared at her profile, memorizing her face, just in case I lost her again. She watched the suitcases tumble down the shoot that led to the rotating conveyor belt. I couldn't wait to be in my Jeep with her, away from the eyes of the crowd. It took forever for her green duffel bag to arrive on the moving belt. She packed like she was staying for a year.

"I'm sorry it's so heavy," she said. "Let me show you how to drag it."

She found a hidden strap and handed it to me to hook on the end to pull the bag. I put on my sunglasses and we walked outside. The sun was bright. We got the walk signal to cross from the airport to the parking garage. When we approached the Jeep, I pointed out the letters AVJY in the license plate.

"Did you pick the letters?"

"No, but when I got the title at DMV, there it was, your initials beside mine. Angel Vickers Jeremiah Young. A sign from God."

In the Jeep, we French kissed. My tongue explored her warm mouth like a snake, continuing our first kiss, as if no time had elapsed.

I liked how she looked at me.

She held me tight, her breasts against me. I drove out of the airport, tapping the gas. I stroked her thigh.

I remembered she suggested on the phone I find something close to the airport that wasn't expensive. Something simple, she'd said. I drove to Harmony Hotel on Foothill Boulevard.

The hotel clerk was from India. "Can we see the room first?" Angel asked.

"Sure." He led us through the maze of craters in the parking lot.

"Are all these places run by foreigners?" Angel asked me in a whisper.

"Guess so. Like the 7-Elevens."

He opened the door on the simple room that was good enough for me, but not Angel. She wasn't satisfied because the room didn't have a phone.

"My husband wants the phone number where I'm staying." I winced as she elaborated. "A number that rings directly into our room, not a switchboard."

Our official story was that she was at a woman's retreat. "On many retreats, they don't allow contact from family, and the cabins don't have phones," I said.

"He'll never buy it."

We drove away from Harmony Hotel. She didn't like the Tujunga-Sunland area north of the airport where Spiritos lived.

"I'm not too impressed. I couldn't take this traffic. Mount Olympus is the armpit of the east, but I'm at home in a small town. We only have two short blocks of stores. That's it. It's a far drive just to find a department store."

"What can I do to make you happy, Angel?"

"This area feels seedy. I don't want to feel like we're shacking up. I want to keep it as pure as possible. Let's go to a place near the ocean," she said.

The congestion was heavier at evening rush. I headed west on the 210 and missed the 118. I checked the Thomas Guide to get back on course to head south. We hit the 405 and more standstill traffic. The jeep became a mobile prison of a failed mission. We got to the ocean after a couple hours, but the hotels along Pacific Coast Highway were two hundred dollars a night.

"Too expensive," she said.

I found myself driving aimlessly and unsure, drained and drowning as the good dream became a nightmare. My nerves felt like a snail crawling on the edge of a razor.

The trip was planned to consummate our relationship, but she turned away when I tried to kiss her again. She pushed me back with the palm of her hand.

"Feeling guilty?" I asked.

"Yeah, this isn't right."

"It's a disaster, isn't it?"

"Oh, please. Don't exaggerate, Jeremiah. You'll feel better when you've eaten something."

After spending four hours looking for a suitable place, we settled into the Paradise Palms Lodge in the 12000 block of Ventura Boulevard, just a couple blocks from my apartment.    I couldn't bring Angel home with Savannah crouching upstairs like a dragon.    We split the room cost between us.    We paid two-hundred seventy dollars cash for two nights, but making the reservation in her name on her Master Card.

"Room 21," the clerk said, handing me the keys.

*Twenty-one.   A sign.*

I glanced at the bed when we entered.    The room was about three hundred square feet.

*Finally alone.*

The bed sheet was red print.    I took my shoes off and felt the thick brown carpet under my toes, hoping I'd soon remove more than my shoes.    She glanced at the walls.

"Beige," she said.    "These walls need painted."

The TV sat on top of a brown dresser, next to the phone. Within seconds of her spotting the phone, she asked for privacy and called Tiger.    I sat on the toilet but listened through the door.

"I love you" she said to him.    *Ouch.*    I punched the door. She hung up, knowing I'd overheard.    "I'm sorry, Jeremiah.    He kept saying it, so I had to say it back.    I didn't want to.    I had to. This way he won't be suspicious."

Her mother Shara called next.    Angel accidentally hit the speaker phone button and for a few seconds and I heard her.

"I told Tiger, something fishy's going on," Mrs. Vickers said.

After the call, Angel panicked.    "Mother and Tiger think I'm with you.    I need to go home early," she said.    "I was raised in the church, with morals.    This is wrong, you know it's wrong."    She slid away from me.

"I can't believe you want to go home early."

"Like I said before, I don't want to. I have to. I'm sorry."

I felt the strong grasp of her family like walls closing in and suffocating me.

That night, I couldn't sleep or eat. I laid over her and kissed her. She wore a black bra with scarlet red pajamas. I trembled. I swallowed and looked down at the tremor in my right hand.

We tried to merge in the middle of the night, but faces from my past passed through my mind.

Father McCormick.

Mordecai.

I couldn't hold an erection inside Angel, or will a hard-on. My penis was in retreat. The more I wanted to, the less I could.

"What's wrong? Is it me?" she asked.

"No."

"What then?"

"I'm nervous."

"You just have to relax."

"I feel so much pressure and we have so little time. Especially now that you're leaving. Let's just go to sleep."

I rolled over on my back, avoiding eye contact. She counted the tiles on the ceiling with her fingers. Moments passed. I was sweating and she sensed I was upset.

"Are you sure nothing's wrong?" she whispered against my shoulder.

"No," I lied. "Go to sleep."

I turned over, my back now to her. She tapped the fingers of both hands, counting two, four, six, eight...

"It's okay," she said.

She turned me towards her and kissed me. We made out for a while. "Don't leave," I said.

Angel faced me. She swallowed. "I'm sorry. I need to go home. My family's freaking out. They don't believe the retreat story. And my husband, he's crazy. He'll kill us both."

"Like hell he will."

I walked into the bathroom to keep myself from saying something I might regret. I snapped the rubber band against my wrist and resisted the thought that I was a worthless failure and it was just no use.

I glanced for a moment in the mirror and clowned at my reflection, imitating Nixon by raising both my arms in peace signs and saying, "I am not a crook," as I shook my jowls.

I stared at my glass twin, and it occurred to me that being with her might be a longing to go back to the nostalgia of a simple time. I defined myself and my first love by memory, but the reflection exposed the dream. I'd changed. The mirror echoed my mortality, waking me like a cold slap. I ignored the reflector, in an act of self preservation, and remembered her face in the moment from 1980 when she was burned into my mind. The Angel of my dreams returned to my thoughts, the woods and the hours of adolescent love.

I overheard her call American Airlines and pay eight hundred twenty-seven dollars to fly home, cutting her trip from a week to three days. After I brooded in silence for a while, I walked toward her and put my hand on her shoulder.

"My nerves are giving way now too," she said.

She broke down and had a cigarette on the balcony, despite her pride in telling me she'd quit the habit. She exhaled smoke in two streams. I sat beside her on a white patio chair. I didn't want to add to her stress.

"I'm sorry.  I just need this one," she said.

"It's okay.  No big deal."

"I had a slip last week.  Tiger caught me.  He went ballistic.  He slammed my head into the window of the car."

"What?"

"We made a pact together.  He quit and I quit.  When he found out I slipped, he went berserk."  She sucked another drag.  Her soft inhale was a sigh, the air pregnant with her imprisonment.  "I didn't want to tell you about-"

"How often does he hurt you?"

"I don't want to answer because-"

"How often?  You led me to believe that hadn't happened in a while."

"Why do you want to know?  It's only going to torment you."  The tip of her cigarette glowed, the ashes long on the end.  She noticed and tapped the excess in the ashtray.

"What's the truth?"

"Once or twice a month."

"He hits you?"

"Sometimes.  Other times he pulls my hair or grabs my arm or shoves me.  It's been going on for years.  I told you."

"But you said it's been a while and that it doesn't happen anymore.  You lied to me."

"I'm sorry.  I didn't want you to worry."

"Why do you still stay?"

"I don't know.  I need his help to pay the mortgage, I guess.  He's a good man, except for this one side.  Good things have always been there.  When the monster comes out, it's hard to appreciate the good.  But he has a fun and a funny side, really.  He apologizes, makes me laugh, and I go back."

I felt the foolishness of her loyalty towards him. I wondered how this radiant girl, my muse all those years, had settled down with this sick man. I judged her a fool for staying and I hated and envied him. I wanted her to transfer her loyalty to me. I deserved it and would treat her right.

She cupped her hand beneath the cigarette to catch falling ash before putting it out in the ashtray.

Her voice turned fragile and hoarse. "We don't have the money to end the relationship. And he scares me. Maybe it's time to take me down off the pedestal, Jeremiah. This is me. This is my life." She inhaled, than exhaled. "I'm getting older too, you know."

"You look even lovelier than you did then. You're ageless." I smiled, coaxing a half-grin out of her.

"Oh, stop."

"I worry for your safety now."

"Don't. That's why I didn't want to tell you." She touched my cheek. "Don't worry."

It was too late for that. I sank into her sweet swamp of quicksand.

*****

I stared at the lengthy shadow that ran from her cheek to her brow. I kissed her on the cheek, inhaling femininity, lotion, and cigarette smoke.

At the crack of dawn, I was a jumble of nerves so she took the thick neck of my instrument in her hands and played me. Her touch transported me as she leaned forward to grip me stronger. I savored the sight of her nakedness.

I exploded.

She smiled, than glided gracefully to the bathroom and brought back a warm wet washrag and cleaned me, wiping off my belly.

She looked down at her legs. Her smile became a scowl. "I don't like my thighs," she said, slapping and pinching the flesh.

"I like them. They're perfect."

"Oh stop. Tiger tells me they're chubby." She grabbed the flesh of her legs again.

"Don't listen to that jerk. They're practically perfect," I said, remembering she didn't like to be told she was perfect.

I had good dreams the next night. Images of Clemente making a basket catch at the right field wall of Three Rivers Stadium filled my head. Then I dreamt of her. My first love still hung like a photograph on the walls of my subconscious.

"Hey there handsome," she said, waking me.

"Hey, Angel." Make the best of the second day, I thought. Salvage the remaining time and don't discuss her departure.

Angel washed her hands several times. She dressed, putting on blue jeans and a blue blouse. Her eyes seemed browner than ever in the morning sunlight. The light accented tints of burgundy in her hair.

We left. I locked the hotel door and we scurried to my jeep. We drove the scenic route to Santa Monica. I drove with my left hand on the wheel and my right hand on her inner thigh.

She caught me up on her life.

"I like my work as a home care giver. Before that, I had my own business."

"Yeah? Doing what?"

"I opened a bridal shop for a while.   I think it was a way to hold on to the idea of love, you know?   I dreamt of a happy marriage, but I didn't have one.   I felt married and single at the same time.   Tiger and I were together alone, like married singles.   When I closed the shop I decided to-"

"What made you close it?"

"Well, it was hard to make a profit.   People kept pressuring me for a discount.   You know it's always the people who had money that were the worst.   But there was this poor couple one time.   She had missing teeth and he had cross-eyes.   They were backwoods. Total hicks.   But they had this connection, this chemistry between them that made me think of us."   I smiled.

We reached the parking lot at the Santa Monica pier.   The sun blinded our eyes.

We picnicked at the beach.   I took Angel's hand in mine and squeezed it.   The Malibu mountains were to the right, the Santa Monica Pier to the left.   The rollercoaster and Ferris wheel at the pier made me recall West View Park.   I told her how Danceland burned down, the summer after we were there.

"That's too bad," she said.

"Everything changes," I said.

We cast bread from the pier, then walked the beach hand in hand in the blaze of the cleansing sunlight.   The ocean made a low heavy rolling sound.   The water shimmered.   The sand felt cold and wet on our feet as we strolled along the shore.   The foam washed over our toes.   A strong wave brought in a mishmash of shells, rocks, and plastic toys.

I looked at her.   I liked the way she was backlit, the shining sun behind her.   Her skin was translucent.

We passed tourists, some young and some old. The old walked in pairs in dark shades, straw hats, Bermuda shorts and Hawaiian shirts. Blue veins sprouted from their legs and their faces were puffy and white. The young had skin like rubber, smooth and tan. Girls with small breasts and boys with tiny behinds ran to the water with boogie-boards. We watched the kids horse around with their boards in the water then walked by a Mexican family, mother, father, and a small girl playing with a volleyball and speaking Spanish.

We rented a tandem bike and rode on the sidewalk parallel to the beach. Seagulls soared out over the ocean as it rolled majestically in and out. We rode to Venice and back again, passing incense vendors, sidewalk painters, and palm readers. We stopped on the way back at the pier for a carousel ride. After returning the tandem, we kissed again, her lips yielding to me. Then I smiled at her.

"I like it when you smile," she said. "Have I ever told you?"

"Several times."

"What were you smiling about?"

"I know what heaven is," I said. "It's quite different from what Sister Ruth told me."

"It is?" she asked.

"But we probably shouldn't tell her."

"No. She wouldn't understand."

After eating blue shaved ice at the Playland Arcade, we headed back to the beach. We walked around the trash, syringes, and fast food cups mixed with the seaweed on the shore. We wrote our names in the sand.

"There's a Bob Dylan song I play over and over," she said. "*I Shall Be Released.* You've given me the courage to believe I'll be released, Jeremiah. One day, I'll divorce Tiger, you'll see."

"Sure you will. I believe in you."

I smiled at a small boy and girl splashing in the water. I puffed on a cigar Spiritos had given me, watching the vaporous smoke rings float away and disappear. When it was finished, I extinguished my cigar underfoot.

We danced on the beach. She waved her arms and turned around in circles. I watched her buttocks as she jiggled. We drifted towards Ocean Avenue in the soft moonlight.

*****

Back at the hotel, we watched TV and talked, sprawled out on the bed. "I live on a hill," she said.

"I know. I've been there." I told her how I saw her for several seconds, walking from her house to the garage.

"You stalked me," she said, playfully slapping my leg.

"Yeah. Does it bother you?"

"No, you weren't a dangerous stalker, so it doesn't bother me. It's flattering, actually."

"What's flattering about it?"

"That you were so curious and couldn't stay away."

She told me more about her childhood and her father. "Paulo was his name, he was a Harley guy," she said, stroking my brow. She glanced to the angel tattoo on my left bicep. "I'm thinking of getting a tattoo with the Harley wings and Sarah's name." She told me her father sired nine daughters with various women.

Her lips had a downward twist and were soft as cushions. I stared at her in a post-kiss daze.

"Play me a song," she said. We sat up on the bed and I strummed my Washburn. "I like watching your fingers move from chord to chord." The smoothness as I transitioned from G to E minor to C to D fascinated her.

She helped me pick the songs to put on my next album. I sang the words I wrote for her.

*"All my life I wanted to love you/I didn't know if you were real/Is there a light, Angel, above you?/Is there a hope for what I feel?"*

"Yes there is hope," she said, smiling. "You're such an amazing songwriter. I hear in your voice the same longing I feel in your lips when you kiss me, baby."

"It's all for you. Every single song." I gave her a tape of my music she could take with her. "This will pass the time on the way home."

She reciprocated, removing a cassette from her duffel bag. "I made this for you. It has all our songs."

*"Baby, I Love Your Way?"*

"How did you know?"

"Lucky guess."

She unpacked her pink Barbie doll tape player and put the tape on. *Baby I Love Your Way* was the first song, followed by *What a Wonderful World,* and *Chances Are.*

I relaxed. She gave me a hand massage. It felt good to my fingers, wearied from playing guitar.

"I used to give manicures," she said. "I learned how to give great hand massages."

When the tape finished playing, we watched *Magnum P.I.*

"This is nice, even the little things, like watching TV with you," I said.

"That's because we don't get to do the every day things," she said.  "If we were together every day, you'd get used to it.  It wouldn't be such a big deal."

"Every second with you is a big deal."

"I couldn't live up to your dream if you saw me up close every day."

"That *is* my dream, to be with you night and day."

"You don't know me, Jeremiah."  She paused.  "I need to tell you about the procedure."  She swallowed and looked to me for approval.

"Go on," I said reluctantly.

"Tiger beat me.  He told me he wasn't paying for a kid and he didn't want me getting fat.  He bullied me into it.  I'm not saying I wasn't responsible.  I think about her all the time.  It's like a wound under a Band-Aid.  I'll never forgive myself, and I'll never forgive Tiger."

"You've got to forgive yourself."

"I don't know how to."

I told her about my dream, how Sarah told me she forgave Angel.

She started to cry.  "I've been praying that if Sarah ever forgave me, she'd let me know.  Thank you, Jeremiah.  You don't know how much that means to me."

We kissed again and things heated up.  She rewound the tape to play Frampton again.  *Suddenly the day turns into night, far away from the city...*

She pressed her body against mine.  My strength, though diminished, returned.  After some initial trouble when I first entered her, I stiffened.

I was Clemente, about to hit Jon Matlock's pitch for the three thousandth hit.   This was the peak moment I'd longed for all my life.

I liked how she felt underneath.   I tasted her and she was on fire.   I inhaled the scent of her flesh.

*Don't hesitate, 'cause your love won't wait...*

I danced in and out of her.   Angel's wings wrapped around me and we waltzed into the land of milk and honey.   She shook in the darkness, surrendering.

Our muscles relaxed.   I held her tight in my arms like it was never-ending.

"Sleepy?" she asked.

"Yeah.   You?"

"Yeah."   She smiled and looked into my eyes. "Goodnight, baby.   Pleasant dreams."

We slept together curled up like spoons.

*****

Hours later, she stirred and woke me.   I reached down below her stomach, rubbing her between her legs until she shuddered.

*What a miracle.   Like the bud of a rose opening, wet and lovely.   They were naked and not ashamed, and it was very good.*

"Jeremiah?" she said.

"Hmmm?"

"I love you."

Angel slept beside me.   The neon signs of the Paradise Palms Lodge flashed red light on the window.     I looked at her and smiled.   My eyes started to swell.   Eden was ours.

*****

She looked angelic in the morning.   I gazed at her as she emerged from her sleepy haze.   Her eyes opened with wetness, and her lips shone with saliva. I leaned in and kissed her cheek, still feverish from dreams.

"Good morning, baby. I sensed your stare," she said.

She got up and walked to the bathroom. I heard her pee, splash cold water on her face, and wash her hands. After she came back into bed, we fondled each other for a while.

Angel hopped up and put on Mickey Mouse ears that she'd kept in one of her bags. Her eyes enlarged when she had a plan brewing.

"Since we met when we were kids," she said, "why don't we play like happy, carefree children of a loving God?"

"Are you taking me on a date, Angel Vickers?"

"Its part of a promise I made to you years ago."

"What promise?"

"When you took me to West View Park, I promised you I'd take you to a special place one day."

"You have a good memory."

"Today is the day."

"Where's our date, Angel?"

"The happiest place on earth. But if you really want to go, you need to be a good boy and get all cleaned up for Mama. Follow me." She beckoned me with her finger.

I followed her to the tub. "There's no bubble bath," she said. "Can you ask for some at the front desk?"

"Sure."

I ran down the hallway and flew into the elevator just as the doors closed. I formed a funny face at my reflection in the silver elevator doors. I maneuvered around an old couple arguing in the lobby, then whisked by a lonely heart girl who threw me a buck-toothed smile.

The desk clerk was a plump man in a fancy vest, surrounded by key cards and china-white telephones. He didn't have any bubble bath so I took shampoo instead.

I rushed back to Angel.

"That'll work," she said as I caught my breath.

We shared a bath and talked in the tub, soaking in the hot water and shampoo suds. After a while, we dressed for our day of fun and frolic.

*****

Angel and I glided in on the Monorail, than rode a horse drawn carriage down Main Street USA, passing the floats and Disney characters. We smiled and waved to Pluto and Goofy.

We stepped down from the carriage and skipped to the entrance. She talked and it was easy to listen to her.

She delighted in telling me funny things she did. There was laughter and self parody in her tales. We entered Disneyland and boarded the merry-go round, riding the carousel horses. I assisted her down from her purple horse when the ride ended.

We rode Snow White's scary adventures, letting our hands glide over each other when it was dark. We met Mickey Mouse at his house.

"This is the most fun I've ever had," she said. "You look like something's on your mind." She paused. "Penny?"

"Penny?"

"For your thoughts."

"I was thinking about how I couldn't get over the fact I lost you. I know normal guys forget their first love and grow and move on, but I never could. I fought it every second, every minute, every hour. I couldn't forget. I couldn't let go."

She reached for my hand. "Neither could I. I was missing you bad a while back. I had some kind of breakdown and Tiger wanted to put me in a madhouse. He said he wanted me to get shock treatments if that would remove you from my head. My mother and grandmother came over the house and prayed with me. The doctor put me on antidepressants. So I guess we both were crazy, and somehow we got stuck in the summer of 1980."

We held hands and walked to the white columned Haunted House. The line was long, wrapping serpentine around the southern-plantation mansion. I felt grace in these simple things. Her hands contained more restorative power than the hands of any healing evangelist. Visions of her were more powerful to me than my Pentecostal past. We walked past gravestones with inscriptions like "Tomb, Sweet Tomb," and "R.I.P."

We made it to the front and into the parlor of the haunted mansion. The Victorian Gothic wallpaper was bandaged in "Ashes of Rose." The lights went out to start the ride. A scream echoed through the chamber and a corpse swung like a pendulum from the ceiling. I seized the opportunity of the darkness and pulled her close.

The lights came back on and we approached our seats for the ride. We stepped into the Doom Buggy as it glided on the conveyor belt. I pulled the steel safety bar tight to our chest. We floated through the dusty cobwebs, passing the portrait gallery where an Egyptian lady in repose transformed into a tiger. We watched the ghostly apparitions dance in the ballroom.

I caressed her.

Our clam-like doom car curved around the bend where books moved in and out of their shelves, than we rode through animatronic spooks and sinister talking busts warning us.

"Beware…take care…" they warned us.

Next, we soared through the ominous séance room with Madame Leota and her moonlit spell book, turned to page 1313. We passed through baroque shadows of idiosyncratic hobgoblins, and exited the Stretching Gallery. Gargoyles clutched flickering candles in their claws and spouted warnings.

"Stay Together…"

A specter flashed Angel a grim grin and she squeezed the blood out of my arm.

*****

In line for Big Thunder Mountain, we stood behind a small, sweaty girl. She was petite with dishwater hair. I thought about Angel as a girl, how her innocence was stolen.

"How long, Mommy?" the girl whined. "Why's it taking so long?"

"The best things we have to wait for. And waiting is hard, isn't it?" her mother said, wiping the sweat off her daughter's forehead with a handkerchief.

"Yes, waiting is hard," I whispered, looking at Angel.

When the next ride ended, we sat in the Enchanted Tiki Room. I watched the singing birds and orchids.

After catching our breath, we ran to the Pirates of the Caribbean in the scorching summer afternoon. The boats carried us past the robotic pirates.

"Hands inside the boat at all times," a voice instructed over the loud speaker.

We felt the water with our fingers in defiance of the prohibition. The boat floated by the Blue Bayou restaurant, a diner where it was always twilight time.   We coursed through the dark and the pirate song played '*yo-ho, yo-ho, a pirate's life for me.*'

When the park closed, we drove back to Paradise Palms and cuddled naked in our room.

"Pleasant dreams, Jeremiah," she said.

For one last transitory moment, we were together.   Like a dream, we knew it would soon be gone in the reality of the morning.

***** 

I woke a few hours later in the dark room.   I pressed my flank against hers.   We were both on our backs.   I heard her howl in pain.   She pressed her hand to her belly.

"What's wrong?"

"My stomach."   She inhaled, her face crunching in agony. "I've been seeing a doctor."

"What's he say?"

"I've got ulcers and problems going to the bathroom, something with my colon."

"When did the pains first begin?"

"When Sarah died.   I had a nightmare she was still here." She sat up and exhaled.   "At first, it started in the middle of the night.   Sudden, stabbing pains hitting my stomach while I was half-asleep.   I thought it was Tiger punching me with his knuckles. Then, I woke up and saw he was snoring.   I realized the stabbing pains came from *inside* my stomach, not outside.   They came quicker, one after another like corn popping in a pot."

"You think of her a lot don't you?"

"How can I not?   Sarah's been stalking me.   Sometimes, when I'm driving, I see a small girl standing in the center of the road, and I jam on my brakes.   And then she vanishes.   Last week, I was at the park having lunch with a couple friends and I saw her there, standing a few feet behind my friends. I told them. They turned around and couldn't see her. She called out, 'Mommy, Mommy…'"

"Sarah's been stalking you because she wants to tell you its okay."

"I hope so. I want the pain to stop."

I thought about what Spiritos said about Kathryn Kuhlman. *Even though healing prayer doesn't always work, sometimes it still does.*

A memory returned to my mind of Kathryn touching my hands when I was a little boy. I remembered the intense heat tingling in my fingers and Kathryn telling me I got the gift. "Can I pray for you?" I asked.

"Sure, baby," she said, looking surprised. She closed her eyes.

I placed my hand on her stomach, and kept my eyes open to observe any effect. I concentrated every ounce of love into her midsection.

"I speak to the pain in Angel's abdomen, commanding guilt to be gone. I pray her stomach will produce acid in normal levels. I declare the ulcers are now dissolved, and the tissues affected are healed. I decree a new stomach lining is forming. I speak healing and cleansing to the colon, for the nerves controlling it to be loosed."

I took her pain into my own body for a moment. Her face relaxed.

"Omigod, I feel a burning heat all through my stomach," she said. "Your hand's really hot, Jeremiah."

"Don't worry. It won't burn you."

"Why is it so hot?"

"Maybe it's like laser surgery, concentrated light and heat."

"The pain's gone. Omigod, the pain's gone."

I moved my hand from her stomach to her forehead. "Most of all, I speak peace and forgiveness into her mind and heart. Help Angel forgive herself the way you forgive her and the way Sarah forgives her."

"Thanks, baby."

"You're welcome, Angel."

Angel slept with a smile and I soon followed her.

# 31

Angel was away for three days visiting her sister in Atlanta, so I flew to Mount Olympus to do what I had to do.  Everything was packed.  The Stick Man mask.  My Roberto Clemente bat.

I drove the rental car from the Buffalo airport, across the New York state line into Pennsylvania.  There wasn't much traffic to speak of, a world of difference from the sprawling congestion of Los Angeles.  An occasional pick-up passed with a redneck blaring country music.

I parked a few blocks away from the Ogerman house.  I tiptoed over the gravel road and hid in some brush to scan the situation.  I saw the number on the white house with blue shudders, 43 Reginal Creek Road.  Dogs barked.  To the side of the house, sat an RV and a rusted pick-up truck.  The bumper was covered with NASCAR stickers.  Beer cans were strewn in the parched grass around the truck.  The front yard looked like an auto salvage yard.  The smell of gasoline was in the air.  I watched Tiger walk from the house to the pick-up truck, a fresh brew in his greasy hand.

I reached into my faded brown duffel bag and felt my wooden Stick Man mask.  Tiger cranked up the southern rock anthem *Freebird* on speakers mounted outside the kitchen windows.  I felt heat inside the mask when I slipped it over my head.  Sweat stung my eyes.  I gripped the handle of my Clemente bat.  I waited for Tiger to go inside the house again.

Tiger adjusted an engine and lowered it into the truck, making a loud clanging sound.  He looked down at his hands and noticed they were black with grease.  He wiped his brow, leaving marks on his face.  He took a bite of his sandwich.

Tiger sauntered into his house, home alone.   My heart pounded like heavy-metal chords.

*It's now or never.*

I crept to the front door and slowly opened it.   The house smelled of cat piss and spoiled food.   Clutter was everywhere. With Angel away, he'd let the place go.

My heart pounded as I approached closer.

Tiger heard the screen door and walked out.   Seeing me in the Stick Man mask, he was startled.

"What the fuck..." he said.

Tiger dashed to the mantel above the living room fireplace and grabbed his pistol from the ledge below his mounted eight-foot buck.   I took advantage of Tiger's pause.   I had the instincts of Clemente reacting to a fastball and swung my bat, connecting with Tiger's right arm and sending the pistol sailing to the other side of the room.   The strains of electric guitar lead notes from *Free Bird* filtered through the window.   The song built to its climactic fanfare, repeating the G, Bb, and C chords as the two lead guitarists bent the notes higher and higher.   The snare drum beat out the quarter notes like a hammer on steel.

Thunder rumbled in the black sky overhead.   "I know what you've been doing to Angel," I said.

"Who the fuck are you?"

"Someone who's telling you the way it is."

"Let me tell *you* the way it is.   Eve is mine.   She doesn't want you.   And she's going to be upset that you came here."

"You tell her I was here, I break your legs and arms.   If you touch her again, I'll kill you."

Tiger lunged at me and I waved the bat. It merged with my arm, an extended wooden limb striking him on the skull. It sounded like the smashing of a coconut.

"Please don't kill me," he begged. "I won't ever hurt her again."

"You won't hurt her for a long time, because you're going to be hurting for a long time," I said, striking him across the face.

Blood splattered from his temple. Tiger crouched on the floor, shaking. He raised his hands and arms to shield his face.

"You were given a woman with a heart of gold and you treated her like shit," I said. "You don't appreciate her. You're nothing but a scared little boy hiding behind your macho façade. You want everyone to think you're the life of the party, but when I see you, you know what I see?" I waited a moment for Tiger to answer, but he was too stunned. "Nothing but a pathetic," I paused to draw out the words, "insecure bully."

"Plea-," Tiger struggled to get out a word before I interrupted him, smashing a wobbly wooden coffee table with a stroke of my bat.

"You hurt her. Don't you know you hurt her?"

"I'm sorry. Please. You can have her. Is that what you want? Just don't kill me. Please."

His bravado was gone. I felt pity for a moment and lowered the bat to my side. Tiger maneuvered to the phone and dialed 911. I noticed out of the corner of my eyes, having excellent peripheral vision.

Tiger whispered into the phone. "He's crazy. I don't know who he is."

I swung again, breaking Tiger's finger and smashing the phone in one fell swoop. I crowed a triumphant guttural roar.

Bang.

I swung again, and Tiger's blood spattered over my hands.

The blood the blood the blood the blood the blood the blood the blood the blood.

*"YOU'LL NEVER HURT HER AGAIN!!!!"* I said, screaming in triumph. *"TELL THEM STICK MAN'S HERE, MOTHERFUCKER!"*

# 32

In the morning, I rubbed my eyes and saw her standing over me, looking down and smiling.

"Wake up, birthday boy.   The nightmare's over, baby."

I looked at my hands and was startled to see there was no blood on them.   She wore the same red dress she dazzled me with in 1980.   She spun like a top sending the edges of the dress billowing upward, showing off her matching red panties and dancing shoes. Her brown eyes were morning misty, like a foggy evening on the California coast.

The golden morning poured through the curtains and shone on her.   She had an apple in her hand and tossed it in the air.   The apple twirled through the sunlit motel room before she caught it. She cut a slice and fed it to me.

"An apple a day keeps the doctor away," she said.

"I can't believe you kept the dress."

She sat down on the bed beside me and played with her apple. She bit into the apple, than wiped her lips with the back of her hand. I lightly caressed and savored her sunburned legs.

"I never should've changed my flight," she said.   "Play guitar for me one last time."

I strummed my Washburn and sang the lyrics I wrote to her when I was seventeen.   *'Angel, why do you have to go?   Angel, I'm going to miss you so.'*

She took another bite of her apple and sang along through the juice in her mouth.   The pungent summer heat was heavy in the hotel room.   She finished the apple and twisted her round bottom to aim for the waste can and toss the apple core in the tin bucket.

"Two points," she said.

I felt my nerves naked with pleasure, a level of awareness beyond my conscious state. I anticipated another trip with her to paradise.

I rested my Washburn against the wall and my hand crept up her thigh again, finding the warm cavity. Her head arched back. My mouth reached her neck. She stretched out on the bed.

I kissed her. Descending, dropping, swirling. I played her, moving my hands and mouth, sliding from fret to fret through an entire octave until I reached the highest notes of her strings. I strummed her faster and faster in rhythm, discovering the perfect pitch.

She tugged me forward with her remaining strength and looked into my face. Angel wrapped her wings around my waist. Her arching force pressed me into her warm capaciousness until I rose to a trembling encore.

We finished the song, and lay in bed.

*****

Time passed. Angel came to and walked into the bathroom to wash her hands and get dressed.

I lay on the bed, writing a poem about her in my journal. I hid it in my suitcase, not wanting to show her until I knew it was the final draft.

I walked into the bathroom and watched her brush her brown hair. I snuck up behind her and kissed her on the back of her neck.

"That's one of my hot spots," she said.

"I know."

"Can I ask you something?" she said.

"Sure."

"When you woke up this morning, you seemed upset, like you were having a nightmare."

"I was."

I wasn't sure if I should tell her, but in a moment of impulse I described the dream about my revenge on Tiger.

Her smile evaporated. "As much as he's hurt me, I don't want to see that happen to him. I would stop you if you ever tried to kill him."

"It's only a dream." She was shaking. "I'm sorry I upset you, Angel."

"I'm bothered by the violence, but it's not just that. You have a false vision. He's not like you portray him. You make him out to be trailer trash with beer cans and cat piss on the floor. He rarely drinks at home, maybe if a friend visits, he'll offer them a beer. If that's what you think of my house and my husband, than that reflects poorly on me."

This hit home.

"I still haven't forgiven him completely. But I've only told you the bad things about him. Like I said before, he's a good man. He's hilarious sometimes. I'm not a sick individual for staying. There are good reasons why I love him." She caught herself saying love in the present tense. "I meant *loved* him."

"So he's a good man because he hasn't pushed your head into a plate glass window for a few days?" I asked. "Does a good sense of humor make up for how he's damaged you?"

"Oh, please. You don't want to hear anything good about him. You read into things and assume the worse."

I felt accused. Something about the way she said the word 'you' was a slap in my face. "Put yourself in my shoes. Don't you see how crazy it is?" I said.

My legs felt numb. My fantasy of Eden fell away, trampled underfoot by her treasure-trove of secrets and pathologies.

"Yeah, I see. Look, I don't want it to end like this. Enough of that. Let's get breakfast, Mister. My treat, since you turn twenty-one today."

*****

We ate breakfast in the Caribou, the patio café at Paradise Palms. The place was crowded. People around us sat and talked, eating eggs and drinking coffee. The large windows surrounding the café had a view of a pond with swans swimming in circles.

The waitress surprised us, catching us holding hands and staring. She was heavy-set, with frizzy hair. Her voice was extra-loud.

"Nice to see two people in love," she said.

I read her name tag, white with "Shirley" in blue capital letters.

"Thanks, Shirley." I said.

Angel smiled at her and ordered pancakes. "I like tasting the butter and the pancakes too. That's why I don't use too much syrup."

"Just the right mix," I said.

I watched her soak her teabag, then lift it up and dip it again. I noticed her lips counting as she dunked it in and out.

I didn't like needing her so much, knowing my fragile heart was in her hands.

"I guess in a way, I'm a hypocrite," I said. "I hate Tiger for cheating on you and how he treats you. But I'm doing the same thing with a married woman. I justify it in my mind." I sipped my coffee. "When I first saw you, we were so young. Who knew the feelings would last this long?"

"One time Tiger told me the only reason another man would ever want me is for sex.   But I know, with us, that's not true.   It's not just sex, it's the connection.   The way we talk."

"When we're old and grey, you'll still be my friend," I said.

She chuckled.   "You're my best friend, Jeremiah."   Shirley brought the food and slipped it on the table, not wanting to interrupt our conversation.

"And you're my best friend."

"I can't bear the thought of you not in my life, baby."

She ripped into the pancake like a lioness and took large gulps of tea.   I smiled at this.

*****

I drove her to LAX on the 405.   My favorite Partridge Family song played on the radio.   *"We've been traveling in circles such a long long time, trying to say hello, Ho..."*

Angel yelled, "Ho!" in sync with the song and laughed.

*"I'll meet you halfway, that's better than no way,"* David Cassidy sang.   The DJ was playing all the right songs.

She asked me to stop at a grocery store on Century Boulevard and wait in the car.   She returned with a white baker's box and told me to drive on.

I pulled in front of LAX, by the sign for departing flights. "Is Tiger picking you up in Buffalo?"

"He better."

Before dropping her off and saying goodbye, I put my arms around her and kissed her one last time.   A deep, long kiss.

"Do me a favor," she said.   "Eat healthy.   And keep painting and writing songs."

"Okay.   I will."   Her wet lips were cool.   The inside of her mouth was hot.   "I'm glad I found you again."

"You not only found me. You helped me find me," Angel said. She gave me the white baker's box. "Open it. Hurry."

Inside was a large chocolate cup cake with a blue candle and the number twenty-one in white icing. "Thanks, Angel."

"You're welcome. Happy Birthday, baby. Bubbye." She kissed me, shut the door and walked away.

A sharp pain seized my chest. I felt like a boy, lost in a supermarket, unsure where my mom was. I convulsed, feeling the relief of salty streams and grief noises that were pent up for years. I looked down at my fingers, as if by staring I could stop the tremors.

She checked in at the curb. Car horns blared, honking at me to move so they could drop off their passengers.

"Move the goddamned car," a mustached man yelled from behind.

I looked at him in my rearview mirror for a second, but didn't budge. I looked over to Angel and couldn't stop staring, in case it was the last time I'd see her. She saw my mental meltdown from afar and ran back to me.

"It's okay," she said, rushing into my jeep.

"I lost you once, now I'm losing you again." My face was smeared.

"But I'm here now, baby. I'm with you this time." She embraced me, stroking my hair. "Let it all out, sweetheart. Mama's here. Take a deep breath."

"All that time, I never knew why."

"I know, I know. It may not be any consolation, but my heart's breaking now too."

I calmed down.

"Don't miss your plane," I said.

"I love your way," she said as she left for the last time.

"Baby, I love your way," I said.

Through my rear window, I watched her walk inside the airport. Her checkered shorts cradled her behind as she drifted away. She moved with a new confidence. A migraine hammered my head. I pressed the gas pedal and drove away, merging into traffic between a blue shuttle van and a white limo.

I turned on the car radio, hoping for the right song. *Baby, I Love Your Way* by Frampton was playing. *Thanks, God.*

I loved her way. The way she dipped her teabag in her cup. The way she brought me a moist towel and cleaned me. The way she counted with her fingers, tapping them in unison..two...four...six...eight...ten. The way she shrugged off my compliments and said, "Oh, stop." The way she sang along with the car radio and shouted out the lyrics. The look in her eyes when I played my guitar for her. The way her small hand fit into mine.

*I can see the sunset in your eyes, brown and grey and blue besides...*

She flew home to Tiger Ogerman in Mount Olympus. I hoped she'd leave him if he ever hurt her again. I held the picture of Angel from my seventeenth summer in my memory, before she forgot who she was.

I drove back to my apartment on Laurel Canyon.

*****

The next day, the Musician's Union held a get-together at the Paradise Palms Lodge. The gathering was in the Waterfall Room, a banquet area seating a couple hundred people.

A tawdry MC impressionist mimicked Sean Connery, James Cagney, and Jack Nicholson. The audience sat at round tables, covered by ivory linens. The room was surrounded by a glass window looking out towards an outside garden with a bridge. A drop down ivory curtain covered the walls.

I stayed for fifteen minutes than decided to leave. The place was too painful a reminder of her. I thought about how we were just there, in Room 21. I didn't want to break down in public. On the way out, I stopped at the Caribou Cafe. I went to the same table, and sat. I heard her laughing and saw her happy brown eyes. I remembered how she'd ate her pancakes, blending the butter and maple syrup with her fork. I looked out the large windows to the pond with the swans gliding by.

"You look like you're drowning. Where's your lady friend?" a female voice said.

I looked up and saw Shirley the waitress scratching her bushy hair. "Had to go back home."

"I'm sorry. You look as down as down can be." Her face was sympathetic. "What can I get you, to pick you up? A cup of joe? On the house."

"No, thanks, Shirley. I just wanted to sit here for a moment."

"A hopeless romantic. My kind of man. You sit here as long as you need to." She touched my hand and the look on her face told me she understood.

"That's okay. I'll be going. I don't want to take a table from your paying customers."

I drove north on Coldwater to get lunch. Through a restaurant window I saw a teenage boy and his girlfriend talking up a storm at a booth at Norm's Restaurant on Sherman Way. I stopped in and sat at the table beside them. The girl had a slight resemblance to Angel. Shoulder-length dark hair, brown eyes.

"Ghosts." I said aloud to myself. "Everywhere I look."

The boy complimented her. "Oh, please. Stop," the girl said, dipping her teabag.

I wished for a moment I could trade places, and turn back time to the summer of my first love.

I tried to hold myself together, stirring more milk into my coffee. The blush of infatuation was on their faces. I wanted to eat of Eve's apple again, with its illusory promise of Eden. I realized I spent more time wanting her than having her, but maybe in some ways, wanting was more powerful than having.

Suddenly, a Mexican busboy dropped a tray of dishes. The patrons applauded. Embarrassed, he cleaned up the mess of broken china and food. I wanted to slug the customers who were clapping. I paid my bill and left.

I drove back on Sherman Way. At the intersection of Sherman and Fulton, I stopped to let an elderly Armenian woman cross the street. This caused a yuppie behind me to roll down his window and yell. He beeped at me to speed up, so I drove slower, tapping my brakes to irritate my newfound nemesis. The normie passed and gave me the finger, honking his horn. I waved at him and smiled like we were best buddies.

Over the next few blocks, I tried to forget this when a large dog barked and leapt in the air. I drove past the corner and saw the dog was a German Shepherd in a black collar, walking his owner across the intersection, a Farrah Fawcett blonde in a pink jogging suit. At the corner across the street, a Spanish man sold roses out of a white bucket and bags of fresh oranges. I smelled hot dogs from a second Mexican man beside him with a small food cart on wheels. It made me think of the circus, the smell of wieners and innocence wafting through the canvas tent, over the sawdust trail.

There was a circus in my mind, thoughts firing like firecrackers. I pictured myself as a clown, with white-face and a red-bulb nose as I made a right on Coldwater. Mordecai Rawlings invaded my thoughts, dressed as a ringmaster.

"Hurry, hurry, step right up..." he said, cracking his whip and chaining me with papier-mâché, devouring me like a sharp-fanged lion, tearing me to ribbons of ruin. I rolled down my window and exhaled.

Evening approached. I drove Mulholland with the windows down, smelling the jasmine and jacaranda blossoms at twilight and taking in the 360-degree jetliner view from the overlook. I thought perhaps it was all a dream. But the taste of her was still on my lips. The smell of her perfume was still on my face. No, it was no dream.

I veered off to a wooded picnic area and pulled up to an open barbecue pit. The air was thick. I opened the trunk door on my Jeep and held it ajar while I removed the Stick Man mask from a plastic 7-Eleven bag and set it on the ground. I checked my gasoline can that I kept in the car. I shook it and was relieved to find there was a little gas left. I tossed the wooden mask in the pit, doused it, and lit the face that haunted me for years, watching it burn.

*I guess that's the last of you.*

I watched the flames. Nothing remained of Stick Man. There was only the dusk and the thick smell of smoke. I stood alone, weeping in the shadows, remembering my father Saul, the storyteller.

*"Tell us a story," I said, shaking Dad from his stupor. We lay beside him in bed.*

*Dad's voice was raw from singing for the barflies from ten p.m. till two in the morning. He smelled of Pall Mall cigarettes and Old Spice.*

He whispered, "Once upon a time, there were two little boys. Jeremiah and Walker. They set off for a walk through the woods. They got lost. The day dragged on and it got very dark." At this, we sat up. Walker clenched his fist. "They came to a haunted house. The windows were boarded up. No one knew what was inside."

"I ain't afraid of ghosts," Walker said.

"Inside the house they saw a monster with a wooden mask."

"Stick Man," I said.

"Stick Man. Than Jeremiah climbed the stairs, up into the attic. There was a magic mirror next to the door. When Jeremiah and Walker gazed into the mirror, they couldn't see their faces. They saw the face of Stick Man in the mirror. Laughing." Dad cackled. "Jeremiah opened the door. He found the key to unlock Stick Man's mask, and learn the truth about who he was."

"What happened when he took Stick Man's mask off?" Walker asked.

"They saw that Stick Man was sad because everyone was afraid of him. 'I don't mean to do the things I do,' he said. 'Forgive me."

Mom was in the doorway eavesdropping. "I don't want you scaring them right now, Saul," she said, coming in with fresh washrags. "Jeremiah has bad dreams as it is."

"Finish the story, Daddy," Walker said.

"Why don't you finish the story, Jeremiah?" Dad asked. "You need to figure out the ending since you're the one who sees Stick Man."

"There are ghosts in the house, but we fight them and chase them away. And Stick Man is gone from our dreams forever," I said. "That'll be the end."

I searched the ashes for scraps, any fragment of Stick Man that may have survived the fire.  His face turned to ash as I wept.  I heard the stern sound of my father commanding me to stop my tears.

I walked to my Jeep and felt relieved it was over.  I imagined the circus again and pictured myself leaping from the trapeze.  My slippery fingers released the restraints of religion, leaving Mordecai back on the platform of fear-based faith.

I coasted Mulholland, sailing mid-air.  I soared between certainty and God-knows-what.  I decided to embrace mystery, a tentative toilet-paper faith, not confined by creeds, but defined by deeds.

I made the left on Coldwater Canyon, at the Tree People environmental preservation lot.  Traffic was light, and soon I passed the liquor store on Riverside Drive.  I turned left off Riverside on to Laurel Canyon.  A few raindrops sprinkled on my windshield.  I clicked the wipers and watched the blades move from left to right.

I reached the 5000 block of Laurel Canyon.  I reached up to the visor on the driver's side and pressed my garage opener, triggering the lift on the security gate.  I drove into the underground garage, than walked up the sidewalk where I stopped to admire the flowers.  The scent of honeysuckle rode the soft breeze.  The fountain flowing between the naked cherubs made me think of Angel.

*Naked and not ashamed*, I thought, as I unlocked my apartment door and walked into my living room.

The sun finished her final chorus and the moon emerged for the night refrain.  I shuffled to my closet and found my paintbrushes.  I set them out on the table, then opened the top drawer of my dresser and found yellow legal pads and four pencils.  I placed the pads and pencils by the painting supplies then scribbled a reminder:

*Paint a portrait of me and Angel walking the beach at Santa Monica.*

I retired to my bedroom earlier than usual. I set my alarm for an early call-time. I looked forward to working at my painting again, which I hoped would be a form of prayer.

I wasn't sure what the future held, but I had new memories and moments to ponder. The circus barker in my brain bellowed again. The balloons waved, flying in faithful tandem. I reached for the popcorn landing on the other side of Angel.

I pushed away the disturbing thought that I didn't really have her, that she was sleeping beside Tiger that night instead of me. I had to face the sobering truth that she stayed yoked to a stultifying marriage, existing under the thumb of an under-evolved man.

I wondered if I created Angel out of Eve Vickers just as I created my paintings and my songs. Maybe I was sleeping like Adam when she was fashioned from the rib of my dreams.

I knew her in reality now, in the ordinariness of her life, rather than her celestial glory as my angelic muse. I faced the disparity that Angel grew more in my imagination than she grew in her own life.

I crawled into bed, wearing my Batman boxers and purple Lakers tee-shirt. I heard the rumbling cars outside rolling out like waves kissing Santa Monica beach. My chest rose and fell to the rhythm. I pulled the sheet over my belly and reached for my cupcake. After lighting my 21$^{st}$ birthday candle, I said a prayer, recounting the good things I was grateful for.

"Thank You God for a great day in Hollywood. For my friends, and that I got to see Angel again. Thank you for the talents You've entrusted to me and that my creativity is a small part of Your creativity. I glorify You with my art and music as an act of worship.

Release me from the bondage of the extremes of grandiosity and inferiority, that I may affect others with my work and carry Your message forward. Heal my childhood wounds. I realize now, this healing isn't something You do to me, but through me, and in me. I surrender my talents to You, knowing You will flow through them in just the right way. I open myself to Your direction and abundance that I may know joy and peace in my work. Please let me set aside everything that I think I know about You, for an open mind and a new experience with You...Amen."

I remembered Spiritos telling me prayer was more for our sake than for God's. I rolled over on my side, wrapping my green blanket around my shoulder and recalling the verse from Corinthians about becoming a man and letting go of childish things. The corridor between childhood and maturity illuminated before me.

Mid-air in my mental trapeze between fundamentalism and freedom, the wind whispered, "Choose grace, not guilt, sweet clown. Compassion, not condemnation. Love, not legalism..."

I cast off my childhood concept of God, the punitive ogre threatening me that my affair with Angel would damn me forever in the flames of incineration. *If God exists, He must be pure love and He'll save and forgive us.* With this shift, the bi-polar heavenly Father faded from me.

The avenging wooden Christ figure was gone from my consciousness. It was replaced by a Good Shepherd, defending and protecting me with His rod and staff. In a moment of absolution, I knew I was forgiven, freed from mortal sin. I soaked in the serene silence.

The heavy darkness that shrouded me lifted and I could feel joy again. A sense of clarity seized me, fixing my attention to an awareness that was pure. For a moment, I glimpsed the richness and resilience of my own soul.

*It wasn't Angel's love that made me whole or banished Stick Man. I know. I finally know. What I was looking for was inside me all along.*

I heard the voices of other tenants on the patio outside my window as they settled in for the night. I realized I was able to let Angel go. I let my father go. I accepted their departure with the grace of a man, not the grief of a child.

"Good night, Shadow," I said to my furry friend, who purred on my chest and hadn't bit me for a while. Next to us, under the covers, was the stuffed German Shepherd Mom had given me years ago.

I heard a girl laughing outside my window. I sat up and saw her through the blinds. She was a new tenant moving into Apartment Eight. Her strawberry-blonde hair hung down the sides of her gossamer granny dress, and she carried a lamp in one hand and a poster of James Dean in the other.

*Hmmm...maybe we'll be friends.*

A Goth guy helped her. He carried a Casio keyboard and a bag of books and videos. He spoke with a nondescript European accent, something about the U-Haul. I wanted to see her movies and books. If the James Dean poster was any indication, she had good tastes. I thought about Natalie Wood, the celluloid version of Angel.

Then I remembered dreaming of a half-heart, floating like a kite through a storm. A warm wind blew Angel's matching half-heart to me. Like two pieces of a jig-saw puzzle, we seemed to fit together perfectly.

But I knew now, two halves could never make a whole. Only two whole people can sustain a partnership for a lifetime.

For as long as I could remember, a solitary pain, bleak and basic, made me terrified to face being alone.   I noticed, for the first time, I liked being by myself.   I enjoyed the quiet of my apartment in a way I never had before.   I listened to the sound of my own breathing and experienced the magnificence of my own solitude.

For several years, I'd tried to fix the world without fixing myself.   I looked for peace through Mordecai's ministry, through my music, and through my muse.   When I poured out for everyone else, I had nothing left to give back.   I had to get filled, too.

In my trapeze leap from guilt to grace, the net below caught me like a faithless flounder when I fell.   I landed in a safe womb when I strayed from the narrow way.

*Ta-dah!*

Lyrics leapt into my mind, so I grabbed one of the legal pads and scribbled them down:

*"Lose it all/In a great big fall*
*And there you find/Love was there all the time."*

# 33

Dear Angel,

It's three a.m. here, six a.m. your time.    I just woke up from a beautiful dream.    I don't remember everything exactly, but I was a boy again.    You were there, and so was Dad, both of you together with me and Mom and Walker at our old house.

The dream started with Dad and me listening to my new album, the songs I've written about you that he never lived to hear. Dad turned to me and said, "Most musicians live their whole life and never write music that good."

Then you and Mom came in, and Mom said that you'd been lost, looking for me in the North Hills of Pittsburgh.    You called the operator who gave you Mom's number.    You sat across from me and our eyes met in the stare, the sparkling eye connection like we did in 1980.

I'm enjoying the sweet silence of the night and savoring my dream.

Don't worry, one day you will be released.    I hope you're alright, that Tiger doesn't hurt you again.    I know life can hurt.    At times, memories of past pain pierce through me and become present again.    But these invasive remnants have become less paralyzing. They're distant, not devastating.

If Father McCormick's right about Purgatory, maybe Dad hasn't reached the light quite yet.    Maybe he's passing through the refining fire of God's purifying love, transforming him into the holiness of heaven.    Just in case, I'm praying every night for Dad to make it through okay.    I know he'll be okay, because I love him and want him to be okay, and if God is love then He's supposed to love Dad even more than I do.

*I'm not out of the woods yet, either. Perfect love hasn't completely banished my fear. I still fear some things, like death. I'm mad at death, and that Dad's body is decaying. I wonder what his body looks like. I hope the bugs haven't got into his coffin. Dad never liked bugs. He used to swat the flies and brush the ants off the picnic table when we had cook-outs at West View Park. "Lousy flies," he'd say. "Dammit anyway."*

*It's still hard to believe he's really dead. The poor guy's body is under the ground. I know people say the body is only a shell and his soul is with the Lord, but it's my Dad's face that's rotting away in the cemetery. The same face I looked at for twenty years growing up as the face of my Dad.*

*I hope to God heaven's true, that Dad's alive somewhere and it's not all bullshit, but I have moments sometimes when I worry that heaven's another fairy tale and that there's nothing but non-existence and non-consciousness after we pass. I think I fear this more than being tortured in hell. Hell doesn't make sense to me anyways. Remember when you told me, "If Mordecai's right that God will burn and torture ninety-five percent of humanity forever, then God is worse than Nebuchadnezzar and Hitler combined?" I never forgot that. I doubt Mordecai's genocidal god theory is true, but what if Savannah's right and this life is all there is?*

*The bible says the dead have "fallen asleep in the Lord." Spiritos told me he dislikes death but he doesn't fear death. "Why fear losing consciousness? It happens to us every night when we sleep," he said.*

*But when I sleep, I'm still awake and aware. There are dreams, like the wonderful world I went to last night that took me back to Pittsburgh and to you as my girlfriend. If in death the heart stops and the brain dies, how can I even dream? It's just nothing. Zero. Zilch. Zip. I hate to think about death.*

*I believe the resurrection most of the time. It's more likely, based on the evidence, Jesus rose from the dead. I don't want to give up on God and Jesus even though I don't believe a lot of the Mordecai stuff anymore. But I still don't understand death. If Christ's resurrection reversed the curse of death, why do we still have to die? I hope I can be lucky enough to be here when Christ sets up his thousand year kingdom on earth and I can live a long life-span of a thousand years, like the patriarchs in Genesis.*

*The California sunset was gorgeous last night. I thought about how the same sunset can be experienced differently by each person. It touches those with primitive understanding who don't know about what causes sunsets scientifically. Mordecai trembles at what he believes is the Almighty Word. Is it possible Mordecai and I experience the same God even though we differ in much of our thinking? I don't know. His god seems like a completely different one from mine.*

*I went to the Griffith Observatory a few weeks ago, the same place where James Dean shot Rebel. I thought about the solar system and how we're floating in space. The concept of heaven "up there" in the clouds doesn't make much sense to me anymore. Jesus talked about heaven being among us and in us. Einstein said time is merely an illusion, because everything's happening all at once. Maybe heaven is here now, not separate from us. This is the only life I'm sure I'll ever have, so I'm so lucky to be alive. Maybe I really did reach heaven when I kissed you, Angel.*

*I've been living with the unknown since the moment I slid down the birth canal. If I've coped with uncertainty so far, there's no reason to think I won't be able to face leaving the womb of this earth to be born into eternal life like Dad.*

*Looking back over the last few years, I've grown up a lot. The contentment I feel from believing I'm enfolded by perfect love is like a light inside me that dispels the darkness more and more.*

*When I was younger, time crawled like a turtle through my enchanted childhood, burning our first love into my memory. I'm realizing my idealization of another time is a trick to avoid the reality of my life today.*

*Sometimes, late at night when I'm in bed by myself, I remember Mom teaching me words from the dictionary. I remember her reading the word 'transcendence' to me and then I realize that's what religion was all about for me. I wanted to transcend the limitations of this world. But that's what you were about, too. Falling in love with you was a spiritual quest. In your arms, I hoped to find God. I think for a brief moment I did. You were my Jesus. And maybe I was yours. For four years, I carried my cross. I gave up my life to redeem you. Dying, crying, bleeding and needing you.*

*I still feel lonely sometimes. Even though Adam was in paradise, walking and talking with God, it still wasn't good for him to be alone. But I'm reaching for wholeness now. I want to reach a point where I no longer need something or someone outside myself, a religion or a relationship, to be the key to my happiness.*

*I read a poem by Emily Dickinson recently. She wrote:*

*The props assist the House*
*Until the house is built*
*And then the props withdraw*
*And adequate, erect,*
*The House supports itself*

*And cease to recollect*
*The Auger and the Carpenter*

*Just such a retrospect*
*Hath the perfected life*
*A past of Plank and Nail*
*And slowness-*
*Then the Scaffolds drop*
*Affirming it a Soul*

    *I think what she was saying is that it's really an amazing thing to grow up. Part of me wishes we could stay young forever, remaining idealistic and forward looking, but now I can look back and be thankful for my youth and for those I shared it with, like you and Red and Walker and Savannah.*

    *Do you remember at BBC summer camp how Mordecai taught us feelings are the caboose of the train, that we need to be led by faith and facts instead? My feelings for you are strong, but I don't believe they're deceitful and wicked. When I was around Mordecai, my emotions were frozen and pushed down. My theory is that Mordecai's feelings were distorted, unexpressed anger that turned into self-righteousness.*

    *God is restoring my soul. I'm learning to know the still, small voice, the language of my own heart. Mordecai taught me to be suspicious of inner guidance, but I'm learning to trust my intuition now to help me decide what to do. My perceptions are accurate far more often than I realized.*

    *I've decide to reject Mordecai's value system and come up with my own. That's one of the benefits to growing up. To know how I feel adds richness to my life. I see in color what he sees in black and white. I guess there are occasions when my feelings aren't facts, like when my imagination tells me there is danger when there is none. And some feelings are negative, like fear, guilt, shame, anxiety, rage, and especially the black hole of despair. I sank into that downward suicide spiral after Mordecai broke us up. It was difficult to feel those feelings. But they were part of my life too, and they were the exception and not the rule. There's no joy without some sorrow. I've decided to believe that most of the time, my feelings are from my heart and what my soul wants to tell me.*

*Negative feelings have lessened since I started thinking for myself and disagreeing with Mordecai's indoctrination. Remember how he manipulated us with that silly chant of 'Spirit over self, Spirit over self...?' That's another example of the fundamentalist bullshit I've outgrown. It's a shoe that doesn't fit me anymore. I need to stop being down on my self, and value and nurture myself instead. I'm not talking about some extreme self-will run riot, a narcissism that harms others who get in my way. But Mordecai's whole mantra of 'spirit over self' set up a lot of the unhealthy thinking endemic to fundamentalism, the guilt, the self-loathing, the feeling I could never be good enough. He had our heads bowed in shame instead of looking up in grace. Feelings aren't the caboose. They're there to be listened to. Cues from the engineer to signal where the train is going and what fuel is needed to get down the track. I've decided from here on in, I'm gonna trust my gut feeling when I need to make a decision.*

*My feelings for you were a guide. You gave me a gift, that I could feel these things, that I have this ability, this capability and capacity to love clear and strong. Thanks Angel for awakening this in me, for turning the light on for me. You showed me that feelings aren't hokey movie stuff, that there can be real love. For that experience, I'm eternally grateful.    Thanks to you, I get misty-eyed watching chick flicks now.*

*I was blocked by nightmares of Stick Man, but you started me feeling something powerful.    The gift you gave me, the experience of someone totally getting who I am, let me know it can happen.    It's not just a dumb dream.    Love is real and it happened to me.    Thanks to you, I finally understand experientially those songs on the radio, like 'I'll Meet You Halfway' and 'Baby, I Love Your Way.'    Thanks for giving that to me.*

*First loves still hang on the walls of my subconscious like photographs.    The colors are bright as ever.    You.    Mom.    Dad.*

*I wish I'd never lost you, but you're still always with me.    I won't ever forget my memories of you.    They will last a lifetime. But now, sometimes when I'm alone, I'm aware of a love that preceded all of these.    A first love flowing from deep down inside like a warm healing river whose source is in me, yet beyond me.    An endless love that brought me into being.    A love within me that is unconditional and reflected back to me in other people. A love that predates the universe.    A love so big it can save all souls.    I'm coming to believe in this well-spring that fills me with an inner dignity.    It flows through me, on into my life and into the world outside.    I know I have experience an eternal Grace.*

*Whatever happens in the future, I'll always hold you in my heart and be grateful for our first love.*

*Unconditional love always,*

   *Jeremiah       xoxo*


I folded the letter and sealed the envelope.    After licking a postage stamp and placing it upside-down in the corner of the envelope, I put the letter on the nightstand and lay back in my bed.

I thought about how Reverend Rawlings was still praying on his knees for me to return to the three rivers of Pittsburgh and come back home to his Baptist church.

*I'm coming home all right, Mordecai. But home isn't a geographic place.*

I turned out the light, and realized I was a better pastor to my own soul than Mordecai could ever be. I felt I could finally forgive him, choosing to believe he wasn't a bad man, but a sick one.

I drifted towards slumber again, accompanied by the music of the traffic on Laurel Canyon.

*Maybe I can water my own soul, and heal myself from within*

This thought felt like a homecoming to me.

As the traffic on Laurel Canyon abated, darkness fell like a theatre curtain. I closed my eyes and I was no longer afraid to dream. I realized I hadn't thought about or seen Stick Man for some time.

**The End**

CPSIA information can be obtained at www.ICGtesting.com
Printed in the USA
LVOW091507170112

264288LV00001B/176/P

9 781456 368685